****

Battlefield Kore:

Book Two of the Red Storm Series

By
James Rosone & Miranda Watson
****

Published in conjunction with Front Line Publishing, Inc.

Disclaimer

This is a fictional story. All characters in this book are imagined, and any opinions that they express are simply that, fictional thoughts of literary characters. Although policies mentioned in the book may be similar to reality, they are by no means a factual representation of the news. Please enjoy this work as it is, a story to escape the part of life that can sometimes weigh us down in mundaneness or busyness.

Copyright Information

ISBN: 978-1-957634-10-4
Sun City Center, Florida, USA
Library of Congress Control Number: 2022904177

Table of Contents

Foreword

Battlefield Korea picks up right where *Battlefield Ukraine* ended so that we can learn about the fate of the US forces stuck in Kiev. However, the next chapter takes a jump back in time, and begins about eighteen months prior to the start of hostilities in Ukraine. The timeline moves forward from there as the story goes on. We took this leap backward so that some of the additional backstory to the conflict in Korea could be explained, and so we could focus more of each of these first two books on the battle theater after which it was named. We hope you will enjoy this second book in our Red Storm Series.

Chapter 1
Surrounded - Nuts

Kiev, Ukraine

Lieutenant Taylor looked at the remnants of his platoon, sprawled out in the back room of the store, trying to get some sleep. He wished he could join them. He was exhausted, but his presence had been requested by the area commander, a major from one of the 173rd Airborne units that was also trapped in Kiev. The Russians had broken through the Ukrainian and NATO defensive line and rushed units around the city in hopes of trapping the retreating forces before they could escape. Their speed and exceptional air support had allowed them to trap nearly a third of the Allied forces in the city.

A German tank and infantry battalion was trapped in Kiev, along with part of a British armored unit, a battalion from the US 1st Armor Division, a battalion of paratroopers from the 173rd, a battalion from the 82nd Airborne, and what was left of the 2nd Cavalry Regiment.

Lieutenant Taylor poked his head out of the door in the alleyway, doing a quick check to make sure he didn't see or hear any Russian helicopters or aircraft, then walked out into the alley to head to a building not far from where his platoon was sheltering. As he ambled through the alleyway, Taylor looked up and saw a new storm rolling in.

Great, more rain, he grumbled to himself.

He crossed the alleyway and entered the back door of another building. Inside, he was guided down to the basement by a sentry to where a makeshift headquarters had been set up.

As he walked into the main room, several soldiers were talking on a couple of different radio systems to some group or another. Taylor hoped they were talking to someone outside the city.

Maybe we'll get lucky and they can figure out how to relieve us before we run out of ammunition, he hoped.

A captain waved to get Lieutenant Taylor's attention. They were meeting in a nearby room and he wanted Taylor to join them. As he walked in, he received a warm welcome.

"Lieutenant Taylor, I'm glad you were able to make it. For a little while, we thought your platoon might have gotten cut off," said

Major Graham, an Airborne officer from the 173rd who was acting as their battalion commander.

Nearly all of the units trapped in the city were at 50% to 60% strength and short on officers and experienced NCOs. Major Graham just happened to be the most senior officer in this sector of the city they were held up in. He had summarily assumed command of the units operating in his area. The prior evening, Taylor's platoon had carried out a dangerous mission to blow up one of the major bridges crossing into the city. They had been successful, but they had lost three more soldiers and had nearly been cut off by a nearby Russian unit.

Lieutenant Taylor just nodded, too tired to say much. All he wanted right now was to get some sleep. He had been running on fumes since they'd arrived in Kiev. He didn't know how his platoon sergeant could run on so little rest. He had to remind himself that he was also a former Ranger; it was probably his Special Forces training that enabled him to be able to operate on so little sleep.

Turning back to the rest of the officers, Major Graham began the meeting. "OK, here's the situation. We've been cut off now for five days. The Russians seem to be more intent on chasing the remaining NATO forces out of Ukraine than they are on finishing us off. Our drones and the intelligence we're receiving from the outside have confirmed that several Russian divisions have gone around our positions and begun to move throughout the rest of the country. They're not massing for a major attack on us, at least not right now."

The room filled with a collective sigh of relief at this news.

"This morning, General Fenzol received an offer for surrender from the Russian commander. Well, just like General McAuliffe from the 101st told the Germans during the Battle of the Bulge, Fenzol said, 'Nuts,' and sent them packing."

Everyone started laughing at that reference. During the Battle of the Bulge, the Germans had had the 101st Airborne Division surrounded in Bastogne. German General Heinrich Freiherr von Lüttwitz had issued General McAuliffe an ultimatum to surrender or be destroyed. The American general had simply sent back a one-word reply: "Nuts."

Returning to a serious tone again, the major continued, "General Fenzol is working to organize a breakout. With the Russians placing so much focus on other parts of Ukraine, they've left a few points in their defensive line weak. Tonight, under the cover of darkness, the few armored vehicles and tanks we have will move towards those parts of the line and attempt to punch a hole for us to go through. Even before that attack though, our group has been tasked with trying to infiltrate the line to see what kind of chaos we can cause. We're specifically going to look for antitank guns or other strong points that might cause the armor some problems."

A British captain interrupted to ask, "So once we start this 'chaos,' is that when our armor attack is going to start?"

Major Graham nodded "Exactly. Once we start to sow disorder and confusion, the armored units will make their move while the Russians are distracted with what's going on behind them. If things go well, they'll be able to punch a large enough hole through the enemy positions for the other units to collapse the outer perimeter and escape through the hole in the line we'll have created."

He sighed for a second, taking a drink of some water while everyone appeared to be hanging on to his every word. "I'm not going to sugarcoat this. If we're not successful, then a lot of us are probably going to die, and everyone will most likely have to surrender at some point. I, for one, would rather try and break ourselves out of this cursed city than have to surrender to the Russians."

Major Graham could also see the tired looks on their long faces. These men were exhausted, and he was about to demand a lot from them tonight. He knew they would need some sleep before the festivities started. "We push off for the attack around 1800, and we'll cross into the Russian lines around 2100 hours. Right now, I want everyone to go back to your units and get some rest. Just have your men moved to this location and ready to push off at 1800 hours. Understood?"

The meeting broke up after a few more orders were handed down. Lieutenant Taylor walked back to where his platoon was sleeping, planning on joining them. However, upon approaching the alleyway door to the back room where his platoon was sacking out, he suddenly smelled something amazing. He entered the room, and Sergeant Childers walked up to him, handing him a bowl of some piping hot borscht.

"Where did you get this?" Taylor asked as he gratefully took the bowl and spoon being offered.

Smiling, Sergeant Childers replied, "One of the families staying above us came down with a potful and even brought some bowls. There's some bread over there, and some beer if you want it." He pointed to a table where several of his soldiers who should have been sleeping were helping themselves to some bread. One of the soldiers held out a beer for him as he walked towards them.

"I suppose General Order Number One doesn't really matter if you're surrounded by a division of Russian soldiers, does it?" the lieutenant said jokingly as he took the beer, lifting it to his lips and taking a long drink.

Typically, US forces weren't allowed to consume alcohol in a combat zone—being surrounded and cut off from the world did have its advantages.

As the soldiers enjoyed their soup, bread and beer, their exhaustion returned. Many of the men who had finished eating now found a spot to curl up on the floor and quickly went to sleep. Soon, Sergeant Childers was the only person left at the table with him.

Lieutenant Taylor thought back to a conversation they'd had a couple of days ago. "Hey, you never did get to finish telling me why you joined the Army. I told you my story," he joked, taking another drink of his beer.

"I suppose it's only fair. I still can't believe you went to Yale, and here you are, leading a platoon of infantry in Ukraine," Childers replied in jest. He sighed before continuing, staring out the window as he remembered back. "Before September 11th, I was a mess. I was in my sophomore year at Texas A&M. I had no idea what I was doing with my life. I spent most of my time partying, getting drunk or smoking weed. Then, one day, I got in trouble on campus and it looked like I was going to get expelled. Somehow, I managed to talk my way out of that problem, but I was still unsure of what I really wanted to do. I decided to take a year off school and get a job."

"My uncle worked for an oil company, drilling wells. He offered to help get me a job so I could make some money and figure out if I really wanted to finish college or just work with him. I was making good money too, $35 an hour, but it was backbreaking work. I'd been working with him for almost three months when the towers were hit. I couldn't believe someone had attacked us like that. Watching those people on the top floors jumping out of the windows, falling to their deaths like that…well, it angered me. I made up my mind that I was going to join the Army."

Pausing for a second to polish off his beer, Childers continued, "My father had served in Vietnam, and my grandfather had served in World War II, so it wasn't an uncommon thing for people in my family to volunteer. When I joined, I said I wanted to be a Ranger. My recruiter laughed at me but signed me up for it anyway. After completing infantry school and jump school, I was sent to Ranger school. After a few grueling months of selection training, I made it. I was placed with the 75th Ranger Battalion, just in time to deploy to Iraq for the invasion."

Sergeant Childers rubbed his eyes for a second, looking out the window again, lost in thought. "Following the invasion of Iraq, my unit deployed to Afghanistan. We lost a couple of guys on that deployment. Then we were sent back to Iraq again in 2006 and 2007. During the Surge, my unit was deployed up in Mosul. We were out on a mission to snatch a high-value target, some Al Qaeda leader. When we broke into the guy's house, I was moving up the stairs to the clear the second floor with a couple of other guys. As I rounded the top of the stairs, I saw several flashes from a muzzle. I felt something hit me in the chest and legs. I went down immediately, before I could get a shot off. The guy following behind me shot the attacker."

Childers began to rub his left thigh, which seemed to be having phantom pain from the memory he was talking about. "I was out. The next thing I knew, I woke up in a hospital in Balad. They said I had been shot twice in my left leg, shattering my femur. One round hit me in my right shoulder. The docs told me they were flying me back to Germany to have my leg fixed. I ended up spending the next eighteen months rehabilitating my leg. I wasn't able to put any weight on it for nearly six months while the bone healed. They had to put a rod and a lot of screws in there to hold everything together. Unfortunately, my jump days were over, so I was out of the Rangers."

He sighed. "After I was released back to active duty again, they sent me to be a drill sergeant. I did that for a couple of years, continuing to strengthen my leg and shoulder, and then I got orders to the 2nd Cav. I couldn't have been happier. I was going to pin on master sergeant in a couple more weeks before we got sent over here. I suppose my promotion has probably come through," he said, snickering.

Lieutenant Taylor let out a soft whistle. "Man, that's a crazy story, Luke. Well, I for one am glad you made it out of Iraq all right; we'd be in rough shape without you here with us."

Childers nodded slightly, the left side of his mouth coming up in a half smile. He didn't really know how to respond to direct praise like that.

"So, what's the scoop from the meeting?" the sergeant asked, changing topics.

Lieutenant Taylor pulled out a map and showed Childers the rally point where they would be linking up near the Russian lines. Taylor spent a little bit of time bringing him up to speed on the details of the night mission, and then the two of them joined the rest of their men in getting a few hours of shuteye before the action started.

****

It was nearly 1800 hours as Lieutenant Taylor's platoon approached what remained of their company and another American unit that would be going through the tunnel first. When they'd entered Ukraine, they had started with one hundred twenty-eight soldiers in their company. Now they were down to just thirty-nine. All the others had either been killed or wounded.

Taylor saw Major Graham walking towards him. "What's going on, Sir?" He hoped nothing was wrong.

"I just wanted to make sure your guys are ready. Do you have full loads of ammo and grenades? We have some extra over near that Humvee," Graham explained, pointing to a vehicle a small group of soldiers had congregated around.

"No, we loaded up earlier," Lieutenant Taylor answered. "My guys are ready to go. Do you still want my platoon to lead the way?" He secretly hoped that another unit might have been chosen instead.

Graham just nodded. "Yeah, I want your group to try and penetrate through that area," he said, pointing to a spot on the map. "That old guy we talked about earlier said there's a bar there that was run by the Ukrainian mafia. It has a tunnel running underneath it. The passageway connects to another bar on the other side of the Russian lines, here," he said, pointing to the two locations.

"Once your men get through, I want your group to try and identify any antitank guns and take them out. If you can, I want your guys to hit those objectives quietly. Once the shooting officially starts, that platoon of German tanks over there is going to try and push through to your location."

Major Graham spent another ten minutes going over everything with Lieutenant Taylor and Sergeant Childers. Following their platoon would be the rest of their company, and then a British infantry unit would pick up the tail. The one thing that gave them pause was the uncertainty of whether or not the Russians had a quick-reaction force or QRF nearby to rush to that position once the gunfire began.

Childers looked at the map and then back up at Major Graham. "We'll cause some chaos, Sir. Just make sure those tanks press their attack home once the shooting starts. If there *is* a Russian QRF, we won't last long without backup."

The major nodded and then moved down to another unit that was also forming up to let them know what their part in the operation would be. If their attack was successful, the entire NATO force trapped in Kiev might be able to break out.
****

An hour later, Sergeant Childers led his platoon down the stairs in the back room of that mafia-run bar to the basement. When they reached the basement, a crusty older man, probably the owner, was there to greet them.

"Good evening, gentlemen," he said in thickly accented English, a smile broadly gleaming on his face. As he flashed his teeth, the group saw that one of his incisors had been boldly covered in gold. The man's rolled up sleeves showed off arms that were covered in tattoos from wrist to elbow. It was obvious without asking that he was a member of the Ukrainian mafia. Under any other circumstances, meeting this man would have been extremely dangerous, but since he hated the Russian military as much as or more than they did, today he was a friend.

Without being told, he guided them down the dark, damp passageway and led them through it. After what felt like an hour but was probably no more than ten or fifteen minutes, they made it to the end of the tunnel, which led up to another door.

The old man told them, "The exit leads to the basement of another mafia-run bar. Hopefully, it will be empty."

Childers calmly directed the man, "Please step aside, Sir. We will need to clear the room."

He passed the word to the soldiers behind him to turn their flashlights off and get their night vision goggles on. They would start to use light discipline now that they were going to enter an unknown building. Childers reached down and grabbed the six-inch knife he carried on the side of his right leg, near his pistol holster. He slowly opened the door. As he panned from left to right, he saw that the room was indeed empty and let out a short sigh of relief.

"We're clear," he announced, signaling with his hands to let the others still in the tunnel know it was safe to enter the room. As the soldiers emptied out of the tunnel, he directed several of them to follow him up the stairs to clear the ground floor and see where they were at.

When they got to the ground floor, the men systematically cleared the various rooms in the bar, cautiously making sure there were no signs of Russian soldiers. All they found were piles of broken and empty beer and vodka bottles.

"The Russians have definitely been here," said Childers, "but it looks like they've cleaned the place out of whatever it was they were looking for."

While one of his soldiers went downstairs to let the others know it was safe to come up, Childers carefully peered out one of the windows near the entrance. About two blocks away, near the entrance of the intersection, he spotted what appeared to be a Russian tank. He wasn't sure what type of tank, but he could clearly make out the turret and the barrel. Looking above the tank, in the windows of the buildings adjacent to the intersection, Childers saw that several balconies had been piled high with sandbags and then topped with heavy machine guns. Those spots would make fairly effective makeshift machine gun bunkers; they had excellent fields of fire, protecting each other and the tank below them.

"Sergeant, what do you have for me?" asked Lieutenant Taylor as he approached Childers.

Childers signaled for them to walk away from the window before he spoke. "Down the block at the corner, there's a tank. There may be another armored vehicle, but I can't fully see it from this vantage point. What I could definitely make out though, are the machine gun bunkers on the balconies of the apartments that overlook that intersection. We're going to need to take out those gun emplacements before we disable that tank."

As they were talking, the ground floor of the bar was starting to fill up with soldiers coming up from the tunnel. Major Graham was among the soldiers exiting the basement. He immediately walked over to Lieutenant Taylor and Sergeant Childers, who brought him up to speed on what they had seen outside.

"I assume you have a plan to deal with those machine gun positions," Major Graham asserted, looking pointedly at Childers.

Sergeant Childers shot him a devilish grin. "When does a Ranger not have a plan?" he snickered, causing the others to let out a soft laugh. The comment cut through the palpable tension in the air, at least a little bit.

After a brief pause, Major Graham replied, "All right, Childers…so, what is it?"

"I'm going to take Sergeant Crockett, Specialist Duncan, and Specialist Cross with me to disable those guns." He pulled out a map and pointed to where they were. "We'll use the alleyway behind us to sneak up to this building here, right at the corner. The backs of these buildings all have drainpipes that come down from the roof above. We're going to scale the side of one of these buildings here and gain entry over here."

"Once inside, we'll make our way to the first machine gun position. We'll take them out silently and then move into position to hit the others. I want two of the guys coming with me to have M203s. When the time comes, they'll fire them directly across the intersection into the other gun positions and take them out. The third guy needs to be carrying one of the AT4s. He'll be able to lean over the edge of the balcony and hit that tank from the top, where the armor is weakest. We won't have much time, but we shouldn't need it if we hit all these positions at once," Sergeant Childers finished.

Several of the soldiers around him nodded in approval. They knew if anyone could pull this off, it would be Sergeant Childers. The guy had more combat experience than anyone in their regiment.

Thinking about the plan for a second, Graham smiled and nodded in approval. "It's bold, I'll give you that. I think it just might work. Get your crew ready and stand by. We need to figure out what we're going to do about these other two blocks before you guys head out. We need to try and sync this attack as much as possible. Once the shooting starts, all hell is going to break loose. We need to make sure we hit these guys hard, right off the bat," the major added.

****

15

Thirty minutes later, the ground floor of the bar was really becoming packed. A lot of soldiers had filtered through the tunnel, and many more were still waiting below ground.

"Luke, you want me to come with you on this mission?" asked Lieutenant Taylor.

Childers looked up at the young lieutenant; he could see genuine concern about this mission on his face.

The fact that Taylor was offering to come along on what was obviously a dangerous mission caused Childers to suddenly view him with more respect. *He's grown up a lot as an infantry officer*, he thought. Even though he had a wife and a baby to go home to, he was willing to put himself in harm's way so one of his soldiers wouldn't have to.

"No, Sir. I think it would be best for you to stay here with the rest of the platoon. Once you hear the fireworks, get to the corner and secure it quickly. We'll do what we can to cover you from above in the gun position," he told his platoon leader, entrusting him with a task just as important as the one he was about to head out on.

Childers turned to look at the three other soldiers who would be proceeding on the mission with him—a sergeant he barely knew from a different platoon, and two specialists that he trusted completely. The sergeant would be carrying the AT4 with him, while the two specialists had swapped out their M4s with two other soldiers' weapons. They needed the M203 grenade launchers for this mission. They each pocketed three additional grenade rounds in their cargo pants, in case they needed more than the one shot.

"OK, it's time. Let's head out," Childers announced to his team.

They quickly followed him into the alleyway behind the bar. Several other small attack teams also filtered into the alleyway, heading to their own objectives. So far, no Russian soldiers had been seen patrolling the streets nearby.

Major Graham had placed a couple of sentries near the exits of the alleyways, their M4s equipped with silencers. Those were few and far between, but if they needed to use them, they would.

I wish we had extra silencers. I sure could use them on this little mission, Childers thought as he approached the guards. He shrugged off the disadvantage and continued to lead his small team to the end of the alleyway, next to the sentry who was keeping watch.

"Spotted anything recently?" he inquired.

"Nothing, Sergeant. Everything looks clear. I've been watching this spot for nearly thirty minutes. I haven't seen anyone moving around, and I haven't spotted anything suspicious in any of the windows or down either end of the street," the soldier replied. This was definitely good news.

As they prepared to cross the street to hustle into the next alleyway, a soft mist started to fall. Then, the sky broke open and the air was filled with the percussion of large raindrops falling.

Sergeant Childers had never been so happy to see rain in his life. It would help cover any noise they made while they moved into position.

Childers looked back at his team and signaled for them to follow him across the street. One by one, they made their way through the darkened alley. Once there, they moved slowly and cautiously along the back edge of the buildings, until they were at the other end of the alleyway, near the next street. It only took them a few minutes to reach the targeted building.

Sergeant Childers looked up and saw what he was looking for— the pipe that allowed the water from the roof to drain down to the alleyway below. He grabbed the pipe and gave it a slight tug, then a harder shake. He smiled, satisfied that the structure was firmly attached to the wall of the building.

He let his rifle hang by its sling and pushed it behind his body, so it wouldn't brush against the wall. Then he grabbed the metal pipe and positioned one of his legs against an indent in the wall. Slowly, he scaled the wall.

As he reached the top of the balcony opening, he slowly lifted his head cautiously above it to see if anyone was visible. When he didn't see anyone, he turned to check the nearby windows. Confirming that the coast was clear, he hoisted himself the rest of the way up, crawling over the balcony wall until his feet were once again on solid ground.

Childers unhooked the rope he had brought with him, tied it off and let it drop to the others below. They used the rope and the metal pipe to climb up to the patio and join him.

As Specialist Cross made it over the patio wall, he quietly told him, "I'm going to go into the building and clear the first room. I want you to wait for me to come back and let you know it's safe to go inside."

17

The young soldier just nodded and went back to helping his comrades get onto the patio.

Sergeant Childers reached down and grabbed his knife with his right hand. He left his M4 slung behind him as he slowly opened the patio door.

Thank God, it's unlocked, he thought as he turned the handle and entered the building.

With his night vision goggles still on, he could clearly see that he was in the kitchen. He crept to a hallway and peered into it. There were two rooms down one end of the hallway, along with a bathroom. Down the other end, it looked like the door opened into a living room, which would probably lead him to the front balcony, where the gun position was.

Childers turned back to the patio and gestured for the other soldiers to enter the kitchen with him, slowly and quietly. They did as instructed and waited.

He signaled for Sergeant Crockett and one of the specialists to head down one direction of the hallway and see if it was clear. If they found any Russian soldiers in the rooms, they were to do their best to kill them silently, with their knives. He and Specialist Duncan would sneak their way towards the living room.

Sergeant Childers slowly crept down the hallway until he reached the entrance to the living room. As soon as he could see inside the door, he stopped dead in his tracks. Nearly two feet away was a recliner with a Russian soldier sleeping in it. He signaled for Specialist Duncan to stay put for the moment.

Childers quietly tiptoed towards the slumbering enemy combatant. He moved his left hand to cover the soldier's mouth while he moved his knife into position. In one swift motion, his hand grabbed the Russian soldier's mouth as he pushed his blade right through the side of the soldier's neck, directly into his throat. Blood instantly gushed through Sergeant Childers' fingers.

The well-muscled man tried to fight briefly, making a gurgling sound when he tried to scream, until Childers twisted the knife in the soldier's neck, severing his spinal cord and killing him instantly.

Sergeant Childers withdrew his knife and moved away from the now-lifeless soldier. Just as he was about to stand back up and slip deeper into the living room, a Russian soldier walked into the room from where the balcony must have been.

As he spotted his friend covered in blood and an American soldier half-crouched, half standing, with a large knife in his hand, the Russian managed to shout one word before Childers' knife flew across the room and hit him in the upper chest, just below his throat. The soldier instantly collapsed backwards to the floor from the shock of impact.

Sergeant Childers sprang to his feet and rushed over to the Russian before he could get up. He jerked his knife out of the man's chest with one hand while placing his other over the enemy soldier's mouth before he could say another word. He quickly stabbed the fighter several more times, until he could feel the life drain from him.

Specialist Duncan became concerned when he heard the second man yell and rushed into the room just as Childers was finishing off the second soldier. He was momentarily stunned as he realized that Sergeant Childers had just killed the two Russians in front of him with his knife.

Just as Duncan began to move towards Childers, who was now on his knees, another Russian soldier walked into the room and immediately spotted Specialist Duncan. The Russian moved faster than Childers could, and he fired a quick burst from his AK-74 right into Duncan's chest. Duncan fell backwards and slumped to the floor, dead before he knew what had happened.

This third Russian soldier hadn't initially seen Childers, until he lunged at him, plunging his knife deep into the man's sternum. Sergeant Childers pushed the man to the wall and stabbed him three more times in quick succession.

Sergeant Crockett and Specialist Cross came running into the room when they heard the gunfire. "Toss me Duncan's rifle!" Childers yelled to them as he looked into the room that led to the patio. Sergeant Childers turned back just in time to catch Duncan's M4 with the grenade launcher and ran into the next room, yelling at Crockett and Cross to follow and take out the machine gun positions on the opposite sides of the street corner.

Sergeant Childers covered the short distance through the room to the balcony just as another Russian was about to enter. He fired several quick shots into the man's chest, then pushed him through the entrance and right over the balcony. Childers looked up and saw several shocked Russian soldiers across the street on the other balconies, also manning machine gun positions. He took quick aim with the M203 and fired the high-explosive fragmentation grenade right into the first gun position, no more than 100 feet away.

As the blast exploded, Specialist Cross made it onto the balcony with Sergeant Childers and fired his M203 at another machine gun position, killing the soldiers who had been manning that stronghold as well.

Just as the soldiers in the third balcony began to turn their heavy machine on Sergeant Childers, he grabbed the machine gun that had been sitting on the sandbag position in front of him and fired a quick burst at them, killing the two Russian soldiers instantly. He then took aim at the walls and room behind them and fired a long string of bullets into the area, ensuring he had killed anyone else who might have been lingering further back in the building.

While he was doing this, Sergeant Crockett had unslung his AT4 and rushed to the balcony edge. He leaned over and aimed the AT4 at the top of the tank. Just as he was about to fire the rocket, a Russian soldier from one of the balconies across the way fired several rounds from his AK-74 and hit Crockett in the head, killing him instantly.

Sergeant Childers turned the machine gun on the Russian and riddled him with bullets. "Grab the AT4 and take that tank out!" Childers yelled to Specialist Cross.

The young soldier ran to Crockett's now-lifeless body and grabbed the AT4 from him. He aimed at the tank below and squeezed the trigger. The rocket leapt from the launcher and hit the top of the turret less than forty feet below, blowing a small hole through it into the compartment below. In less than a second, the tank rounds inside the turret began to cook off, causing a much larger explosion. A piece of shrapnel flew back and hit Cross in his left shoulder, knocking him to the ground as he screamed in pain.

While the chaos was unfolding around them, the rest of Childers' platoon was now moving down the street heading towards the building where Cross and Childers were, engaging Russian soldiers along the way as they saw them. Then, several Russians began to pour out of one of the buildings not far from his platoon; within moments, they had managed to pin down Lieutenant Taylor and his men. Sergeant Childers turned the heavy machine gun and opened fire at the backs of the Russian soldiers below, killing many of them outright.

Childers looked back to the road in front of them when Cross, who'd managed to bandage himself up, pointed to more enemy soldiers.

Childers turned the machine gun loose on them as well, cutting many of them down before they realized their own gun positions had been compromised.

"Cross, get me more ammo," Sergeant Childers ordered with a sense of urgency. "We need to keep providing covering fire for the rest of the platoon."

As Specialist Cross was grabbing an ammo can near the edge of the balcony, a hand grenade flew towards them. Without thinking, Sergeant Childers grabbed his M4, which was still slung behind him, and swung it towards the grenade like a baseball bat. He hit the grenade, sending it flying away from the balcony; in seconds, it exploded over the center of the intersection. A piece of hot shrapnel hit Childers on his cheek and his left arm, knocking him to the ground briefly.

Specialist Cross ran over to him. "Are you all right, Sergeant Childers?" he asked, genuinely concerned despite his own shrapnel wound.

Childers was holding his left arm as pain shot down it to his hand and fingers. He could feel some blood starting to ooze through his fingers. "Yeah, I'll be all right. I think I just got clipped. Get the machine gun reloaded. We need to keep providing covering fire." He pulled open a bandage from his tactical vest and began to wrap his wound. He didn't dwell on the injury very long, moving back to the machine gun just as soon Cross got it reloaded for him.

With another 100-round belt attached, Childers began to lay down covering fire for the rest of the American soldiers still moving to the corner below them. While they were shooting away at the Russians, they could hear what sounded like a cacophony of machine gun fire echoing from the various cross streets.

It was pure chaos as they saw green and red tracer fire zig-zagging back and forth between the various groups of soldiers. Above the din, Childers could also hear the roar of a lot of vehicles starting their engines, and the unmistakable sound of tank treads as they rumbled down the city streets.

While Sergeant Childers was keeping a group of Russian soldiers pinned down, he suddenly saw a tank rumbling in their direction.

When the turret began to turn towards them, he knew they had seconds to vacate the area before that 125mm gun fired.

Childers got up and grabbed Specialist Cross by his individual body armor or IBA. "Run back into the building!" he yelled.

They had made it a couple of feet into the living room when the balcony exploded from the high-explosive round the tank had just fired. Childers had been running through the living room when he felt the sudden pressure change in the air around him, then the immense heat from the explosion. His body was thrown to the floor by the concussion of the blast. Specialist Cross was just slightly in front of him, so Sergeant Childers had absorbed most of the blast, preventing him from being too seriously injured.

As Childers lay there on the floor, he fought to keep his mind from drifting off into la-la land and succumbing to the blackness that was beckoning him. He felt a sharp burning pain in his legs and lower back, though he could still feel his toes and wiggle them. "*That's a good sign*," he thought.

Specialist Cross got up and moved to Sergeant Childers. He applied a couple of bandages to his legs and tried to help him up. "We need to get you out of here, Sarge. You're hit pretty bad," he said in an anxious and shaken voice.

"Agreed. Let's try and move down the stairs over there and get to the ground floor. The rest of the platoon should be here by now," Childers replied through gritted teeth.

As they made their way to the ground floor, several American soldiers entered the house and advanced to several of the windows, working to set up a couple of machine guns.

"Hey, we need a medic over here!" Cross yelled to the soldiers who had just entered the room.

When the men turned and saw that the injured soldier was Sergeant Childers, they instantly yelled out for the platoon's only medic to come help them. A minute later, the medic came in with several other soldiers, many of them wounded. They immediately began to place the wounded on the chairs and couches, turning the first floor of the building into a makeshift aid station.

Lieutenant Taylor walked into the room, carrying another wounded soldier. He saw Childers and came over to him. "How bad are you hurt, Luke?" he asked as he surveyed his comrade.

"I think they got my legs and my left shoulder pretty good. How is the rest of the attack going? Are we breaking out of the city yet?" Sergeant Childers asked, hoping all their efforts hadn't been in vain as he continued to fight to stay conscious.

"It's starting to look like it's going to work," Taylor answered. "I saw a couple of the German tanks just a couple of blocks away. I think we're going to bust out of this hole, so you just hang in there. We'll get help and hopefully a medevac for the wounded, once we're able to place some distance between the city and the Russian lines."

****

The fighting was fierce and hard, often devolving into hand-to-hand combat and close quarter action. The mixed NATO units fought like men possessed along this part of the Russian line.

Within the first thirty minutes of heavy fighting, the German tank unit that was leading the charge broke through the Russian positions. They were swiftly followed by a battalion of tanks from the 1st Armored Division who followed the Germans through the hole they created.

Next came dozens of Strykers and other armored vehicles and trucks. When a group of transport vehicles drove towards Lieutenant Taylor's position, a group of soldiers hopped out of one of the vehicles to load up the wounded. The rest of the platoon and company piled into the remaining transport vehicles.

The fighting lasted through the night and into the early hours of the morning as the NATO forces opened a wide hole in the Russian lines. The Ukrainian units that were trapped with NATO were fighting with everything in them to try and roll up the Russian positions, giving the rest of NATO more time to get their soldiers out of the city. The NATO tank units were doing their best to support the Ukrainians and give their forces as much time as possible to get out as well.

Just prior to the breakout, General Fenzol had contacted Lieutenant General Isaac Zotti, the Commander of Three Corps and the NATO Ground Commander near Novohrad-Volynskyi. He had informed Lieutenant General Zotti of their plan to break out of the city and requested as much air support as he could possibly get. In response, Zotti had told General Fenzol that if he could get his force to the city of

Kmytiv, roughly 110 kilometers west of Kiev, they would try to get him additional reinforcements, supplies and medevacs.

While NATO and Russian aircraft battled over the skies of Kiev and the surrounding area, roughly 80 Blackhawks, Chinooks, and British Puma helicopters headed towards the cities of Kmytiv and Zhytomyr. Once the area had been secured, the Air Force would send in a few dozen C-130 cargo aircraft to drop the fuel, munitions, and other supplies Fenzol had requested.

General Zotti was under no illusions; he realized that this was purely a rescue effort, not an attempt to grab this city from the Russians and hold it. He estimated the Russians would launch a massive counterattack against Kiev and try to encircle General Fenzol's meager force once again. They needed to get munitions and fuel to his force ASAP and hope they could keep on the move long enough to get back to the NATO lines.

****

22,000 Feet Above Zhytomyr, Ukraine

Major Dale "Honey Badger" Young was cruising along at 650 knots with his wingman, Captain Jorge "Iceman" Montoya were looking for targets. Below them were 80-plus NATO helicopters and close to 30 C-130 Hercules cargo aircraft, all vigorously carrying out a daring rescue operation. The past several hours had been absolute chaos as their fighter squadron had scrambled to get airborne and support this last-minute operation.

Major Young had no idea who had drawn this operation up, but it was clear it was being done by the seat of their pants.

Their airborne warning and control system or AWACS support aircraft buzzed through on the satellite link. "Raptor 66, this is Looking Glass. We are tracking ten MiGs heading towards your location from Rostov-on-Don. Their altitude is roughly 100 meters, moving at 680 knots. How copy, over?"

"This is Raptor 66. We copy. Send the targeting data. We're going to descend to 5,000 feet and will engage the MiGs shortly," Major Young said calmly as he led his wingman down through the cloud cover on their attack. They were three minutes away from being within

24

weapons' range, and they needed to lose a lot of altitude if they were going to get in position.

Young and his wingman descended quickly, lining up for their attack. They needed to intercept these MiGs before they got in range of the helicopter force. Above Raptor 66, another flight of four F-15s was swooping in to help support them. It was a risky move for the US to vector in those F-15s; NATO had already lost twenty-nine aircraft from Russian surface-to-air missiles (SAMs) in the area. Unfortunately, the F-16s performing the Wild Weasel missions had been getting hammered hard trying to suppress the SAMs.

"Iceman, I only have three missiles left," Major Young explained to his wingman. "I want you to fire your remaining missiles at the same time that I do. Then we'll head back to base, rearm, and get back on station again. How copy?"

"Copy that, Honey Badger. Between my four missiles and your three, hopefully we'll scare these guys off from their attack," Iceman replied.

Major Young wished the rest of his squadron hadn't gotten rerouted to Kiev. If only these Russian Su-25 ground attack aircraft hadn't started mauling the Ukrainian armored vehicles along the E-40 highway.

As they descended to 5,000 feet, their AWACs sent them the targeting data they needed for their missiles. Major Young had missile lock with all three missiles. He depressed the firing button three separate times.

In rapid succession, each missile dropped from his internal missile bay and streaked towards the incoming MiGs. Major Young and his wingman banked hard to their left and headed in the direction of Kiev.

They watched briefly as their missiles shot across the sky towards the Russian MiGs. Once the enemy aircraft detected the missiles, they initiated evasive maneuvers, trying their best to survive.

Four of their seven missiles struck the MiGs dead-on, exploding the aircraft in glorious balls of fire. Three of the missiles exploded without connecting with their targets; the evasive maneuvers had been successful for a few of the Russian aircraft. Now it was up to the F-15s to finish off the remaining six MiGs.

As they leveled out over the E-40 highway, their radar display began to show a series of SAMs firing at the F-15s. Major Young watched in horror as he counted twelve missiles from at least two SA-21 missile batteries streaking across the sky to destroy the F-15s that had been sent to help them.

My God, I wish I'd known there was an SA-21 in the area, Major Young lamented. *I would have warned them!*

He was simultaneously grateful that his F-22 was largely invisible to radar and sick to his stomach that the F-15s had just been led to their death like lambs to the slaughter. An ire boiled up inside him at the Russian SA-21s–they had been wreaking havoc on the American's ability to secure air supremacy since the beginning of the war.

As he was wrestling with these competing thoughts, his wingman's voice came over the radio. "Where are we going, Honey Badger? The base is in the other direction," he joked.

"I know. I just want to head up the E-40 for a little bit and see if we can spot the convoy we're providing air support for," he replied.

As they flew along the highway, they eventually spotted the ragtag group that had busted their way out of Kiev. The convoy stretched for miles. Nearly any vehicle that could drive and carry soldiers was on the road. It was a mix of military vehicles, busses, taxis, and civilian vehicles. Towards the end of the convoy, they saw dozens upon dozens of pyres of black smoke rising into the sky. It looked like the images Young had seen as a child of the so-called "Highway of Death" in Kuwait.

During the Persian Gulf War in 1991, the US Air Force had caught a couple of Iraqi divisions fleeing Kuwait to Iraq and had wasted no time in sending nearly everything they could to wipe them out. After the attack, the highway had been renamed the "Highway of Death" for all the burned-out vehicles and charred bodies strewn across the road. It was a gruesome sight. It looked like the Russians had delivered their own version on the E-40.

Geez—I wonder how many people we lost during this air raid? Major Young wondered. *I wish we could have been prevented this.*

Helpless, Honey Badger turned his aircraft around and headed towards home. He began to add altitude, bringing their aircraft up to roughly 20,000 feet, their optimal cruising altitude, and they steadily made their way back to the NATO air base in western Poland they were now flying out of.

****

Sergeant Childers had been utterly exhausted when they had loaded him into the back of a truck after he had been wounded. Even though he heard the near-constant sound of gunfire, tanks, explosions, helicopters, aircraft, and the occasional bullet hitting their vehicle as they drove out of the city and onto the E-40 highway, he had soon fallen asleep.

The medics yelled at him, "Sergeant! You need to stay awake!"

"Well, you shouldn't have given me a shot of morphine, then," Childers grumbled in a sleepy haze, and then he had gone right back to the world of dreams.

****

When he woke up next, he felt comfortable and strangely clean. As he slowly opened his eyes, he saw white ceiling tiles above him and a light shining overhead. As he regained more of his senses, he realized his head was resting against a pillow and he had a blanket over him. He raised his right arm to rub his eyes. He felt some stitches on his left cheek and saw an IV in his right wrist.

I must be in a hospital, he realized. *But where, and what day is it?*

Just then, a nurse walked over to the side of his bed. "Ah. Hello, Master Sergeant Childers. Glad to see you're awake. I'll go get the doctor," she said kindly and then darted off before he had a chance to ask her anything.

A few minutes later, a clinician walked into his room and came over to his bed. "Good afternoon, Master Sergeant. It's good to see you up. You were unconscious for a while," the doctor said, reading from his medical chart as he spoke.

Sergeant Childers could see he was a military doctor, and an American, which meant they had broken out of the Russian lines and made it back to safety, or at least *he* had somehow.

"How long have I been out? What about the others in my unit?" he blurted out impatiently.

The doctor held up a hand. "I know you have a lot of questions, and I'll do my best to pass along what little information I know. You were brought to Germany two days ago, along with several hundred additional soldiers who escaped from Kiev. I cannot tell you anything about your unit, or who else made it out. I only know that many hundreds of wounded soldiers were evacuated."

Childers processed that information for a moment as he formulated his next question. "How bad am I hurt, and how soon can I get back to my unit?"

The doctor smiled at the spunk of the man in front of him. "The good news is you aren't in that bad a shape. You needed a few stitches on your left cheek and left arm from what appeared to be a shrapnel wound. You had several pieces of shrapnel in both of your legs that we took out, and a bad contusion on your lower back. You're going to be sore and will need some time to recuperate, but with a little bit of physical therapy, you should be able to return to duty within a month, maybe two, pending nothing gets infected."

Childers let out a sigh of relief.

Just as the doctor was about to leave, he turned around and said one more thing. "By the way, congratulations on your promotion, Master Sergeant. I was told you had been in constant contact with the enemy the last month and a half, but the promotion came through nearly a month ago." The doctor shook his hand and then left to go see the next patient on his rounds.

Childers lay there for a minute, just thinking. Another voice interrupted his thoughts, and then he suddenly realized that there were two other patients in the same room with him. He hadn't even noticed them up to this point.

He overheard one telling the other, "Hey, I just read in this newspaper the nurse gave me that a lot of NATO units that had been trapped in Kiev broke out and made it back to the NATO lines." The two soldiers chatted with each other about it, speaking as if some sort of miracle had occurred.

Childers felt better, knowing that a lot of his unit had probably made it out. Filled with a renewed sense of peace, he closed his eyes. Almost instantaneously, he fell asleep. He did have six weeks of sleep deprivation to recover from, after all.

Chapter 2
Election Meddling

Moscow, Russia
Hotel Savoy
18 Months Prior to the Start of Hostilities in Ukraine

It was a beautiful day in Moscow. The sun had finally broken through the clouds, and the summer flowers were in full bloom. Zhang Dejiang made a mental note to find time to take a short walk outside to enjoy the sun on his face, even if just for a few minutes, before he boarded his plane back to Beijing. He finished tucking his shirt into his pants and slipped on his black dress shoes, freshly polished for that day's meeting.

This was the last day of a three-day trip to Moscow to discuss a wide range of security issues, to include the American general election. This afternoon, however, was reserved specifically for discussing the final details of the post-American election world and what it would look like. More importantly, they were to strategize how Russia and China were going to assert their national wills on a greatly weakened America.

As he finished getting dressed, he motioned for his secretary, a beautiful young woman who had accompanied him on this trip far from home, to check that he had his tie on straight. She made sure he looked polished, which was one of her primary duties. He gave her a quick nod of acknowledgment, which was the highest form of praise she received from him.

"Make sure my belongings and gifts are brought to my aircraft while I head off to my final meeting," he directed.

"Yes, Sir."

Zhang walked through the elegantly decorated lobby of the hotel and stopped for just a minute to marvel at the intricate crown molding and designs on the walls and ceiling. He really enjoyed staying at this particular hotel when he traveled to Moscow.

One of these days, I'll bring my wife here, he thought.

His deputy, a man named Liang Wei, signaled that their vehicle was ready to take them to their next meeting. Zhang joined Liang, and the two of them left the lobby and entered the covered entrance where their vehicle was waiting. One of the hotel doormen held the door open for them as both men approached, gently closing it as the vehicle began to pull away.

Zhang hoped for some reassurance from his counterpart, Liang. "Is everything ready on our end? Is there anything I need to be concerned about before we meet with the Russians?" he asked curtly.

While their upcoming meeting was to discuss the post-election policy their two governments would adopt, Zhang also knew they would be discussing the Russian plans for Ukraine, as well as China's plan for Mongolia and Southeast Asia. It was imperative that the two countries coordinate their operations so they could all benefit from the West's inability to respond to multiple crises at one time.

"Yes, Chairman. Everything is in order, and has been prepared as requested," his deputy responded with confidence.

Zhang trusted every word that came out of Liang's mouth, on any topic. Liang was a brilliant and politically savvy man. Zhang was grooming him to become his successor one day, which was why he had been brought along on this trip and given such a high-profile position within his office.

As the Chairman of the Standing Committee of the National People's Congress, Zhang was the third-highest ranking person in China. He was a man with great power and influence. Zhang was also the deputy and de facto head of the National Security Commission, which was why he was meeting with his Russian counterpart at the Russian Federal Security Service or FSB.

As their vehicle pulled up to the side entrance of Lubyanka, several security guards motioned for the vehicle to stop. One of the guards walked forward and proceeded to open the passenger-side door for Zhang to exit.

Several minutes passed while they cleared security, then Zhang and his deputy Liang were escorted into a secured conference room to meet with Ivan Vasilev.

Ivan had a long history both within the FSB and its predecessor, the KGB. He was trusted by both Prime Minister Mikhailov and President Petrov, which said a lot, considering how selective those men were in attributing confidence.

The three men exchanged pleasantries and then got right down to business. They all knew that Zhang only had four hours before he needed to head to the airport.

Zhang had been working with Ivan for nearly six years; he was comfortable with him and knew him to be a straight shooter. He liked to get down to business and wasted little time on small talk.

"I am glad we were able to meet. I wanted to ask you about the American election." He leaned forward. "Is it true that you have a copy of the former Secretary of State's government emails?" Zhang asked, hoping the rumors being spread in the press were actually true.

Ivan's lip curled up mischievously. "Let us just say if she wins, controlling her won't be a problem," he replied.

"And what if that flamboyant billionaire wins? Can you control him as well?" Zhang shot back.

"Zhang, it really does not matter who wins the American election. We have people in place to plant enough rumors and misinformation to call into question the legitimacy of the election results, whoever wins."

He snickered before continuing, "The Americans love scandal, and they eat conspiracy theories up. We just need to drop a few breadcrumbs here, a few there, and their media will have the public so consumed with election tampering and collusion, they won't know what hit them. That confusion we're going to cause will allow both of our nations a freer hand to make our moves."

Ivan then pulled out a cigarette from the beautiful jade carrying case Zhang had given him when they'd first met, many years ago.

Seeing the flash of jade, Zhang smiled, and his eyebrow rose in surprise. "You still carry that case, Ivan?" Zhang asked.

Ivan chuckled. "Only when I'm going to meet with you."

The two men laughed for a moment, then returned to business. "So, how soon will you move on Ukraine?" Zhang asked.

Ivan sat forward in his chair with his cigarette hanging out of his mouth. "Soon. We have stepped up our training of separatist fighters and moved heavier weapons into the disputed territories. We're going to push for a referendum vote towards the end of next summer. This will give us the time needed to get the 1st Tank Army fully outfitted with the new equipment and allow many more months of hard training."

Ivan took a long pull from his cigarette, then tapped the ashes into the tray on his desk. "How are the plans moving along on your end?"

"As discussed previously, we're engineering unrest in Mongolia. We now have more Chinese guest workers living in Mongolia than there are native Mongolians. As the violence against our peaceful workers continues to escalate, we'll look to intervene. We will, however, wait until Russia initiates the referendum vote in Ukraine. We want all eyes to be on Europe when our tanks roll across the Mongolian border," Zhang said smugly.

Ivan snorted. "You really think anyone in the West, or the rest of the world, even knows where Mongolia is? They aren't going to care about a landlocked country with a small population that looks Chinese. What I want to know is how you are going to pull off the acquisition of Myanmar and the rest of Southeast Asia, not to mention Taiwan," Ivan retorted, a bit skeptical.

"Laos will be easy. We are communist brothers, and we're already responsible for nearly 70% of their exports, as well as providing them with enormous amounts of financial aid. We're already working to integrate them as a Chinese province as we speak. Right now, we provide them with security guarantees against Vietnam. Given the history between the two neighbors, they'll welcome us."

"Will Myanmar be as easy, though?" inquired Ivan, probing to gain some additional information like a good spy master would.

Zhang smiled for a second, knowing exactly what Ivan was doing. "We are allies. Let me tell you about Myanmar. They're a terribly impoverished country. Even now, we're providing additional aid to the people in the major cities and small villages to build up our support. Their military leaders are being recruited and paid off to not interfere when the time comes. As a matter of fact, with Myanmar and Laos, we plan on integrating their military into our own as an additional selling point to get them to comply. The plan has been well thought through, and we're confident it will work," Zhang replied.

His smile fell slightly as he continued, "The trickier part is going to be Vietnam. For the last several years, we have been slowly creating a food shortage problem in southeast China. This has caused food prices to rise sharply and placed a heavy burden on those living in the big cities. We have also ensured the media slowly mentions the enormous food production in Vietnam, and the rest of Southeast Asia, while we struggle to produce food for our people. The stories usually also explain that Vietnam won't sell their abundant rice supplies or other food stocks to China, and when they do, they sell it to us at huge markups. Public opinion of Vietnam over the last several years has eroded, and attitudes have become hostile. Next spring, the food shortage will become even worse for those living in the cities," Zhang explained.

"Be careful, my friend," cautioned Ivan. "I don't want you to create a monster you cannot control."

Zhang continued, "We're even going so far as to organize demonstrations and food riots in the southern provinces. Of course, everything will be monitored and controlled, my friend, but it will drive people to action. Then, we'll instigate violence in Vietnam against Chinese tourists and workers, which will be the catalyst used to drive our intervention. We will, however, wait until either NATO withdraws from Ukraine or Russia invades. With the West's eyes focused on Russia, there'll be little they can do about us."

Zhang handed a tablet over to Ivan, who extended his hand and took the device from him. He began to swipe through various pages on the screen, each showing a timeline of their objectives, digesting the information quickly.

"This is impressive," Ivan said after just a few moments. "I must commend you, Zhang. You have really thought through this intervention. How are you going to ensure India won't cause you problems? Your two nations are not exactly friends."

Drinking some of his tea before it got cold, Zhang replied. "That is trickier. But we have a plan for that as well. Pakistan has been one of our military trading partners for many decades, mainly to just annoy the Indians. However, Pakistan has been harboring Islamic militant groups that are now starting to cause problems for us in China. We have asked them to handle this for the past decade, but they have been either unable, or unwilling to do so. Because of this, we are going to cut off our relationship with Pakistan. Of course, Pakistan does not know this is about to happen, and it will be used as a bargaining chip for our renewed efforts at improved relations with India."

Taking the tablet back from Ivan briefly, Zhang opened up another folder before handing it back. "Our plan is simple," he explained. "We declare to India that our state of hostilities between our two countries has gone on long enough. We agree to withdraw our military forces from the region and sever our ties with Pakistan, and in exchange, they agree to leave Southeast Asia alone as a part of China's sphere of influence."

Pulling out another cigarette to replace the one he had just finished, Ivan responded, "Just be cautious with the Indians. They are probably the only country that can cause you problems in Asia. We have some influence there as well. I will see what we can do to try and strengthen our economic and military ties with them. Perhaps we can use that relationship to keep them on the sidelines of your adventure when the time comes."

Russia was in the midst of concluding a large arms sale with India. The Indian Air Force had just signed a deal to purchase one hundred and sixty-four Su-34 Fullbacks and one hundred Su-57 stealth fighters in their bid to modernize their air force. Once the Americans sold the Pakistanis' F-16s to fight the Taliban, the Indians had felt that they needed to upgrade their air force after decades of neglect.

The two men continued to talk for several more hours about the finer points of the plans.

President Vladimir Petrov was on board with everything they had discussed; the trick was going to be getting President Xi to go along with the plan. That task was what concerned Ivan. If Zhang was not able to sway him, then he would need to be removed. As the afternoon turned into early evening, the meeting concluded, and the two men shook hands and said their good byes.

A sinister look stretched across Zhang's face. "So, we will meet again in three months," he said. "By then, we should know if Xi has agreed to be a part of the new world order, or if he is going to have an 'accident' somewhere along the way."

Ivan chuckled. "I always did like how you think, my friend."
****

When the Chinese group left the secretive meeting room, Ivan pulled a folder labeled "Red Storm" from his secured vault. Not trusting electronic documents, Ivan kept the details of the operation in a folder he regularly worked from. Everything was compartmentalized electronically in pieces, never revealing the whole picture. When one piece was finished, it was printed and added to his master folder, which held all the pieces of the puzzle together that painted the grand scheme of what was going to happen starting in the fall of 2017.

****

During the flight back to Beijing, Liang leaned over to ask his boss a question. "Mr. Chairman, do you believe the Russians can pull off their part of the plan?"

Zhang quietly put his book down and then sat up even straighter in his leather chair. "Yes, Liang. I believe the Russians can and will."

He sighed briefly before adding, "What gives me pause is wondering who will win the American election. The former Secretary of State is more of a hawk on foreign policy and more likely to intervene in Ukraine and Asia. I don't know enough about the other candidate to know how he will respond. That is something I task you with finding out."

Liang seemed a bit unnerved by the question.

Zhang continued, "I want you to put together a full dossier on this other candidate. Try to understand him. See if we can figure out how he can be manipulated to stay out of Asia, or if he will pose a threat to our plans. Our fight is not with the American people. But we will fight them if we have to."

"Of course, Mr. Chairman," responded Liang dutifully.

Chapter 3
Preparations for a New World Power

Shanghai, China
Jiangnan Shipyard

It was a cool autumn morning as Chairman Zhang walked out the sliding door to the observation deck. He was on the top of the Jiangnan Shipyard Headquarters building at the edge of the shipyard. It provided him with an exceptional view of the second *Kuznetsov*-class aircraft carrier that China was finalizing construction on. Like its sister ship, the *Liaoning*, it leveraged a ski jump takeoff system. While this limited the number and type of aircraft it could launch, it provided China with the ability to project power beyond its national borders as it developed its first blue-water strike group. It also improved tremendously on the *Liaoning*, with a stronger propulsion system, more modern electronics, and a tougher air-defense capability.

Zhang was there to meet with Wen Jiabao, the director of China's shipyards. Once the two men had exchanged the necessary polite conversation, Zhang jumped right in. "When will the *Mao Zedong* be operational?" he asked somewhat gruffly, feeling impatient.

The *Mao Zedong* was going to be China's first supercarrier to displace more than 110,000 tons. It would be similar in size to the American *Nimitz*-class supercarrier, but not as large as the new *Ford*-class.

Wen smiled, knowing he had good news to share. "Mr. Chairman, the *Mao* was officially launched as of two days ago by the Dalian shipyard. Per the committee's instructions, we have restricted all access to the ship and kept it hidden under a construction dome. Since we have also placed all Panamax freighters under construction domes, no one has suspected a thing."

Wen was proud of his idea to hide the construction of such a large ship in plain sight was working. They were building a host of new warships right under everyone's noses.

Zhang nodded in approval.

It was a brilliant idea to move the construction of all of the Panamax freighters under construction domes three years ago, he thought. *It allowed us to start building the* Mao *without anyone knowing about it.* He smiled wistfully at the thought that China would soon unveil its very own supercarrier.

Zhang offered some rare praise. "The President and the Ruling Committee are most pleased with your clever idea of the dome, Wen. How soon until the *Mao* will be able to join her two sister ships?" Zhang asked.

"The delivery is still on schedule," Wen insisted. "I have four construction shifts working on the *Mao* around the clock, seven days a week. We have even incentivized the workers by rewarding them with extra pay for completing various tasks ahead of time."

Wen held up a hand before Zhang could respond to his last statement. "I know that's against party doctrine, but please, hear me out. I conducted an experiment. The crews that were given this incentive worked twice as hard as the ones without the incentive, and the quality of their work was better. I know this goes against the teachings of the Communist Party, but the timeline must be met. The *Mao* is too important to our future. I hope you will forgive me this transgression." Wen lowered his head, completely unsure how Zhang would respond.

Zhang considered the situation for a minute, then nodded in agreement. *Wen has broken party doctrine, but it was only in service to the party,* he thought. He was willing to overlook this sin, as long as it did not spread to other areas of the country. While China had become more of a capitalist version of communism, it still relied heavily on the ideology of collectivism.

People should be motivated to serve the party and China because it is the right thing to do, not because of money, Zhang thought.

"Wen, the *Mao* is important. Please keep this idea to yourself, but I'll allow it to continue. When will the *Mao* be ready for its sea trials?"

Sighing out of relief, Wen responded, "We'll be ready to unveil the *Mao* to the world on May 1st, during the May Day celebration. It will be ready to begin sea trials that same week. It'll then be up to the Navy as to when it'll be combat ready," he announced proudly.

"Excellent. And the submarines? How are they coming?" asked Zhang, moving on to the next platform they would need to control the Pacific.

China had deployed the Type 093 nuclear-powered fast-attack submarine in the mid-2000s. NATO called these ships the *Shang*-class.

The improved version, the Type 093G, had been introduced in the mid-2010s and provided China with a fast-attack submarine that was on par with the American *Los Angeles*-class of submarines in terms of its quietness and ability to stalk its prey. The Type 093G subs were of great concern to the Americans, who had gone to great lengths to try and infiltrate the program to learn more about them, albeit rather unsuccessfully.

"We have quietly completed construction of five new *Shang*-class subs. By May of next year, we'll have eight more delivered to the Navy for deployment." Pausing for a second, Wen dared to ask, "Will these thirteen submarines be enough?"

The wind at the shipyard picked up, as if it somehow recognized Zhang's change in demeanor. "Wen—you are but one piece of the great puzzle we're assembling. I need you to focus on your piece and allow others to focus on theirs. Don't concern yourself with 'if' your piece will be enough. Your piece, combined with others will be more than enough," he replied, giving him a tempered but firm rebuke for asking for more information than he needed to know.

Wen bowed his head slightly, realizing he had overstepped his bounds. "My apologies. Is there anything else you would like to see at the shipyard before you depart?"

Zhang turned to his deputy, Liang Wei, who nodded slightly, then back to Wen. "No, I have seen enough. You are on track, which is what I needed to know. Please continue with your work. Do not disappoint us, Wen." He left with his deputy in tow.
****

As Chairman Zhang and his deputy, Liang, settled into the vehicle that would take them to their next meeting, Zhang saw the questioning look on his protégé's face. Liang would never outwardly challenge him, but he decided to turn this last meeting into a teaching point.

"Liang, as I groom you for higher office, there are certain things you must know, and things you must recognize in people," Zhang began.

"First, don't let any of your subordinates know too much. Second, don't immediately dismiss an idea just because it goes against party doctrine. Examine it first, then determine if the indiscretion would further or hurt the party. If it furthers it, then find a way to bend the rules without breaking them."

He paused for a second as Liang looked at him attentively. "Information is power. Information in the wrong hands can also mean disaster. If Wen knows too much about our plans and accidentally slips, saying something at the wrong time or place, it could be pieced together by an intelligence organization. A piece here, a piece there, and soon, the enemy can see a picture."

Liang nodded diligently. His boss was an astute man. He had to be to rise to the position of Chairman and essentially the head of state security. Balancing the military, economy and political realities was a daunting task. Zhang was juggling many balls in many different courts. Liang felt honored that he had been chosen to be Zhang's replacement, assuming of course that Zhang continued to stay in power long enough to retire or one day become president himself.

Chapter 4
Stir Fry

Beijing, China
US Embassy

When Vincent Jones had graduated Georgetown, he had known he wanted to work for the State Department, and specifically to be an expert on the region of China. He was fluent in both the major languages of the mainland and had done a study abroad program in China his sophomore year, which had really cemented his career choice. After finishing college, he had been accepted into the prestigious diplomatic corps and elected to pursue the economic track. He had minored in economics, and he knew China was going to be the new economic power of the 21st century. He wanted to be a part of it.

After his initial years in training, his first overseas assignment had been to Hong Kong. Living there had been a rich learning experience and further reinforced his desire to make China his career track. Following that three-year assignment in Hong Kong, he'd returned to Washington, D.C., and spent two years at headquarters, where he'd met his beautiful bride, Leslie.

Leslie had worked for a consulting firm that specialized in helping American firms looking to globalize their offices to include work in China. She was also fluent in both Mandarin and Cantonese and, like him, had traveled to China many times. Their interests were so aligned that it was really a whirlwind romance. They had gotten married quickly, and she had been eager to return with him on his next overseas assignment in Shanghai.

Vincent counted himself lucky to have been working overseas during the last election cycle. He hated Washington, D.C., and all the politics that went with it. It truly was a quagmire in every sense of the word. He just wanted to further the interests of the American worker; he couldn't care less about the politics so many people consumed their daily lives with. When he got his next assignment to Beijing, he was ecstatic. He'd thought he might have had to do another tour back in DC, but he'd managed to dodge that proverbial bullet—although he did have to pull this tour as the political officer in order to round out his career.

Before he'd become the political officer, Vincent had helped to broker dozens of trade deals and assist in the globalization of multiple American firms, bringing jobs to both countries. Because Vincent and his wife both had exceptional language skills, he had become highly respected by his Chinese counterparts and was routinely invited to many of the cocktail networking events between US and Chinese firms.

Now that he was the political officer, his duties had changed. He was to monitor the political activities of China and alert the State Department on how those actions might impact the United States, whether positively or negatively. He was more focused on the overarching developing changes in the China-India relationship and the souring of the China-Pakistan relationship.

Viewing these diplomatic developments through the economic lens he used, Vincent saw the reason for the shifts. The Chinese had more to gain financially by having a better trading relationship with India than they ever would with Pakistan. Plus, the Pakistanis hadn't exactly been helpful to either the US or China when it came to dealing with Islamic extremists.

Another economic and political challenge for China was its growing population. The growing swarm of people had reached almost 1.4 billion people by 2015 and would continue to grow at a much higher rate than the populations of Europe and the US. With the relaxation of the One Child Policy beginning in November of 2013, the PRC was about to experience an entirely new baby boom.

The sheer volume of food products to be consumed by a population this size was a daunting challenge, especially given China's geography and lack of arable fertile farmlands. Despite the country's large territory, it did not have a "breadbasket" region like the Midwest of the United States. China had become a massive importer of food products from abroad, especially from America. This had only increased since the year 2000, when the population of China had begun to move closer to the cities in droves, slipping away from the rural regions altogether.

The incredible economic boom China had experienced over the last thirty years had created an enormous demand for energy and other natural resources, which was something that the Chinese weren't able to satisfy with their own domestic production.

They had taken full advantage of the cheap coal that was being sold by the United States and other countries to solve their energy needs. However, burning that much coal had resulted in poor air quality. The pollution levels in major cities were simply unsustainable. People were getting sick, and the dirty air was also beginning to affect the land and soil so desperately needed for food production. Vincent had a HEPA filter system in his home just to try and cut down on some of his own exposure. While China continued to move in the direction of renewable energy, it was going to be decades before they were able to produce enough power to eliminate the need for coal.

Since arriving in Beijing, Vincent had also been monitoring the political situations in Mongolia, Myanmar, Cambodia, Laos, and Vietnam. These were all areas the PRC saw as lost provinces, which they considered to be part of "Greater China."

The more he continued to keep an eye on the situations there, the more he thought something just wasn't quite adding up. With all the activity taking place there between these countries and Chinese diplomats and the security personnel, something was afoot; he just didn't know what.

One day, Vincent was walking towards the cafeteria for lunch when he ran into one of the regional security officers, or RSOs, Orlando Martinez. He smiled broadly, always happy to see this man who had become his friend.

Vincent waved. "Hey, Orlando, how are you doing today?"

The two of them fell in step, both walking towards the cafeteria. The smell of stir fry was wafting through the hallway as they approached it.

"Oh, I'm fine. The wife and kids just got back from the new Disney Shanghai Resort. They had a great time. I wish I could have gone with them," Orlando replied, a bit sullen.

"I'm sorry you weren't able to join them," Vincent remarked, taken aback. "Something keep you here?"

He was curious to know what could have kept his friend from this trip. The poor guy had been planning that vacation for months. It was all he had talked about.

The two of them got in line for the cafeteria's special of the day. Orlando sighed. "You know Mika, that new RSO that joined us two months ago?"

"Yeah, smart woman, and fluent in the language, too," Vincent replied.

Most RSOs rotated from one geographical region to another, so very few of them became truly proficient in the language of the host nation to which they were assigned. Vincent always thought it was a missed opportunity to not allow the RSOs to specialize in geographical regions so that they could establish those critical language skills and law enforcement connections.

"Well, her mother died suddenly in a car accident. She had to fly back for the funeral and help out with some family matters. Then, Tim's wife went into labor a month early, so he had to be with her. That meant we were down two RSOs. Normally, I wouldn't have needed to stay, but with the tensions as high as they are with the elections back home, the ambassador wanted me here," Orlando replied, a bit glum.

"That's really too bad, Orlando. Why is the ambassador concerned about the election? From everything in the polls, it looks like our old boss, the former Secretary of State is going to win."

Vincent placed some cabbage, carrots, and a few other veggies in a bowl before handing it to the grill cook to stir-fry up for him. He loved stir-fry day at the cafeteria. He especially liked the hot spicy garlic sauce they added to everything.

Orlando reached out and grabbed his steaming hot plate of food from the cook before responding. "There's been a lot of hacking activity going on in the US and Europe," he explained. "Most of it's been coming from Russia. But that latest batch of Wikileaks documents shows some connection to a Chinese state-run organization. The FBI has been investigating it, and so has our office. I'll just be glad when the election is over and we can all go back to doing our jobs again."

In his twelve years as an RSO, he had never had his time off canceled by an ambassador. Then again, there had never been a concerted effort by foreign actors to try and influence the US elections to this degree either. The internet and social media had completely transferred the social landscape of not just the US, but the world.

As the two men paid for their lunch, Orlando signaled for Vincent to join him at a quiet table along the wall.

As Orlando had finished a bite of food, he leaned forward and spoke softly. "Vincent, I have a question for you. What do you know about any Chinese government involvement in Mongolia?"

Vincent thought that was kind of an odd question. China had always had some government involvement in Mongolia. "Well, it's interesting that you bring that up. Recently, we've seen a lot of interest from the Chinese security service in Mongolia. What are *you* thinking, Orlando?"

"Well, there've been some issues there lately. A friend of mine owns a private equity firm in Mongolia, so he provides me with a lot of good insight into the happenings. As you know, Rio Tinto has that $7 billion copper mine under construction. They also have a new uranium mine under construction that has caught the Chinese interest."

Vincent nodded. Orlando paused long enough to take another bite of his lunch before continuing, "Most of the labor for the mines comes from China. However, over the last two years, there's been a lot of tension between Chinese and Mongolian workers. While Mongolia needs the Chinese laborers, there has been a deep-seated resentment and distrust between the two factions. The Mongolians believe the Chinese are trying to assimilate Mongolia into China by flooding the country with its own citizens."

"Do you think there's any truth to that rumor?" asked Vincent.

After shoveling another bite into his mouth, Orlando answered, "Well, Mongolia has roughly three million people. Yet there are five million Chinese workers living in the country, and another six hundred thousand non-Asian expatriates. In just the last six months, there have been a dozen attacks against Chinese workers. While it's not certain that all the attackers have been Mongols, the rate of violence between Chinese and Mongols has been increasing significantly. Have you heard anything about the Chinese government's intentions regarding Mongolia? I mean, I know it's kind of a broad question I'm asking, but any little bit would help."

Vincent took a long drink of water, giving him time to think for a second before responding. "I'll admit, I wasn't aware of some of those situations—though it does make sense why there's been an increase in the number of security service interactions with the Mongolians. I know there are a lot of mining interests in Mongolia, and the Chinese covet the fertile farmlands as well." He paused for a second to consider something else.

"For centuries, China has considered Mongolia to be a part of Greater China, but they also think that of most of Siberia and Southeast

Asia. Look, I have a meeting with my counterpart next week. I'll make a note to ask them about Mongolia and get back to you," Vincent replied, pulling out his smartphone to make a quick note.

Once he finished typing, Vincent leaned forward. "Orlando, perhaps you can help me with a similar question. For decades, China has been buying large quantities of rice from Vietnam, Laos, and Cambodia, but I've noticed that it tapered off about two years ago. Do you happen to know if there's a diplomatic row between these countries and China?"

Orlando sat back in his chair, raising his left eyebrow in surprise. "Surely you remember the dispute between the two countries over the Paracel and Spratly Islands in the South China Sea—those large oil and natural gas findings. Then there was that situation with the oil rigs in the Gulf of Tonkin."

Vietnam had discovered pockets of oil and natural gas that showed great promise. The resources were clearly in Vietnamese-controlled areas, but the Chinese had swooped in to claim territorial rights over them. Vietnam had then taken the dispute before the World Trade Organization, which had ultimately sided with Vietnam. China, however, had refused to recognize the verdict and severed trade relations with Vietnam.

Vincent snickered before responding, "Man, you sure know how to make a guy feel like an idiot. Remember, I'm new to the political officer side of the house. I was an econ guy for most of my career."

Orlando smiled.

Vincent laughed at how stupid his question sounded now. "I don't know how I'd forgotten that. I've been trying to figure out this food shortage problem that started about two years ago. The tonnage of food being imported in hasn't changed, but the volume of tonnage consumed has. I'd overlooked the rice deal China and Vietnam used to have. I owe you a beer for helping me solve a problem that was right in front of me."

Orlando's mouth curled up on one side. "It's Ok, man. I'm sure you'll get me back sometime."

The two chatted on between mouthfuls of stir fry, putting pieces together, but still blissfully unaware of the larger plots at play.

Chapter 5
CMC and Politburo Pow Wow

Beijing, China
Great Hall of the People

The weather had finally turned cold and the fall leaves were nearly all gone. Winter would come soon enough, and then the smog would once again intensify as the 21 million residents of the city began to heat their homes and apartments. As Zhang walked into the private entrance to the Great Hall of the People, he removed his HEPA filter mask. He hated wearing that thing, but the smog this time of year made it a necessity.

It wasn't often that a meeting was called by the Central Military Commission or CMC in which the members of the Politburo Standing Committee were also in attendance, but this was not an ordinary meeting. Today was the meeting that would decide whether or not China would move forward with Chairman Zhang's plan to reassert Greater China and implement a new world order.

After everyone had gone through an extensive security check, which included a thorough sweep of electronic devices, the group was allowed to enter the secured briefing room in the bowels of the building. The secretive chamber was a suite of technology wizardry. One wall of the room was filled with large digital displays that could show PowerPoint briefings, live satellite feeds, drone or other video feeds. The opposite wall had a large map of China, Asia, and the rest of the world. There were also several monitors that had various news outlets on.

Once everyone had entered the room, the eight members of the CMC and the six members of the Politburo Standing Committee took their seats at the elegantly hand-carved board table to discuss the future of China and the world. As Chairman Zhang had organized this joint meeting, he'd made sure to arrange the name placards on the table so there would be a member of the military sitting between each member of the Politburo. He wanted everyone to be involved in the discussion.

Of course, his deputy, Liang Wei, was sitting against the back wall and would note each person who was against moving forward with the plan. Each person who raised objections would be dealt with separately, to include the President if need be. The future of China and the world was too important for one or two men to stand in the way of progress. Zhang would see to that.

President Xi knew Chairman Zhang was working behind the scenes on a grand and elaborate plan with the Russians. While he knew most of what Zhang had been working on, this meeting would bring to light the full scope of it. President Xi was no fool; he knew there were structural problems within the Chinese society that needed to be solved. The size of their population, the lack of eligible single women for the hundreds of millions of single men, and the food and natural resource shortages were proving to be more than challenging to manage. The time for China to break out of its shackles was quickly approaching.

Zhang cleared his throat before beginning. "Mr. President, Generals, Politburo members, thank you for your time today as we discuss the future of China. As you know, I have been working behind the scenes to develop a plan to realize the dream of a Greater China— one where our lost provinces are returned and where we can see China fulfill our true destiny."

The various generals and politicians at the table all rustled a little in their seats. Many of the generals and politicians at the table, while not outwardly against such a notion, were reluctant to risk their stature and position to further China as a nation. They were comfortable with the status quo, which was why Zhang needed to identify who the holdouts would be, so they could be dealt with and replaced.

President Xi interrupted, "—Generals, gentlemen, Chairman Zhang has developed quite a comprehensive plan. I believe everyone should hear him out before passing judgment." He nodded slightly to Zhang. That was about as much support as he would provide until Zhang convinced the others to endorse his plan.

Zhang bowed slightly to President Xi as if to thank him, then continued, "The increased activity of Islamic militants in Xinjiang Province has become a national concern as the number of attacks across the region has increased to nearly one a week. The majority of these militants are being supported and trained in Afghanistan and Pakistan.

"For years, we have been pressuring the Pakistanis to deal with this problem. However, they are either unwilling or unable to deal with this situation. Therefore, the time has come for us to sever military and economic ties with the nation of Pakistan." Zhang saw several heads nod in approval. If there was a threat to the Communist party in the rural areas of China, it was radical Islamic terrorism. They would not allow it to spread any further than it already had, even if it meant sacrificing a marginal ally.

"The end of our relationship with Pakistan will give China an opportunity to resolve our longstanding dispute with the people of India." A few of the eyebrows in the room rose in surprise. Zhang continued, unhindered. "As of two days ago, we have settled that issue. We have given up our territorial disputes with India, and ending our military support to Pakistan was then sufficient enough for them to agree to a thawing of relations."

Zhang continued, knowing that some of these points had already been gone over the day before by the foreign minister. "India has also agreed to cede Southeast Asia as China's sole sphere of influence, while we turn a blind eye to India's brewing conflict with Pakistan." This gained more nods of agreement and smiles. They were probably thinking about the enormous activity that would be spurred between the countries now that their seemingly intractable issues had been resolved.

Now comes the tough part, thought Zhang. *Time to sell them on moving forward with the actual plan of Greater China.*

"We have some tough choices to make going forward," he told the group sternly. "As you know, for the past several years, violence against our people working in Mongolia has continued to increase. Our people are essentially treated like slaves in Mongolia. They're not allowed to own property, they're not allowed to marry women from Mongolia, and they're not treated with basic human respect and dignity."

Zhang could see the Politburo men nodding their heads, even some of the generals agreed. "Mongolia continues to thumb its nose at us, believing that their newfound wealth allows them to rise above their station. I would like to draw your attention to the folder being given to you on how we may deal with Mongolia," Chairman Zhang announced as Liang walked around the table, giving each member a folder with a political, military, and economic plan to deal with Mongolia.

Several hours passed as Zhang painstakingly put forward the benefits of his plan. The group then discussed the future of Mongolia and ultimately concluded that China should move forward with its acquisition of the country under the guise of protecting their own citizens. As the talks continued, tea was eventually brought in for everyone to share.

As the stewards left the room, Zhang turned towards the People's Liberation Army ground commander. "General Liu's forces will absorb Mongolia in a single day."

Liu puffed his chest out at being mentioned in such a strong light.

"During the dark of night, our airborne forces will secure the various airports across the country in a swift and decisive move. While their people sleep, our Special Forces will capture the TV and radio stations, along with other key targets throughout the city. They'll also capture the Mongolian president and prime minister." There were even more nods of approval and smiles from the generals. They loved to have their egos stroked, and Zhang made sure each general was mentioned in glowing terms in front of the Politburo members.

"While our armed forces are capturing their objectives, our cyber-warfare and electronic communication groups will seal the country off electronically. By the time the sun comes up, the entire country of Mongolia will be cut off physically and electronically from the rest of the world."

General Liu smiled broadly at the thought of his forces being given this great honor; he would be given the opportunity to show the world how powerful the Chinese military had become.

One of the Politburo members, Huang Li Jun, signaled that he wanted to speak. Zhang nodded towards him to take the floor. "Mr. Chairman, while I support the overall premise of Greater China, the Americans just elected a new president. Many of us do not know who he is, or how his government would respond to China's provocative move. From what he has said during the campaign, he appears to want to take a hardline stance with China."

Zhang had known this question would be asked and had prepared a response for it. He signaled for Liang to present the next set of folders for everyone to review. "We have done a detailed assessment of the new American president. His interests are largely related to trade deals, jobs, and currency values. His agenda is heavily slanted towards domestic politics and going after Islamic terrorism, not Asia. As a matter of fact, we have it on good authority that his new ambassador to China will be none other than Governor Max Bryant."

Zhang gestured to President Xi. "Mr. President, I believe you know Governor Bryant well. Do you believe he will be a problem for our

Greater China strategy?" he asked, hoping to get the president to place his stamp of approval on his plan once and for all.

The president smiled. He knew exactly what Zhang was doing, but at this point he was already on board with the plan. Looking at the others at the table, Xi replied, "No. I do not believe he'll be a problem. Max is going to be focused on increasing trade and reducing their trade imbalance with us."

Xi sighed, then continued, "What most people don't realize, or don't want to believe, is that America is not the tiger it used to be. Their forces are spread out fighting in the Middle East. Their military members are tired from nearly two decades of war. Their equipment, aircraft and ships are also nearing the end of their service life."

He paused for a second to let that sink in before continuing, "When the Russians initiate their plans in Ukraine, the US will have to decide if they're going to come to the Europeans' aid or not. If they do come to Europe's aid, then they won't have the ability to stop us in Asia. We'll have a finite amount of time to implement our Greater China strategy. 'Possession is nine-tenths of the law,' as the Americans say. Once we have control of Southeast Asia and Mongolia, the Americans won't be able to do anything about it. They'll just have to accept it and deal with us, just as they'll have to deal with Russia once they control eastern Ukraine."

Seeing that everyone was agreeing with what he had just said, he moved forward with his recommendation. "I commend Chairman Zhang on his work organizing our efforts to initiate the Greater China strategy. I want everyone at this table to begin their part of the preparations. We have less than nine months to be ready to initiate the plan."

He had danced around approval for hours, but with this last statement, Xi had officially announced his support of Zhang's strategic initiative. It was now incumbent on the others to do their part and get the country ready to expand its national borders.

Chapter 6
Good Morning Vietnam

Hanoi, People's Republic of Vietnam
US Embassy

Lieutenant Colonel Lisa Kowalski worked in the US Army's Office of Defense Cooperation or ODC at the US embassy in the People's Republic of Vietnam. She had been assigned there about a year ago, after a stint at the embassy in Jakarta, Indonesia.

After the previous administration had announced a military "pivot" to the Pacific, the US had expanded its military training opportunities and exchange programs with several of the countries that the US had traditionally excluded, like Vietnam, Laos, Cambodia, and Myanmar. This included sales of equipment and training opportunities in countries that had previously been less than friendly with the United States. The new president had kept up this policy, which was applying pressure in a roundabout way to the Chinese.

Lisa was the perfect person for a role in the ODC. She was energetic and outgoing, the consummate salesperson. She loved her job, even though it was a bit complicated to explain what she did every day. As a key player in establishing the China containment policy, her office was coordinating several naval port calls that should start to take place at the end of 2017 and into 2018, along with a potential US naval exercise with the Vietnamese navy. She had a way of getting even the most reserved people to talk to her. While some men in Asian cultures tended to treat her with some disregard as a woman; she didn't let it bother her. Despite the cultural differences, she managed to develop good friendships and relationships within Vietnam that were opening up opportunities.

One of Kowalski's primary goals in Vietnam was to establish a series of Joint Combined Exchange Training or JCET opportunities. These exercises were designed to benefit the host countries while also helping the United States behind the scenes. What would typically happen was that a group of military members would come in and demonstrate equipment that would be available for sale, as well as conduct training about possible scenarios that the host country might be interested in. Covertly, while they were training the foreign militaries, they would also be assessing where some of the country's weak spots were in terms of defense.

After nine months, Lisa had broken through the different layers of bureaucracy in Vietnam and had gained approval for the first of what she hoped would be several JCETs in her host county.

The first JCET would take place in the end of August and would bring in a US Special Forces group and a Navy SEAL team as well. The Army SF team would provide training on counterinsurgency operations, while the SEALs would provide training on how to raid and secure an oil platform.

The Vietnamese were very interested in these demonstrations as these were two very real scenarios that the Vietnamese continued to train for, in case hostilities with China should ever resume. Ever since Vietnam had discovered a series of oil and natural gas deposits in the Gulf of Tonkin and the South China Sea, tensions had been high. As China continued to lay out new territorial claims, it was only be a matter of time until a conflict over one of them broke out.

The main person Lisa had to convince to approve the JCET had been a hard nut to crack, but really, it was more out of general stubbornness that he had ever turned down the invitation. Once he was fully aware of the opportunity, he was actually excited about the upcoming JCET, even if he never managed to publicly crack a smile. Lisa didn't care; she was used to working with crusty people. It was almost like a contest for her to see how quickly she could get someone over to her side.

While Lieutenant Colonel Kowalski was coordinating Vietnam's JCET, her counterparts at the US embassies in Laos, Cambodia, and Myanmar were doing the same. Several JCETs would all be happening around the same time, which meant the Army Special Forces battalion and SEAL team stationed in Okinawa, Japan would be very busy in the end of August and into September.

Chapter 7
Great Day to be a Paratrooper

Gansu Province, Inner Mongolia China
Jinchang Military Training Grounds

Captain Ma Qiliang had just stood up in the back of the Xian Y-20 transport aircraft as his airborne company neared the drop zone. This was the best part of being a paratrooper—the lead-up to the jump out of the aircraft into the abyss below. This would be their tenth jump in four weeks, which was more than they had conducted the previous year, let alone in a single month.

The first few drops had been on a practice range to get the division used to dropping as a single unit. Nearly 11,000 paratroopers from the 43rd Airborne Division were participating in the jumps, the largest exercise in the history of the organization. The first two brigades would jump in and secure the objective; then the second wave with the last two brigades would follow with additional equipment and supplies.

Tonight's jump was on a simulated hostile airfield, which his battalion would secure and prepare to receive the additional heavy equipment that could not just be thrown out the back of an aircraft. It would be a timed event with observers, just like the last two jumps.

As he checked the parachute of the man in front of him, he could feel the man behind him doing the same. Then, the proverbial red light came on, letting them know they were almost to the drop zone. The jump master standing near the exit opened the door where they would be jumping out. Wind started to buffet their faces as they psyched themselves up.

A few minutes later, the green light came on, and the jump master signaled for everyone to start moving through the exit. One by one, the men of Captain Ma's company walked out the side entrance of the aircraft, their chutes opening seconds later.

In less than a minute, he had joined his men, rushing through the air. He felt his chute snap open, jerking his body from freefall to a soft, gentle floating sensation. As he looked around, the light of the moon allowed him to make out the white parachutes of the rest of the soldiers from his company, descending with him to the airfield below. Further out to his left and right, he could see the other companies of the battalion descending towards their objectives as well.

His group had been tasked with securing the terminal and the nearby hangars. Other teams would secure the control tower, the entrances to the airport, the runways, and the surrounding areas. His battalion had been training hard for the past several months leading up to this exercise. They had spent more time at the range over the last few weeks than he could remember. Just a month ago, his unit had been fully equipped with night vision goggles and body armor, which they now used during all their jumps. He almost felt like his unit had been transformed into one of the elite Special Forces units he used to read about as a child.

As he neared the ground, he prepped his body for the landing, bending his knees slightly and preparing to roll. His feet made contact with the earth below as he bent and rolled just as he had been taught and had done so many times before. In seconds, he was down on the ground, disconnecting his parachute, rolling it up as fast as he could while his eyes searched for his drop bag, which held his rucksack and extra ammunition. His rifle had been strapped to his body armor, so he had been ready for combat from the moment he had jumped out of the plane.

In less than five minutes, the majority of his soldiers had their gear on and were moving to secure their primary objectives. He left one of his sergeants to round up the stragglers and get them moving when they were ready. His soldiers moved to their various primary and secondary objectives, just as they had trained dozens of times before this jump, to the point that it was becoming second nature. As the observers watched and took notes, his men deftly moved to neutralize each of the mannequins that had been dressed like guards. Now that they knew where each entrance was from memory, his soldiers gained control of both their primary and secondary objectives in less than ten minutes, a new record.

After they had secured the objectives and met the training exercise goals, their observers went over everything they had done right and wrong. They spent the next two days working on their various approaches, training for how they would respond if a guard opened fire or additional security arrived at the airport. Once they had gone through a series of new challenges meted out by their observers, they were given one final jump. This would be their last jump before they would be certified as combat ready for whatever special mission their superiors were cooking up.

Captain Ma had no idea why they had been given so much training and specialized equipment these past few months, but it thrilled him. This was why he had wanted to become a paratrooper, to be a part of an elite force that could jump into any country and secure any objective given to them. He only hoped that after all this intense training and additional equipment, they would get to put their training to a real test soon.

Chapter 8
Intelligence Gap

Washington, D.C.
White House Situation Room

Dr. John Winters had been a key foreign policy advisor during the president's campaign, advocating for a hardline stance when it came to dealing with Islamic extremists. Despite popular opinion, President Gates was really not a military hawk or an interventionist. He believed America should refrain from foreign engagements, but if the US had to engage militarily, then it should do so with little restraint, fighting all out in order to win quickly.

As Dr. Winters sat through the CIA and DIA briefing on Russia and China, he started to get frustrated and dismissive of the information being provided. When it came to Asia, neither the CIA nor the DIA could agree on what was going on inside China or the Democratic People's Republic of Korea. China had just completed a several-month-long naval live-fire training exercise with both Russia and North Korea. Russia and China had also carried out a series of joint armored and airborne training exercises and were currently completing a series of air combat exercises.

While this wasn't the first time these nations had done joint military exercises, it was the first time either country had done them to this level. Nearly 250,000 troops on all sides had participated in the ground warfare exercises. In the case of North Korea, China and Russia had provided with them with a massive surge of money, munitions, fuel, food and new weapons. Individually, these situations were alarming. Collectively, they were of grave concern.

While the Asian desks at the CIA and DIA could not fully agree on what China and the DPRK were up to, there was no dispute about Russia. The Russians were providing additional heavy weapons and munitions to the separatists in Ukraine. They had even moved a few air-defense systems, armored vehicles and a couple dozen tanks to the Donetsk People's Republic. Of course, the Ukrainian central government did not recognize the Donetsk People's Republic, or any of the separatist groups demands or self-elected governments.

As the briefing ended, Dr. Winters raised his hand. "I appreciate your organizations' time and effort in developing this comprehensive brief. However, before we end this meeting, I'd like to clarify a few things. My first question is, what's the motivation behind this sudden increase in military activity in Asia? How do we know that this isn't just a distraction on the part of China or Russia? All this activity could just be a smokescreen for what's happening in Ukraine and the Middle East."

Both of the directors seemed a bit put off by the questions, partially because they were stumped by what it all meant as well.

The Director of the CIA finally admitted, "We don't know why there has been such a run-up of activity in China and Russia, at least not yet."

"Well, at least you're being honest with me," answered Dr. Winters. "It's important that we know if the Chinese are moving troops or heavy equipment to the border regions. We also need to know if they're shuffling around any major air wings; all of that could be an indicator of what's about to happen. Unless we know some of that information, then it will be hard for us to determine what their intentions are and what we tell the President...I want both of your agencies to figure this out and come back with an updated briefing within the next thirty days," he ordered.

There was some grumbling that was barely audible around the table, but the directors eventually agreed to collect additional information and meet with Dr. Winters again.

As he left the room, Dr. Winters was frustrated by the lack of preparation he had seen. The President had asked for a comprehensive strategy on Ukraine and how the country should deal with Russia. If the National Security Council wasn't giving him the best possible information, they could end up with a diplomatic misstep or an accidental conflict.

He decided that in addition to sending the intelligence agencies out to complete their previously inadequate work, he would make some phone calls of his own. He was a very connected man. Everyone he knew had a connection to someone with the information he sought.

Chapter 9
Mongolian Airborne

Ulaanbaatar, Mongolia
Chinggis Khaan International Airport

The Xian Y-20 was a beautiful heavy-lift, jet-powered aircraft, similar to the American C-17. Nearly every Y-20 in the Chinese Air Force inventory was in formation as they carried the 43rd Airborne Division to their first ever combat jump.

Captain Ma and his company had been in the air for nearly two and a half hours as they approached their drop zone, the Chinggis Khaan International Airport in Mongolia. Ma had had no idea that the fictitious airport they had been training to capture for months on end was an exact replica of this very place until two days ago. That was when he'd been told the target of their first live mission.

Captain Ma didn't know why China would invade Mongolia; he only knew that his division would be conducting combat jumps all across the country, and he had a job to do.

As the aircraft droned on, word came down from the flight crew. "We're approaching the drop zone," they announced.

The lights inside the cavernous aircraft switched from a soft blue to red as the jump master prepared to open the side doors. Then, the doors opened. The cool summer air began to circulate throughout the aircraft as they descended to 3,000 feet and made their final adjustments. The jump master signaled for everyone to stand up and get ready.

Captain Ma stood up along with the rest of his men and began to do a final check of their gear. Then the lights near the open doors turned from red to green, and the troops immediately began to exit the aircraft, just as they had done dozens of times before in training. In less than a minute, Captain Ma was shuffling towards the exit as he followed the man in front of him out of the aircraft. All 110 paratroopers from his company were now descending on the airport below them.

Ma immediately felt the rush of air around his body as he leapt from the aircraft and began his freefall towards the ground below. As his chute opened, he surveyed his landing site beneath him. The airport lights were still out.

So far, so good, he thought.

He and his men had been told that the cyber-warfare guys would be turning the lights out across the country. Most of the officers in his division had seemed skeptical, but surely they would be believers now. In minutes, his troopers would be on the ground, moving to secure their various objectives, along with the rest of their brigade.

It was nearly 0330 hours, making it the ideal time for them to capture the airport and the country. However, as Captain Ma reached the height of around 1,000 feet off the ground, he suddenly saw dozens of figures running around on the ground near the military side of the airport. While Ma's company was responsible for capturing the civilian side, he felt a sense of panic as he realized that his sister company might be about to meet some serious resistance. Then, all hell broke loose.

Near one of the military hangars, Captain Ma made out the distinct sound of an armored vehicle starting up. Shortly afterwards, another one roared to life. Their floodlights turned on, and suddenly, several large-caliber machine guns opened fire on the paratroopers descending towards to the earth.

BANG! BANG! BANG!

Green tracers crisscrossed through the night sky, reaching out for the falling soldiers.

Captain Ma was almost to the ground. He knew he had to focus on his unit's objectives; he couldn't think about the shooting going on at the other end of the airport.

In what felt like an instant, he found himself down on the ground, rolling up his parachute while his eyes quickly located his drop bag. He ran for it. As he did, he heard his senior sergeant call out to him.

"Captain Ma! Over here. We're forming up over here," his senior sergeant, Xe, announced.

Ma ran towards the small cluster of his soldiers, who quickly formed up into their platoons and moved towards their objectives. Just as they had practiced, they headed rapidly towards their various points, securing the civilian side of the airport. They encountered several security guards as they secured the terminal, but they quickly surrendered without putting up a fight.

While his company continued to secure their various objectives, Captain Ma was comforted as he heard the shooting die down on the military side. Clearly, the other company had subdued the enemy vehicles and had the situation under control.

While their battalion captured the international airport, the rest of their brigade was landing all around the capital. Several Special Forces units were hitting key targets within the city, capturing the president and the prime minister along with other key members within the government. When the sun came up on Sunday, August 21, 2017, the people of Mongolia woke to the sight of Chinese paratroopers walking the streets of the major cities across the country.

In just a single day, the 43rd Airborne Division of the People's Liberation Army Airborne Forces had essentially captured the entire power structure of Mongolia. However, the rest of the world wouldn't fully react to the news until much later. Information on the takeover was heavily controlled by the Chinese press, and the major world powers were far too distracted by the situation in eastern Ukraine, where the Russians had just instituted a no-fly zone. Not to mention, the majority of Americans could not identify Mongolia on a map. The victory was swift and somehow almost unnoticed, even though it happened in plain sight.

Chapter 10
War in Europe

Beijing, China
US Embassy, Chancellery Building

Ambassador Max Bryant had been appointed by the new president to be the US ambassador to China because he was a lifelong friend of China's President Xi. It was hoped that this friendship would give the US a competitive edge in the looming trade negotiations. As Ambassador Bryant sat in his office reviewing the latest State Department intelligence summary, he could not believe what he was reading. The Russians had shot down several NATO aircraft over Ukraine, and now they were demanding that US and NATO forces withdraw from the country or face severe consequences.

His deputy chief of mission or DCM had called an emergency meeting down in "the box" in an hour to discuss these developments. He hoped that once they got to the secured facility inside the embassy, his DCM and CIA station chief would be able to provide him with some better insight as to what was going on in eastern Europe and how it would affect things there in China.

Then of course there was the situation in Mongolia, which he had also recently learned about. *The President put out a statement condemning the Chinese takeover of Mongolia, but what exactly does that mean?* he wondered. *What does the President want me to do about it?*

Secretary of State Johnson had asked his team to determine what the Chinese government's intentions were with Mongolia and if this was just a temporary incursion or something more permanent. Ambassador Bryant placed the intelligence summary in the folder on the right side of his desk and grabbed his notepad as he left the office and headed for the bowels of the embassy. As he walked down the hall and got into the elevator, the senior defense official, Major General Robert Kip, joined him.

Major General Kip was the senior defense official stationed at the embassy and was responsible for helping the DCM and ambassador address and deal with the abundance of defense issues and challenges between the US and China. His insight into and knowledge of military affairs had proven invaluable during the eighteen months he had been stationed at the embassy. While his tour in Beijing was ending in six months, Ambassador Bryant planned on leveraging his expertise as often as he could.

While they were still moving from floor to floor, Ambassador Bryant asked, "What do you make of the situation happening in Europe?"

Pondering the question for a minute, General Kip answered, "I think things are heating up with Russia, and I'm not sure how our folks in Washington are going to deal with it," he said honestly.

The elevator dinged, letting them know they had reached the basement of the building, where the "box" was located. Inside of each US embassy was a Sensitive Compartmented Information Facility, where there was a top-secret computer and connection to both the intelligence community and headquarters back home. The SCIF at this new embassy building (which had been built in 2008) had a larger secured facility than most. The CIA used the chamber often to communicate with their home agency and kept this room staffed nearly 24 hours a day.

The two gentlemen walked down the hallway to a large cavernous room that was slightly raised above the ground and enclosed in a copper mesh. They walked in and saw the rest of the leadership team for the embassy already assembled.

There was the head Regional Security Office, the FBI's legal attaché, the senior political officer, the CIA's chief of station, the Defense Intelligence Agency representative, the deputy chief of mission, who was the senior career diplomat, and the senior defense official, who walked in with Ambassador Bryant.

With everyone seated, the meeting began. Deputy Chief of Mission Tim Gilmore started the discussion. "Well, ladies and gentlemen, the Russians have issued an ultimatum to NATO. They've given NATO until the end of the week to withdraw their forces back across the Dnieper River or they'll be forcibly removed. Then, they have another week to withdraw completely from Ukraine. While Europe is not our area of responsibility, we need to consider how the Russian actions are playing out here in Asia, and China in particular."

The others in the room looked around at each other and then back at the DCM. The political officer, Vincent Jones, spoke up next.

"Well, I'm not sure how the whole Russian angle fits into this, but I met with my counterpart yesterday afternoon, and it appears that China is not considering the situation with Mongolia a short-term problem. They insist that the Mongolian government has been complicit in the violence against their citizens, and more importantly, they believe that Mongolia is a part of Greater China—a lost province that they're bringing back into the fold."

Snorting before responding, the chief of station retorted, "China has been going on and on about their 'Greater China' policy for decades. They still believe in the Qing Dynasty, which encompasses Mongolia and most of Southeast Asia." He sighed before continuing, "Look, my agency does not believe there's a link between what is going on in Europe and the sudden annexation of Mongolia, but I do. I think the Chinese are using the situation in Europe to expand their territory and return to the borders that existed prior to 1911."

Ambassador Bryant signaled that he wanted to add something. "I've known President Xi for more than thirty years. I don't believe he would lead China towards a confrontation with the US. He wants to improve relations with America and focus on jobs. What evidence do we have that China is moving towards a greater military confrontation?" he asked, sounding skeptical.

The DCM held up his hand before anyone could get another word in edgewise. "I'd like to get our military members in on the discussion now. What are your thoughts, gentlemen?"

The senior Defense Intelligence Agency representative, Terry Bell, interjected, "—Look, we have seen an enormous increase in Chinese military activity. I've been stationed here in China for fifteen years. I'd like to think I know a thing or two about how they operate and what they're doing. I'm just going to address the military perspective and leave the politics to you professionals. Over the last two decades, the Chinese have spent an inordinate amount of money modernizing their force. They know where they're weak and where we are strong. They've built their force structure around those strengths and weaknesses."

"Right now, they're moving entire army groups from one part of the country to another for 'training exercises.' That's a load of crock. The entire airborne force that captured Mongolia has already been replaced by regular soldiers and transferred down south. They've moved nearly 500,000 soldiers towards the borders of Vietnam, Laos, and

Myanmar. They've shifted nearly 70% of their entire air force to bases within striking range of those countries. Never in the fifteen years I've been here in China have I seen them move this many soldiers or this much equipment from one part of the country to the other for an 'exercise.'"

Major General Kip added, "The unique thing about these moves by the Chinese military is that they're intentionally avoiding the appearance of any hostility towards Taiwan. They're even drawing from forces stationed in that area to be moved further south. I believe they're doing this because they want to assure the US that any future military moves they make are not directed at any US allies. They are focusing on what they have traditionally viewed as 'internal affairs' within China."

The DCM brought everyone's thoughts back to the initial question. "So, what is our opinion, then, that we want to transmit back to headquarters and the National Security Council?"

Everyone thought about that for a moment, and then slowly, each of them gave their opinion. The consensus was that China, while certainly acting provocatively towards its neighbors, was not directly threatening the United States, global trade, or any US allies...*yet*. China might move on Laos, Vietnam, and Myanmar, but would not attack Taiwan, Japan or South Korea. They decided to write up a report to this effect and send it back to D.C.

As to how to proceed, the people in the room simply could not come to an agreement. The debate over what their official response should be and what their positions should be behind the scenes remained cordial, even though there were strong disagreements. Although the meeting was originally only supposed to last for an hour or two, they were there for over four hours. Ultimately, they could not come to an agreement and decided to wait on directions from the higher-ups on how the US government should respond to China.

Chapter 11
Canceled Party in the Jungle

Okinawa, Japan
Torii Station

Chief Warrant Officer Four Charles "Chucky" Lee was excited about the planned trip to Vietnam at the end of the week. They had been planning this JCET for nearly a year with the ODC, a female lieutenant colonel from the embassy in Hanoi.

As Chucky was finalizing the contents of his pack, his battalion commander, Lieutenant Colonel Hank Mitchel, knocked on the door to his office. "You got a second, Chief?" he asked. "We need to talk."

"Sure thing, Sir," he replied, placing the last item in his bag before closing it up. He walked around his desk and shook Colonel Mitchel's hand. "What can I do for you, Sir?"

"I believe the JCET is going to be canceled, and I wanted to go over the change with you," he said.

"And here I thought we were going to get an all-expenses-paid vacation to Vietnam!" Chucky replied with a wide grin, trying to lighten the mood. He knew the colonel had been looking forward to the JCET as well. He didn't typically go with the teams that often, but he had planned on being a part of this one to help with the country assessment.

Laughing at Chucky's comment, Colonel Mitchel replied, "You know, my dad wouldn't have called it a 'vacation' when he went to Vietnam in the summer of '67, but I do appreciate your attempt at humor." He signaled for them to walk to his office and talk further once they got there.

As they walked through the door, Chucky saw Major Lance Witten, the battalion's intelligence officer waiting for them there as well. The colonel gestured to him. "Major Witten has some intelligence updates that you should be aware of," Mitchel said as he walked around the desk to get to his seat.

Looking behind the colonel's desk and out the window, Chief Lee could see the wind was really starting to pick up. There was supposed to be a tropical storm moving through the area in a couple of days, so the island was starting to experience some of the outer bands.

Major Witten raised his hand a bit and made sure he had Lee's attention. "Chief, we have a problem right now in China. As you have likely already heard, Chinese airborne forces invaded Mongolia a week ago."

Chief Lee snorted. "Sir, with all due respect, they didn't just invade Mongolia a week ago—they captured the entire country in twenty-four hours. That's a feat we did not believe was possible, at least not according to you intelligence weenies," Chief Lee retorted. He hated it when intelligence officers liked to state the obvious without adding anything of value. This was Special Forces, not the regular Army; they didn't need to be spoon-fed intelligence.

Major Witten smiled at the feisty response before continuing, "Yes, they secured the entire country in twenty-four hours. Now it appears they're getting ready to gobble up a couple more countries."

"So, what does that have to do with us and our JCET?" Chief Lee asked again, a bit annoyed at being led to an answer rather than just told it.

"One of the countries they're looking to annex next appears to be Vietnam." He paused for a second to let that sink in. "Then most likely they'll go after Laos and Myanmar. As of right now, they don't appear to be threatening Taiwan, Japan, or South Korea. Thailand and Cambodia also don't appear to be in their crosshairs either," he explained.

"Before you ask, we don't know when they're planning to invade, but we anticipate it to be very soon, which is why we're recommending to Group Headquarters that the JCET be canceled. We don't want you guys to be caught in country if they're invaded."

"Does this have anything to do with what's going on in Europe?" Chief Lee asked. He had friends in 10th Special Forces Group, which was now fully deployed to Germany as tensions with Russia grew. Nearly half of 10th Group was already in Ukraine as advisors.

Shoot, half of my unit wants to transfer to Europe to fight the Russians, he thought.

Major Witten leaned forward, speaking in a lower voice. "Look, this needs to stay between us. The consensus is split right now. The CIA and State Department believe the Russians are just posturing right now, that at the end of the day, they'll blink. However, the DIA and even the ambassador on the ground in Ukraine believe otherwise, and so does the

Secretary of Defense. As to China, no one knows for certain. If I were the Chinese, I'd be using the situation in Ukraine to my advantage. Have either of you heard of the term 'Greater China'?" he asked.

Both men shook their heads.

"OK, up until 1911, the Chinese national border used to encompass Mongolia, parts of Vietnam, Laos, Taiwan, Myanmar, and the Koreas. They lost a lot of that territory during the two world wars and their own civil war. The intelligence sources on the ground are hearing that Chinese officials have been saying that they want to unite Greater China once again. Until now, no one really took them seriously, but with their recent annexation of Mongolia and the massive troop movements to those border countries, it now looks like they're going to move in that direction."

Lieutenant Colonel Mitchel held his hand up for a second and interrupted, "Wait, I thought you just said the Koreas and Taiwan are also part of this Greater China...they're not moving forces to those border areas like you mentioned?"

"No, they're not," Major Witten replied. The intelligence reports I've read from DIA about this, as well as a report from the Beijing embassy DIA rep, which I believe is probably the most accurate, conclude that the Chinese don't want a direct confrontation with the US, at least not yet. They're leaving traditional US allies alone for the time being and going after countries we don't have a strong relationship with."

It makes sense, thought Chief Lee. The US was less likely to get militarily involved in preventing China from annexing Vietnam or Myanmar than they would be if there were action in Taiwan, Japan, or South Korea.

"OK, so let's assume the JCET is canceled. What do you want us to do with this information? Should we start preparing to deploy to these countries, or just concentrate on our allied nations?" Chief Lee asked.

Lieutenant Colonel Mitchel jumped in. "Right now, Chief, keep training the men like we're heading to war with China, just like we always do. Whether we get sent to South Korea or Vietnam won't matter. We'll still be facing the same enemy. The terrain may be different, but the Chinese soldiers we face won't be. Also, we're not getting those two replacement captains we thought we would. Apparently, a lot of the SF qualified officers have been rerouted to 10th Group to support operations in Ukraine. It looks like you and Chief Limski are going have to remain in command of your two teams for the time being."

With that, the meeting broke up and Chief Lee went down to the team room to break the news to his soldiers. There would be a lot of broken hearts over not going to Vietnam.

Chapter 12
Start of Red Storm

Pingxiang, China
110 Miles Northeast of Hanoi, Vietnam

General Yang Yin looked out the helicopter window as they approached his headquarters building. In nearly every direction, he could see the various units that made up his army group encampment, uncertain of what would come next.

Yang had been rigorously training his group for four long months. In that time, they had spent more time at the range honing their shooting abilities than they had in the past two years. In addition, they spent part of every day down at the field simulators, working small unit tactics and practicing combat in a combined arms environment. His generals, colonels, and majors had devoted hours of classroom time to watching videos and conducting tabletop exercises on how to effectively employ armor, artillery, and mechanized infantry forces into an attack.

They had also watched countless videos of the American invasion of Iraq and the earlier Persian Gulf War, examining how various tactics had been used to great effect. For all their faults and misgivings, the Americans were the masters of warfare in the air, on the sea, and on the ground. No nation on earth knew how to kill people more efficiently than the Americans. It was for that reason that General Yang placed such a heavy emphasis on learning their tactics and then working to implement them in his own army group. While other army groups trained their men according to standard Chinese military doctrine, he opted for an unconventional and more aggressive plan. His efforts would be tested soon, and he would either prove to be a brilliant military leader or be replaced for not trusting in the traditional military doctrine.

Yang's helicopter began to circle the landing pad, coming in for its final approach before settling down on the grassy knoll not far from the building he had commandeered as his forward headquarters command. It had been a quick, whirlwind meeting with the People's Liberation Army General Staff in Beijing. He was eager to get his part of the operation moving and prove to his superiors that his training program would work.

General Yang was not like a lot of the traditional Chinese generals. He came from an aristocratic family, but unlike many other generals, he had grown up in the United States. His father had been a wealthy businessman and owned several factories in the US and China. During his teenage years in America, he'd expressed an interest in serving in the Chinese military when they returned to home one day, so his father had enrolled him in a military school in America.

His father had encouraged this interest and had done whatever he could to give his son a competitive edge when entering the People's Liberation Army. However, when Yang had graduated high school, instead of returning to China to join a Chinese military academy, he'd applied to and been accepted by a prestigious American military academy, the Citadel.

During his four years of study at the Citadel, he'd attended the US Army jump school and had been among the few students selected to attend Ranger School. Being a foreign student, he was given a lot of opportunities that most students wouldn't have gotten until after they had joined the active-duty military. Yang had kept quiet about his goal of returning to China. It wasn't that he didn't like—even love—living in America. He did. Yang had many American friends, but his true love was his ancestral homeland, China.

He wanted to see China succeed and become the dominant world power. While he loved many aspects of American culture, he deeply resented the culture of identity politics, various forms of racism, and the never-ending pursuit of money at the expense of others in society. The Americans seemed to value making money over taking care of their own people. In Yang's eyes, while China might have a lot of problems, it provided its people with free education, free healthcare and a stable government that didn't swing from one end of the political spectrum to the other with each election. It provided what Yang thought was the most important—stability.

After completing his studies at the Citadel, Yang had re-joined his family in China and been introduced to several high-ranking party officials and military generals that his father routinely did a lot of business with. His father's factories produced a lot of military equipment, so he was well connected in those circles. Once they'd learned that Yang had not only attended one of the top American military academies but had gone through the Army Ranger School, Yang's stock in these powerful men's eyes had increased substantially. It had been decided that they would become Yang's patrons and help mentor and guide Yang through his career in the military to become a general and a leader in the new PLA.

Twenty years later, Yang was now the Commanding General for the Southern Theater of Operations. When he had been read in to Operation Red Storm, he'd moved his headquarters to Pingxiang to be closer to his command when the annexation of Vietnam eventually began. Unlike a lot of other generals, Yang wanted to be near the action so he could adjust tactics quickly if the situation warranted it.

General Yang's force, Army Group A, consisted of the 14th Army, 41st Army and the 42nd Army. He had roughly 69,000 soldiers spread across six divisions, all ready to roll across the border. He had been told his objective was to secure Hanoi and the surrounding area, then let General Sheng's Army Group B—which consisted of the 20th Army, the 27th Army, and the 38th Army—pass through his lines as they moved further south and secured the next set of objectives.

Never in his entire military career had General Yang seen such a large display of Chinese military might in one place, ready to be sprung. When he had been recalled to Beijing four weeks ago, he'd thought he was going to be replaced. Yang was a relatively young general by Chinese standards—only forty-four. However, his patrons in the Politburo had been advocating for years to update the military, not just in terms of weapons and equipment, but also in bringing in a younger generation of generals who were tuned into modern technology and tactics. Unfortunately, one of his key patrons had suffered a heart attack a few months ago, and that had left Yang uncertain of his future as the youngest army group commander since the revolution.

When General Yang had arrived in Beijing, instead of the nasty surprise firing he had anticipated, he had been read into a secret military operation that had been put together by Chairman Zhang, arguably China's most forward-looking leader. He might be the third-ranked person in the Chinese government, but he was probably the most powerful.

As General Yang had read through his portion of Red Storm, his eyes had grown wide with excitement. China was finally going to ascend the global stage as a real superpower—not just an economic superpower, but a military superpower and the dominant leader of Asia.

This was why he had wanted to join the military, to help lead his country into that glorious future.

As General Yang exited his helicopter and walked towards his command building, a commandeered government building, he signaled to his officers that he wanted them to follow him to his office. Once he had walked into the room that had been designated as his, he neatly placed his bag down in an almost robotic way and then grabbed the water bottle next to his computer. After taking a long drink, he looked at his executive officer and six division commanders, who were staring at him, waiting for instructions.

"We've been given the orders," Yang began. "We are to invade Vietnam in 48 hours. I want you to get your divisions ready." He paused long enough to pull out several folders from his bag, handing one to each of the division commanders and another to his executive officer.

"These are your division orders and objectives," he informed the division commanders.

The men nodded, beginning to pore over the flood of new information.

Pointing to his XO's folder, he said, "Your folder holds our army group orders and objectives. Obviously, I want them gone over by our planners to make sure we have everything covered."

Yang sighed. "Before you ask, I don't know what the other divisions or army groups are doing. I only know *our* orders and what *we* are supposed to accomplish. Please move to have your soldiers prepare to carry out the orders given to us. The eyes of China and the world will be upon us. We cannot fail."

His future, his life, depended on the ability of the men in front of him to execute the orders they had just been given. The PLA didn't look fondly on failure, and neither did the generals above him. He would be equally hard on his own generals and their officers. The state must prevail at all costs.

Chapter 13
Basement Dwellers

Hanoi, People's Republic of Vietnam
US Embassy

Lieutenant Colonel Lisa Kowalski was overwhelmed by the continued screaming of the air raid sirens, which continued to wail all around her. Another wave of Chinese bombers began to hit strategic areas around the city. Several bombs landed close enough to the embassy that it caused the building to shake violently, even from Lisa's vantage point in the basement. Fortunately, the reinforced bulletproof windows were holding so far, and none of them had burst from the impacts.

As Lisa looked around the basement of the embassy, she could see fear written across the faces of those huddled under the various tables and desks. Like her, the CIA station chief sat in a chair, trying to read a book and wait out the bombing. Others looked at them like they were crazy for not trying to hide and take further shelter.

The CIA guy got tired of the looks and asked, "Do you really think a table or desk is going to save you if the floor above us collapses?" Then he went right back to reading his book.

Lisa giggled at the interaction. She had been deployed several times to Iraq and Afghanistan during the height of the war, so she remembered what it was like to wait out a rocket or mortar attack. There really wasn't much point to hiding under a table or desk if the multi-ton floor above you collapsed; it was just as likely to kill you whether you were under a desk or sitting in a chair reading a book.

The embassy had been warned by the DIA about 48 hours ago that the Chinese might attack Vietnam. The State Department, however, insisted that China was just making a show of force along the border, that they would not invade.

Two hours ago, when the first bombs and missiles had begun to hit the capital city of Hanoi, the ambassador had sent an urgent message to headquarters asking what to do. They had been directed to get all nonessential personnel out of the country as best they could and to hunker down in the basement of the embassy. Supposedly, headquarters was working on coordinating things with the Chinese government to make sure the embassy and its staff weren't targeted by whatever the

Chinese were currently doing, but that brought little comfort to those in the basement with Lisa. There wasn't anything to do but wait, whether nervously or curled up with a book.

Chapter 14
Run Pappi, Run

Nasva, Russia

Lieutenant Colonel Rob Fortney ("Pappi") was exhausted. He had been trudging through the woods, farm fields, dirt roads, and streams, evading Russian search parties for nearly a week. He wasn't sure how far he had traveled on foot, but at some point, he'd stopped hearing dogs and helicopters, so he figured he must have moved far enough away from the search party that they had lost him.

I hope Ricky made it out, he thought as he surveyed a farmhouse not far from the edge of the woods, squinting to see if the inhabitants had a vehicle. He knew he would never be able to walk out of Russia, but it occurred to him that unlike in the Soviet Union, a person could drive from one region to another within Russia without special papers. He figured he could hotwire a car, drive it as close to the Latvian border as possible, and then cross on foot. He had been scoping out this farmhouse for hours now, waiting to see if there was any activity, and wondering if someone might come home later in the day.

Around 1900 hours, he saw a middle-aged man pull into the drive in a Lada Priora. He intuitively knew he had found what he was looking for. The man got out of the vehicle carrying what appeared to be a bag of groceries and walked into the house. Several lights turned on inside as the man began his evening routine. Pappi waited almost three more hours, until the lights slowly began to turn off and he believed that the man was now in bed, asleep.

To be absolutely certain, Pappi waited another hour before he moved cautiously towards the Lada. As he approached, he gently lifted the door handle, hoping with everything in him that no car alarm would go off. As he lifted it, the door slowly opened without incident.

No alarm, thank God, he thought.

Pappi knew if he started the car in the driveway, chances were the owner would hear it. Instead, he placed the vehicle in neutral and released the parking brake. Then he positioned his hands on the frame of the driver's-side door and gently pushed the car backwards down the driveway. As he neared the road, he turned the steering wheel slightly, angling the car onto the road.

Once the vehicle was on the road, he pushed it a little further, to make sure he wasn't directly in front of the house he had just stolen it from. With the coast clear, he looked for the wires under the steering column that would allow him to hotwire the car. It took him a few minutes and a few false starts to find the right wires, but eventually the engine of the Lada Priora roared to life.

With the vehicle running, he hopped in and opened the glove box. Inside, he found a couple of maps, which he quickly began to look over. He had to estimate where he was since he had no GPS and hadn't had access to coordinates for some time, but he saw he wasn't too far from a road that would lead him down to the M-9. If he had calculated correctly, that road would turn into the E-22, which would lead directly to Latvia.

It was roughly 0000 hours, and Pappi knew he had roughly eight hours or so until the sun came up. If he was going to make his break for it, he needed to do it at night, while there was limited traffic on the roads. After getting turned around once, he found a sign that led him to the M-9. From there, he drove for roughly an hour and then the road turned into the E-22.

He glanced nervously at the fuel gauge. There was a little more than three quarters of a tank, but he wasn't sure how far that would take him.

After nearly two hours on the road, he drove through a couple of small cities and towns. He had seen very few vehicles, and the only ones he did observe were military transport trucks. Many of them were carrying soldiers, towing artillery pieces or carrying other tools of war. He made sure to keep his distance; he was too close to making it out of Russia to get pulled over for tailgating a military truck or trying to pass one.

As he got closer to the Latvian-Russian border crossing at Terehova, he spotted a small gas station on the right and pulled over. He was less than a mile from the Latvian border and freedom, but he still wasn't sure how to get across the border without being stopped by the Russians. Because Latvia was a NATO member state, there were a number of Russian infantry fighting vehicles and armored personnel carriers, BMPs and BTRs, blocking the road at the border. Neither side was actively shooting at each other—at the moment, both sides were content to hope the war would stay in Ukraine and not involve them all the way up here.

Pappi parked the Lada behind the gas station and pulled out the map. He didn't want to get any closer to the border with those Russian soldiers guarding it. He needed to figure out another way across without being seen.

As he continued to search the map, he found a little dirt road that looked like it ran along the border. Pappi looked up, and sure enough, roughly 50 meters from the gas station, there it was—a small, unassuming dirt road. In that moment, he decided to drive the Lada along that road. He would try to get as close to the border as he could that way and then either cross on foot or try to ram the vehicle through the border fence if he thought he could.

Keeping the headlights off, he slowly moved down the dirt road, driving towards freedom. After traveling the small unkept road for a few minutes, he began to see the divide between the two countries. The area wasn't lit by lights along the border, but a clearing had been cut and a fence ran between it, clearly outlining the demarcation. Pappi pulled the car over off the road and turned it off, angling it slightly so he could get back into the vehicle in a hurry if he needed to.

He walked through the wooded area towards the demarcation line; he wanted to see with his own eyes if there were any guard towers or roving patrols. As he approached the edge of the trees, he came upon the demarcation line. Looking left and then right, he spotted two guard towers, roughly 500 meters away from him in either direction. The fence was roughly twelve feet high but didn't look to be reinforced with any antivehicle rails or traps.

I wish I could walk out there and inspect the fence, Pappi thought. *Maybe I should just go back to the car and try to ram through it.*

After spending some time considering his options, Pappi glanced down at his watch and saw that it was roughly 0430 hours. He knew he needed to decide what he was going to do soon. The sun would be up in a few more hours. Pappi walked back to the Lada and started the vehicle. As he fastened his seat belt, he heard a noise.

Several Russian soldiers were approaching his vehicle from behind. They started to yell out to him. Pappi didn't speak a lick of

Russian, but he could tell by the tone of their voices that they weren't happy with him.

In that moment, Pappi knew he needed to make a run for it or he'd become a prisoner of war. He slipped the car into gear and then floored it. As he sped through first gear and started shifting into second gear, the soldiers behind him opened fire with their AK-74s.

Bullets shattered the rear windows of the Lada. In his driver's-side side-view mirror, he saw one soldier talking on a radio while several others fired more rounds into the car. Then the mirror suddenly shattered as it was hit by one of the bullets.

As shots continued to fire, his rear tires blew out. Pappi charged ahead, adrenaline racing. The engine was roaring as he shifted into third gear and continued racing down the road. He was less than a hundred meters from the fence as he drove his car into the cleared demarcation line.

Suddenly, the passenger-side window exploded in a cloud of glass and flying shrapnel. More bullets punched their way through the passenger side of the vehicle as he neared the fence, shifting into fourth gear.

As the Lada rammed into the fence, the front of the vehicle nearly came to a halt, catapulting the rear of the car into the air, bending the fence and landing upside down. The engine emitted a horrible sound, and smoke began to fill the car.

Pappi unclipped his seat belt and fell to the roof of the vehicle. He quickly crawled out the driver's-side window and ran for his life into the tree line on the Latvian side of the border. As he sprinted, he heard bullets whiz past his head and body, kicking up dirt near his feet.

Just as he was about to make it into the woods, he felt something hot and hard slam into the back of his right shoulder, throwing him to the ground. As he lay there on the ground, trying to catch his breath, bullets continued to whip overhead, hitting branches and trees, sending flakes of wooden shrapnel flying all around him.

As he recovered from the shock of being hit, he slowly crawled into the woods and away from the gunfire. As he dragged his body along the ground, he heard more shouting. Several vehicles roared towards him. He could tell they were closing in on him, but there was nothing he could do at that point. If these were the Russians, then they had him.

A small group of soldiers ran towards him with their weapons raised. As he saw their uniforms, a huge wave of euphoria washed over him. They were Americans.

An unknown man knelt next to him and spoke in English. "Are you American?" he asked incredulously.

At that moment, Pappi knew he had made it to safety. He smiled and answered, "Yes. I'm Lieutenant Colonel Rob Fortney, US Air Force." Then he passed out from his injuries.

****

When he woke up two days later, he discovered he had been transported to the military hospital at Landstuhl in Germany.

One of the doctors walked in after learning he had regained consciousness. "You are one lucky soldier, son," he said. From his wrinkles and grey hair, the doctor looked like he had been kept in the military a little longer than normal—he had definitely seen his share of war wounds.

Pappi was still orienting himself to what was even wrong with his body. He could see plenty of bandages, but at the moment he wasn't sure how serious it actually was. "What happened to me, Doc?" he asked.

"You were shot in the back of the shoulder. It required a series of surgeries to put everything back together. You're stable now, of course. You're going to be flown back to the US for additional surgery and recovery. You are going to have a metal plate where your shoulder blade used to be, and you will need extensive physical therapy, but honestly, all things considered, it could've been a lot worse."

The doctor let that sink in for a few moments before he said, "Listen, there's an Air Force intelligence officer waiting outside that wants to ask you some questions about how you got out of there. I told him he'd have to wait until you were up to it. So, take your time, but when you feel like you can tell your story, go ahead and hit this button to turn on your call light."

Pappi nodded. Once he felt like he had his head back on straight, he signaled for the officer to come on into the room. He explained how he had evaded the search party and then eventually stolen a Lada and driven to the border. The officer asked him several questions to clarify, but the conversation was friendly.

At the end of the interview, Pappi asked, "Hey, do you know anything about my copilot?"

The Air Force officer's face fell. "There's no easy way to tell you this. The Russians captured him and have him listed as a prisoner of war. I can't provide you with any further information."

Chapter 15
Enemies Within

Following Morning
Washington, D.C.
White House, Oval Office

It was a beautiful September morning as the leaders of both the Republican and Democrat parties from the House and Senate walked into the Oval Office. It was unusual for them to be called to the White House so early in the day. As they entered the Oval, they all immediately observed that several additional chairs had been brought in so that there would be room for everyone. They could tell it was a serious meeting, seeing that the Director of the FBI and the Attorney General—neither of whom looked very happy—were also in attendance.

As the congressional leaders took their seats opposite each other on the couches, the President took his seat in the head armchair, opposite the AG and FBI Director. His face was somber, and it looked like he had aged a year or two within a few days.

"Thank you for coming so early in the morning, everyone," the President began. "I've asked you all to be here today because I felt it was important to make sure the leaders of Congress knew what was about to happen and why. As you know, there have been an unprecedented number of intelligence leaks since I have taken office. We have worked to address those leaks, and this morning is the first step toward doing just that."

The President paused and looked at the AG and FBI Director before continuing, "I've asked the Director of the FBI and the AG to be here to explain the facts of the case. The evidence has been collected, and now it's time to walk you all through it. This is too big a deal for me not to bring your offices into the loop."

Concern was written over all the faces in the room. They knew things hadn't been going well with the war in Ukraine, but this move had them wondering what shoe was about to drop.

The Director of the FBI and the AG began to lay out the evidence against the three congressmen and one senator who had been caught committing espionage against the country. At first, the Senate and Congressional minority leaders thought this was a partisan witch hunt, until they heard the audio records, watched the videos, and read the highlighted portions of both emails and text messages. As the President spoke, the reality of what had happened began to set in. They could not believe that members of Congress could commit such open acts of treason against the people they had been elected to represent. The Speaker of the House was equally appalled that one of his caucus, a member of the Armed Services Committee, no less, had committed acts of espionage, especially during a war that had resulted in the deaths of US service members. He was seething with anger.

They were further aghast at hearing the number of other high-level government officials who had been identified in the dragnet. "What is being done about all of this?" asked the Speaker, horrified.

The AG answered, "These individuals are being arrested right now, while this meeting is taking place. A press conference is being scheduled to take place within an hour, at which time the President will announce the findings. The FBI Director and I will also speak to the press."

The President looked intently at both of the party leaders. "I want to assure both sides that despite what we've learned today, the war is still going on. The country and our military still need your support. I ask that we put aside our differences and come together as one country, one people, to defeat the Russians and ensure the Chinese don't threaten our allies."

When the meeting broke up, everyone headed to the White House press room to watch the President give his address. The media largely sat there in stunned silence, shocked by the information the President had just given them. Many suddenly realized they had been played by Russian intelligence, that they had unwittingly been pawns of a foreign power. When the AG and the Director of the FBI laid out the evidence, it suddenly became clear how they had also been complicit in all of this.

Once the statements were complete, there was about fifteen seconds of complete silence. However, as soon as the first journalist raised their hand to start asking a question, the room erupted into a din of hungry wolves, each trying to speak over one another to get their words heard above the others. The Attorney General and the Director of the FBI managed to stay professional despite the ravenous crowd.

The American people were enraged by these revelations. On social media, the country was fuming, railing against the Russians and the Chinese for their involvement. People were demanding a response, calling for action. Most of all, people wanted revenge.

Chapter 16
Pacific Pivot

50 Miles East of Okinawa, Japan

Rear Admiral James Lomas was spoiling for a fight as the USS *Carl Vinson* raced towards Okinawa. His good friend, Rear Admiral Munch, had been killed the other day when the remnants of his carrier strike group had been destroyed in the Black Sea. It was bad enough to suffer the defeat of the *Bush* carrier group—losing his friend and several thousand sailors, many of whom he had served with, only added to the insult.

Unfortunately, his strike group wasn't being transferred to the Atlantic to fight the Russians. They had been ordered to leave San Diego and head for Okinawa. They were going to link up with the *Reagan* carrier strike group and bolster the US presence in the Pacific. If things didn't turn into unmitigated conflict with the Chinese, then they might head up to the North Pacific and attack the Russian Pacific fleet. A couple of Russian submarines had already been sunk in the Pacific since the start of the war.

Captain Michael Richards, the captain of the *Carl Vinson* supercarrier, walked up to the admiral, handing him a report that had just come in from one of their destroyers. "Sir, one of the destroyers is reporting a submarine contact, roughly sixty miles from our current position," he announced.

Admiral Lomas took the report and digested the information quickly. Sixty miles was still outside their designated protective bubble. "Do we know if it's Russian or Chinese?" he asked.

"It appears to be Chinese. A Yuan-class, one of their newest and quietest diesel submarines. I ordered additional antisubmarine warfare assets to the area," the captain said.

"Excellent job, Captain. Send a message over to the *Reagan* and let them know of the contact as well," the admiral instructed. "I want to make sure they're tracking the submarine. The last thing we need is for one of our carriers to get ambushed by a Russian or Chinese submarine."

Admiral Lomas turned to find his operations officer. "Commander Ryan, what's the status of the Chinese fleet in the area?" he asked.

Commander Ryan had been the operations officer on the *Carl Vinson* for two years. Prior to that, he had done a tour at US Pacific Command. Much of his naval career had been spent in the Pacific, so he was well-versed in what the People's Liberation Army Navy was capable of.

"Sir, in our area, they appear to have only a handful of destroyers and roughly a dozen submarines," Commander Ryan replied. "The majority of their ships, including their three carriers, are south of us, off the coast of Vietnam, supporting their ground forces." As he spoke, Ryan pointed out the locations of the various ships on the digital map board.

The admiral took a moment to zoom in on the different types of Chinese subs for himself. *Hmm...*, he thought. *This seems odd.*

"Why do you suppose they have nearly all their advanced submarines up north here with us, as opposed to down south with the bulk of their fleet?" Lomas asked.

"I thought about that earlier today. The best assumption I could come up with is that they know their surface ships wouldn't fare well against ours. It's their submarines that can cause us some damage. They're most likely keeping their prized subs in our area, in case they feel a need to use them. Frankly, Admiral, I don't believe them to be a threat right now. They've stripped most of the land-based aircraft from our area of responsibility and sent them down south to support their ground operations in Vietnam. If they were planning something against our fleet, I don't think they would have stripped away so many of their land-based air support units, along with nearly half of their sub fleet," Commander Ryan responded. He sounded confident, but the admiral could tell that he was just offering up his best educated guess.

Thinking for a minute and then examining the map further, Admiral Lomas had to agree with that assessment as well. It appeared that the Chinese were going to gobble up some of their neighbors, knowing full well that the Americans were powerless to stop them for the time being, with the Russian war raging on. It angered him to realize how impotent the US had become. There was a time when the US had had the ability to fight two major armed conflicts at the same time; those days appeared to be gone.

Admiral Lomas' strike group continued on to Okinawa, linking up with the *Reagan* strike group and providing a power deterrent against a Chinese incursion towards Japan and more than enough of a force to keep the North Koreans in check. If they needed to, they could shift further south and support Taiwan, but that would leave South Korea and Japan essentially on their own, and China knew that as well.

Chapter 17
New Commander, New Strategy

Washington, D.C.
White House

Admiral Peter Meyers had taken over as the Chairman of the Joint Chiefs following the dismissal of General Joe Hillman. Of course, he didn't agree with this decision, but he understood why the President had made it. The United States had been caught completely off guard by the sudden turn of events in Ukraine, which had now led to a full-scale war between NATO and the Russian Federation. The fact that most of the intelligence community and the military had underestimated the Russians' resolve to go to war over Ukraine was a supreme miscalculation. Thus far, that tragic decision had led to some disastrous defeats.

The siege of Kiev, with nearly 9,000 NATO forces trapped in the city, was a media nightmare. Then, China had annexed Mongolia, and two weeks later, invaded the countries of Laos, Vietnam, and Myanmar.

When it was discovered that several members of Congress and dozens of senior government officials had been caught leaking highly classified intelligence, some of which had been used directly against US and NATO forces, the President had been left with no other move than to come down hard on the leakers and try to right the war before defeatism set in.

Admiral Meyers' first priority was making sure the war fighters had everything they needed to win this war that America now found itself in. His first order of business was to assess the losses and then determine how quickly they could replace them.

Today's White House meeting was going to involve a morning meet with the National Security Advisor and the President to obtain permission to acquire the needed equipment, and gain authorization for a full mobilization of the military's strategic reserves. He also wanted to push for a draft to quickly bolster the size of the US military. He knew this would be controversial, but he was also not sure how else they could fill the ranks of the military as quickly as they needed to. The war with

Russia could quickly turn into a war with North Korea and China at any moment, so time was not on their side.

It was turning into a beautiful autumn morning as his driver stopped their vehicle right in front of the side entrance to the White House.

I was going to retire at the end of the year. It looks like I'm going to have to put that off for a few more years now, Admiral Meyers bemoaned to himself.

Meyers cleared security quickly and made his way to McMillan's office. He wanted to go over a few things with him first before he briefed the President. As he approached his office, he saw McMillan getting up and heading out the door to greet him.

"Good morning, Admiral. You ready for today's meeting?" he asked jovially as he led the way down to the Oval Office. This was Admiral Meyers' second visit to see the President since taking over as the Chairman of the Joint Chiefs. He had only been appointed CJC three days ago, so it had been a whirlwind getting caught up on everything that was going on.

Prior to being appointed to take over as the Chairman, Meyers had been in charge of the Navy's procurement program, which, he had concluded, was a complete mess. It was one of the reasons he had planned on retiring. He was just tired of the bureaucracy and how mismanaged the procurement process had become. He had tried on numerous occasions to improve it but had been met with stiff resistance from various members of Congress and the lifelong bureaucrats who resided at the Department of Defense. He missed serving in the Fleet. He'd loved the smell of JP-8 as it wafted across the bridge from the flight deck of a carrier.

Suddenly, Admiral Meyers was jolted from his reminiscent thoughts. "Are you ready for the meeting?" asked Tom McMillan, the National Security Advisor, as he shook Meyers' hand.

"I'm ready. I've spent the last two days reviewing the combat losses and mission requirements being sent to our office. It's been a mind-numbing experience, but I believe I'm prepared to start making recommendations. Then again, I'm not 100% sure how the boss is going to take them," Meyers explained, realizing as he spoke that he didn't know the President very well.

"Just be honest and direct with your assessment," assured McMillan. "The President doesn't like BS, and he can smell it a mile away. He's very direct and to the point, which makes him pretty easy to work with. If you see Saunders or Rosenblatt in the room, be careful—not that they'll gun for you, but they hold a lot of sway. Sometimes you almost have to win *them* over before you can win the boss over. They're smart, good guys, but their agendas aren't always the same as the President's agenda," McMillan offered as they approached the outer door to the Oval Office.

Admiral Meyers nodded. He appreciated the insight into the office politics since he was so new in his position.

The President's secretary waved them on in and held the door open for them. As they walked into the room, they immediately saw the President's Chief of Staff, Saunders, and Rosenblatt sitting on the couch waiting for them, along with the Secretary of Defense, Jim Castle. They all stood up and gave the obligatory greetings before getting down to business.

The President opened the meeting, saying, "I know we've kind of thrown you into the deep end of the pool having to take over for General Hillman, but I need to know where we stand with the war, and what needs to happen to win it."

The NSA was right—the President likes to get right to it, Meyers thought.

The admiral scooted over and took his seat on the couch next to the SecDef. "Mr. President, I'll be blunt. The war is not going well right now, and if it keeps on its current track, we are going to lose. I have some recommendations. In my military opinion, I believe these actions are needed to turn things around and win this fight," Admiral Meyers said.

The SecDef gave an affirmative nod. The two of them had talked late into the evening the night before about what Meyers was going to propose at this meeting. Castle was fully on board and would back him up.

Rosenblatt, the President's advisor, seemed a bit taken aback that so much had been apparently missed under General Hillman's leadership.

The President leaned forward in his chair and looked the admiral in the eye. "That's why I placed you in charge. I don't want any fluff and nonsense. I want to know what you need to win, and I don't mean in a few years. You and I know the American public will only support a war for a finite amount of time before they'll lose patience with it. We need to win this fight quick."

Nodding in agreement, the admiral continued, "I agree, Mr. President. The first order of business is I need your permission to activate the military's strategic arms reserve. All the branches of the military have a strategic reserve of aircraft, tanks, ships, etc., that we keep in dry storage in case of a national emergency. With the equipment losses we've sustained in Europe and may potentially sustain in Asia, we need to get that equipment out of storage and brought up to full readiness immediately." He handed out several documents, which listed some of the critical equipment each service needed.

Gates looked at the documents briefly and then nodded. "Done. You have permission to get this equipment activated immediately. What else do you need?" he asked.

"We need troops, Mr. President. We need a lot of soldiers to fill the new units we're creating." He held up a hand for everyone to give him a chance to finish his thought. "I know General Hillman had authorized the activation of the entire military reserve and the National Guard, but they're not going to be enough. Even with 50,000 people volunteering to join the military in the past two weeks, it's still not going to be adequate. I believe we need to reinstitute an immediate draft, and do it *now* so we can get their training started."

There was a moment of silence after the mention of the word "draft." Then he saw Stephen Saunders nod in agreement. Rosenblatt's expression remained flat, almost dismissive. Admiral Meyers knew in that moment that he already had Saunders on board but would need to find a way to convince Jonathan that this had to happen.

"We have 460,000 troops on active duty, with another 530,000 personnel in the Reserves and National Guard. While that sounds like a lot of soldiers, it's not nearly enough to accomplish the task of winning this new war. Most of these soldiers aren't direct combat soldiers— they're largely support units. We badly need active ground forces. We also cannot have our entire armed forces deployed to Europe, nor can we leave the Pacific and our allies there unprotected. If hostilities do break out with North Korea or China, then we're certain to lose in our current state." Admiral Meyers spoke passionately. He really wanted to persuade the President to agree to ramp up the military immediately, while they still had time.

Stephen Saunders jumped in before anyone else could speak. "Mr. President, while I don't like the sound of a draft, the admiral is right. It takes time to train an army and time to equip one. Right now, we're still operating with the depleted military that existed when you took office. We can't change that, but we can do what's needed to get the country ready to win this war. Remember, during World War II, it took the US nearly eighteen months to raise and train an army before it was ready to start fighting. We don't have that much time. This war with Russia is serious. They have nearly four times as many soldiers in Ukraine as we do. We cannot rely on NATO to step up to the plate on this. We need to institute a draft and a massive rebuilding of our military."

Jonathan Rosenblatt then jumped in. "I'm not sure a draft is the right call. I agree with the idea that we need to rapidly rebuild the military—that has to happen—but I think we can get enough people to volunteer without having to institute a draft. If we go that route, the press is going to eat us for lunch," he said, disgusted at the options they appeared to be left with.

Steve snorted before retorting, "The press has never been on our side, so what difference would it make if they agreed with us on a draft or not? They're going to report whatever they're going to report. We need to focus on the business of the country and not what they're going to say or think. We have to assume they're going to be against us no matter what decision we make."

The President's left eyebrow went up. With his usual voices of reason at odds, he turned towards Admiral Meyers, NSA McMillan, and SecDef Castle. "Gentlemen, what is your recommendation for how many forces we should draft should we move in that direction?"

Castle nodded towards Admiral Meyers to continue. The two of them had briefly talked about how many soldiers they would need the night before. McMillan thought they could get by with a much lower number but was willing to let the admiral make the case for the larger number he wanted.

"Mr. President, I believe we should announce a draft of five million men and women. It's going to take us time to get them trained, and until we have the proper facilities up and running, we'll have to draft people in stages." As he finished his point, he pulled out a sheet of paper that outlined how many people he would like to draft into each of the military branches.

Rosenblatt scoffed at the number, almost laughing out loud. The President's Chief of Staff did audibly chuckle at the number being proposed. McMillan leaned back in his chair, waiting to let the admiral make his case for why he felt the US needed such a large number of draftees. However, before he could even begin, Saunders offered, "You know, Mr. President, this kind of army would allow us to right a few wrongs and bring some true peace to the world."

At that comment, Ishaan Patel, the President's Chief of Staff, jumped in. "Steve, this isn't some crusade we're talking about. You can't just build up a multimillion-man army and start invading countries you disagree with."

Saunders bristled. He didn't like it when people openly disagreed with him.

The Chief of Staff brushed off the obvious disdain that Stephen was dishing out with his deadly stare. He turned to the President. "Sir, I agree that we need to build up the military, and maybe drafting a few million people is what we need to do…but we need to be cautious with this. If we announce too large of a draft, it'll send the wrong message overseas."

This time the President interrupted, "—You mean it'll tell the Chinese and Russians that we aren't screwing around? That we mean business? Or that the mentally unstable little dictator in North Korea had better get in line or he may be next? That kind of message?" Sarcasm dripped from the President's voice.

Gates was obviously irritated at this point. "Honestly, I'm tired of this crap. The Russians invaded Ukraine and attacked NATO because they believed us to be weak. The Chinese invaded Southeast Asia because we don't have the military capability to tell them to back off. North Korea has developed ICBMs because we lack the ability to stop them. Enough is enough. We're going to send a message loud and clear to the rest of the world that this kind of annexation of their neighbors is over. I don't want President Xi to think for even a second that he can invade and take Taiwan next because we lack the troops or resources to stop him."

The President got up from his chair and began to pace back and forth. He signaled for everyone to stay seated. "I'm stepping outside for a minute to calm down and clear my head. I want you all to stay here. Think this problem through for a minute—don't talk to each other, just work your way through the problem quietly. Try to figure it out...if we do this draft, how would we use these forces? What would be our end state, and how do we message it? When I come back, I'll want some options from you guys." Gates opened the side door to the portico and walked outside to get some air and think without distractions.

The others in the room sat there for a minute, not saying anything as they thought about what he had just said. Ishaan and Jonathan immediately began to write several things down on their notepads. Saunders got up and pace around the office himself, mulling over the finer points of messaging. McMillan just smirked as he looked at Admiral Meyers and nodded.

Less than five minutes later, the President walked back into the Oval Office with a determined look on his face. He looked at Saunders first and asked, "So, how do we present our new strategy and the draft to the public?"

Without missing a beat, Steve confidently responded, "We look back at President Reagan's speech about the Evil Empire—those words galvanized the nation. Of course, we'll need to work on updating it to our current time and situation, but we'll go with something along those lines."

Gates gave a half nod. He didn't like the thought of stealing ideas, but he knew Saunders well enough to know that his finished work would be acceptably original.

The President then turned to his senior advisor, Jonathan Rosenblatt. "Thoughts on end state? What do we want it to look like?" He knew Jon wasn't in favor of this option, but he also knew Jon would identify a set of objectives that was feasible, and not some "pie in the sky" idea that Steve might want to try and unsuccessfully pursue.

"For the record, Mr. President, I don't agree with this decision," Jonathan began, taking one last opportunity to put his two cents in. "However, I have identified what I believe to be a suitable end state given that this is the direction you want to move towards. We should use this war with Russia and the massive buildup of our forces to deal with North Korea also. They've been a problem since the end of the Korean War in

1953, and they can no longer be allowed to continue on their current path. They now have ICBMs that can hit the West Coast, and if given more time, they'll be able to equip those missiles with nuclear weapons. Heck, they might be able to do that now. We cannot allow the US or our allies to be faced with nuclear blackmail for the foreseeable future."

The President nodded, and Jonathan continued with his assessment. "Presently, we cannot do anything about the Chinese annexation of Laos, Vietnam, or Myanmar, but we can let them know that we won't tolerate the annexation of Thailand, Cambodia, the Philippines, or Taiwan. If we're going to stand up to China and the rest of the world, then we need to stand strong and be willing to use our growing military. A lot of countries are going to test us over the next few months. Some may even attack our allies, knowing that we aren't in a position to stop them. If we move forward with this draft and military buildup, we may be able to deter them from those ambitions, even if just for a short while."

No one in the room had any objections to anything Rosenblatt had just said, so Gates signaled to his Chief of Staff to speak next. "Ishaan, how do we get Congress to get on board with this and approve the draft, along with the equipment and money we'll need to make this happen?"

Ishaan sighed deeply before responding, "Very carefully, Mr. President. Congress just officially declared war on Russia last week. The defense spending authorization bill is nearing completion right now. I believe we should try to get them to tack on the draft Admiral Meyers is requesting along with the additional monies that will be needed for the war. However, the real problem is going to be figuring out how to pay for it. The conservatives are going to cry foul on the cost because we're probably talking about a defense bill that is going to be over one trillion dollars. The liberals are going to cry foul on the draft and what they'll see as an expansion of the war. Even if the war is currently against Russia, they're going to see this as a stepping stone to additional wars."

Gates walked around to the chair he had previously been sitting in and sat down. He looked at Steve and said, "Well, there's one way to make sure we get both the liberals and conservatives on board. We raise a war tax to help pay for the war, thus ensuring that the draft doesn't disproportionately hit minorities or the poor. What are your thoughts on how we do that?"

Ishaan nodded in agreement but wanted to hear Saunders' ideas before he jumped back into the conversation. Stephen crossed his arms somewhat defensively before he admitted, "Mr. President, the tax is absolutely necessary. This war is going to be costly, and we cannot just run up the debt on this one. During World War II, Congress instituted a war tax, and they also heavily pushed government war bonds. I think current circumstances would point us towards doing the same thing now. To make sure the conservatives stay on board, we can put a sunset clause on the tax. That way the tax will end when the conflict has finished or the debt from the war has been fully repaid."

The President raised his hand to stop Steve. "While the discussion of a tax is something we should talk over further, I want to stay focused on the draft," Gates said as he signaled for Admiral Meyers and the NSA to continue talking.

McMillan jumped back in to provide his own input with regard to the draft. He couldn't let the good admiral have all the credit. "Steve brought up a good point about the draft not being directed at the poor and minorities like it appeared to have been in the past. When we announce the draft, we should also ensure that there are no deferments. No one should get out of it because they're able to afford college while others are not. If someone is in college and gets drafted, then I think they should have the option of going in as an officer if they're beyond their sophomore year. We also make sure there are no exceptions that can be handed out by those who are politically connected."

Gates nodded in approval. McMillan took the green light to keep going. "I'd even go one step further, Mr. President. If any member of Congress has a son or daughter of military age, then at least one member of their family should be drafted and have to serve. This will ensure that people aren't able to get out of service to their country because their parent is a political figure and thus able to shield them. This war is a threat against our country's very survival; the burden of fighting it should be shouldered by every social and economic class," Tom concluded.

Admiral Meyers was smiling from ear to ear.

The President also smiled at that idea. He turned to Ishaan and Admiral Meyers and ordered, "Gentlemen, make it happen. Admiral, I want you to begin procuring the equipment and tools you need. Now, onto the strategy. How are we going to defeat the Russians and ensure the Chinese don't annex any additional countries?"

Admiral Meyers jumped into answering this question, probably before he should have; McMillan really should have been the one to lead off since he was the National Security Advisor. "Sir, I believe the NSA and I should sit down with some of the other generals and military planners to come up with a strategy for how to do that now that you've given us the authorization to increase our military buildup. With these additional resources, we'll need some time to collectively develop a winning strategy. Can I propose that we meet again in a couple of weeks to go over an initial outline?" he asked.

Gates overlooked the breach of etiquette and replied, "Of course, Admiral. Let's plan to reconvene in two weeks to go over your plans. In the meantime, we'll move forward with the draft and the other orders we talked about today." Satisfied with how the meeting had just gone, he got up and signaled that it was time to wrap things up.

Gates did have other pressing matters to attend to. They had been discussing this matter for nearly two hours and had gone well over their scheduled time. He rushed off down the hall; he was going to be speaking with a trade delegation from Brazil in another hour and he still needed to prep for that meeting and grab some lunch.

As the meeting ended, McMillan and Admiral Meyers left the Oval and headed towards Meyers' new White House office, with the SecDef following. In a rare moment of transparency, McMillan turned to Admiral Meyers and told him, "I'm envious of you. As a retired general, I wish I could do what you're about to do with the military and direct a real buildup—not a ragtag group to fight off some terrorists, but a real standing army." The men continued down the hall in silence as they thought about what to do next.

Chapter 18
A Message of Hope

Washington, D.C.
White House, Oval Office

The two previous days had been a whirlwind of activity, both in the US and abroad. The previous week, the President had announced the arrest of four congressional members, and dozens of government officials and military members. The case had been clearly laid out as to how these defectors had been leaking classified intelligence to the media and to America's enemies, and how those leaks had resulted in lives lost. These revelations had rocked the public's trust in the government and the media, leading to hundreds of protests and rallies across the country.

In the Ukraine, the US-led NATO force had been cut off and surrounded in Kiev. A large contingent of US and NATO forces were marshaling to attempt to break them out, but that offensive had not yet started. Meanwhile, continued live footage of the house-to-house fighting in the suburbs of Kiev was emotionally numbing for those who tuned in on social media to watch as the city was being torn apart.

Once the Chinese launched their surprise invasion of Vietnam, Laos, and Myanmar, things at home and abroad started to spiral out of control. The President knew he needed to calm the nerves of both his allies and citizens and take control of the situation before defeat set in.

As it turned out, not all of those who were leaking information to the media from the White House had been identified. News started to leak out of the President's desire to draft a new army, which sent the media into a complete frenzy. In response, the White House announced an upcoming presidential address to the nation that would air at 10 a.m. eastern time on Saturday and requested that all the major networks air the broadcast.

As President Gates prepared to give what would perhaps be his biggest speech yet, he knew he needed to accomplish two things. First, he needed to reassure the American people that America wasn't defeated, that the United States could win this war with Russia and defend its allies. Second, he needed to send a message to China, North Korea, and Iran that the US would defend its allies and was building a military force sufficient to do just that.

****

The makeup artist finished the final touches on the President's face and then ran to the side just as the lights turned on. The camera light turned red, indicating that the message was now broadcasting live to the country and the world.

"My fellow Americans, I come to you today with a heavy heart and a message of hope. During the last several weeks, America and our allies in NATO were savagely attacked by the Russian Federation while defending the freedom-loving people of Ukraine. During the lead-up to that dastardly attack, it was discovered that a number of high-ranking government officials and even members of congress were leaking classified intelligence to the media and our enemies, with the express intent of hurting this administration and undermining the national security of our great nation for selfish political purposes."

"I understand that many of you did not vote for me and disagree with my policies. We can agree to disagree on issues. That's what democracy is all about. Our country, however, is at war. A war that was not of our choosing but was thrust upon us. A war that we did not start, but will finish." He paused for a minute, looking down and then back at the camera.

"Let's set the record straight. There is no argument over what would be the desirable choice between peace and war, but there is only one guaranteed way you can have instantaneous peace—surrender. Admittedly, there is a risk in any other course we would follow, but every lesson in history tells us that the greater risk lies in appeasement. We saw that in World War II with Hitler and we saw it in the post war with Stalin and the Soviets. If we continue to accommodate, continue to retreat, then eventually we have to face the final demand, the ultimatum. And what then?"

The President again paused, giving the audience time to think before continuing, "Petrov and Xi have undoubtedly told their people that they know what our answer will be. They are likely having conversations in smoke-filled rooms right now, saying that we are retreating under the pressure of this war and that one day, when the final ultimatum is delivered, our surrender will be voluntary because we no longer have the stomach to fight on. They believe this because of the many voices they have heard in our media, pleading for peace at any price. Protestors are out in the streets saying, 'Better alive on our knees than dead.' However, those voices don't speak for the rest of us. You and I don't believe that peace is so sweet as to be purchased at the price of our own slavery."

"I ask you this: should Moses have told the children of Israel to continue to live under the oppression of the pharaohs? Should Christ have refused the cross? Should the patriots at Concord Bridge have thrown down their guns and refused to fire the 'shot heard around the world'? The martyrs of history were not fools, and our honored dead who gave their lives to stop the advance of the Nazis didn't die in vain. Like these heroes before us, we must find the courage deep within our souls and stand up to our enemies; they must know that there are lines we are not willing to cross. There is a point beyond which they must not advance."

"Winston Churchill said that the destiny of man is not measured by material computation, and that when great forces are on the move in the world, we learn we are spirits, not animals.[1] He told us that there is something going on in time and space, and beyond time and space, which—whether we like it or not—spells duty. You and I have a rendezvous with destiny. We will preserve for our children this, the last best hope of man on earth, or we will sentence them to take the last step into a thousand years of darkness." [2]

"Today, I am officially announcing the rebuilding of our armed forces and a retooling of our economy to provide the tools of war necessary to *win*. During a midnight session of both the Congress and the Senate, a nearly unanimous vote was held to reinstate the draft. I have that bill before me now, and I stand ready to sign it to initiate the draft, which will begin today at 4 p.m., Eastern Standard Time. Despite the tens of thousands of young men and women who have volunteered to join the armed forces this past week, the military ranks need to grow immensely if we are to defeat the Russians and ensure the Chinese do not threaten our allies in the Pacific. It is for that reason that I am directing the Selective Service Board to draft five million men and women to serve in our armed forces during our country's greatest hour of need."

---

[1] http://ww2today.com/16th-june-1941-churchill-addresses-the-u-s-a
[2] http://voicesofdemocracy.umd.edu/reagan-evil-empire-speech-text/

"Unlike the drafts of the past, women, who have continued to serve in more and more combat roles in the military and served with distinction in Iraq and Afghanistan, will also be required to enroll in the Selective Service, effective immediately, just as all men reaching the age of eighteen are required by law. The first draft, which will be held today, will draft the first one million men. Women under the age of twenty-six will have one month to register for the draft. There is no set criteria or quota for the number of women who can or will be drafted; they will be selected based on their birthday and year, just as the men are."

"The Selective Service will hold a draft on the first Saturday of each month, drafting one million young men and women into the military. That number may be reduced, depending on the number of volunteers who willingly join the service prior to each draft date." He paused for a second, feeling the weight of what he had just announced.

"It pains me that I have to be the first President since the Vietnam War to have to institute a draft for military service, but make no mistake, the world is at a turning point. The democracies of the world will either rise to the challenge of our age and defeat these autocratic dictatorships that threaten our survival, or we will collectively fail, falling prey to these violent regimes that threaten our values, freedoms, and very way of life."

"We are not Republicans or Democrats. We are Americans. We must unite as one people, under the cause of freedom, defend our country and fight for the allies who are depending upon us. I ask for your prayers and the Lord's guidance to help me make the right decisions and guide our nation through this perilous time. Thank you for your time today. God bless the United States of America and its people." With that, the red light on the camera turned off and the transmission ended.

There was a collective sigh of relief as the speech ended. Several people in the room came up to the President to shake his hand and congratulate him on a rousing speech.

Secretly, the President thought, *I just hope this draft will be enough and the Chinese won't seek a confrontation with the US.*

He'd been pressing the Chinese ambassador hard lately to keep them from attacking any American allies, but Gates just didn't know how much good that was doing. The last time he'd spoken to President Xi, it hadn't gone well.

Chapter 19
The Marines Are Coming

Camp Pendleton, California

Once Lieutenant General Roy Cutter got off the phone with the Secretary of Defense, he let out a soft whistle. His executive officer and the rest of his staff stopped talking amongst themselves. All eyes were on him.

"Well," Cutter announced, "we're deploying the entire Marine Expeditionary Force to the Pacific. The SecDef says he wants us deployed to Japan immediately." He knew that his entire staff would have to get to work immediately if they were going to make the deadline they had just been given.

"What's the timeline for when he wants us to be in Okinawa?" asked his G3, the head of his operations staff.

Lieutenant General Cutter smiled the half-crazy grin of a man on the verge of maniacal laughter. "We have a week, but we aren't going to Okinawa. He wants us deployed to Japan proper and be prepared to move out from there, to either South Korea or Taiwan. So, once we get to Japan, we'll need to stay packed and ready to ship out. We'll be essentially acting as the United States' quick-reaction force for the Pacific."

"What about the third Marine Expeditionary Force? They're already in Okinawa. What will they be doing?" asked the G2, his intelligence officer.

"The SecDef plans on having them ready to deploy to Taiwan or South Korea, depending on how the situation evolves."

Cutter leaned back in his chair, reflecting. A more genuine smile spread across his face. "The Pacific is going to be a Marine war, if and when it happens," he said proudly.

"It does seem like a bit of karma, doesn't it, Sir? The Marines originally made their name in the Pacific during World War II, and now they'll be the main fighting force there again," said the G2.

"One more thing before we break and start to get the ball rolling on our deployment," Cutter announced. "As you know, the President has initiated a draft. The Marines are going to be growing by roughly one million. That's nearly eight times our current size, even with the reserves. I'm going to need you to identify two sergeants from each platoon and one officer from each company who can stay behind. They'll be assigned to the Marine Recruit Depot and will assist in the training of this new force."

Sensing that there was about to be some pushback, he held up a hand to stop the questions. "I've also been authorized to give any sergeant who volunteers for this duty two bumps in grade, and the officers will get one bump in grade. We're going to need a lot more sergeants and officers as our force grows, so start identifying your up-and-comers and get them ready to fill in when the time comes. As these new recruits complete training and start to fill out our ranks, a lot of people are going to start receiving promotions and new assignments," he concluded.

Suddenly, everyone in the room was smiling. It had been getting harder to get promoted in a shrinking Marine Corps, so an increase of this size meant a fast track to the senior ranks.

Chapter 20
Greater China

Beijing, China

Chairman Zhang didn't usually attend the secretive meetings of the CMC, but President Xi had been including him in them since the start of Operation Red Storm. Zhang was responsible for state security and was the lead facilitator between China and Russia. He was also a shrewd political operative as the Chairman of the National People's Congress, and someone Xi wanted to keep a close eye on.

As the military leaders of China began to take their seats for the meeting, Chairman Zhang took his seat next to the President. As the stewards brought everyone their drink, President Xi brought the meeting to order. His bodyguards quickly led the stewards out of the room, so the location was completely secured. No electronic devices were allowed in the room, aside from what the security service had already inspected and deemed secured. Any presentations that were to be given had to be cleared first by the information technology security group, to ensure the files didn't have any malware or other spy software attached to them. The IT department under Zhang's State Security was completely paranoid about the NSA's spy capabilities and scrutinized everything.

"General Wei Liu, please bring us up-to-date on the progress of the annexation of Vietnam, Laos and Myanmar," President Xi requested as a way to open up the meeting. He had been briefed on the progress a couple of hours ago by the Defense Minister, General Kuang Li Jun, but for the sake of everyone else, he felt it important to reiterate the information.

General Wei cleared his throat before he began, then signaled for his aide to begin the PowerPoint presentation. The first slide showed a map of Myanmar, with various unit symbols and arrows pointing in different directions. The military incursion there was now in its second week and was showing some real progress. Already, a third of the country had been occupied, to include the capital. Naypyidaw, the capital city, had been captured the first day by PLA airborne forces.

"Mr. President, our airborne forces were officially relieved two days ago by elements of the 31st Army. We have traditionally had good relations with Myanmar prior to our incursion, and we have used that relationship to our benefit. Our social media campaign was very effective in painting our forces as saviors to the needy of the nation, and as our troops have moved across the border, we have been distributing food and offering free medical clinics in each of the villages and cities our forces enter."

"Before our invasion of Myanmar, we liaised with their military and informed them that as long as they don't resist, we'll integrate their army into the PLA as a colonial army. We even offered to pay them in Chinese Yuan in accordance with their ranks. This has proven to be exceptionally effective, to the point that we have only had eight armed confrontations. Three of our soldiers have been killed, while close to one hundred have been injured, but this was mostly from a bridge that collapsed when several troop transports crossed what they thought was a stable bridge. Aside from these few engagements, the majority of the military and the political leaders of Myanmar have welcomed us with open arms."

The other members of the CMC asked a variety of questions about the operation but otherwise appeared content with the progress being made in Myanmar. In less than a month, the rest of the country would be occupied by the PLA, and then the integration of their economy and armed forces would begin. One of the first priorities would be to bring in a vast amount of specialized farming equipment to increase the country's rice and other agricultural production to maximum capacity. China would also begin a series of massive infrastructure projects, connecting the rail lines in western Yunnan Province with the ports in Yangon and the other major cities in the country.

Once additional farming equipment and proper infrastructure were developed in Myanmar, the country would be able to provide up to 11% of China's demand for rice and 14% of its demand for other agricultural products. Myanmar would also provide China with a seaport on the Indian Ocean, greatly shortening the transportation time of moving goods to and from Europe.

As the group finished discussing the situation in Myanmar, General Wei moved on to the next slide in his presentation, which showed a map of Laos, a fellow communist country. Unlike Myanmar, Laos had a souring relationship with Vietnam. Throughout the late 1970s and into the 1980s, Vietnam had invaded and occupied parts of Laos. It wasn't until the late 1990s that Vietnam had fully withdrawn its forces from the country.

General Wei explained, "As you know, the People's Republic of China has spent the better part of the last seven years developing enhanced economic relations with Laos. The commitments we've made there to increased foreign aid and economic development seem to be paying off. We implemented the same strategy with Laos as we did with Myanmar in terms of offering to pay any Laotian armed forces that are cooperative in Chinese Yuan. We also bribed key senior military and political officials there when we found a holdout or it was needed to smooth the transition."

General Wei nodded in acknowledgement towards Foreign Minister Yong. "Our compatriot here also spoke with key state officials in Laos to make it clear that once Laos was successfully annexed, all of its foreign debts to China would be forgiven and its other international debts would be taken care of by the People's Republic."

"So, how is the military advancement going there, given these enticements?" asked a more cantankerous advisor.

"The 12th Army moved throughout the country unhindered and has secured their armed forces. We have encountered virtually no resistance to the annexation there. The rest of the Laotian government should be fully integrated over the coming weeks. Once the military actions are complete, both Laos and Myanmar will become provinces of China; the leaders of each respective country will remain in power as long as they support the authority of the Chinese government. As soon as these countries come under the umbrella of our authority, we'll all begin to benefit; our minister of agriculture is confident that his department will be able to start integrating Laos' food production into our economy starting next week."

The various advisors and political officials in the room all nodded, happy with every word that had just come out of General Wei's mouth.

Then the next slide in the presentation came up, and a collective groan could be heard. Even the stoic men before him couldn't help but express some frustration at the sight of a map of Vietnam.

China and Vietnam had had a troubled relationship since the end of the American war with Vietnam in the mid-1970s. Soon after that conflict, Vietnam had interfered in Laos, and since China maintained close political ties with Laos, they had invaded Vietnam to "teach them a lesson." That military incursion had lasted for several years and resulted in a humiliating defeat for the Chinese Army. The Vietnamese had become extremely battle-hardened after fighting France and the United States. They had also been militarily backed by the Soviet Union, which had provided them with numerous military advisors and a significant amount of military equipment. The result was a drawn-out war that had resulted in the PLA's humiliation at the hands of a much smaller nation.

The PLA had an axe to grind with Vietnam, especially since their country had somehow managed to thaw their relationship with the US and were actively considering allowing the US to build a naval base in their country. Vietnam had also laid claim to the Spratly Islands, which were clearly part of China and held vast oil and natural gas reserves. General Wei wasn't at all surprised by the change of mood in the room.

Wei glanced at the slide; the picture wasn't pleasant. Unlike Myanmar and Laos, several regions of Vietnam were bogged down in heavy fighting. He took a deep breath before he began. "Mr. President, we invaded Vietnam with the forces from the Southern Theater of Operations, led by General Yang. We bolstered his army group with 100,000 militia forces. Because of this, our army has been able to capture Hanoi and the surrounding area in less than two weeks. Our airborne forces have secured the critical port area of Hai Phong, which will allow us to better supply our military there and bring in additional ground forces."

He then moved to a slide that showed the southern half of Vietnam. "The PLAN was able to offload their naval infantry to secure the coastal cities of Huế and Da Nang. We also landed a substantial force not far from Ho Chi Minh City, which they should secure by the end of next week. Our three carriers have been providing exceptional air support to the naval infantry and proving they can operate as an effective combined air, land, and naval force." As he spoke proudly about the achievements of the Navy, its leader, who was several seats away, swelled with pride.

President Xi smiled. "Congratulations are in order to Vice Admiral Ning Sheng. Your efforts to modernize our navy and turn it into a fully integrated combined arms force have clearly been very fruitful."

The President turned to the Commander of the Chinese Air Force, General Xu Ding, and asked, "How have our new aircraft and bombers been performing in Vietnam?"

General Xu smiled proudly. "The Chengdu J-20 has performed beyond our expectations. During the opening hours of the war, it successfully shot down twelve Vietnamese fighters that attempted to interdict our airborne forces. It has continued to provide exceptional air superiority over Vietnam, shooting down another fourteen aircraft."

He switched over to a couple of his own slides to discuss some of the assessments they had conducted during the war. "We were able to successfully test the effectiveness of several of our naval cruise missiles from the Xian H-6 bomber. These missiles are now going to go into full production. We tested several air-to-ground standoff cruise missiles and guided munitions with the bomber as well. This was critical, as this was the first time we were able to see how a number of our missile and bomb platforms would perform during a live combat scenario. This combat drill also proved that we can effectively engage and sink a foreign naval force with our anti-ship cruise missiles." As he spoke, he showed several images of the H-6 firing a variety of different missile platforms.

Before he concluded, a devilish smile curled up on the left side of his face. "Unbeknownst to the West and the rest of the world, we also successfully tested the H-20, our subsonic stealth bomber that has some similar characteristics to the American B-2 Spirit. The H-20 penetrated the Vietnamese airspace undetected during the opening hours of the incursion and carried out a series of strikes. We have continued to test various bombing tactics and ordnance with the H-20 in Vietnam and believe we have identified the few remaining flaws in the system. If we need to use it against the Americans, we now know it'll be effective."

Chapter 21
Setting the Trap

North Atlantic

Captain Yuri Popov drank his coffee, lost for a moment in his thoughts. *I still can't believe that I'm here*, he marveled.

He had hoped that cooler heads would prevail and war could be avoided, but now that their brothers in the Black Sea had sunk an American supercarrier, the Russians might actually have a chance at winning. The American Navy had the best equipment and technology money could buy, but maybe they weren't as good as everyone thought if the Russians could sink one of its supercarriers.

Well, if the Black Sea fleet could sink a carrier, then surely our little wolfpack can sink a few freighters in the Atlantic.

Captain Popov reached the bottom of his cup of joe and moved back into action, signaling for his executive officer to join him at the map table while they discussed the plan of attack.

"To review, once we get in range of our cruise missiles, we're going to be the first to fire. Then, as the NATO antisubmarine forces move towards us, our two *Akula* submarines will close in on the convoy and attack with their torpedoes."

Mikhail, the XO, nodded.

Popov continued, "I want you to send a message to the *Akulas*. Tell them to position themselves in this area here." He pointed to a spot on the map, roughly 140 miles from the mouth of New York Harbor.

"Aye, Sir," Mikhail responded.

The captain went on, "Our last intelligence report, which is only two hours old, said a group of fifteen freighters left Baltimore Harbor yesterday, and a group of six US Navy ships left Norfolk about the same time. Both groups are headed to New York, most likely to link up with this other group of twelve freighters and four additional naval ships. Altogether, that makes twenty-seven freighters being guarded by ten navy ships. Of the ten naval ships, three of them are amphibious assault ships, so they won't pose a serious threat to us."

"The *Akulas* should be ready to commence their attack as soon as they hear our cruise missiles launch. If they have a clear shot, they should target the amphibious troop ships first. If not, then they should take out the largest freighters they can—those will most likely be the roll-on, roll-off ships that would be carrying the heavy armor units." Captain Popov paused for a moment to allow his XO to catch up; he had been taking notes, and he was getting a little behind.

Pointing to another position roughly 150 miles off the coast of Nova Scotia, Popov resumed his explanation. "When everyone has carried out their attacks, we'll rendezvous at this location here. Then we'll regroup and determine what Moscow wants us to do next," he said with a smile.

Mikhail's mouth also curled up to one side mischievously. "Sounds good, Sir. I'll get these instructions written up and sent off within the next two hours."

Prior to the conflict, the Russian Navy had equipped their submarines with a new buoy communication system. At certain times on different days, the subs would raise the buoy to just below the surface and send or receive a set of messages. The buoy would stay just below the surface, extending several small antennas above the water for no more than sixty seconds, just long enough to send and receive a burst message and then dip back below the waves. The time window to send this next set of instructions was rapidly approaching.

"Good," Popov responded. "We need to get moving if we're going to be in position to attack the convoy when it leaves for Europe tomorrow. We're set to make contact in less than 24 hours."

Chapter 22
Retirement Canceled

Atlantic Ocean

Captain Patrick Gilbert had just taken over as the commodore of the first major NATO supply convoy to leave the US for Europe. They had just finished assembling outside of New York Harbor and would make the transatlantic journey shortly.

Captain Gilbert had been nearing retirement when the situation in Europe had turned sour. He had been less than eighty days away from retirement when he'd received a call from the Chief of Naval Operations Office, informing him that his retirement had just been rescinded and he was to take over as Commodore of NATO Convoy Group Alpha. He was to take command of the USS *Churchill*, a guided-missile destroyer that had just completed a series of repairs at Norfolk to act as the command ship for the convoy.

Upon receiving his orders, he'd hopped in his Ford F-150 and driven down to the pier where his new ship was docked. He had been greeted by the executive officer and the outgoing captain, a Commander Richard Owens, who was being assigned to a staff position.

It was an impromptu change of command, as there was a lot to get done and not a lot of time to get it all accomplished. They had fifteen hours to get everything straightened out before they needed to be on their way to New York to link up with the convoy.

Captain Gilbert would have a total of six guided-missile destroyers as part of his squadron to defend the convoy. They really needed about ten to do the job effectively, but the rest of the available ships had already been detailed off to the carriers that were putting to sea. With the loss of one carrier in the Black Sea, the Navy wasn't taking any chances with the Russian submarines and had beefed up the carrier strike group's complement. He would have to make do with what he had.
****

Captain Gilbert lifted his mug to his mouth and took a long drink of the freshly brewed coffee that the steward had just brought to the bridge. After nearly thirty years in the Navy, Pat had become a bit of a java snob and had developed the uncanny ability to balance the hot liquid in his cup no matter how rough the water got. Before the ship had left port, he'd brought his personal stash aboard—forty pounds of Calle San Juan coffee beans, telling the stewards this was the *only* coffee he wanted brought to the bridge and CIC when he was on duty. The rest of the officers and enlisted personnel who worked on the bridge also became fans as of the sweet-toned Costa Rican java, which had a rich, spicy floral note. It sure beat the garbage the Navy issued.

Lieutenant Commander Tiffany Brewster walked out on the bridge wing and joined the captain as he drank his coffee. In the distance, she could see the coast of Delaware as they moved to where the convoy was forming up.

Tiffany had joined the Navy because she'd wanted to follow in her grandfather's footsteps. He had been an officer in the Navy during World War II, and as a child, she used to listen to him tell her stories of what it was like during the war, riding a destroyer as they provided convoy duty in the Atlantic. His tales of hunting German U-boats had been scary but also exciting.

When she was old enough, she'd applied and been accepted to the Naval Academy at Annapolis. It had taken years of effort and a lot of career planning, but she had finally made executive officer of the *Churchill*, a guided-missile destroyer. Her goal was to get a command of her own when she was eligible for her next promotion in two years.

When she'd heard the *Churchill* was going to be commanded by a senior captain, she had been excited. This was an opportunity for her to shine and prove she was ready for a command of her own. A senior captain could hopefully help influence the selection board in her favor when the time came. She didn't know a lot about Captain Gilbert, other than the fact that he had been months away from retirement when he'd been ordered to take command, but he had a solid reputation in the destroyer world as a very capable captain and mentor.

As the two of them looked off in the distance, she asked, "Do you think the Russians are going to try and attack the convoy?"

Pat took another sip of his coffee, savoring the flavor as his ship crested another wave before plowing its way down the small trough.

He turned and looked at his XO. "If I were the Russians, I certainly would. The bigger question is, are we capable of stopping them if they try?"

She pondered this question for a minute before responding, not sure if this was some sort of test. "I think it's going to be challenging for us to guard twenty-seven freighters and three marine amphibs with six escorts. I know we're supposed to have P-8 Poseidon support for the duration of the trip, but that's a lot of ocean for us to have to cover."

Captain Gilbert nodded and she felt that she had passed an exam.

"Good answer, XO," he replied. "The P-8s will be helpful, but we're going to have to rely on our helicopters and our towed sonar arrays. I'm going to want to have the squadron deploy with two ships always racing in front of the convoy: one listening with the towed array while the other moves ahead to get in position to do the same. They'll pretty much leapfrog each other all the way to Europe, clearing a path for us. The ones on the flanks will have to stay ready to move to where we think we have a possible sub. We'll have one ship trailing the convoy, and our ship will remain near the center of the convoy with our towed array deployed."

Gilbert took another sip of his coffee before continuing, "The fastest ship we have in the convoy can only make ten knots. So that will unfortunately be the max speed the convoy can make."

"How do you want to deploy the helos?" Tiffany asked, wanting to know if the ship's two helicopters would need to have some sort of special schedule.

"We have twelve ASW helos in our group. We'll look to keep two of them in the air at all times. That way we can keep two more on standby, and the rest will alternate in three-hour shifts. I spoke with the captains of the amphibs. They're going to have several of their helicopters readied for ASW work in case we need additional support. Our helicopters are going to be flying a lot—hopefully we won't have any maintenance problems on the voyage over," Pat replied as he looked off at the clear skies in the horizon.

At least the weather forecast looks good for the next four of five days, he thought.

"I'll make sure the air boss knows what kind of schedule to set," Brewster responded. Captain Gilbert didn't say anything, so she asserted, "I'll be back on the bridge if you need me, Sir."

She left the captain alone with his thoughts. The next couple of weeks were going to be busy, and she figured he probably wanted some time to think before the tempo picked up. Once they got to New York, the convoy would set sail. The other escorts had already arrived, and the three Marine ships were following the *Churchill* up the East Coast.

Chapter 23
Hunting in the Atlantic

North Atlantic

Captain Yuri Popov was sitting in his captain's chair, taking a few minutes to read a book that his wife had given him before they'd left port. He was growing impatient as he waited for the American convoy to head towards him. However, the latest satellite intelligence showed the convoy had finally left New York and should transit through their ambush soon.

Captain Second Rank Mikhail Borodin had been the executive officer of the *Orel* for nearly a year when they'd set sail three weeks ago. He glanced over at Captain Popov and decided to pull out a book of his own—a textbook on naval strategy he wanted to study.

As he got settled, he thought about what a privilege is was to sail under such an experienced and respected commander as Popov. *I'd like to get my own command in the next few years, if the Russian Navy would ever stop decommissioning the submarine fleet*, he thought. It was becoming harder and harder to get promoted in a shrinking navy. He wondered pessimistically if he'd ever be able to follow in his father's footsteps and have his own ship.

"Con, Sonar. We have possible surface contacts," announced the sonar room, breaking the quiet.

If NATO knew we had stolen the blueprints to the newest British sonar systems, they'd be breaking out in hives, thought Captain Popov with amusement.

The British had developed a new advanced sonar array that could detect ships hundreds of miles away. The Russians had naturally found a way to pilfer the designs rather than invent their own version of this technology. The key to this new sonar system was the intricate software that analyzed the hundreds of acoustical noises and distilled them down to determine which ones were probably man-made. Those noises could then be further isolated and analyzed to provide a fairly accurate assessment of what they were looking at.

Captain Popov tucked his book away in his jacket pocket, then turned to one of his officers. "Take us to periscope depth. I want as much targeting data as we can get from the RORSAT," he ordered.

A few minutes later, the submarine leveled off and the periscope ascended. Captain Popov squatted down and performed an awkward circling duckwalk with his eyes glued to the scope as he performed a quick 360-degree search of the horizon, making sure there wasn't a helicopter nearby, or a ship that had somehow snuck up on them.

Nodding in approval, he ordered, "Raise the periscope the rest of the way up, as well as the detection antenna."

They had the scope up for less than thirty seconds, just long enough for them to see where the ships were and obtain the targeting solutions they would need from the RORSAT above them.

The captain looked at his communications officer. "Deploy the buoy," Popov ordered. "I want as much targeting data as possible."

The Americans and the rest of NATO had been under the assumption that the Russians had ended their RORSAT program shortly after the fall of the Soviet Union. However, the People's Republic of China and the Russian Federation had worked together to develop a much more accurate means for their navies to track and monitor their mutual enemies. They had even built a system that could use their data to guide their anti-ship cruise missiles to their targets, just as the Americans had done with their satellites.

The tension in the submarine mounted as the reality began to set in that they were about to attack the American Navy. This was something they had all trained for, but most had honestly never thought it would happen.

"Captain Popov, it looks like they have two destroyers in the lead. One is located here," explained Captain Borodin, pointing at the location on the map board. The RORSAT had provided them with excellent targeting data. "The other is here. Looking at the satellite images, it looks like they have one on each flank, one in the center, and one pulling up the rear."

Popov could see that they had identified the locations of six destroyers. "Where are the *Akulas* on this map?" he asked.

Borodin brought up the coordinates for the *Akulas'* projected locations and plotted them in relation to the convoy and the destroyers. "They should be right here, just at the outer edge of the left side of the convoy. They're not quite in range of their torpedoes, but they're not that far outside of range either."

115

"Weapons—what targeting solutions do you have for our missiles?" Popov asked his weapons officer.

The *Orel* was equipped with 72 SS-N-26/P-800 "Strobile" anti-ship missiles. Each missile was nine meters in length, and their ramjet engines could propel them at a surface speed of Mach 2, nearly 750 meters a second. Each missile carried a relatively small 300-kiloton warhead, which would detonate shortly after its armored tip punctured the hull or bulkhead of a ship for maximum damage.

What NATO didn't know about the new Strobile, which had come into service with the Russian Navy in early 2017, was that it was fitted with an improved radar homing head. The Strobile used an all-weather monopulse active-passive radar with frequency-hopping capabilities, which meant it would be nearly impossible for an adversary to jam its satellite guidance system once it had been launched.

The Russians typically would have stood off and fired their missiles from a range in excess of ninety miles. However, if they snuck up on the convoy and fired them closer, there would be little chance of their missiles being intercepted before they struck their marks. They also needed to create a distraction for the *Akulas* to get in close and do the real damage with their torpedoes.

The weapons officer had calculated all of this into his response. "Captain, I recommend we launch our first barrage of twenty missiles at this location here," he said, pointing to a position not far from where they were. "Then I recommend that we move to a new position here," he explained, pointing to another position roughly thirty-five miles away. "This will allow us to fire off another volley at the American convoy as they move away from the first attack."

Captain Popov looked at the firing positions thoughtfully. *This should still leave us plenty of time to try and evade the Americans*, he thought, *and it should enable the Akulas to get in their attack*.

He liked the idea of repositioning for a second attack as the convoy tried to escape from the first one. The trick would be making sure that the American antisubmarine warfare helicopters and destroyers didn't find them after they launched their missiles. Once they fired, the Yankees would have a pretty good fix on where they were.

Nodding in agreement, Popov signaled for his weapons officer to get the missiles ready for launch.

It's time to teach NATO a lesson, he thought. *One they won't soon forget.*

It took them roughly five minutes to get the ship and the missiles ready to fire. As the ship leveled off at its launch depth, the weapons officer and the captain anxiously watched the launch timer count down. *Ten...seven...four...two...launch!* They both turned the launch key as the other weapons officer began to fire off the missiles, one through twenty.

The ship shuddered slightly after each missile was ejected from the vertical launch pods behind the main sail of the submarine. Every two seconds, another missile was ejected from the launch pods to the surface. As each missile broke through the water, its scramjet engine ignited, followed quickly by the nose cone's stabilizer rockets, which leveled the missile off. The engines quickly brought each missile up to its final speed of a little over Mach 2 as they headed towards the convoy. In less than a minute, twenty anti-ship missiles were racing towards the freighters and American escorts less than 35 miles away.

"Bring us down to three hundred meters. All ahead full speed!" yelled the captain to his men. They needed to get below the thermal layer and put some distance between themselves and the launch site. The Americans would have spotted roughly where the missiles had originated from, and there would surely be a helicopter on its way to try and find them. Now it was time to see if they were good enough to evade the American Navy and get in position to fire another volley of missiles off.
****

Captain Gilbert left the bridge to walk down to the combat information center and check in on the crew there. He was observing the men and women manning the controls of the AN/SPY-1D 3D radar and the AN/SQS-53C sonar array as they diligently monitored the three-dimensional perimeter of the convoy. These were the men and women responsible for identifying any potential submarines, air, or missile attacks against the convoy, and they would coordinate any necessary defense with the complex Aegis Combat System. He was proud of how well the crew was handling their duties, knowing that a Russian submarine force might be out there, stalking them.

Man, I wish we had a few submarines with us on this crossing, Gilbert thought as he looked at the protective bubble. He saw several glaring holes in it, and he knew he had no chance of patching them up.

It was roughly 1030 hours, with another ninety minutes before shift change. The mess hall would start serving lunch soon for those who would be starting their afternoon shifts, while the morning crew would get a chance to get something to eat before starting their daily maintenance work and then sacking out for the evening. Today was the second day of their transatlantic journey, and so far, they hadn't encountered any Russian subs. Pat wasn't sure how much longer that would last but was content to hope that maybe, just maybe, the Russians might not try to interdict his convoy.

Suddenly, one of the petty officers that had been manning the radar system nearly jumped out of his chair. "Vampires! Vampires! Vampires!" he shouted as the threat board on the wall of the CIC suddenly showed one, then two, then dozens of anti-ship missiles as they emerged from the sea.

"Set Condition-1! All hands, man your battle stations. Incoming missiles!" yelled a voice over the 1MC.

"Start engaging those missiles! Get our helos airborne and heading to that point of origin now!" Captain Gilbert bellowed.

The petty officer manning the ship's RIM-156 SM-2 missiles immediately began to target the incoming missiles.

The crew sent a flash message to the freighters, telling them to go to maximum speed and take evasive maneuvers. Another flash message was sent to Norfolk, letting them know they were under attack.

As the ship moved to battle stations, the engine revved up to full speed as the *Churchill* made best speed towards the launch point of the enemy missiles and positioned themselves between the missiles and the convoy.

"Do we know what type of missiles are coming at us?" asked one of the targeting officers in the CIC.

A petty officer manning one of the radar terminals answered. "They appear to be...crap. They're the new SS-N-26 'Strobile' missiles," he said.

Another petty officer explained, "The missiles are hitting their terminal speed, Mach 2. Three of the missiles appear to be heading right for the *Gravely*. They're engaging them with their missiles and point defense systems right now."

"The *Mahan* is steaming straight for the suspected launch site and engaging the enemy missiles with their SM-2s and close-in weapons system," shouted Lieutenant Sheehan, one of the CIC battle managers.
****

Over on the bridge, Lieutenant Commander Brewster was also involved in responding to this attack. From her vantage point, she could see in the distance that both the *Mahan* and the *Gravely* were firing off their missiles as quickly as they could to intercept the Russian missiles. Seconds later, she heard the roar of their MH-60 Seahawk helicopters as they gained altitude and raced towards the location where the enemy missiles had been launched from. She assumed the other helicopters in their convoy were converging on that point as well.

The ship shuddered as its own frontal vertical launch tubes spat out a series of SM-2s from the *Churchill*'s forward magazine, heading straight for the incoming missiles. The *Gravely* was still several miles in front of their position, but they could see the enemy missiles now converging on the convoy.

The *Gravely*'s CIWS threw a wall of depleted uranium rounds at the incoming missiles, scoring a hit on two of them. As they exploded a few thousand feet in front of the ship, the detonation sprayed the ship with a layer of shrapnel.

The third missile that had been targeted at the *Gravely* flew right past the ship's 5-inch gun and plowed into the forward superstructure, one deck below the bridge. The armor penetrator on the missile, combined with the super-sonic speed upon impact, forced the missile warhead to punch nearly ten feet into the ship before its 300-kiloton warhead exploded inside the ship's CIC, instantly killing everyone in it.

A large fireball burst from the superstructure and was visible several miles away from the impact. The side walls of the front superstructure exploded outwards, adding to the debris and shrapnel. Fire erupted from the various holes in the forward part of the ship, and the vessel lost power and came to a stop, billowing black smoke and flames into the air.

119

Lieutenant Commander Brewster lifted her hand to her mouth in shock. She couldn't believe what she had just seen. It was too surreal. Then the loud thunderclap of the explosion rocked the *Churchill*, shaking it with the force of the soundwave. Another series of explosions could be seen and heard rolling in as nearly a dozen SM-2s found their marks. She looked to her left just in time to see the freighter *Anne Marie* take a direct hit from one of the missiles, right at the waterline. A sizable hole was punched through by the impact.

One of the officers on the bridge of the *Churchill* was speaking to the CIC when he suddenly yelled, "Everyone, brace for impact!"

In that second, they heard their own CIWS open fire. A loud boom echoed through the halls as fragments of the missile that had just been streaking towards them disintegrated from the hail of bullets it had flown into. The ship took a few minor hits from the flying debris, but it didn't appear that it had caused any significant damage other than to its paint job.

****

In less than five minutes, the sudden and violent attack was over. Captain Gilbert came running up to the bridge from the CIC and immediately grabbed one of the pairs of binoculars. Through the windows, he scanned the horizon, looking to see which of the ships had been hit. He quickly confirmed what had been reported to him by the CIC. The *Gravely* had been hit, along with five freighters. In all, they had intercepted fourteen of the incoming missiles.

The captain grabbed one of the mics. "Sonar, Bridge. Do you have anything on sonar? There may be additional submarines out there trying to sneak up on us."

"Bridge, Sonar. We're moving too fast to tell. If you can slow us down and redeploy the towed array, we can see if we can spot anything."

Pat could see off in the distance that one of the helos was dipping his sonar into the water, trying to get a fix on the enemy submarine that had just carried out this attack. "Slow the ships down, and get the towed array back online," Captain Gilbert ordered. "We need to figure out if there are additional submarines in the area."

Then he turned to his communications officer. "I want a full report from the escorts," he ordered. "Get their helicopters airborne and start actively pinging away." He had a sickening feeling that the attack wasn't over.

Five minutes later, an urgent call brought everyone back to a state of heightened alert.

"Bridge, Sonar," came a voice over the mic. "We have contact bearing 204, eight miles, depth three hundred meters. It's an *Akula*..." Seconds later, he yelled, "Torpedoes in the water! We count six torpedoes!"

Several of the officers on the bridge immediately shifted their gaze in the direction of the new threat to see what ships were over there. To their horror, they saw the amphibious assault ship, the USS *Essex*. The *Essex* was carrying 1,800 US Marines and their full complement of equipment.

"Send a flash message to the *Essex* and let them know that they have torpedoes in the water heading towards them," ordered the captain.

"Bridge, Con. We have six more torpedoes in the water. Bearing 318, nine miles out," the CIC reported.

Captain Gilbert let loose a string of obscenities, speaking to no one in particular. He just needed to vent his anger.

"Bridge, CIC. We have an antisubmarine rocket firing solution on one of the subs."

The captain nearly ripped the mic off the hook and yelled down to the CIC, "Fire now! Take that sub out!"

A second later, the ASROC fired and headed towards the submarine. Off in the distance, they saw several additional ASROCs fire from the other escort ships. Two of the helos also dropped their own ASW torpedoes.

Lieutenant Commander Brewster turned to look at the *Essex* in time to watch two of the torpedoes impact against the side of the ship. A huge geyser of water shot up in the air, intermixed with heavy black smoke and flames. She could see the ship rock slightly from the impact; then it lost speed and started to list to one side. Dark smoke and flames continued to billow forth from several areas of the ship.

The *Anne Marie*, which had already taken a hit from one of the anti-ship missiles earlier, was also struck by a torpedo. The ship had already starting to list slightly from the previous blow; now it tilted more heavily to one side as water rushed into the new hole, courtesy of the Russian Navy. The *Anne Marie* was quickly sinking.

"Bridge, Sonar. We can hear multiple impacts against a sub's hull. We're hearing crush sounds. We got them!" they yelled excitedly.

No one on the bridge felt excited, though. As the officers and enlisted men and women looked out the bridge windows, they saw nearly a dozen ships with smoke billowing from them.

"Order the helos to begin rescue operations. Deploy our own rescue boats and let's get our people out of the water," the captain ordered.

The other two amphibious assault ships had thankfully survived unscathed and immediately deployed their helicopters to the *Essex* to help evacuate the ship. In the meantime, the crew of the ship desperately tried to save her from sinking. The vessel continued to list to one side but was still level enough for its helicopters to operate.

****

Five Hours Later
42 Miles Northeast of NATO Convoy Alpha

Captain Popov was both elated at the success of their attack and disheartened at the loss of both *Akulas*. After they had launched their cruise missile attack, the American destroyer escorts had come after his ship with a vengeance. They probably would have been caught had the *Akulas* not launched their attacks. However, once the Americans had realized the two Russian subs had snuck up inside the convoy, it had been too late to stop them.

When the *Orel* had raised its communications buoy to the surface twenty minutes ago, they'd received a burst message from their RORSAT, providing them with a detailed view and disposition of the NATO convoy. They could clearly see one of the American amphibious assault ships had been heavily damaged, as were a guided-missile destroyer, and two other freighters. From the images and what their sonar was able to piece together, they had been able to determine that seven freighters had been sunk by the *Akulas'* torpedoes, while two others had been sunk from their own cruise missile attack.

Thinking for a minute on how to proceed next, Popov looked at the map of the North Atlantic. They had three options: they could make their way back to their home port and take on supplies and rearm, move to a better position and try to attack the convoy a second time, or head towards New York Harbor and launch an attack on the shipping route along the US East Coast.

Tracing his fingers across the map to a point not far from their current location, he ordered, "Let's reposition here. This places us roughly 60 miles from the three damaged ships, and 72 miles from the rest of the convoy. If we launch a barrage of twenty missiles at those damaged ships, we should be able to sink them. We can launch the remainder of our missiles at the rest of the convoy. The Americans only have five escort ships left that can engage our missiles, so more of them should get through this time."

One of the weapons officers asserted, "I know this is risky, but I believe we should raise our targeting radar mast before we launch. This way we can get a positive lock on the critical ships in the convoy and then target our remaining missiles to attack them."

Captain Popov raised an eyebrow at the suggestion. "Please elaborate."

"Captain, the convoy has four large medium-speed roll-on/roll-off ships, which are most likely transporting main battle tanks and other heavily armored vehicles to Europe. I recommend that we focus a large number of our missiles at these ships. They also have several large dry cargo transport ships with the fleet, along with two additional *Wasp*-class amphibious assault ships. My point is, there are a lot of cargo ships and freighters in the convoy, but some of them are a lot more valuable than others. It is my recommendation that we focus our attack on the high-value ones, Captain," the young targeting officer explained.

The captain and the XO could see his idea had merit. They could not stop the convoy. With the loss of both *Akulas*, this was probably going to be their best chance at hurting NATO. They weren't likely to get replacements for the two lost *Akulas*. Most of the fleet's submarines were in the North Sea, preventing the Americans from moving a carrier battle group into the Baltic Sea.

The captain nodded.

"OK, we'll move forward with your plan. How long will you need the radar operational to identify and target the specific ships you mentioned?" Once they activated their radar, the Americans would be able to zero in on them quickly.

"Operating in conjunction with the RORSAT, we shouldn't need more than one pass. Once the coordinates are locked in, the

RORSAT will help guide them to the targets," the targeting officer said with confidence.

The group of officers smiled at the thought of being able to sink a few more ships.

Chapter 24
More Bad News

Mons, Belgium
NATO Headquarters – SHAPE

General James Cotton was not having a good day. The Navy had just given him a report on a second attack against the NATO convoy six hours ago. There was no way around it—it was appalling. A Russian *Oscar II* nuclear-powered cruise missile submarine had delivered yet another devastating attack against a desperately needed supply convoy. Not only had the *Essex* (a *Wasp*-class amphibious assault ship) been lost, they'd lost two of the four roll-on/roll-off transports and two additional heavy transports. The loss of the sailors and Marines was bad enough, but the equipment loss would hurt them more.

General Cotton walked into the operations center to discuss the equipment and manpower issues with his operations staff and several officers from the supply and logistics group. As he sat down, a steward brought a fresh pot of coffee to the table, along with several mugs. The steward kindly poured the general a cup of piping-hot coffee as the others joined him at the table.

Cotton daydreamed for a moment over his mug of java as he waited for everyone to file in. Once everyone was seated, he was jolted back to reality, and without even the usual pleasantries he blurted out, "How bad are these losses from the convoy going to be? What exactly did we lose?"

An American naval officer from the US Navy's Military Sealift Command, who managed the logistics and supply aspect of Operation Reforger spoke up to answer this question. "The roll-on/roll-off ships that sank were carrying a mix of Abrams battle tanks and self-propelled artillery guns, equipment that is typically too heavy to transport by air. We lost an entire battalion of Paladin artillery guns and two battalions of main battle tanks. Intermixed with those armored vehicles were another 60 Stryker vehicles."

Groans from the other officers filled the room.

"And the freighters? What did we lose when they went down?" General Cotton asked.

The naval officer shuffled through a few papers to find the one he was looking for. "The freighters we lost were transporting roughly 132,000 tons of munitions and 43,000 tons of MREs and other military equipment. It was roughly about 38% of the munitions and 26% of the MREs and other military equipment the convoy was transporting that we lost."

The naval officer continued to be the bearer of bad news. "Then, there is the loss of the *Essex*. Three hundred and forty-six Marines and 124 sailors were killed when the torpedoes hit. Roughly twice that number were injured. We ultimately lost the ship. One of the other amphibious assault ships sustained two missile hits, which killed another 160 sailors and Marines. It also destroyed nearly half of their helicopters when one of the missiles detonated inside the hangar deck. If those missiles had been the older Shipwreck missiles, the convoy probably would have lost a few more ships."

General Cotton pondered the bad news. These were some tough losses, but not insurmountable. The Navy was already hard at work getting Convoy Bravo ready to sail from New York Harbor in a few more days, and that convoy was going to be more heavily guarded than the last one.

"OK, there's nothing we can do about the convoy," Cotton said. "So let's focus on the other tasks at hand. What's the status of the counterattack? Are we still on schedule?"

A Dutch officer responded to General Cotton's question. "The German 1st Panzer Division arrived last night and moved to the jump points this morning. The French 3rd Armored Division will arrive tomorrow and should be ready to join the offensive if we achieve a breakthrough—otherwise, they're going to act as the reserve force."

A British general asked, "What does that bring our troop count to, with the French division?"

The Dutch officer looked at the unit strengths and did some quick addition. "It brings the NATO troop levels to roughly 68,000 troops, with another 53,000 Ukrainian soldiers."

"What do we want to do with the units that broke out of Kiev?" asked the same British general. "There are around 7,600 NATO troops that made it out of the city, and roughly 19,000 Ukrainians. Nearly all those units are at 40% or less troop strength, though. How do you want to use them, General Cotton?"

126

General Cotton thought about that for a minute. "I want those units to return to Germany to regroup and reequip. They've been fighting nearly nonstop since the start of the war almost six weeks ago. They need to be taken off the line for a while and allowed some time to rest."

Cotton turned to his operations officer and added, "When those units get back to Germany. I want every soldier and officer given a seven-day pass of R&R. These men need to rest and decompress so we can get them ready for combat again. Make sure promotions and awards are handled. Also, give those units top priority for replacements coming in from the US. Is that understood?"

"Yes, Sir. I'll see to the orders myself," the colonel answered with a smile. These guys were heroes in the eyes of the NATO leadership—they planned on making sure everyone knew it, too. The NATO member states needed a poster child for victory, and it had been determined the group that broke out of the Kiev pocket was going to be it.

Turning back to face his air boss, General Cotton asked, "How are we doing with taking out the Russian SAMs?"

The British air marshal who was in charge of NATO's air power cleared his throat before responding, "We lost 47 aircraft during the rescue operation, and most of the aircraft losses were due to Russian SAMs. These SA-21s are brutal. They are mauling our attempts to take them out. We're trying a couple of new tactics. For one, we've dedicated a lot more surveillance to the suspected sites. As we identify their positions, we're starting to use more standoff cruise missile strikes against them. These strikes are forcing them to use a lot more of their missiles to try and intercept the cruise missiles, which is going to start having a supply-and-demand effect on them. We also aren't risking aircraft when we do these types of attacks."

"When it comes to Wild Weasel missiles, we're strictly limiting those now to direct air support missions. When we have a large air mission going, that's when we have the Weasels go in. We're working with a variety of Special Forces units to help us track down and then neutralize these sites. The SF teams are either calling in a cruise missile strike or just taking out the sites themselves. They've had some success disabling the radar systems with their .50-caliber sniper rifles."

The air marshal sighed briefly before continuing, "It's hard going right now, General, but by God, we'll get those SAMs thinned out."

General Cotton nodded. He knew it was going to be a tough road ahead gaining air superiority from the Russians. The US, and NATO in general, had woefully underestimated the capability of the SA-21. The US had believed its electronic warfare capabilities would be enough to spoof the Russian SAMs, but within the first few hours of the war, they had quickly learned how inadequate those defenses were—they were paying for it now.

Cotton tapped his knuckles on the desk as he thought of how to respond to the officers around him. "I'm going to be straight with everyone," he began. "I'm under a lot of pressure from Washington to hit the Russians and hit them hard. Aside from General Fenzol's force busting their way out of Kiev, the Russians have been hitting us nonstop. The President wants us to start hitting back."

He stood, looking each person in the eye as he tried to motivate them to action. "We have over 100,000 troops marshaled and ready. We're going to go ahead and move forward with Operation Thunder and try to push the Russians back to the Dnieper River. We've been planning this for a few weeks. Now it's time to execute."

Chapter 25
Counterattack

It had been a rough couple of weeks for the men of Alpha Troop. Their troop had been separated from the rest of their regiment during the retreat from the Kiev line, and nearly the entire regiment remained trapped in the city. Their unit had tried to hold off a much larger Russian force to keep the lines of retreat open, but they had been unsuccessful in preventing the Russians from fully encircling the NATO forces. Since their long retreat, they had been consolidated with the 35th Armored Regiment, a sister unit in their brigade combat team.

When they'd heard their old unit had busted out of Kiev, they had thought they might fold back in with them. However, the leadership had determined that this group was too badly mauled and wouldn't be combat-effective for some time. They were going to be moved to Germany to regroup and reequip, which meant Sergeant Dukes' ragtag unit was going to stay put with the 35th.

****

Lieutenant Colonel Tim Webb's 35th Armored Regiment hadn't seen any combat yet but was itching for a fight. They gladly welcomed Sergeant Dukes' ten tanks; his tankers had seen the Elephant and had fought the vaunted T-14 Armatas and survived. His officers and NCOs had been picking their brains on a near-daily basis for details on how the T-14s fought and how the Russian armor units attacked, trying to gain as much information from them as possible. They had proven to be a wealth of information.

Lieutenant Colonel Webb walked over to Sergeant First Class Joe Dukes, who was just hopping out of his tank near the ammunition point to top off their stores before the coming battle. Webb signaled for him to join him and his command sergeant major.

Dukes, or "JD" as his friends called him, saw his new battalion commander wave for him to come over. *The sergeant major is with him too—I don't know if this is a good thing or a bad thing*, he thought.

JD tapped his gunner on the shoulder. "Hey, I need you to get the tank topped off with fuel and ammunition while I go talk to the battalion CG for a minute."

The gunner just nodded and said, "Good luck." He was too exhausted to say much else.

JD walked up to the officers without saluting, since they weren't far from the front lines and separatist militia units had been sniping at NATO soldiers on and off for the past week. "Sir, how can I be of assistance?" he asked innocently enough.

Smiling for the first time in days, Lieutenant Colonel Webb replied, "Sergeant First Class Dukes, I've talked with several of the NCOs and soldiers in your troop, and I've also talked with a few of the other units that have worked with your unit since the start of the war. A British captain from the 20th Armored Infantry Brigade said your troop was responsible for most of their unit being able to escape from Kiev. He told me that without your troop, most of their brigade would have been trapped in the city."

JD was surprised by what he was hearing. From his perspective, he was just doing his job—trying to keep his men alive and help as many others as he could during the retreat. He saw his CSM was smiling from ear to ear as the colonel kept talking.

Webb continued, "We've received nothing but glowing praise for your gallantry and ability to lead while under heavy enemy fire. I wanted to be the first to let you know the division commander is awarding you the Distinguished Service Cross, and a Purple Heart for that gash on the side of your head."

He held up a hand before JD could reply, adding, "I know you're going to say you were just doing your job, but I want to tell you something, Sergeant. You went far above and beyond your job. You helped save several thousand soldiers from being trapped in Kiev and blunted a Russian motorized division from completely encircling our forces. The command sergeant major, the British captain and I have all written a letter to the SACEUR to have your medal upgraded to the Medal of Honor. I'm not sure when or if that will happen, but we'll let you know. You can bet there are a lot of people pushing for it."

"Um…I don't even know what to say, Sir," JD said humbly. "It wasn't just me out there…I'd like my men to be recognized as well. They all earned it, and it was a team effort. I couldn't have done it without them."

The CSM jumped in at this point. "Everyone in your troop is being awarded Bronze Stars with V Devices for Valor. You can choose eight soldiers to receive the Silver Star—and don't worry, your troop commander, Captain Lillith, is being awarded the Silver Star posthumously as well."

They could see JD was a little bewildered at the news they had just shared with him but wanted to assure him he had done a great job and, more importantly, let him know that his troop's actions were becoming a rallying cry for the rest of the division.

The colonel had one other piece of good news to add. "I've also received permission from the division commander to give you an official battlefield promotion to first lieutenant. You're going to take over as the Alpha Troop commander, effective immediately," Webb said with a genuine smile on his face.

This was one of the more gratifying moments he had experienced as a commander, to let one of his soldiers know that he was being publicly recognized for a heroic act and being given a battlefield promotion. They needed more leaders and heroes like him, especially since the Army was about to triple in size. The sergeant major was also smiling as he reached out and took JD's hand and shook it hard.

"I couldn't be prouder of one of my NCOs…you earned this, Dukes," said the CSM. "Now, we only have a day before your unit needs to move forward to the front, so I need you to figure out who else is going to get those Silver Stars. I also need a list of those who were injured since the start of the conflict, along with the details of when, where, and how those injuries occurred, so we can go ahead and get those Purple Hearts taken care of."

"Uh, Ok—I mean, yes, Sir," JD replied.

"You're going to be an officer now. You need to make sure that you're properly recognizing your soldiers in addition to taking care of their needs," the CSM explained.

As the impromptu meeting ended, JD walked back to his tank, a bit surprised and still in shock at what he had been told. He couldn't be more happy and excited, yet he also felt a bit ashamed that he had survived and would be awarded these prestigious medals, when so many others had died saving his own life and those of his men.

How many aircraft were shot down providing air support for my men? he wondered. *How many infantrymen died defending my tank from enemy missile teams?*

131

His gunner, Sergeant Jay Smokes, a.k.a. "Smokey," saw him approach. "How'd the meeting go? Anything we need to know about?" he asked.

JD snorted. "Yeah, a few things, Smokey," he replied as he reached up and grabbed a handle to help him climb back on his tank. The other two guys from his crew looked up at him, waiting for him to finish his explanation.

"First, I'm being promoted to first lieutenant and officially taking over as the Alpha Troop commander," he said nonchalantly.

Several men nearby let out a hoot, and a couple shouted, "Congrats!"

Ignoring the fanfare, Dukes went on. "Second, they said everyone in the troop is being awarded a Bronze Star, and I have to pick eight individuals to receive a Silver Star. I also need to get a tally of who all was injured since the start of the war and collect all the details so that I can get that information over to the CSM for their Purple Hearts. Apparently, before we kick off this next assault, they want to get decorations in order," he finished as the guys started to smile.

The Army and its paperwork doesn't care about when an attack was going to start. It wants its t's crossed and its i's dotted, thought JD, laughing to himself.

Dukes cleared his throat and got back to business. "I need to go talk with the other tank commanders and have them start working on the CSM's request. In the meantime, we need to get the tanks ready. It looks like this new offensive is going to start soon, so be ready to move," he announced.

The soldiers around him got back to work, and he stepped down from the tank to go find another tank commander. As he watched his guys scurrying around, he thought about the change in responsibilities. *They're going to have to handle a lot more of the tank duties; I've got ten tanks and crews that I'm now officially in charge of*, he realized.
****

After a series of "hurry up and wait" announcements, two days had passed. Then, all of a sudden, the offensive finally started.

JD's tank slowly moved through a farm field towards a tree line, where his troop would form up with another tank battalion. They were going to act as a mobile reserve for the coming attack. Once the Germans and British units broke through the Russian lines, the Americans would rush a full battalion of tanks and mechanized infantry through the breach, followed quickly by the French division that had just arrived in country. The overall objective of the offensive was to break through the Russian lines and push them back to the Dnieper River.

As their tank came to a halt at the edge of a cornfield, they could hear the hum of aircraft flying low overhead towards the Russian lines. The Air Force was working the Russian lines over before the main attack started. JD and Smokey were sitting in the turret, getting their crew-served weapons loaded and ready. The order to move forward would probably come shortly after the main attack started, and they wanted to be ready.

Off in the distance, they saw several large explosions as the attacking aircraft delivered a series of bombs. Then, a tremendous amount of tracer fire leaped up from the ground, heading in the direction of the attacking aircraft. Judging by the clatter of the machine guns and the volume of tracer fire being thrown at the fighters, the Russians must have had some anti-aircraft vehicles equipped with 25mm or 30mm guns nearby. It sounded like hundreds of sheets of fabric were being ripped apart, over and over.

As they watched the tracer fire, they saw nearly a dozen missiles streak from the frontlines for the aircraft as well. An A-10 took a direct hit from a missile, and one of its engines exploded in a spectacular fashion. The aircraft left a trail of black smoke as it turned towards friendly lines, somehow still able to stay aloft. A pair of F-16s didn't appear to be so lucky; both aircraft were hit by one of the dozens of SAMs being fired at them and burst into enormous fireballs that rained debris and aviation fuel across the ground below.

"It looks like the Air Force is laying it on thick," Smokey said with a whistle. "They're hammering the Russians." He secured the ammunition box next to his weapon, pulling the charging handle back as he made sure he had a belt properly fed into the machine gun.

"Yeah, they are, but they also look like they're taking some losses. You see that A-10 limping away," JD replied as he surveyed the sky. Additional air battles continued well above them. In the distance, helicopters brought their own fire and brimstone to the Russians.

The radio came alive with chatter as the ground battle started. The crew listened in for nearly an hour, wondering if they would receive

133

the call to exploit a breakthrough, but it never came. Then, out of nowhere, they heard the unmistakable sound of incoming rockets shrieking through the sky towards them. Without needing to be told, the tanks around them began to button up their turrets. No one wanted to be caught outside their tank during an artillery barrage.

Explosions rocked the area around their tanks. Pieces of shrapnel could be heard hitting their armor as the ground shook from each explosion. Suddenly, the radio sputtered to life and JD's battalion commander gave them their final instructions. "Alpha Troop, move your tanks to grids 975 457 and support the German assault. The Russians are moving additional units forward, so be on the lookout for a possible flanking attack."

Finally, we're being moved forward to attack, JD thought as they moved forward, out of the artillery barrage.

Lieutenant Dukes passed the orders down to the rest of his new command as he ordered his own tank forward. He could see by the looks of the faces around him that the men around him felt the same way he did—it was time to get some payback.

As his tank moved across the original frontline, he could see dozens of destroyed German Marder infantry fighting vehicles and Leopard Tanks, intermixed with Russian T-80 and T-90 tanks and dozens of armored troop carriers. The field they were traveling through had become a burning cemetery of armored vehicles and charred bodies.

"I see the Germans, 5,000 yards to our front, LT," declared Sergeant Smokes as he began to scan the area for enemy tanks. As they approached the German lines, they made contact with them on the radio.

"We're coming up from behind you, and we'll pass through your lines as we advance to engage the enemy," Lieutenant Dukes explained.

The German commander sent them a warning. "You're about to encounter the new T-14 Armatas," he cautioned.

Lieutenant Dukes' troop came parallel with the German unit, just as a pair of A-10s swooped in and released several cluster bombs on the enemy positions.

"I've got enemy tanks 3,000 yards to our front!" yelled Smokey.

Keying his mic for the rest of the troop, Lieutenant Dukes announced, "Listen up, Alpha. We have enemy tanks to our front. The

Germans are reporting T-14s in the area, so stay frosty. Our A-10s just lit them up, and a pair of Dutch F-16s are about to make a run at them. Once we see their bombs hit, I want everyone to charge forward. Call out your targets and I'll see you all on the other side of Hill 785."

Hill 785 was their primary target; if they could capture that hill line, it would give them a commanding view of the surrounding area. As JD sat in his tank, looking through his viewfinder, the F-16s came screaming in, releasing a series of 500-pound bombs across the hill. He took a deep breath, and then he saw what he was looking for—several secondary explosions lit up the horizon, letting him know that a few important vehicles had been hit.

"Let's move, Alpha! Engage!" Dukes yelled as he ordered his driver to charge the enemy position. "Smokey, find us some targets to kill and take 'em out!"

"T-90 at 2,800 yards! Load sabot!" yelled Smokey to their gunner, cuing up the depleted uranium penetrator rounds.

"Sabot up!" Specialist Jones responded as he slammed the breach shut and stepped aside, bracing for the recoil of the gun.

BOOM! The cannon fired the sabot round, which flew across the open ground and slammed into the front armor of the T-90, punching a hole right into the crew compartment. A second later, the turret blew right off the chassis of the tank, flipping end over end in the air. It was a spectacular sight.

Suddenly, they heard a loud *THWAP!* as a Russian tank round slapped into their frontal armor. The hit jarred everyone in the tank, but they continued to race across the open field towards Hill 785. Several explosions erupted nearby from enemy artillery rounds as the Russians started to bombard the field they were racing across.

"T-90, 2,400 yards at our three o'clock. Load sabot!" yelled Smokey as he found another tank for them to attack.

Specialist Jones hit the lever to open the ammunition compartment and grabbed another sabot round out of the stores, slamming it into the breach. "Sabot up!" he yelled back as he secured everything.

"Turn right!" Lieutenant Dukes screamed to his driver, overriding everyone else in the tank. Specialist Miller turned the tank sharply, just as a Russian T-14 fired a round at them. It barely missed them, plowing into the ground not far from where they had just been.

"Gunner, target that T-14!" yelled Dukes as he switched their target to the more dangerous tank. As his gunner moved to engage the T-14, they saw several additional T-14s emerge from a small copse of trees near Hill 785.

BOOM! Their tank fired their Sabot round at the Armata, just as the enemy tank fired another round at them. Their Sabot flew flat and true, slamming into the T-14's rear engine compartment, exploding the rear half of the tank. The Armata quickly ground to a halt, although the turret turned and began to track another one of his tankers. As the round from JD's tank hit the Armata, the enemy round hit the right side of his tank, throwing them sideways a bit and destroying several of their tank wheels. Their track quickly blew apart as their tank came to a halt, smoking badly.

"We're hit! Blow the smokescreen and grab your weapons. We need to bail out before we get hit again!" ordered Lieutenant Dukes, hoping with everything in him that they could get out of the vehicle and somehow make a run for it back to the German positions.

JD quickly grabbed his short-barrel M4, lifted his commander's hatch open and climbed out. The gunner's hatch flipped open a second later as Smokey started to get out of the tank as well. His driver was already halfway out of the vehicle when a second tank round hit their front armor, exploding, and throwing shrapnel everywhere. The blast ripped his driver, Specialist Miller, nearly in half as his lifeless body crumpled to the ground.

The detonation threw JD several feet into the air and off the back of the tank, into the grassy field his tank had just driven through. He lay flat on the ground for a second, struggling to breathe. He'd had the wind knocked out of him by the impact, and he suddenly felt panicked as he fought to get air into his lungs. After he eventually managed to take a couple of deep breaths, he began to check his body for injuries. He had some bruised ribs and a few cuts, but he could still move his arms and legs. He slowly rolled over and looked around him for the rest of his crew.

Not far from him, Sergeant Smokes was lying on the ground, slumped on his side. JD crawled over to him. He was unconscious but looked to be OK. He shook him, trying to wake him up. Smokey jolted his eyes open. "My God—what happened?" he asked in a panic.

Just then, another explosion detonated near them, throwing additional dirt in the air, and showering them with grass and pebbles. JD heard a moan, and then someone called for help. As the dust particles settled a little, Lieutenant Dukes wiped his face and made out Specialist Jones, his loader; he had been thrown from the tank and was maybe twenty feet away from him and Smokey. He ran over to Jones and quickly saw that his loader's left hand had been ripped off and his left leg was in bad shape.

JD immediately grabbed Jones' first aid kit and tied a tourniquet on his left forearm, just below the elbow; he hoped he had tied it tight enough to stop the bleeding. Then he applied a pressure dressing on Jones' leg wound. As he worked, bullets continued to zip all around him, striking the dirt and shrubs nearby.

"Smokey, Jones is hurt bad," JD yelled to his gunner. "I'm going to carry him out of here, but I need you to help give me some covering fire. Miller's dead, so don't try to find him. I saw him go down—he isn't coming back."

Smokey just nodded and fired his weapon in the direction of the Russians.

JD reached down and threw Jones over his shoulder. He grabbed his M4 and ran back towards the German positions. Smokey provided some cover fire for him with his M4 and waved to the Germans, who were roughly 1,000 yards away, to help them.

Several German soldiers jumped out of their positions and ran towards the Americans, firing their rifles at the Russian soldiers, who were now sending a lot of lead in their direction. One of the German Marder infantry fighting vehicles turned its turret towards the Russian lines and sprayed 25mm cannon fire into the Russian positions to help keep their heads down.

Just as JD had made it to the German positions, a round clipped his right leg and he went down hard. He tried to get up with Jones still on his shoulder, but his leg gave out from the pain. One of the German soldiers quickly grabbed Jones and carried him further behind their lines to the medics, who were already working on several wounded soldiers. Another German grabbed JD, pulled his right arm over his shoulder and helped carry him to the makeshift aid station. Meanwhile, the soldiers and infantry fighting vehicles continued to fight back against what was quickly becoming a Russian counterattack. Antitank missiles could be

137

seen streaking from their lines, slamming into several of the Russian tanks and armored vehicles, slowing their advance.

"I need a radio!" JD yelled above the cacophony of machine gun fire and explosions.

As he lay there bleeding, waiting for a medic to make his way over to him, one of the German soldiers asked him, "Why?"

"That's my tank troop out there. I need to know how they're doing and what's going on," JD pleaded.

The soldier looked sad in that moment. Then he said, "All of the American tanks were destroyed. We're helping the few crewmen who got out of their tanks make their way back to our lines. I was told as soon as we have them, we're going to pull back. The new Russian tanks are hitting the entire NATO lines." The German was visibly disheartened.

In that moment, JD laid his head back down on the grass, not sure how to respond. He stared off into the sky above him. Nearly everyone he knew in his battalion, and now his own command, had been effectively wiped out. He fought back tears.

One of the medics came up to him and ripped his pant leg open. He wiped away some of the blood with some water from a canteen. JD saw the wound; it looked like the bullet had just grazed his leg, though he would probably need some stitches. Several Germans helped to load the wounded soldiers into an armored ambulance that quickly whisked them away to the rear of the fighting lines, where they could be better treated.

It took nearly an hour for their ambulance to arrive at a local field hospital roughly thirty miles behind the front lines. Several medics helped to move the wounded to waiting cots, where they were being triaged. JD saw several medevac helicopters landing at the far side of the field hospital. Dozens of medics were busily rushing the most seriously wounded soldiers towards the waiting angels of mercy who would carry them to a higher-level trauma center.

One of the medics walked up to JD and examined his leg. "This isn't too deep, but it's going to need stitches. I think we can try the glue, which might work better, but you're going to have to take it easy on the leg for at least two weeks or it'll reopen. Do you want to try the glue or the stitches?" asked the medic.

"If the glue will get me back into the fight sooner, then let's go that route," replied JD.

After six hours of heavy fighting, the offensive stalled. Eventually the ground force commander called a halt until the Air Force could reestablish air superiority and suppress the Russian artillery and the new Russian tanks that had begun to flood the area.

Chapter 26
Reinforcements

Donetsk, East Ukraine
1st Tank Army Field Headquarters

Lieutenant General Mikhail Chayko could not be happier with his forces after they beat back the most recent NATO counterattack. After being humiliated by one of his division commanders, who had somehow managed to let a significantly smaller NATO force break their way out of Kiev, he needed a big win. He'd summarily fired that division commander and replaced him with a much younger, more aggressive commander.

After breaking out of Kiev, NATO had been falsely lulled into thinking that they could break through his 4th Guard's Tank Division since they had an influx of additional aircraft and troops. General Chayko's plan was to let the 4th Guard appear weak, overstretched, and open to a counterattack. Once NATO launched their attack, the 6th Tank Brigade, which had been largely equipped with the new T-14 Armatas, carried out their own counterattack, demolishing the NATO attack.

The 53rd Anti-Aircraft Rocket Brigade moved a dozen SA-21 batteries towards the frontlines, shooting down 47 NATO aircraft with a loss of only seven SA-21 batteries. His forces could sustain the losses in SAMs. NATO, on the other hand, could not sustain these kinds of losses in advanced aircraft—they took a long time to manufacture and replace, and this conflict, though only about six weeks old, had already chewed through nearly 500 NATO frontline aircraft.

One of the communications officers handed him a secured phone. "General, headquarters is on the line for you," he said. Then he walked away, out of earshot.

"Chayko here," the general declared.

"General, congratulations are in order. Your forces stopped NATO yet again," General Boris Egorkin, the head of the Russian Army, commended him. He had already chewed General Chayko out for the Kiev debacle earlier, so there was no need to dwell on it now.

Chayko grunted. "It was a close battle, comrade. We nearly lost. These Americans are tough fighters, and they won't give up easily. If I am to defeat NATO and push them out of Ukraine, I need those forces from the 6th Tank Army, or I'm not going to be able to hold my own positions for much longer."

General Chayko sighed. "I've lost nearly half of my T-14s since the start of this conflict, and my SAM batteries are starting to get wiped out," he said, hoping that General Egorkin understood the gravity of the situation. His victory was tenuous, and wouldn't last if NATO pressed him hard again.

General Egorkin groaned inwardly. *Chayko is right, of course*, he thought. He needed to release more units to Ukraine if they were going to hold on to the ground they'd already captured. *And yet...*"

"I cannot release any additional units from the 6th Tank Army," Egorkin grumbled. "They're tying down the entire Polish Army and the American airborne forces they moved into the Baltic States. We need to keep that threat real and viable or they'll release those additional forces to Ukraine, which will place you in even more trouble."

Knowing that he had just delivered news that his subordinate wouldn't be happy to hear, he sighed audibly before continuing. "I've spoken to the President. He's authorized me to release the 2nd Guard's Tank Army, the 58th Army and the 49th Army. That gives you an additional 98,000 soldiers and 2,100 additional tanks on top of what you already have. As to the T-14s, the President has personally met with the manufacturers, and they're running round-the-clock to turn out more tanks. We should produce 48 new units this month, and up to 200 by the start of the new year. By this time next year, we'll be producing 300 a month."

General Egorkin paused for a moment before continuing. "In response to the American president's military draft, President Petrov has also authorized me to begin raising an auxiliary force of up to two million soldiers. Most of these forces are going to be slated for the infantry and will not be ready until sometime towards spring. Just know that we're working on addressing the troop and equipment shortages."

Chayko then decided to change topics, seeing that there were things that were beyond the control of either of them. "Comrade, have the negotiations started to end hostilities yet? We have met our initial objectives."

If the politicians can work out a cease-fire, then we won't need all of these additional troops, Chayko thought.

Egorkin paused for a moment. "Yes, comrade," he responded. "The negotiations have started...and so has the next phase of Operation Red Storm."

With that, the call ended.

General Chayko took a deep breath and grabbed a swig from the flask of vodka at his desk. *Things are about to get really intense soon,* he thought. He hoped his reinforcements would arrive quickly. He was going to need them if NATO didn't accept their cease-fire terms.

Chapter 27
Tough Decisions

Mons, Belgium
SHAPE Headquarters

General Cotton sat down at the briefing table, angry and defeated. "What the hell happened with our offensive?!" he yelled at his senior staff, losing some of his professional restraint.

They had spent the better part of ten days moving troops and aircraft from across Europe to engineer a breakthrough and push the Russians back across the Dnieper River. Instead, the effort had ended in abysmal failure and substantial casualties.

A French general spoke up first. "We were beaten, General. They laid a trap for our forces, and we fell for it," he explained in a defeated voice.

General Major Ulrich Laubenthal, the senior Bundeswehr officer at NATO, cleared his throat. "Enough of this defeatist talk! We lost a battle, not the war!" he shouted at his fellow generals and colonels.

Laubenthal scowled at the other officers, who had hung their heads low when the French general had given his prognosis of the battle. "We rushed our attack before we were ready. We should have waited until we had air superiority and additional armor units. There are two American armor brigades en-route to Ukraine that should have been part of the attack. We have to slow the war down while we regroup and consolidate our forces to launch a proper attack," he said passionately.

Brigadier Barney Wall, the senior British officer, added, "The Sixteen Air Assault Brigade should arrive in Ukraine tomorrow. That'll add 8,000 additional troops. The rest of the British 1st Armor should finish arriving tomorrow as well. If we add in the two American brigades and the additional Belgium and Dutch units, that should bring our forces back up to around 103,000 troops." He spoke with a level of confidence that another offensive could begin shortly.

General Cotton let them continue to discuss and argue amongst themselves for a few minutes longer before asking more questions himself. Looking at the French general who had spoken up first, he asked, "What was our final casualty count, General?"

143

The French general pulled a couple of pieces of paper out of his folder. "Our casualties were high. We lost 3,456 killed in action, and nearly three times that number wounded. Another 850 soldiers had been captured during one of the Russian counterattacks. In terms of equipment, we lost 235 tanks and another 700 infantry fighting vehicles. A total of 47 fighter aircraft were shot down, and another 51 sustained some sort of damage," he said.

General Cotton just nodded. He had known the casualties were high but hearing them out loud like this seemed to make it worse. He calculated that NATO was averaging close to eight aircraft losses a day. His men were still shooting down more Russian aircraft per day than they were losing, but the Russians could absorb these losses, and they could not.

Looking to his air marshal, Cotton directed, "We need to keep going after their SAMs. We have to bring their numbers down if our air forces are going to be able to support future offensives. We cannot continue to sustain these kinds of aircraft losses, or our ground forces will soon have to fight without air support."

The SACEUR was frustrated. It seemed like he kept having the same conversation with the French and British generals, with little progress to show for it. *Most of these Europeans have not had to fight a serious war since World War II, and it's showing*, he thought in exasperation. Their lack of equipment and training was becoming more apparent the longer the war dragged on. Even with additional men and equipment, they might not be able to achieve more than a short-burst attack.

Sighing, General Cotton announced, "I've received word from US European Command that most of Three Corps has officially arrived and formed up in Germany. They'll begin to move as a unit towards Poland tonight and should start to arrive tomorrow."

"Three Corps brings with them 49,000 soldiers from the 1st Infantry Division, 1st Cavalry Division, 1st Armored Division and the 4th Infantry Division. The Pentagon also said they just reactivated V Corps, which will make up the second major wave of US forces to arrive in Europe. Unfortunately, they won't arrive until sometime in early November."

He looked at his French and German counterparts. "We're going to need your nations to release additional forces to NATO. After

144

this last offensive failure, we're going to hold our current positions and wait until additional European and US forces arrive before we consider another offensive. As it stands, we're now entering early October. We're going to start moving into the winter months in Eastern Europe, which everyone knows is a tough time to fight. I want to gather our strength now, so we can launch a massive offensive operation in early November. If things work out, we may be able to liberate Ukraine before the end of the year and bring this war to an end on our terms," Cotton announced.

The two men nodded. No one wanted to fight a winter war with Russia.

While the group continued to discuss the military situation, an aide walked up to General Cotton and handed him a note. He quickly read the paper and raised an eyebrow, not sure what to make of it. Everyone at the table stopped talking and looked at him, hoping he might let them in on what new development must have transpired.

General Cotton cleared his throat. "I just received word from our political counterparts. The Russian government has asked for a cease-fire to discuss terms to end the war. Thoughts on this latest development?"

Chapter 28
Red Storm Update

Kremlin, Moscow

The cool October air was starting to move across Moscow, letting everyone know that autumn had arrived, and winter was just around the corner. President Petrov was in a good mood as he looked at his foreign minister, Dmitry Kozlov. NATO had just agreed to a short-term cease-fire earlier this morning, which would give his forces more time to consolidate their positions and move additional troops into Ukraine.

If NATO didn't agree to his terms, then he would have the forces necessary to push NATO out of the rest of Ukraine and open an additional front in Poland and the Baltic States. Up to this point, Russian forces hadn't invaded a NATO member—but all of that might be about to change.

Kozlov smiled broadly as the President sipped his tea. It was a long shot getting NATO to agree to a cease-fire, but pressure from many of the NATO members made it nearly impossible for the Americans not to at least agree to a short-term pause in the war. Now, the hard part would be convincing America and the other NATO members that Ukraine should be partitioned off.

"Dmitry, now that the negotiations are going to start, what do you believe our chances are at ending this war on our terms?" asked Petrov, hoping for his honest assessment.

Kozlov put his cup down on the table, then looked up at the President, full of thought. "I would like to think our chances are better than fifty percent," he began. "We've hurt NATO badly in the last six weeks. Our intelligence operation has also been incredibly effective. Portugal, Hungary, Greece, and Turkey are effectively out of NATO, and there is the possibility that several other nations will be kicked out of the alliance if they don't start to contribute the forces the Supreme Allied Commander has continued to ask for. Our effort to destroy and destabilize NATO through this disinformation campaign has proven incredibly effective."

He raised a hand to stop the President from interrupting him. "What should not be underestimated, Mr. President, is the will of the new

American president. He has publicly chastised his military leaders for their failures and replaced them with significantly more aggressive generals. Our attack on the American LNG facilities was also a major setback. The opinion of the American public had been going heavily in our favor until the Spetsnaz attack on those LNG terminals was caught on video. A physical attack on American soil that led to the deaths of several civilians rattled and scared them tremendously. It also infuriated them. The President has announced a major buildup in American forces as a response. In just the last week, the new American Defense Authorization Bill jumped from $688 billion to $1.3 trillion. Based on all this, I don't believe the American president is going to agree to any of our terms," concluded Kozlov sadly.

The other men in the room nodded in agreement—all except the FSB Director, Ivan Vasilev, who promptly made his opinion known. "When the Chinese launch the next phase of Operation Red Storm, the American president won't have a choice. He will *have to* accept our terms. The Americans have let their military diminish in size, to a point where they can no longer wage two major wars at once. They also don't have the equipment or ships to carry out such a war. They'll have to choose which theater of operation they want to fight and win."

"What makes you think they won't choose *our* theater of operations?" asked one of the generals at the table. Everyone turned back to Vasilev to see what he would say.

"During the last presidential campaign, the President chided his European counterparts for not doing more to defend their own countries. America has come to the aid of Europe during the last two world wars; they're not keen on having to do it a third time. If Japan, Korea, and Taiwan are threatened, I believe the Americans will come to their aid over the Europeans, who can defend themselves but have thus far simply chosen not to," Vasilev explained.

President Petrov pondered what had just been said. It made a lot of sense, but he just didn't believe the Americans would leave Europe entirely defenseless.

Petrov decided to play devil's advocate. "What if the Americans decide to just buy time until they're able to build up their forces enough to refocus their energies on us? Right now, they have a little over 100,000 soldiers in Europe—that number is going to double in a week, two tops. They could leave Asia to China while they focus on defeating us, then turn their attentions to China once they're ready."

The generals in the room suddenly looked nervous. Ivan Vasilev, however, didn't look even the slightest bit nervous. He just smiled while the others seemed unsure of themselves. The President noticed this and inquired, "Ivan—why are you smiling?"

"Mr. President, we have been working on Operation Red Storm for years. I have gone over nearly every possible scenario with Chairman Zhang. The Americans may decide to focus on Russia as opposed to China. If they do that, then China will be able to secure Taiwan, the Koreas, and Japan. Their position in Asia will be too strong for even the Americans to remove them. At that point, the Chinese will send troops to aid us in our war against NATO," Vasilev responded.

His answer surprised a few, and confused others. No one else believed the Chinese would actually send troops to aid Russia. Though China and Russia had been communist partners in the past, they had a rocky relationship and at times had even been adversaries.

"Let us hope it does not come to that, Comrade. In the meantime, I want our forces to continue to consolidate our gains and bring in additional reinforcements. Hostilities could resume at any time, and we must be ready for that," Petrov said, trying to appease all of the parties in the room at once.

Chapter 29
Pecking Order

Beijing, China
Ministry of National Defense HQ
August First Building

The Chinese takeover of Myanmar and Laos had shocked the world. Their capture was nearly bloodless, which made it even more astounding. The invasion of Vietnam was a bit more of a concern for the Asian Pacific nations, who still remembered how Japan had nearly conquered most of the Pacific 70 years prior. The Vietnamese were putting up one heck of a fight, but it looked like they would probably fold within another week or two.

It had taken the PLA two weeks to capture Hanoi and begin to move down the rest of the country, but Ho Chi Minh City had collapsed after the People's Liberation Army Navy had launched a successful seaborne invasion that no Western military expert would have ever imagined they could pull off. The performance of the Chinese Navy's blue water force had been a tremendous surprise. The Navy had shown that it could effectively support a ground invasion with both naval guns and cruise missiles. What had caught the Western militaries off guard the most was the introduction of a series of new cruise missiles, smart munitions, and aircraft. The PLA was using the invasion of Vietnam to test a series of new weapon platforms that the US, Australia, and Japan had been completely unaware of up to that point.

Now that the operations in Vietnam were complete, the CMC decided to meet to discuss initiating phase two of Operation Red Storm.

As the leaders took their seats, President Xi smiled happily. "I want to congratulate all of the generals and everyone else present on the success of phase one," he opened. "The annexation of Myanmar and Laos have gone smoothly, and we'll soon begin our projects there to increase the agricultural production and improve infrastructure of our new provinces."

Then Xi cleared his throat, and his voice took a much more serious turn. Turning to the generals, he inquired, "How soon can North Korea begin their attack?"

The Defense Minister, General Kuang, replied, "They can commence operations within four days of us giving them the order…however, before we do that, I would like permission to begin transferring additional fuel and munitions to them now, so they'll be in place prior to the attack."

The other generals at the table nodded in agreement. When the attack did finally start, the North Koreans would chew through enormous amounts of ammunition and fuel. It was imperative that their attack succeed, as it would tie down tens of thousands of additional US forces and pull the Japanese into the conflict.

Chairman Zhang felt he should ask a question, as this was a critical aspect of Operation Red Storm. "What if the North Koreans use their nuclear weapons?" he dared.

The generals at the table turned and looked at Zhang, surprised that he would pose such a question or even think the North Koreans would use their nukes without seeking permission first from China.

General Wei Liu leaned forward in his chair and addressed this question. "Mr. Chairman, we have told the Koreans they are not to use them, that this war is to stay conventional. If, by chance, the Koreans do use their nuclear weapons, then we need to hope that they succeed in whatever they hit, and it truly hurts the Americans."

"What about the American carriers?" Zhang asked. "Don't they have two of them in Japan, with a third on the way right now? They have also deployed nearly 60,000 Marines to Japan."

The defense minister spoke up this time. "Mr. Chairman, I understand that you have been the brains behind Operation Red Storm and coordinating this effort with Russia. You have given us the political and military goals, and we have developed a series of plans to achieve them. This is a military matter, and we aren't going to share all the details of our operations with you as they don't concern you. We'll continue to keep you informed of the progress of the objectives you have given us, but we won't go into the minutiae of how we're going to execute them."

This was a rather sharp rebuke the defense minister had given to a senior Politburo member, but he had felt the need to intervene before this politician thought he had the authority to get involved in their inner workings.

The President was rather amused to see the drama unfold. He supported Zhang, but he also wanted the Chairman to know that his support had limits, and that Zhang's authority didn't include control of the military or the CMC, despite his status with State Security.

Zhang could feel everyone looking at him and knew he had asked too many questions. The President had given him the opportunity to sit in on the secret military meetings so he could better coordinate things with the Russians. That didn't mean he had any authority to order the generals to do anything they didn't want to do. Only the President had that authority. He lowered his head slightly and acknowledged the defense minister's rebuke.

Go on and gloat, you old goat. When Operation Red Storm succeeds, I'll become the next President of China, Zhang thought as his cheeks burned red with embarrassment.

Xi raised a hand to stop any further discussion. "General Kuang, Chairman Zhang does bring up some valid points about the Koreans' nuclear weapons. I want it reiterated to them that they are *not* to use them unless the Americans use them first."

The Koreans had better not use the ICBMs at Paektu Mountain, or there will be hell to pay, thought Xi.

The President continued, "I want you to move forward with the next phase. Get our frontline units out of Vietnam and start moving them to the Formosa sector. Also, get our northern forces ready to intervene in Korea if needed." He turned and looked at his admiral. "Move your forces into position and execute the plan we discussed."

That evening, several Shang-class nuclear-powered submarines moved closer to the American carrier battlegroups in the Pacific, along with ten Yuan-class advanced diesel submarines. America was about to receive a rude awakening.

151

Chapter 30
Trepidation

Washington, D.C.
Boiling Air Force Base
Defense Intelligence Agency

Angela Peterson had been a Chinese intelligence analyst at the DIA for the past ten years. She had joined the DIA after spending her first four years after college working for Lockheed Martin in their aircraft development department. During her time at the DIA, she had seen China increase funding to the PLA at an alarming rate. The introduction of the Chinese J-20, which strongly resembled the American F-22, had caused a lot of people to question if they had obtained the designs of the F-22 and just copied the blueprints.

When China had invaded Vietnam, her group had observed a series of weapons the Chinese were testing and had become quite concerned. Of particular trepidation was the introduction of the more advanced versions of the YJ-62 anti-ship cruise missile and the CJ-10 land attack cruise missile.

Both of these new missiles could cause considerable problems for the US and its allies in the Pacific. The YJ-18 long-range anti-ship cruise missile had a range of 140 to 340 miles and could carry a 660-pound warhead at an attack speed of between Mach 2.5 to Mach 3 when it began its terminal approach. The cruise missile could also maneuver and evade antimissile interceptors, which made it significantly deadlier than previous models.

As Angela and her team considered all the implications of these new missiles, they realized that this would push out the distance that the Allied carriers needed to be from the shore to keep them out of range of the cruise missiles. This would put the carriers at a point where the aircraft on board wouldn't be as effective, since they would have very limited time over a target before they ran out of fuel. Her group collected all the applicable data and wrote up their findings.

When the tier one PLA frontline units began to withdraw from Vietnam, another analyst on her team became alarmed.

"Hey, Angela," said her coworker, Pamela, as she rolled over to her cubicle in her desk chair. "The war in Vietnam hasn't been fully won yet, so why are they pulling their frontline troops out before the job is done?" she asked.

The hair on Angela's arms suddenly stood up straight. *That just doesn't seem right*, she thought suspiciously.

"Let's check a few more things to see what this might mean," Angela said. For the rest of the day, the two of them began reviewing the raw data, looking for the one fact that would explain why the Chinese would begin to shift their best forces out of Vietnam when the war hadn't been won just yet.

A couple of hours later, while combing through the most recent satellite imagery, Angela suddenly called out, "Pamela, come here and check out my screens. Are you seeing what I'm seeing?"

After staring at the screens for a moment, Pamela exclaimed, "My God—all of the Yuan-class diesel submarines have left their ports. They're all headed in the direction of the US Fleet…"

Chapter 31
I'd Trade My Kingdom for a Horse

Washington, D.C.
White House, Situation Room

The United States was reeling from all the body blows being thrown at it. Several NATO members had failed to honor their commitment to the alliance, which had forced the American president to demand their expulsion from the organization. That, of course, had caused additional rifts and problems among the remaining countries. NATO had been brutally attacked by Russia, the very country the organization had been created to counter, and now, several members had shown their true colors and failed to meet their obligations when the alliance was attacked.

The discovery of nearly three dozen senior government officials as leakers had rocked the public trust in the government. The realization that members of the media had also been caught in this treasonous web caused Americans to suddenly doubt every news story they heard, wondering if there might be an alternate agenda in the reporting.

While the political and domestic front was a disaster, the military front wasn't going any better. The first ten days of the war had seen NATO forces suffer one defeat after another. After being pushed several hundred miles west of Kiev, NATO had launched a massive counterattack. However, less than three days later, they had been forced into another disastrous retreat.

Then, the US had lost its first aircraft carrier since World War II, and nearly two dozen other naval ships. The aircraft and equipment losses during the first four weeks of the war were nothing short of disastrous.
****

The President was fuming internally, but knew he needed to project some sense of calm and right the ship, just as he had with his many businesses. Gates took a short walk in the Rose Garden to help clear his head a bit and calm himself before he went to the Situation Room for the next round of updates and status reports from the various services.

As he approached the side portico door that would lead him back to the Oval Office, he looked back at the perimeter of the White House and the fence that kept the public at bay. He could see a mix of people, some tourists trying to snap a picture of the White House, others were protestors chanting their disdain for the war.

Gates then opened the outer door and walked into the most powerful office in the world. He was summarily greeted by his Chief of Staff, who had been waiting anxiously for him to return.

Ishaan had been working hard these past few weeks, trying to sift through hundreds of personnel decisions and legislation that needed to be completed despite the war that was raging in Europe and the one that was brewing up in Asia. With the firing of so many government officials, there had been a bit of a void in the government, but the leaks had largely stopped, and the officials who remained were finding it a lot easier to get things done when they didn't have others who were actively working against them.

"Mr. President, the others are ready in the Situation Room when you are," he announced.

Gates nodded and headed down the hall. He walked with a sense of purpose, knowing that each decision he made was going to have a profound impact on history and the course of the world.

This war is quickly spiraling out of control. Something needs to be done to stop it, or at least contain it, he thought as he walked. Although part of him just wanted to wash his hands of the whole thing and let the world burn down around me while he focused only on the internal needs of his own country...in the long run, America would suffer from that tactic, and history would certainly not look kindly upon his presidency if he went that route. *I have to defend the people who elected me, even if half of the country wants to surrender.*

The President walked briskly into the Situation Room and signaled for everyone to stay seated as he took his own seat at the head of the table. As per usual with President Gates, he got right down to business, skipping the pleasantries. Looking at Admiral Meyers, the Chairman of the Joint Chiefs, Gates asked, "Where do we stand with replacement equipment for the services?"

Admiral Meyers responded, "We've activated the Navy's reserve fleet, and we've started reactivating nearly 100 additional ships, including the supercarriers we previously mentioned. It'll be some months before they're ready for combat, but we have crews working on them 24/7. The Army has also reactivated their various war stocks and equipment reserves. Similarly, it'll take time to get all the tanks and other vehicles ready for combat but once they do, they'll be ready to outfit several corps worth of troops. The Air Force has started to reactivate several air wings' worth of fighters and cargo aircraft from Davis-Monthan Air Force Base as well."

"What about replacement equipment?" the President inquired. He was glad the services maintained a reserve force, but he was concerned about the replacement of the newer equipment.

"We've spoken with the CEOs of Boeing, Lockheed Martin, Northrop Grumman, and others. They're moving to 24-hour shifts, seven days a week, and will start rapid production of our F-16, F-15, F-18, and A-10 aircraft, along with our entire suite of air-to-air, air-to-ground and cruise missile systems."

Admiral Meyers paused for a second to take a drink of water, clearing his throat and then continuing, "The aircraft manufacturers need to restart the production lines for the F-22s and the B-2s, so it's going to be months before they'll even be able to start work on any of those aircraft. They're also going to ramp up production of our helicopter force. Unfortunately, all of this is going to take months before they're able to start bringing new aircraft off the assembly line, and then there is the issue of pilot training. We're working out the kinks in the programs and calling a lot of pilots who had recently retired or separated from the military back to active duty."

The admiral paused for a second, looking at the others in the room before turning back to face the President. "Sir, I'm not going to sugarcoat it—the military is depleted and nearly spent. We have been at war in Afghanistan and the Middle East for nearly sixteen years. Our aircraft are old and well past their service life, and so is most of our ground warfare equipment. There hasn't been a lot of money spent on replacing old and worn out equipment, aircraft, and ships over the years. We're paying for that right now with this unexpected war with Russia. It's going to take us time to rearm and gear up to win this war."

No one said anything for a moment, waiting to see how the President would respond. For his part, Gates just sat there thinking, trying to figure out what their options were. He sighed as he formulated his response. "Then we have to accept the fact that we're going to have to rebuild. We'll need to stay on defense for the time being, until we're strong enough to win. So, if that's going to be the strategy we need to take, then what does everyone recommend we do with Russia and China?"

The SecDef felt this was a good time to speak up. He was a retired Marine and not one to back down from a fight. "Mr. President, we had hoped this would be a quick war, one in which we could use our advantage in technology to overcome our adversaries. That has obviously not worked out the way we thought it should have, but we can't cry over spilt milk. We have to accept the new reality and deal with it. I have full confidence that we can defeat the Russians, and if necessary, the Chinese. You've given me the troop numbers I've requested. You've given me the monies I need to buy equipment and streamlined the procurement process, so I can get this equipment to the warfighters in a timely manner. What I need now is enough time to train and equip an army that can defeat our enemies," Secretary Castle explained.

The other generals at the table nodded in agreement.

The Secretary of State inquired, "How much time do you need us to buy you?"

Castle calculated for a moment before responding, "I need at least six months to get you the numbers needed to win in Europe. I'll need at least eighteen months to get the troop and ship numbers we'll need to win in the Pacific. That theater is going to rely on the Navy a lot more than Europe. Until we get some of our additional aircraft carriers out of mothballs and their supporting fleets ready, we're going to be hard-pressed to challenge China."

The Secretary of State grimaced but did not say anything. He knew the SecDef was doing his best. *You can't create an army out of thin air overnight*, he realized. *It takes time to draft, train, and equip. Time is unfortunately not on our side.*

The President thought about this for a minute. "The Russians and Chinese really thought this out, didn't they? They knew we were at our weakest point since Pearl Harbor. They've worked feverishly to divide our country and distract us from what their true intentions were.... Well, I'm the wild card in their plan. I'm the one guy they didn't think would become President, and I intend to use that status to throw them off."

He turned to face his secretaries of state and defense with a renewed energy and anger. "Tell Petrov no deal. Either he withdraws his forces from Ukraine, or we'll continue the war. You tell that piece of trash I won't stop until we've removed him from power or reduced his country to rubble."

A few of the mouths in the room dropped open in shock.

The President plowed on. "Tell the rest of our alliance members that they'll either adhere to their alliance requirements, or they can leave NATO. Make it known to them that nations that are kicked out of NATO for not honoring their pledge will face severe economic consequences as well. I want a specific war tax placed on all goods and services those nations provide to the US if they withdraw or offer anything less than full support to the alliance. No more free lunches. If they want to leave the alliance high and dry in its time of need, then they can pay a financial price for it." As he finished that last thought, he slammed his fist on the table.

"As to the military, I want our Air Force to go after the Russian economy. I want their infrastructure destroyed. Then, find a segment of their economy we can thoroughly wreck and take it out. Let them grind to a halt until they're willing to leave Ukraine."

"In the Pacific, I want you to send a strong message to China. If they attack Taiwan, South Korea, or Japan, there will be severe military and economic consequences. They better think hard about what they would be giving up if they choose to go to war with America. Also, tell that pudgy little dictator in North Korea that if he invades the South, bombs Seoul, or launches his ICBMs at the US, I will burn his country to the ground."

The others in the room nodded quietly. Some of them liked his decisive remarks, but many hoped that this was a bit more bluster than his real intentions.

Gates paused for a second, then he looked at the Marine commander. "I want the Marines in Japan, ready to move into Korea if it comes to it. I also want additional cruise missiles and heavy ordnance moved to Japan—and move some of our nukes, just in case we end up having to use them. I have a bad feeling that things with China and North Korea are about to go from bad to worse. They think there isn't a lot that we can do to stop them other than bomb them, but I want to try and project as much strength and resolve with them as possible. Perhaps we

158

can get them to think twice and let calmer heads prevail. If not, then I want the option to bloody them badly when the time comes."

As the meeting concluded, the generals and advisors immediately went to work getting the President's orders issued and sending the appropriate guidance to the various field units and commanders. If the Russians thought this was going to be a quick war, they were in for a rude awaking. The President had no intention of giving in to the Russians, and he was bent on making sure the Chinese understood that a war with America wouldn't go well for them either.

Chapter 32
The Second Korean War

Okinawa, Japan
Camp Butler Marine Base

It was a cool October morning as Lieutenant General Roy Cutter finished his morning run. His command had deployed to Japan two weeks ago, unsure of where they might be headed next. They had only been told to be prepared to move when given the order. Then, two days ago, he had been given overall command of all US Marine ground forces in the Korea-China area of operations and told to be prepared to deploy to South Korea.

I'm glad I got a good run in today, he thought. *Starting tomorrow, things are going to get really busy.*

Intelligence reports from the National Security Agency and the Defense Intelligence Agency showed a massive transfer of ordnance and fuel from China to North Korea. Surveillance also showed an increase in general military activity across North Korea, with military units leaving their bases and heading to the field. This could only mean one thing— North Korea was gearing up to invade the South and was being given a healthy supply of fuel and munitions prior to the start of hostilities.

With the deployment of the First Marine Expeditionary Force to Okinawa, there were now 68,000 Marines in Japan. Now, it was Cutter's job to get them to South Korea and ready to repel one of the largest armies in the world. Fortunately, his Marines wouldn't be the only US forces in Korea. The Army had 28,000 soldiers already in there and another 22,000 more in Japan that were also transferring to Korea.

The South Koreans, unlike their European counterparts, maintained a large standing army and reserve force. The South Koreans had 650,000 soldiers and 3,200,000 reserve soldiers. As the US began to deploy additional troops to the Peninsula in preparation of a North Korean invasion, the country started a full activation of their reserves.

Lieutenant General Cutter was intricately involved with the buildup, every hour of every day. His sleep was starting to suffer. He had been on the battlefield before, but this was the first time he had been in a potential nuclear conflict.

As he went through his cool down routine, he couldn't stop the racing thoughts. What would happen if the North used their weapons of mass destruction? Would they resort to using a nuclear weapon against the US forces in Korea or Japan? Would they try and launch an ICBM against the United States?

Despite his restless tossing and turning the night before, Cutter's run had helped to wake him up a bit. He chugged a thermos of black coffee to bring him back to an alert state. *I don't have time to be tired*, he thought.

****

Seoul, South Korea
Yongsan Garrison

Lieutenant General Cutter had flown into Seoul the night before with his staff for an in-person meeting with General John Bennet, the overall commander of US Forces-Korea. Because this would probably be the last time all the US and Korean military commanders would meet together in one room prior to any potential conflict. It was imperative that the US response to the various situations be gone over. General Bennet also wanted to personally meet with the commanders who would be responsible for the defense of South Korea.

As Lieutenant General Cutter and his staff approached the headquarters, they immediately noticed the increase in security. The buildings had been recently reinforced with sandbags and a few machine gun and other fighting positions. The soldiers on guard around the facility were wearing their full combat loads and had their rifles at the ready. With war a near certainty, General Bennet wasn't taking any chances on potential saboteurs attempting to take out his command facility before hostilities started.

As they walked towards the entrance, several soldiers snapped to attention, and then proceeded to ask for their IDs. The Marines dutifully handed their identification over to the sergeant of the guard, who entered their information into a laptop. Once their IDs were verified, they were all asked to scan their biometrics into the computer for one last check. A few seconds later, they were allowed inside.

Once they entered the building, an Air Force captain met them in the reception entrance and led them into the facility. After a short walk

161

through a couple of hallways, they finally ended up in the conference room.

As Lieutenant General Cutter walked into the briefing room, they took their seats along with their Air Force, Navy and ROK or Republic of Korea counterparts. A minute later, General Bennet walked in and took his seat at the head of the table.

General John Bennet was a new four-star general, having only pinned on his fourth star just two weeks ago. He was part of the new wave of military generals the President and the SecDef had promoted ahead of some of their peers in a move to advance more aggressive military commanders to frontline commands.

After a series of military defeats in Europe, the SecDef and the President had been cleaning house, removing those officers who were placing their careers and political interests above that of the country. Rumor had it that General Bennet was a hard-charging warrior that liked a good fight. He had a solid reputation from his various commands in Iraq and Afghanistan, though Cutter had personally never worked with him before.

General Bennet was a tough-looking African American man, an imposing figure at six foot four and built like a brick house. He looked like the type of guy you wanted on your side in a bar fight.

As Bennet surveyed the room of senior military officers from the various branches of service and the South Korean officers, he took a long drink from his coffee mug, which had a picture of a bulldog dressed as a general on it, along with the words, "Filled with blood, tears, and whiskey."

Oh, I'm going to like this guy, Cutter thought. *This guy should have been a Marine.*

Bennet cleared his throat, and in his harsh gravelly voice, he began, "Listen up. I just got done talking with the heads of DIA and NSA. They have actionable intelligence that says the DPRK is going to initiate hostilities within forty-eight hours. The NSA has intercepted direct communications between the Russians and the Chinese about North Korea initiating an imminent attack against the US, Japan, and South Korea, so we know this to be fact. It's *going* to happen. Additional messages between the Chinese and the DPRK were just intercepted two days ago; the content of those messages was also about directing North Korea to attack the South."

162

He held up his hand to stop any questions. "Before you ask, the NSA only just broke the encryption code on those messages, which is why we're meeting now and not two days ago." The veins on his hands seemed even more visible as he finished this last sentence. It was clear he was personally upset that they were only now getting this critical piece of information.

Bennet paused for a second, surveying the looks of the faces around him. Some were surprised, others excited, and a few were unable to hide an expression of dread. No one wanted a fight with the North Koreans. It was believed that they had over 10,000 artillery pieces aimed at Seoul that could flatten the capital, not to mention their ballistic missiles and ICBMs, all nuclear capable.

Seeing their looks, Bennet got right to the point. "No one wants this war to happen, least of all me. The war in Europe is still going on, and frankly, it's a catastrophe. We cannot afford a war in Korea right now. The Chinese know that, the North Koreans know that, and more importantly, the Russians know that. However, unlike Europe, the Republic of Korea has a substantial military force. Japan has also agreed to support the US and ROK forces, and so has Australia and New Zealand. We have plans in place to deal with the DPRK, and we are going to move forward with them," General Bennet said, eyeing each of his military commanders with a gaze that seemed to see right through them.

Bennet took another sip of coffee before he went on. "Because hostilities are imminent, the President has authorized the Secretary of Defense to initiate Operation Hammer. We're not going to sit here and wait for the North to obliterate Seoul, just so we can feel justified in striking back. During the past two days, the Air Force has moved the remaining B-1s from the US to Japan, and we've relocated our B-2s from Europe to Japan to launch a pre-emptive attack. In twelve hours, the B-2s are going to attempt to decapitate the government. We've identified where the 'Supreme Leader' is meeting with his generals, and we're going to try and take them out with a single strike. I'm going to turn this part of the briefing over to the Air Force, so they can go over the specific strike packages." With that, General Bennet turned to his Air Force counterpart, Lieutenant General Alison Forrester, and signaled for her to begin.

The officers in the room all hoped like crazy that the Air Force was able to take the North Korean leadership out quickly. Then they might get lucky and end the conflict before it turned into a nasty ground war.

One of the aides got a PowerPoint presentation pulled up so General Forrester could have the maps up as she began to go over the targets. "As General Bennet said, we're going to launch a decapitation strike against the civilian and military leadership of the government. The B-2s will be carrying out precision strikes against the entire command and control groups of the DPRK throughout the entire country. They'll also hit the known and suspected ballistic missile silos, along with any sites associated with their nuclear weapons program."

She switched the PowerPoint slide before continuing. "The B-52s are going to launch a series of ground attacks and standoff cruise missiles. These missiles will be targeted at the North's air-defense systems, mostly near the demilitarized zone and their air bases. They will specifically target the enemies' radar and communications systems. We will also have a series of EA-18G Growler aircraft from the Navy, providing us with electronic warfare and countermeasures for the next series of strikes.

"As the cruise missiles are hitting their targets, the B-1s will go after the North's artillery positions aimed at Seoul. They will hit the enemy artillery positions with 2,000-pound bombs intermixed with napalm and cluster bombs. And, yes, I said napalm. At the outset of the war in Russia, the President authorized the production and use of this weapon from the past. Following the B-1 strikes, the B-52s will then continue forward to the frontlines and will conduct a series of arc light missions or carpet-bombing runs against the North's troop formations."

One of the naval officers asked, "What if the North launches their ballistic missiles at the US, Japan, or the South? What is our response going to be?"

Everyone in the room suddenly sat up a little straighter. It was the one question everyone was afraid to ask but still wanted answered. This was one of the big concerns about a war with North Korea. A normal, sane nation state wouldn't willingly destroy its people, even in the face of defeat. North Korea, however, was not a normal, sane state actor.

The Air Force officer paused for a second, as if she had known this question might come but had hoped they wouldn't need to discuss it. "The President has authorized the release of nuclear weapons to the Secretary of Defense and General Bennet, should the North use a nuclear weapon against US or Allied forces. For this purpose, a single B-2 will be held in a holding pattern at an undisclosed location armed with nuclear bombs. The President stressed that the use of nuclear weapons would *only* be released if a nuclear detonation occurs from a DPRK missile."

"Although the North Koreans have tested ICBMs that they claim would effectively reach all of the continental US, our intelligence shows that they have not completed the process of miniaturizing the nuclear warheads capable of reaching the United States. The main concerns right now are Guam, Hawaii, Alaska, Japan, and South Korea."

She paused for a second, then continued, "We're confident the current ballistic missile defense systems we have in place will sufficiently protect our forces. Everyone should be focused on this war staying conventional. Should that situation change, everyone will be notified immediately."

Several people in the room exchanged some nervous glances, but they were glad this apocalyptic scenario had at least been thought through.

The next couple of slides showed specific targets the ground attack aircraft and fighter bombers would support next.

The whole first strike is a risky proposition, thought General Cutter. *We could get lucky and pulverize the North's ability to hit Seoul, or we could end up destroying most of the city.*

An Army general was the next to present his information. "To help us beef up the defense of the city, we've moved dozens of counter-rocket, artillery, and mortar systems to intercept the flight paths the enemy's artillery and missiles would most likely travel to hit Seoul," he began. "We know they most likely won't get all the enemy artillery positions or missile launchers in our initial strike, but by placing defensive systems along the flight paths incoming rounds would have to take, with any luck, we should be able to intercept a large percentage of the enemy's incoming fire. The C-RAM worked exceptionally well at intercepting incoming rockets and mortar rounds in Iraq, Afghanistan, and in Israel, so they're going to be heavily employed in the protection of Seoul."

165

The various generals and aides talked about the most likely scenarios and outcomes each action would have and how they would counter the North's response. At some point there was an uncomfortable moment as they realized that they weren't entirely sure who would be in charge if the decapitation strike worked. One general even asked if they should try to contact the new potential leader to pursue a peace deal before the US launched the ground assault. No consensus was ever reached on this issue though, and they finally decided to put a pin in it and move on.

Lieutenant General Cutter was nervous as he looked at the details of the ground operations for Operation Hammer. While the ROK Army would be the spearhead for the offensive and would likely sustain the largest percentage of casualties, the current plan also called for a large amphibious assault to open a second front. That assault would have to be carried out by his Marines, followed by additional ROK Marines. They would assault North Korea's west coast and land their forces near the cities of Namp'o and Onch'ŏn, placing them less than twenty miles from the enemy's capital. There was also an alternate seaborne invasion plan to land forces on the east coast if the west coast could not be secured or it looked like China might join the festivities.

The west coast assault was a risky invasion in that the first several kilometers inland was mostly rice paddies with limited roads. This would bog down his heavy armor from getting ashore quickly. Intelligence also had very little information about what possible forces or defenses might be on the small island of Ch'o-do, which would have to be secured prior to the main amphibious assault.

Vice Admiral Dan Kinkaid, the 7th Fleet Commander, spoke up next. "Ok, I know any plan is going to have its downfalls, but do you realize that we'll have to sail the bulk of our naval force up the Yellow Sea? That's going to place us precariously close to the Chinese mainland at a time when the Chinese have just relocated the bulk of their air force to that region. It's going to leave my fleet little room to maneuver and place us in range of land-based anti-ship missiles, in addition to the Chinese Air Force."

Lieutenant General Cutter nodded in agreement, then pointed to some of the interactive maps. "Admiral Kinkaid is right. As you can see, the Chinese Navy is still steaming towards Taiwan, and the bulk of the PLA is also marshaling around that area. What concerns me most, though, is the presence of Chinese fighter aircraft in the Jiangsu Province, and the increase in submarines in the Yellow Sea. Both of those factors could have a huge impact on our amphibious assault."

The debate over the risks went on for some time. Ultimately, however, despite their concerns, they concluded that this was the best possible plan if they wanted to end this conflict quickly. General Bennet was convincing as he argued, "We can't let Korea turn into a meat grinder that lasts for months or years. The war with Russia could resume at any time, and the Chinese look as if they might join in. We need to end this conflict, and quick."

At this assertion, any hesitancy that had been present melted away. All that was left was the resolve to win, by whatever means necessary.

The leaders still had many details to work out, and the conversation went on for some time. Just as it seemed that the meeting was wrapping up, a Japanese naval admiral and air force general walked into the room.

General Bennet signaled for everyone to pause their conversations, so they could discuss what the Japanese part in all of this will be. The Korean generals eyed the Japanese with a bit of suspicion, but they weren't going to look a gift horse in the mouth. They knew they would need all the help they could get in dealing with the North.

The Japanese admiral said whatever polite niceties were required in that situation and then got right down to business. He informed the group, "The Japanese navy will be taking up positions in the upper portion of the East China Sea to help act as a guard against any potential Chinese intervention. Our air force will be on standby to assist the US Navy, should they need it. We have also placed 50,000 soldiers on alert, which could be quickly moved to South Korea to aid in its defense. We want to assure the alliance that Japan will stand strong with the US and the South Koreans, should the Chinese intervene."

A sense of renewed hope filled the room. The leaders continued to work out details for another hour, but they all left feeling that they at least had a fighting chance of achieving victory.

Chapter 33
Opening Salvos

Yellow Sea

It was early October, and though the weather was starting to turn cold, the skies were relatively clear and the seas smooth. Rear Admiral James Lomas looked up to the sky and said a small thank you to the Big Man Upstairs for this little bit of good fortune as his naval task force began to steer towards North Korean waters.

Lomas took a deep breath. He was nervous but also anxious to start the action. Nearly 60 US warships had started their trek into uncertainty, flanked by another twenty-two ROK ships. All told, the combined fleet was escorting nearly 70,000 US and ROK Marines to carry out the largest amphibious assault since the last Korean War.

The Rear Admiral felt confident in his men and ships. He hoped that he was right, and this assault behind the North Korean lines would help lead to a quick defeat of the enemy. He felt some comfort as he remembered that despite being one of the largest armies in the world, the average North Korean soldier was underfed and under-equipped, which should play to their advantage.

When the DPRK had launched their surprise invasion of South Korea in 1950, the US and South Korean Forces had been caught completely by surprise. In a matter of months, the Allied forces had been pushed to the Sea of Japan, and it had looked like certain defeat. Then, General Douglas McArthur, the overall commander of US forces in the Pacific, had launched Operation Chromite, storming the shores with 75,000 soldiers at Inchon, less than thirty miles from Seoul and deep behind enemy lines. By threatening the communists' rear area, the Allied forces had forced them to withdraw or be completely cut off. This tremendous victory had saved the allies from almost certain defeat. Now the Americans were hoping to pull a page from history and secure Pyongyang quickly, possibly ending the war before it could really get going.

As the ships moved slowly forward in the night, one of the biggest concerns Admiral Lomas had was the proximity to the Chinese mainland and the possibility of so many warships being near each other. If they wrongly identified a submarine or aircraft threat, it could easily lead to an accident. Submarines were their greatest fear. They had been tracking several Chinese subs for days, but now they also had to be leery of North Korean submarines.

****

Captain Yong-ju's *Sang-O*-class submarine had sailed out to meet the American fleet almost a week ago, after being told that war with the Americans would start soon. His orders had been to move to their attack position and then wait until the appointed time. After days of waiting and mentally preparing themselves, they were now down to less than six hours before they would move to engage the Americans.

For the past day, Captain Yong-ju's crew had been tracking the American fleet as it began to change course and start to head towards them; it looked like they wouldn't have to maneuver very far to get a shot off at the Americans. They were sailing right into their trap.

As the captain reviewed the information on the Conn, the voice of one of the sonar operators suddenly came over his headset. "Conn, Sonar. Submarine identified less than 5,000 yards from our position."

They had been sitting still in that position for more than a day, so it was unlikely that they had made any noise that would have given away their position. *Still...I can't be certain*, thought Yong-ju.

As the captain was calculating his response, the sonar operator suddenly yelled, "Conn, Sonar! I just identified the sound of a torpedo door—it sounds like the submarine is getting ready to launch!"

Captain Yong-ju panicked. *It's not time to launch our attack against the Americans, and now our submarine might be destroyed before we even get our chance.*

He took a deep breath and steeled his nerves. *No, I will not be sunk by some sort of sneak attack by the Americans*, he resolved. The only submarines operating in this area were the Americans and the South Koreans. *I'm going to hit them before they hit us.*

"Fire at the enemy sub!" he ordered. "Then bring us up to full speed and take evasive maneuvers as soon as the torpedoes launch!"

****

Captain Ma had just taken command of one of China's quietest diesel submarines, the *Wu Ling*, a Type 039A Yuan-class attack submarine. His sub had been moving down the Yellow Sea and was

169

going to observe the coming battle between the DPRK and the American-backed ROK naval forces. There were rumors among the other naval officers that a war with the Americans may happen soon.

I hope those are just rumors, thought Ma. *The American Navy is good, and despite our best efforts, I just don't see our forces holding up against them.*

As they moved to their observation point, which was well outside the combat area and in international waters, he wanted to raise their communications buoy to make sure they didn't have any additional orders since he set sail several days ago.

They had one of the new communications buoys that the Russians had developed; Captain Ma hoped it would work as promised and allow his sub to be better able to communicate with the surface fleet while reducing the likelihood of being detected by the Americans.

As Ma overheard his communications officers talking with the enlisted men as they prepared the buoy, a series of events suddenly went wrong.

He heard a loud grating noise and yelled, "What was that?"

One of the officers responded, "The outer door that protects the buoy scraped against something as it opened, Sir."

The sound of rushing air suddenly gurgled in the waters. An enlisted man shouted, "The hose that was supposed to release the air into the buoy at a specific rate must have malfunctioned. This piece of crap is supposed to be silent!"

Clearly, a function check was missed before we left the shipyard, Captain Ma realized. Now they would all be paying for it by alerting nearly everyone in the area of their presence.

Seething with anger, the captain ripped into his officers. "How did this happen?!" he demanded. "What if someone heard us? You idiots—your incompetence may have just put all of our lives at risk!"

A voice came from the sonar room, "Conn, Sonar. We have contact. Submarine less than 5,000 yards from our position."

Everyone in the room froze in that second, unsure of whose submarine it was that had just detected them.

The captain grabbed the handset in a jerking motion. "I want a readout—whose submarine did we stumble onto?" he yelled.

Then, to their horror, the sonar room announced, "A torpedo has just been launched! I spot a second torpedo...the unknown

170

submarine just moved to flank speed and appears to be dropping a noisemaker behind them."

They had precious little time to make their own decision on whether they should respond.

Captain Ma bellowed, "Are there any American submarines in the area?"

"Conn, Sonar. We haven't identified any American subs, but that doesn't mean that there may not be one that slipped by us," came the reply.

The captain made a critical decision in that moment—one that might have been made differently by a more senior captain, but he had just been promoted and this was his first command. *I am not about to lose my sub on my maiden voyage as its commander*, he thought.

"Take us to flank speed," he ordered, "and drop our own noisemaker. Then turn hard to starboard." He hoped to create a knuckle in the water that would confuse the incoming torpedoes.

He turned to his weapons officer. "Prepare one of our own torpedoes to fire."

Seconds later, the sub lurched forward and then turned hard to starboard, just as they had trained a million times. It was a Russian strategy that had played out well in the Atlantic, and the Chinese Navy wasn't at all opposed to adopting a new strategy if it worked.

While still in the middle of their turn, they fired off one torpedo towards the other submarine, which was now running at flank speed and making an inordinate amount of noise for a submarine.

As they picked up speed and moved deeper to get under the next thermal layer, their sonar finally identified the sub that had shot at them. "Sir…" the officer began in disbelief, "it was a *Sang-O*-class North Korean submarine."

Captain Ma was furious that an ally had launched a pair of torpedoes at him. He also felt foolish for launching his own torpedoes so quickly. *If I'd just waited a few more minutes, I would have known it was a North Korean sub and not one from the US or ROK.*

The first North Korean torpedo went straight for the noisemaker and detonated several thousand yards away, rattling everyone in the sub.

A very tense moment passed; the second DPRK torpedo seemed confused and began to head away from them, in the direction of the Americans. They had somehow escaped unscathed.

Their own torpedo, however, was a much more advanced model, with smarter targeting sonar and a processor to help it distinguish between distractions and the sounds of an actual sub. It blew right past the noisemaker and locked onto the *Sang-O* sub. Once it had a solid lock, it increased in speed to close in for the kill.

Minutes later, the torpedoes rammed the *Sang-O* and exploded in spectacular fashion. The submarine crumpled under the pressure and began to sink to the bottom quickly.

Captain Ma turned his attention back to his officers. "What in the hell happened? How did we not know that noisy, clunky diesel was sitting right there—and what in the world happened with that buoy?" he demanded of his officers.

The enlisted men tried to sink a little lower in their chairs to avoid the gaze of their irate captain. They had just survived a very close encounter and were still not 100% out of danger yet. Their position had just been broadcast to every submarine in the area, which is something no submariner ever wants to have happen.

One of the officers stepped forward and offered himself up. "Captain, I take full responsibility for this mistake. Prior to you taking command, when we took the ship out of the shipyard to test the upgrades, the communications buoy made this same noise. We spoke with the engineers about it during the test, and they said it would be corrected when we returned back to the shipyard."

"A week later, the engineers told me the problem had been corrected and tested to make sure it worked. I didn't insist on a second sea trial test before you arrived. I trusted them when they said it was corrected." As he finished his explanation, he hung his head in defeat and humiliation. He was certain he would be shot when they returned to port, if they ever made it back.

Captain Ma was fuming. "*I can't believe that one my officers could be so reckless,*" he moaned to himself. *Ugh—I should have made sure we used the buoy prior to this situation. If we had, we would have discovered the problem sooner.*

They had only been at sea for three days, so they hadn't had a need to use the buoy just yet. So far, they had been able to come to periscope depth and had relied on their main antenna.

This whole deployment was rushed, Ma complained to himself. If the previous captain of this submarine hadn't died unexpectedly of a

172

heart attack two days before the submarine was supposed to put to sea, he would have had the appropriate time to get to know the submarine and check on all the upgrades the sub had just received at the shipyard. *I'm paying the price for that now...*

Just as he was about to tear into his officers, a voice over the speaker yelled, "Conn, Sonar. We have a new contact. It's an American *Virginia*-class attack submarine...Torpedo in the water! Torpedo in the water!"

"Left full rudder. Ahead full speed!" the captain yelled, and the sub driver turned the sub hard and took them to full power.

"Drop countermeasures and let's create another knuckle," he said, hoping the trick that had worked on the Korean submarine might also work on the American submarine.

Turning to his weapons officer, he ordered, "Fire off two torpedoes at the American submarine!"

I'm not about to let those Americans get away with shooting at my sub, he thought. *Plus, I need to have them reacting to my torpedoes if we have any chance of evading theirs.*

There were now four torpedoes in the water, and numerous noisemakers. It was unclear if either submarine would be able to escape, but both captains and crews were giving it their best effort. One of the American torpedoes hit the Chinese noisemaker in the knuckle and exploded. The second torpedo blew through the explosion and continued to hunt for them.

As Captain Ma's submarine rose now to further throw off the torpedo that was still tracking them down, they heard the unmistakable sound of a third torpedo.

"Where did *that* come from?!" yelled the captain to anyone who could give him an answer.

"It was probably dropped from a helicopter," one of the officers responded nervously, a bit of fear in his voice.

This new, smaller torpedo began to speed below three hundred feet at an alarming rate. It immediately triggered its active sonar and went to full speed towards them.

In that moment, Captain Ma knew that they weren't going to be able to get away. This third torpedo had been dropped too close to their position, and they had been rising, not diving, when it had landed in the water.

173

At this point, my only hope is to get this submarine to the surface so that I can give my crew the best possible chance to escape and live, he realized.

Turning to the submarine driver, Ma yelled, "Blow the ballast tanks and surface!"

Then he directed his communications officer, "Send a FLASH message to fleet headquarters. Let them know we've been fired at by an American sub and we're not going to make it."

As their submarine climbed towards the surface, the American torpedo slammed into the forward section of the sub. The whole vessel was rocked by the explosion, and water pushed its way into the confined space of the sub.

Still safely breathing air in the Conn, Captain Ma began receiving reports of the damage. "Sir, there's flooding in the forward compartments, and it's moving towards us!" one officer yelled.

"The ballast systems are failing!" yelled another.

"How far are we from the surface?" Ma shouted.

"Less than a hundred feet now," came the response.

We have to get to the surface, the captain thought. *That's all that matters. I have to save as many of my crew members as possible.*

The submarine broke through to the surface and began to level out immediately. Unfortunately, almost immediately, it slowly tipped back down into the waves because of the gash in the hull.

"Abandon ship!" the captain bellowed. "Get to the life rafts!"

The crew had less than three minutes to push and shove their way out of the escape hatches before the remaining American torpedo hit them. When it impacted, it nearly split the submarine in half. It took less than sixty seconds for the sub to slip below the water, this time for the last time.

Of the one hundred and nine crew members, only eighteen escaped before the sub slipped beneath the waves for the final time. An American helicopter appeared overhead, quickly joined by a second helicopter. They hovered above the sub and threw life preservers down to the survivors while an American destroyer headed towards them to pick them up as prisoners of war.

****

Captain Michael Richards of the USS *Carl Vinson* breathed a sigh of relief when one of the helicopters reported that their torpedo had hit the enemy submarine. It had been a chaotic 34 minutes. Their antisubmarine warfare screen had been tracking a North Korean diesel submarine for some time when, out of nowhere, a new sub had been identified and the two of them had started shooting at each other.

Suddenly, the calm waters of the Yellow Sea had had multiple torpedoes racing through it. At first, they hadn't been sure if the attack was being directed at them. Then the ROK navy had informed them that they had a submarine operating in the area and it could have been one of theirs that was under attack.

It was a confusing moment. *We thought that the first sub we were tracking was North Korean*, thought Captain Richards. *Could we have been wrong?*

Then one of the torpedoes had headed towards one of the American attack submarines, which had fired in retaliation. The fight was on.

At that moment, Richards had realized, *It doesn't matter anymore who fired at who first. All that matters is that American sailors are now in harm's way. The fleet has to defend itself.*

Admiral Lomas had ordered several helicopters to assist the American submarine and neutralize the underwater threats.

The war with North Korea had officially started. Perhaps the Chinese were trying to move into position and they had jumped the gun. In any case, they were about to pay the price for it.

Admiral Lomas turned to Captain Richards. "Order the fleet to engage the North Korean fleet now. We need to sink the rest of their ships before they launch their own attacks."

Lomas then turned to face his Commander Air Group. "I want your aircraft to start hitting their targets and keep an eye out for the Chinese; I think they may try to jump the fleet now that hostilities have officially started," he said, hoping the fleet wasn't sailing into some sort of trap.

He turned to his weapons officer and directed, "Send the signal to the rest of the fleet to start launching their Tomahawk missiles."

We need to start hammering the landing zones and the known enemy positions before the Marines begin their assault from the sea,

Lomas thought. *The seaborne assault isn't scheduled to take place for another day, but we need to start buttering them up now.*

Chapter 34
Cry Havoc and Let Slip the Dogs of War

Paektu Mountain
North Korean-Chinese Border

In the early 2000s, the Chinese had begun to help the North Koreans develop a series of ICBM silos near the base of Paektu Mountain, which stood 9,000 feet high along the Chinese-North Korean border. Technically, Paektu was still considered an active volcano, although there hadn't been any eruptions since 1904. A large crater lake called Heaven Lake was situated in the caldera atop the mountain and had been a tourist destination for several generations, until the North Koreans began to develop a series of underground missile silos.

The Chinese continued to believe a strong and belligerent North Korea could keep the Americans distracted for many years while they focused on their Greater China strategy. While the North Koreans continued to develop their own ballistic missiles, they kept the Western intelligence eyes focused on their more active launch sites and centers. To help keep the focus off them as long as possible, the Chinese had also provided the North with ten Dongfeng 5B ICBMs under a secret deal in 2015.

It had been tricky moving these missiles into their silos without being discovered, but they had found a way. The Chinese had taken the missiles apart and moved them in pieces to the mountain, then reassembled them and lowered them into the silos.

The DF-5B had an operational range of 12,000 to 15,000 kilometers, placing nearly all the continental United States within its range. This variant of the missile given to the Koreans was also MIRV-capable, meaning each missile could carry six independently targetable warheads or decoys. The one flaw to the missiles was the amount of time required to prepare them to launch; from the time the order was given, it would take between 30-40 minutes to fuel them and have them ready to take off.

Despite providing the Koreans with the DF-5B, the Chinese had been unwilling to provide them with nuclear warheads. They had insisted that those had to come from the Koreans themselves. They were willing to provide them with the missile, but they wanted nothing to do with the warheads.

The North did not have sixty nukes to fill all the MIRVs with. Instead, they had taken three of the missiles and loaded them with just a single one-megaton warhead. Those were the largest warheads they had built up to that point. The remaining MIRVs had been loaded with three 25-kiloton warheads and three decoys each.

****

The soldiers manning the entrance to the missile complex looked nervous because of all the heightened security. They had seen many missile drills in the past, but this one seemed different. Lieutenant General Ghim Choi, the Commander of the Strategic Rocket Forces, was there to personally tour the site.

Once he had entered the facility, the guards were instructed to seal the entrance and not allow anyone in afterwards. They had also been ordered to be ready to repel any potential attack on the facility. Rumors had been rampant that war was really going to happen, and soon.

Following an emergency meeting with Supreme Leader Pak Lee and the rest of his senior military advisors, Lieutenant General Ghim Choi had been given a clear set of new orders. He was to change their ICBM targets to a set of selected US military bases, as opposed to only targeting US cities. A few of the cities would remain as targets, but the Supreme Leader wanted to take out some of the bases the US had specifically slated to support any future war effort in Asia. General Ghim had also been told to ensure the mobile launchers carrying their smaller tactical nuclear weapons were targeted at the US fleet amassing off their shores and US bases in South Korea.

Before Ghim had left the meeting with the Supreme Leader, Pak Lee had issued some very specific final instructions. "If the Americans attempt to decapitate the government, you're to ready the missiles. If you're unable to maintain contact with me, and no one else in the government can respond or assume control, then you are directed to launch all the missiles at the predetermined targets."

When the meeting had ended, Ghim had boarded a helicopter that would take him to an obscure base nearby. From there, he would transfer to a jeep and drive to their secretive missile command base on the Paektu Mountain.

As the general cleared security and entered the missile complex, he headed straight for the command center to meet with the facility commander and inform him of their new orders and change in missile targets. He walked briskly down the narrow tunnel, lined with very yellow fluorescent lights that blinked in an irritating fashion.

As Ghim stood in the elevator that would take him several hundred feet below the surface to the launch control center, he couldn't help but think, *I might never see the sun again, or feel the warmth of its rays against my face.*

He almost felt a sense of fear at this revelation, but he knew he had a duty to protect his country.

As the elevator dinged his arrival at the bottom floor, the facility commander met General Ghim at the elevator entrance. He was a colonel, and not someone Ghim personally liked, but he was a smart and capable man, nonetheless.

The colonel greeted him. "General, it is a pleasure to see you. We weren't expecting you. Is something wrong?" he inquired, hoping he wasn't being relieved.

Ghim sized up the colonel before responding, "No, nothing is wrong. The Supreme Leader has instructed me to be here in case the Americans launch an attack against us. We were warned by the Chinese and the Russians that the Americans are planning to launch a preemptive spoiler attack before we invade the South. The Leader fears the Americans may try a decapitation strike to wipe out the government."

He paused for a moment as a couple of missile technicians briefly walked past them before continuing to bring the facility commander up to speed. "If the Americans do try to wipe out the government, and I cannot regain communication with the Leader or whoever takes over, I have been ordered by the Supreme Leader to launch our missiles against the Americans. I also have new targets for the missiles, and I'll need you to input them immediately," he ordered.

The base commander looked surprised for a moment, but then his features hardened as the reality of what this meant for him and his country hit him. He would do his duty at all costs. "Yes, of course," he responded, "we'll get the new targets inputted immediately."

The colonel signaled for some of his other officers to come to him. He took the new targeting list from General Ghim and went over them with his officers.

As he looked at the new targets, he slowly walked closer to the general. In a hushed voice so no one else could hear, he asked, "Have the Chinese given us permission to use our nuclear missiles?"

General Ghim looked dismissive of the colonel's question. "We don't *need* Chinese permission to use our nuclear weapons. If the Americans wipe out our government, then we'll respond by attacking them with the one weapon we have that will equalize our nation with our adversaries and give us a chance to win."

He opened the briefcase that was still handcuffed to his left hand and retrieved a paper from a folder marked Top Secret, handing it to the colonel. "These are the new targets for the ICBMs. The missiles need to be reprogrammed immediately."

The colonel took the document from him and examined the targets. One of the missiles with a MIRV was now to target the American naval facility in San Diego. A second MIRV missile was now supposed to target New York City, as opposed to Chicago.

That makes sense, he thought. New York had one of the largest ports on the East Coast. It was a critical port location for the war in Europe.

A third MIRV missile was to target the American naval facilities in Hawaii. The remaining seven ICBMs were supposed to target military bases in Alaska, Washington State, Utah, Nevada, Texas, and the West Coast port of Oakland, California.

The colonel was satisfied with the new targets. Not that he had much say in the matter, but he was happy to see that these targets were of high military value and would have a large impact on a war with the Americans.

"I'll get the new targets inputted now. Do you want me to start fueling the missiles?" he asked. Although the fueling of the missiles took between thirty and forty minutes, if they weren't launched within six hours, they would have to be emptied. Each time they went through that process, it created its own dangers, and there was always the possibility of a mechanical failure or something else going wrong.

"No, we'll wait until it becomes clear that we need to launch before we fuel the missiles. Keep everyone on alert and ready to launch, should it become necessary," Ghim replied. As long as they didn't lose communication with the other missile sites or their command center in Pyongyang, they would wait.

****

Seoul, South Korea
Yongsan Garrison

General Bennet looked at the wall clock and saw that it was 0255 hours. In five minutes, the Second Korean War would officially kick off, with the US and its allies launching a preemptive attack on the DPRK. They had chosen to start the war at 0300 hours, the darkest possible time of night, and a time when most people would either be asleep or wishing that they were if they were on guard duty.

As John sat in the command bunker, observing the multiple ten-foot by ten-foot computer screen projectors monitoring the disposition of the US and ROK forces, he saw the aircraft and Tomahawk cruise missiles make the slow and steady march towards the border, then cross it. With that act, the war had officially started.

Nearly 600 aircraft were now in the air, heading towards their attack points. The B-2s had just crossed into North Korean air space, headed towards their designated targets. So far, they appeared to have gone completely undetected. In another minute, the B-52s would begin to launch their ground attack cruise missiles, specifically targeting the enemy radar and air-defense systems. This would quickly be followed up by the B-1s, who would begin their bombing runs against the thousands of artillery positions along the border.

On a separate screen, the naval situation began to show a series of attacks underway. Blue aircraft and missile icons were shown on the screen, advancing quickly towards their targets. A confrontation with a North Korean and a Chinese submarine had taken place less than an hour earlier, nearly compromising their preemptive strike. Both submarines had been sunk, but not before the Chinese sub had been able to send an emergency message, and several crew members had escaped from the submarine before it had finally slipped beneath the waves.

One of his senior officers and a diplomat from the embassy were talking with the Chinese about the exchange, trying to explain to them what had happened. General Bennet was hoping to keep the Chinese out of any potential conflict. It was unfortunately looking like they were going to enter the war, no matter what the US did to try and keep them out.

181

One of the naval officers, who had been manning a monitor in the room, suddenly announced, "We've received a FLASH update from the fleet, Sir. They've engaged the North Korean Navy. So far, they've destroyed nine submarines with their opening attack. The ships are now engaging their assigned land targets and getting the landing zones prepped for the Marines."

General Bennet could see the naval front was progressing as predicted. He turned and looked at the display tracking the known Chinese naval and air units. So far, they hadn't moved towards his forces and appeared to be staying in observation mode, which suited him just fine.

Focusing next on the air map, he could see the missiles from the B-52s were starting to hit their targets along the demilitarized zone or DMZ. They were disabling the enemy's radar and communications systems for the next wave of bombers, ground-attack aircraft, and helicopters to start their attack runs soon. The electronic jamming aircraft were now blanketing the entire country in electronic interference in hopes of jumbling up the North Koreans ability to communicate and properly operate their radar systems.

The B-1s would start their bomb runs shortly. With any luck, they would take out the brunt of the enemy artillery and rocket forces that posed such a significant threat to Seoul. Another screen tracking the flights of B-2s showed the bombers were now hitting their targets throughout the country. Pyongyang was being hit especially hard. They were going after the command-and-control function of the military and the civilian government.

As he watched the screens, General Bennet couldn't help but think that the images of the capital from the B-2 runs were both scary and spectacular.

Tracer rounds could be seen crisscrossing the night sky, intermixed with aerial explosions from the heavier caliber air-defense artillery guns. It was clear the enemy had no idea where the bombers were because there was no discernable pattern to the tracer fire. They were firing blind, hoping for that one magical hit.

There was also a squadron of F-117 Nighthawks that had taken out of cold storage at the beginning of the war with Russia. They were circling above North Korea, ready to pounce on targets of opportunity as they were found. The F-117s were placed on standby in case any of the satellite surveillance groups or Special Forces on the ground identified a mobile launcher being moved or set up. If they did, they would call in a surgical strike by one of the stealth fighters, hopefully before they were able to get their missiles off. In addition to the Nighthawks, the Air Force also had several pairs of F-16s circling off the coastlines of Korea, ready to dart in to take out any additional mobile launchers that the Nighthawks couldn't get.

What I wouldn't give for a couple of wings of F-35s, Bennet moaned to himself. *Lousy Russian theater needs them all—yeah, right.* The war in Russia had sapped nearly all the reserve forces that would have normally been surged to his theater of operations, and he wasn't happy about it.

While the air war ramped up, reports were starting to filter in of some sporadic enemy artillery fire hitting US and ROK forces along the DMZ.

"Sir, a handful of rounds have been fired in the direction of Seoul," said one of the analysts. "However, the artillery guns were quickly silenced when the B-1s began their bombing run."

The high-explosive bombs intermixed with cluster munitions and napalm are having the desired effect, thought Bennet with a smile. It looked like the few rounds that did fly toward the metropolis were intercepted by the C-RAM system. It was still too early in the fight to know if the B-1s and B-52s had silenced enough of the enemy artillery from pulverizing the city, or if that carnage was still to come.

One thing that had concerned the military planners was the series of underground tunnel systems the North had built; many of them led directly under the DMZ, with forces ready to blow open a hole behind the American lines. Fortunately, satellite technology had increased immensely, and they had identified what they hoped were all the tunnels. Engineers had drilled some holes a hundred or so meters above the tunnels, placing specialized sonic bombs in them. Once the war started, they detonated them, collapsing the tunnels.

By 0310 hours, nearly everyone in Seoul, and the rest of South Korea, had been jolted out of their blissful sleep by a loud government announcement instructing them to "seek shelter immediately." All South Korean TV and radio programs had begun to broadcast the government's emergency alert message, asking for everyone to head to the various

183

bomb shelters. If they were unable to find one, then they were asked to stay indoors and move away from any windows.

As hundreds of thousands of people sleepily crawled out of their beds to see if this was yet another drill, many saw the flashes of bombs going off in the distance from their various high-rise buildings. Many people recorded the events with their phones, broadcasting them live across Twitter, Snapchat, Facebook, and other social media platforms. The world was getting a firsthand account of the war as it unfolded less than thirty miles away.

The rumble of explosions slowly built throughout the city. The bombing runs being carried out by the B-1s and B-52s were absolutely deafening and terrifying. Thousands of 500-pound and 2,000-pound bombs were dropped on the North Korean positions, intermixed with the thousands of artillery guns and multiple-launch rocket systems being fired into the North. It was a cacophony of death being rained down on the enemy, and it was being live-streamed to the world.
****

Ch'o-do Island

Captain Yi Jang was still in a state of bewilderment. It was a little after 0300 hours, and his garrison's whole world was being rocked by multiple explosions. As another missile or bomb hit nearby, bits of dirt sprinkled down on the men who had made it into the bunker. He scanned the room; it looked like roughly half of his soldiers had made it to the bunker that connected them to their tunnel complex.

As he moved to the command center, one of the officers there rushed up to him. "Sir, the Americans are coming," he announced.

Captain Yi handed the young officer a message from their higher command, ordering them to engage the American ships. The officer rushed off to put some plans into motion.

The smell of cordite and dirt hung in the air. Another explosion rocked the command center, sending reverberations through their chests. The soldiers nearby were all looking at him and seemed to be asking for guidance and assurance. He saw the looks of fear and excitement on their faces at the realization that war was upon them. Yi knew he had a duty to his men and his country and was determined to do his job.

184

"Man your positions!" he yelled. "Prepare the missiles for launch!"

A couple of years prior, the Chinese had helped the Korean People's Army or KPA build a series of ship defense systems on the island. Ch'o-do Island was small, but it had several hills, where a series of reinforced bunkers had been built to house the missiles and protect them from this very type of attack. Inside the underground shelters, they had created several launching points for their anti-ship missiles.

Yi smiled at the idea that he and his men could actually make an impact in this war. The Chinese had provided them with their newest ground-launched, anti-ship missiles, the C-802. NATO called them CSS-N-8 "Saccade," and they were nasty missiles, capable of reaching speeds of over 1100 kilometers per hour within seconds and skimming across the surface of the water at no more than ten meters. Their time-delayed semi-armor-piercing high-explosive warhead weighed over three hundred and fifty pounds and could cause all sorts of problems for a ship, particularly if it punctured the ship at the waterline. Captain Yi looked forward to using them.

As his men moved from their bunkers to the series of tunnels that would take them to their missile sites, a young lieutenant waved for him to look at his monitor. The young officer's screen showed nearly four dozen surface contacts, less than fifty kilometers from their position and well within range of their missiles.

As his missile crews began to report in, Captain Yi realized that only three of the launching points were operational. The others had been destroyed during the bombardment. Thinking for a minute, Yi Jang realized that once they launched their first three missiles, they would probably only have enough time to get maybe one more volley off before the Americans found out where the missiles are coming from and destroyed the launching stations.

We had better make those missiles count.

He looked more closely at the ships on the monitor. "Can we determine what type of ships we're seeing?" he asked.

The lieutenant brought up the camera feed and zoomed in as best he could. "It looks like this ship here is a troop transport of some sort. We could launch our missiles at that ship," he suggested.

Captain Yi nodded. It looked like a good target. They programed the targeting data into the missiles and prepared them to fire.

185

Once the missiles had fired, the rail launcher would pull back inside the bunker and the crews would work feverously to reload another missile onto the rail and get it ready to launch again. Even under the best conditions, it had still taken them three minutes to reload the rail launcher during training exercises.

Once the data had been programed into the missiles, they were immediately fired off. As the missiles leapt from their launchers, they quickly got up to speed, skimming the surface of the water as they streaked towards their targets. It would take less than a minute for the missiles to intercept the ships.

****

As the *Arleigh Burke*-class destroyer sailed to within thirty kilometers of Ch'o-do Island, the Captain of the USS *Howard* began to get nervous. They were screening for the Marine transport ships, which were still moving to get in range of their amphibious assault crafts, and his ship had already fired off half of their Tomahawk and Harpoon cruise missiles in the first fifteen minutes of the war. The KPA artillery had tried to zero in on their positions a few times, but it was hard to hit a ship that could accelerate to thirty-plus knots and zig and zag.

While the captain sipped his coffee, the mundane noise of the CIC was suddenly broken. "Vampires, vampires, vampires!" yelled a petty officer who was manning one of the radar stations.

Three missiles originating from Ch'o-do Island suddenly materialized and accelerated quickly towards their flotilla. One of the weapons officers ordered the ship's missile defense systems to engage the incoming threats. The ship began to fire off their SM-2 missile interceptors in quick succession.

Then, several dozen more land-based missiles appeared from the Namp'o City area, not far from Pyongyang. The USS *Howard*'s integrated defense systems went into overdrive, spitting out SM-2s as fast as it could.

In minutes, the sky was filled with missile interceptors as the destroyer escorts and the four *Ticonderoga*-class guided-missile cruisers did their best to defend the fleet from the incoming threats. The battle was now in the hands of the Aegis Combat System and the extensive training of the crews that were manning it.

Chapter 35
No Time to Iron

Beijing, China
CMC Headquarters

General Kuang called the emergency meeting of the CMC as soon as Vice Admiral Ning informed him that one of their submarines had been attacked and sunk by the Americans in the Yellow Sea. The Americans had managed to preempt the North Koreans invasion of the South by one day, throwing China's timetable off; however, this attack by the Americans on one of their subs might have just given them the pretext for the next phase of their operation.

President Xi walked into the command bunker, feeling a bit disheveled. His hair hadn't been combed, and his shirt was badly wrinkled. He had been sound asleep when he had been rudely awakened from a lovely dream by one of his aides.

The unlucky man informed him, "Sir, there was an incident involving one of our submarines and the US Navy carrier group. Your presence is needed in the bunker."

Once his feet had hit the floor, President Xi had quickly thrown on some pants and a button-down shirt. He'd skipped the tie and jacket; no need to be too formal at this hour of the day. When he'd arrived at the command bunker fifteen minutes later, he saw he wasn't the only one who had chosen speed over formality to get to the bunker.

"What happened?" he asked his Minister of Defense as everyone took their seats. A military aide poured everyone some hot tea as the meeting began.

Vice Admiral Ning spoke up first. "Sir, one of our Yuan-class attack submarines was sunk by a US Navy submarine roughly 90 minutes ago. The submarine had recently completed some upgrades at the shipyard and was en-route to join our other forces in the East China Sea to observe the American carrier battle groups. While transiting to their observation point, it appears they stumbled onto a North Korean submarine, who confused them for an American sub and fired on them."

The men around him exchanged nervous glances. It was obvious they were confused. The admiral held up his hand to signal that there was more to the story.

"Our sub evaded the KPN's torpedo and summarily sank them, rather than risking an enemy sub getting a second shot off at them. One of our torpedoes missed the Korean submarine, and it continued on a trajectory that took it towards an American submarine. At that moment, the Americans engaged our sub and sank them. Eighteen sailors were able to escape and are currently being held on an American destroyer," the admiral concluded.

Foreign Minister Yong Zhang added, "The Americans have reached out to our office and have relayed nearly the exact same information. They said they fired in self-defense of their fleet, believing it was under attack. They have offered to return our sailors as soon as possible and requested to know where we would like them flown."

The others in the room grumbled at this. They didn't like the fact that their sailors had been taken prisoner and over a hundred others had been killed.

General Kuang, the Defense Minister, interjected, "Mr. President, while the loss of our submarine and most of its crew is tragic, it does present us with a unique opportunity." The others in the room looked at him as if he had two heads.

"The next phase of our operation calls for us to reoccupy the province of Formosa, or Taiwan, as they like to call themselves. That action was going to result in a probable confrontation with the US. This incident gives us a precursor situation, allowing us to respond militarily to the Americans and shape the narrative that *they* were the aggressors, that we are merely defending ourselves," he said convincingly.

Foreign Minister Yong jumped in before anyone else could get a word in edgewise. "I would highly caution us against an immediate retaliation against the Americans," he urged. "Our plan calls for us to wait until the United States is fully bogged down in a ground war with North Korea. If they are fully committed in both Korea and Ukraine, they're not going to be *able* to intervene in Taiwan."

The group devolved into several factions, arguing for and against striking back at the Americans right away. The sinking of their submarine did present the perfect pretext to attack them, but they still needed time to shore up their assets before they made that move. The Americans were in an excellent position to retaliate financially against China if they didn't get certain things taken care of first.

President Xi looked at his foreign minister. "How long do you believe we need to dump the remaining treasuries we hold?"

The group all looked intently at Minister Yong. He flipped through some notes, then responded, "At least twenty-four hours. We can take a loss on them, but it would be best if we could wait two days to get a better price. As to the businesses, I have no idea how far along they are at securing themselves from any potential American retribution. They were told they needed to have things ready in eight days, not twenty-four hours."

Sitting back in his chair, Xi reached out and took his cup of tea. He lifted the warm liquid to his lips and sipped slowly, thinking. "The Americans have given us the appropriate pretext to act without appearing to be the aggressor. Some of our corporations may be hurt by an expedited timeline, but that cannot be helped. We must execute. Start Operation Red Storm in twenty-four hours. Move our forces across the North Korean border and secure the peninsula. Then let's bring that belligerent little province Formosa back into the fold."

Everyone in the room smiled; they liked it when their leader was aggressive. Then the room became abuzz with activity as they all sprang to action, issuing orders to the various departments and commands and setting the stage for the next phase of action.

Chapter 36
Ant Hive

East China Sea

The two American supercarriers were either launching or recovering aircraft almost constantly for the past three hours. The Korean War had started just like the Iraq War in 2003, with complete and utter shock and awe, which was a stark contrast to how things had started with Russia. The US had hit North Korea with nearly 1,500 cruise missiles and precision-guided munitions, destroying much of the country's command and control bunkers, air-defense and artillery positions in the first thirty minutes of the war.

The KPA was being pounded from the air, sea, and land by the US and ROK forces in a very well-rehearsed attack plan. Since the end of the Korean War in 1953, the US had kept detailed and up-to-date plans on how they would disable and occupy the North, should it ever come to that. Once it had become clear that a war with North Korea was unavoidable, those plans had been combed over and updated once again. So far, things were basically going according to the grand strategy.

Captain Michael Richards, the captain of the *Carl Vinson*, stood on the bridge, watching as the next wave of aircraft was recovered from a successful bombing run. The pair of F/A-18s coming in for a landing had been hitting suspected artillery positions near the beach area, where the US and ROK Marines would be assaulting once the ground war started.

Richards looked on as the Hornets were guided to the elevators. They would be lowered to the next deck so they could be refueled and rearmed, then returned to the flight deck so they could hit the next target. The whole process moved so quickly that the pilots were only on the ship long enough to use the restroom, rehydrate, and get a brief on their next target before they got back in the air.

The maintenance and ordnance crews below were working feverishly to get the aircraft turned back around and ready for another mission. It was relentlessly hard and backbreaking work getting everything done like this. When things were running smoothly, it was impressive to watch. When things went awry, it could get crazy fast.

Captain Richards picked up a pair of binoculars to catch a glimpse of one of the aircraft coming in. It was streaming smoke from one of its engines. The F/A-18 had taken a hit from some enemy ground fire and was trying to limp its way back home. The aircraft moved a bit awkwardly through the air as it approached the carrier, streaming a light trail of black smoke from one of its engines. He could see it was in a bit of trouble; it was coming in too high and too slow.

The air boss tried to wave the aircraft off, but the pilot was determined to set her down. He descended quickly, thinking he might overshoot. Then, just as the aircraft looked like it was going to make it, its remaining engine stalled out and the F/A-18 slammed into the rear of the ship, just below the flight deck, killing the pilot and injuring nearly a dozen people. Oily black smoke began to billow from the stern. Firefighting groups immediately rushed forward to douse foam and fire retardant on the flames.

"No! The pilot should have gone around or ditched in the water!" yelled Richards. Then the captain let out a long stream of obscenities. He'd mourn the loss of the pilot later; right now, he had other aircraft needing to land, and this foul-up had just cost him precious time.

One of the other officers from the CIC came up to the bridge and got his attention. "Captain, there's a message coming in from the *Reagan*," he said, handing Richards a piece of paper. The officer paused long enough to look out the window and see the black smoke coming from the rear of the carrier, then unceremoniously headed back down to the CIC.

His CAG looked at him. "What's it say, Captain? Anything good?" he asked, trying to take his mind off the pilot he'd just lost.

The captain read it over, then looked up at the CAG. "One of their Hornet pilots spotted a mobile missile launch vehicle moving through a valley where he was bombing some artillery positions. The pilot didn't have any ordnance left but sent the coordinates back to the carrier. Looks like the North may be trying to get in position to launch some ballistic missiles," he replied, which made the bridge crew a bit nervous.

No one knew if the North would try and use their nuclear weapons, or if the missiles would be conventional or possibly chemical in nature. A nuclear missile could just as easily as take out the battle group as a coordinated strike by the Chinese or Russians.

191

Chapter 37
The Unthinkable

North Korean-Chinese Border
Paektu Mountain

Lieutenant General Ghim was furious. The country was under attack, and there was little he could do to stop it. Several of their launch facilities had already been destroyed. Now the Americans were hunting down his mobile launchers far more effectively than he believed possible. Within minutes of the first missiles and bombs hitting Pyongyang, he immediately ordered his mobile missile launchers to disperse. He had a brief call with the Supreme Leader, who ordered him to launch his missiles, but the connection was cut off before he could confirm the order. When he tried to call the command bunker back, the line was dead.

For the last three hours, General Ghim had been trying to get through to the military leadership to confirm his order and to find out if he should have the mobile launchers fire their missiles as well. Finally, he was able to reach one of the alternate command bunkers.

"The Supreme Leader has been injured and is currently in surgery," explained the new Commander of the KPA.

"Should I launch my missiles, Sir?" asked General Ghim.

"Proceed with the launch. Hit the South Korean and American Army and Navy immediately," came the order. Then the line went dead again.

He looked at the phone for a second, wondering if the line had gone dead because the bunker had just been destroyed, or if it was a problem on his end. All he knew was the Americans were bombing his country, and his fellow soldiers were dying by the thousands.

I had better get our missiles airborne, he realized. They were the only thing that would equalize the situation. If at least one of their missiles could get through, then they might be able to destroy enough of the enemy army to allow their guys to hold the line.

He turned to several of his officers. "Have the mobile missile crews launch their missiles at their assigned targets," he instructed matter-of-factly.

The officers began to contact the nearly two dozen missile crews that had managed to get set up and relayed their orders to them. The missile crews would fire their short-and medium-range ballistic missiles, which would rain down on the American naval battle group and several troop concentration points along the DMZ. Their hope was to destroy enough of the Allied forces to keep them from penetrating the DMZ.

While his officers were handling the mobile launchers, General Ghim walked over to the terminal where the technicians who handled the launch of the Dongfeng 5B ICBMs were waiting. They looked at him with grave concern in their eyes. Everyone revered Pak Lee like a deity, and to hear that he had been injured by an American bomb infuriated them.

"Begin fueling the missiles and prepare them to launch," ordered Ghim. "Wait until the last minute to open the launch door."

Chapter 38
Snake Eaters

Woo-shup Eup Village
North Korea

The distant flashes of artillery and explosions were visible in the darkness, followed by the low rumbles of explosions. Despite the sounds of war raging in the distant background, it was quiet in the forested area where the Special Forces operators had set up shop. A few birds could be heard chirping as they began their morning calls to each other. While it was still dark, the predawn light was starting to displace the blackness that enveloped the valley and surrounding area the three Special Forces operators were hiding in.

The air was cool, almost chilly, as Chief Warrant Officer Four Charles "Chucky" Lee slowly moved to the spotting scope and looked down into the valley below at the possible target Maverick had found.

Sergeant First Class Mark "Maverick" Wilson was Chucky's best spotter. The guy had eagle eyes and seemed to have a knack for finding things that didn't belong. Maverick had been using a long-range directional microphone to listen for vehicles traveling into the valley below. If they heard the sound of vehicle engines, they would switch over to using the night vision and thermal scopes to locate and identify the source of the noise.

Chucky's twelve-man Operational Detachment Alpha or ODA team had inserted into the valley seven hours ago via a HALO jump. Shortly after parachuting in, they realized that their original observational post had been compromised when they spotted a company-sized element of enemy soldiers encamped there, forcing them to use an alternate OP.

The observation post they had established themselves on, while not ideal, still had a commanding view of the lower portion of the valley below them. It also provided them with a view of two winding roads that ran through several large nearby ridgelines and a couple of small villages. This valley and the one nearby were both suspected staging sites for the KPA's mobile ballistic missile launchers.

Lee's team had made it in undetected and successfully set up in various over watch positions on the alternate OP, covering several different potential launch sites. Their mission was to observe enemy troop movements and look for possible missile launchers. If they found a target, they had one tactical air control party or TACP with them to call in an air strike.

As Chucky moved next to Maverick, he whispered, "Do you see the launcher being set up?"

Maverick indicated he should move over and look for himself. As he peered through the night vision scope, he could make out several soldiers placing camouflage netting over the mobile missile launcher. He could also see what appeared to be a very menacing-looking ballistic missile.

I wonder if I'm looking at a nuclear warhead on that missile, Chucky thought.

"Yeah, I see it. It looks like they just moved an SA-13 and a ZSU in to guard it as well," he whispered as he panned the scope around the area, looking to see what else was around.

He then turned to look at Technical Sergeant Jordan "Jordy" Mitchel. "How soon can you get us a strike package to hit that launcher?" he asked his TACP.

Jordy had been assigned to their ODA team numerous other times and was a very competent TACP. While deployed in Afghanistan, he had called in a series of air strikes that had saved their lives on more than one occasion. He had the respect of the ODA team—even if he was Air Force.

Jordy looked at his watch and then at the map he had lying on the ground next to him. "Five minutes. We have an F-117 on standby just for missions like this. Let me confirm that's the target we're looking for," he said as he scooched over to Chucky to see the launcher with his own eyes.

After confirming that it was indeed a missile launcher with a missile on it, he moved back to his position. "Before I call this in, Chief, do we have eyes on any additional launchers? A strike will give our position away, so it would be best if we only call in one strike and hit all the launchers we spot at one time," Jordy said.

That's a good question, Chucky thought. He gently pushed the talk button on his throat mic. "Team One has eyes on designated target Alpha. Do any other team elements have eyes on any other designated targets?" he asked his teammates.

A voice calmly came over the radio. "This is Team Two. We have eyes on a small cluster of vehicles moving into a tree line. We count one SA-13 and two ZSUs. We haven't seen a mobile launcher just yet but believe one may be part of the convoy. Out."

Another voice buzzed in. "This is Team Three. We have what appears to be one platoon's worth of enemy soldiers moving below our position, roughly 500 meters. How copy? Over."

Chucky knew the enemy soldiers could pose a serious problem for them if they discovered their locations. Their mission was to observe and report, not engage the enemy. There was no possible extraction for them, at least not until the frontlines moved closer to them.

"Copy that, Team Three. Please keep an eye on them and do not engage. Out."

Maverick turned to look at Chucky. "What do you want to do, Chief?" he asked.

I wish we could see further into the valley, thought Chucky. *There could be additional launchers out there, and we have no way of knowing it.*

"We need to wait to see if a second launcher shows up at Team Two's location," Chucky directed.

"I sure hope we aren't missing other launchers deeper in the valley, Chief," Maverick grunted, still mad that they had to abort their original OP. They had chosen that position because it would have given them a view of the entire valley, as opposed to this location, which only gave them a view of roughly half of it.

"Can it, Maverick. We can't do anything about it," Chucky retorted.

He then turned to his TACP. "Jordy, make sure Henhouse knows what we have, and the coordinates for this launcher. Let them know we may have a second launcher, but we're waiting for confirmation before we call in the strike package. See if they can direct a satellite to this area and try to look for additional launchers at the top end of the valley. Tell them we're out of position to see that area," he directed.

Chucky wanted to make sure their air support had the targeted coordinates now, so when they called in for the strike, they wouldn't have to waste time providing the aircraft with multiple target coordinates all at once.

Jordy just nodded and lifted his handset to his face, whispering into the receiver exactly what Chucky had just told him.

The F-117 pilot on the other end acknowledged the information and said, "I have enough fuel to stay on standby for another fifty minutes before I need to do another midair refueling."

The team sat there for thirty minutes as the predawn light turned to dawn and the light slowly began to illuminate the trees and valley below them. Had they not jumped with long-range listening devices and extremely high-end night vision and thermal-capable spotting scopes, they probably would have missed the mobile launcher moving into the valley. Now, as the sun began to creep into the sky, the light started to reveal more soldiers moving into the valley than they had originally thought were there.

The enemy soldiers and additional military equipment winding their way through the valley were clearly moving towards the sounds of war, further south towards the DMZ. The Air Force was pounding enemy troop positions deep behind the DMZ. They were making sure the reinforcements heading to the front were feeling the heat before they even arrived.

This constant aerial bombardment had its own strange rhythm to it, almost like a bass or kettle drummer pounding out a disjointed beat. From time to time, they could hear the roar of jets high above their heads, moving towards some unknown target. Chucky looked down at his watch and saw the war had started a little over four hours ago.

He was just about to reach for the talk button on his mic when a familiar voice came over the radio. "This is Team Two. We have positive visual on a mobile missile launcher. It looks like they're getting the missile readied for launch. Recommend we call in the strike package now, before they fire. How copy?" asked the team leader.

"Maverick, is our launcher being readied to launch? Team Two just said theirs appears like it's going to be launched soon," Chucky explained. He was hoping that they had not waited too long to call in the strike package. They were supposed to destroy the launchers with the missiles still on them.

Maverick leaned back down to the spotting scope and peered through it. "No, it's still down, although I see some soldiers starting to uncover the camouflage netting around it. They could be getting it readied for launch," he replied.

Chucky keyed up his mic. "Team Two, send the coordinates to Jordy. We'll have them strike your target first. How copy? Over," he said.

A minute passed as the team lead relayed the grid coordinates to their TACP, who typed the information into his targeting computer and transmitted the information to the pilot of the Nighthawk who was loitering somewhere above them.

Jordy then came over the net. "Bombs away. Stand by."

Close to two minutes went by with nothing happening while the SF men lay on their bellies, waiting for the final warning before impact. Then they heard Jordy announce, "Impact in five seconds."

It might have only been five seconds, but it felt like an eternity waiting for the 2,000-pound laser-guided bomb to hit its target.

Team Two had painted the mobile launcher with their laser designator and watched as the bomb dropped right on top of its target. The explosion was thunderous and echoed throughout the valley. Black smoke began to billow upwards as the shockwave expanded outward, destroying everything within a thousand feet of the impact. Trees around the impacted area were flattened, along with three air-defense vehicles that had been meant to protect the launcher from American and ROK aircraft.

The crew manning the mobile launcher Chucky's team had been monitoring suddenly moved with a lot more purpose as they reacted to the explosion. The soldiers pulled and yanked the netting off the launcher as other soldiers began to raise the missile. These guys weren't going to wait around for everything to be perfect. They wanted to get their missile launched and then find a way to escape with their lives.

"Jordy, tell your guy to drop his next bomb. That missile is going to launch!" Chucky said excitedly, hoping that they hadn't somehow fouled up their chance to take this missile out.

What if this missile launcher was carrying a nuclear warhead? thought Chucky in a panic.

"I already did, Chief. The bomb is on the way…should hit in sixty seconds," he replied, much to Chucky's relief.

The seconds ticked by, and then they witnessed an epic explosion as the bomb hit the launcher, obliterating it and everything near it. There was chaos on the ground as enemy soldiers were thrown into trees like ragdolls from the blast's concussion. Flying debris, shrapnel, and flames were injuring many other soldiers, several of whom could be seen running like insane men as their clothes were on fire. Some of their comrades jumped to their aid, throwing them to the ground while they tried to put the fires out.

"We have two inbound fast movers that are going to attack several additional launchers the satellite folks found. Stand by for more impacts," Jordy announced loudly over the mic.

They heard the loud roar of an F-16 as it flew low over their heads into the valley below. Two large objects fell from under the wings of the aircraft. What looked like several cluster bombs detonated over a densely forested area. Two large secondary explosions could be seen billowing upwards, then finally a third fiery blast lit up the skyline as another vehicle exploded.

As the F-16 pulled up from his bombing run to gain altitude, they saw multiple missiles emerge from the tree line, chasing after the aircraft. The F-16 fired off a series of flares and chaff canisters, in an attempt to distract the enemy missiles. Several of the Korean missiles hit the flares, exploding harmlessly as the F-16 continued to gain altitude.

A second F-16 then swooped into the valley from a slightly different angle, gearing up for its own attack run. As the aircraft entered the valley, they saw four SAMs emerge from the tree line, heading straight for the F-16. Before the pilot could even react, two of the missiles slammed into the aircraft, causing it to burst into a fiery comet that rained down jet fuel and debris in a long high-velocity trail from the forward motion of the aircraft.

To their surprise and amazement, the first F-16 swooped in for a second attack run at what Chucky assumed must be another mobile missile launcher.

If it wasn't a launcher, then chances are he would have turned for home and not risked his life a second time, thought Chucky.

Several missiles again rose from the trees and raced towards the F-16, which banked hard while dispersing additional flares and chaff canisters. The pilot released a series of bombs, though it looked like he didn't get as good of an alignment on them as he had the first time around. They burst into flames in the trees, but no secondary explosions could be seen.

The pilot pulled up hard, turning his aircraft nearly vertical while hitting his afterburner. Two additional SAMs leapt from the ridgeline he had just flown over and raced quickly after the aircraft. Just as it looked like he was going to outrun the missiles, they went to terminal velocity and detonated, spraying the F-16 with shrapnel. The aircraft began to disintegrate quickly. Just as it was about to explode, they saw the pilot eject.

While the aircraft began to fall to the earth below in a fiery ball of flames, the pilot began his slow descent to the ground and near-certain captivity—if the KPA didn't kill him outright. Chucky's team was way too far away to get to the pilot quickly, although they would try anyway.

Then, maybe a couple of miles deeper in the valley, they heard the roar of a rocket. They spotted the body of a missile as it began to gain altitude, and they knew it was a ballistic missile that had just launched.

Just as they got ahold of their higher headquarters to report the missile launch and the destruction of the two F-16s, they saw five more launches.

In that moment, they all hung their heads, knowing that despite their best efforts, they had only been able to identify and destroy two missiles while another six more had successfully launched. All they could do now was relay the information to their leaders at Henhouse and pray the vaunted missile defense systems could shoot them down.

Once Chucky had completed the depressing call to the higher-ups, he grabbed his mic and announced, "Everyone, pack up your gear. We're going to head in the direction of the downed pilot and see if we can link up with him before he's captured."

Minutes later, they were on the move towards the pilot as they saw a brief flash rush across the sky. Then they heard a low, deep rumble. What they didn't realize was that they had just witnessed the nuclear detonation that destroyed the South Koreans Northern Air Command on Wonju Air Base.

****

An hour had passed since they had seen the F-16 pilot eject, and they figured they were close to where he should have landed. Chucky told Maverick, "Switch to the pilot's emergency frequency and see if you can make contact with him."

After three attempts, a voice came over the radio, shaken and scared. It was the voice of a woman—the pilot that had been shot down was a female pilot. Her voice was shaky as she relayed her surroundings to Maverick. He asked her a series of questions, trying to get her to describe the surrounding area and explain if there were any KPA soldiers near her.

"I haven't seen any enemy soldiers, although I heard some voices maybe ten minutes ago," she responded.

After identifying a few common landmarks, they figured they were within a mile of each other. Another thirty minutes went by as Maverick and two other members of their ODA team moved through the woods to find her. They spotted her well before she spotted them, and they approached her cautiously. When it was determined there were no additional enemy soldiers in the area, they guided her to them.

As she approached their location, she still hadn't spotted them. When they did reveal themselves, she nearly jumped out of her flight suit at the sight of the three hidden figures that suddenly materialized right in front of her.

These guys are good, she thought as they guided her back to the rest of the team.

Chucky saw her approach their hide and stood up briefly to signal her to come and kneel next to him. He held his hand out and shook hers. "That was some seriously impressive flying Major...Lopez," he said as he read the name tape on her flight suit.

She smiled and quickly replied, "Well, I still got shot down, so I don't know that it was that good." He could see the smirk on her face in the early morning light.

"I still cannot believe you guys found me. I knew there was an ODA team in the area that had found the launchers, but I thought I was going to be captured for sure when I ejected," she said, some fear still perceptible in her voice. "I can't thank you guys enough for rescuing me."

Chucky snickered. "Before you thank us, just realize you're now a part of our team. We're deep behind enemy lines, and our mission is to observe and call in air strikes. I have no idea when we'll be extracted, but you can bet it's going to be at least a week, maybe more, before we're even in helicopter range," he said.

"I'd rather be stuck out here for a few weeks with you guys than a POW. Are there no officers with you guys?" she inquired, hoping she hadn't just insulted the team leader who had rescued her.

Smiling at the question, Chucky answered, "I am an officer." He chortled. "We're short commissioned officers in the teams. One in four of our officers were sent to Europe to replace the losses in the Special Operations Forces prior to this war kicking off. Since I'm a CW4, I'm running the show for A Company."

Major Lopez nodded, understanding full well the extent of the losses from Europe. She had already lost a few friends in Europe, and then today her wingman had been killed. She knew she was going to be stuck with these guys until they could be extracted. Her goal at that point was to make sure she was an asset to them and not a liability.

"What do you want me to do now, Chief?" she asked.

He pulled his rucksack off and unstrapped the Benelli M4 Super 90 combat shotgun he had brought with him as a secondary weapon. He held up the weapon to her and talked quietly. "This is a semiautomatic 12-gauge shotgun. Here's the safety," he said as he pointed to it. Then he walked her briefly through the function of the shotgun. "It has one round in the chamber and seven rounds in the tube. This is the extra ammunition I brought with me. It's also the only additional ammunition we have for it, so use it sparingly." Then he handed her the shotgun and the bandolier of extra ammo.

"Maverick here," he said, pointing to the SF soldier who had fetched her, "will be your body man. I want you to stick closely to him and do exactly what he says. Also, listen to our other teammates. You need to stay quiet. Don't talk above a whisper. Only once Maverick tells you it's Ok can you speak in a normal voice. We're going to move to our next OP and get set up for our next mission. Do you understand everything, Major?" His tone indicated she needed to do as she was told.

She may be a major, but she's on our turf now, and if she wants to live, she needs to listen to us, Chucky thought.

Major Lopez took the shotgun, examining it briefly and placing the extra ammo around her shoulder along with her 9mm pistol. She nodded in acknowledgment. She was just glad *they* had found her and not the KPA. As a woman, she knew if she had been captured, she probably would have been raped mercilessly by the enemy soldiers.

The team started to move to their next observation point, quietly hoping they hadn't been discovered while retrieving the downed pilot. The next several hours were spent moving slowly through the forested hills and valleys of the area, until they reached their next OP. Once there, they spread out and formed a defensive perimeter. They pulled out their spotting scopes and directional microphones and went back to work, looking for mobile missile launchers and targets of opportunity.

Chapter 39
DEFCON One

Colorado Springs, Colorado
Peterson Air Force Base
North American Aerospace Defense Command (NORAD)

While it was 0730 in North Korea, it was roughly 1530 hours the day before at NORAD. The operators of this Cold War-era command center were watching nervously as the opening hours of the war in North Korea held a lot of uncertainty. It was unknown if the Koreans would try to launch their ballistic missiles in response to the US and ROK's preemptive attack.

In addition to the ballistic missile threat, many of the planners at NORAD feared a possible cyber-attack by the North Koreans. It was still early in the morning, so it was hard to fully know if such an attack was still in the works or if the CIA, NSA, and military had been successful in neutralizing that possible threat.

The war with Russia had seen an unprecedented level of cyber-attacks across nearly every aspect of the NATO nations. As a result, the US was rapidly identifying and fixing the vulnerabilities as they were being exploited. The North Koreans might have been disappointed to find that America was much more capable of dealing with a cyber-threat now than they would have been three or four months earlier.

Master Sergeant Lisa Collins was monitoring her computer screen, which presently was showing very detailed real-time satellite images of North Korea, when she spotted a series of small flashes indicating missile launches. In a fraction of a second, the complex computer software that was monitoring the images being fed to it by the satellites alerted her and the rest of the operation center that multiple missile launches had been detected.

Once the klaxon alarms began to sound and the flashing red lights started, everyone in the room knew about the launches from the DPRK.

Not everyone had been monitoring the Korean Peninsula. Many others were monitoring the thousands of satellites in orbit and other potential hotspots like China and Russia, but at that moment, they all looked at the new missile threats.

The primary monitor on the big wall showed the Korean Peninsula and confirmed that twenty-three ballistic missiles had just been launched. Seven of the missiles were starting to track towards the American carrier battlegroup, three were headed towards Seoul, and the other thirteen were heading towards major US and South Korean military bases throughout the peninsula. What no one knew was whether these missiles were carrying nuclear warheads or whether they were simply conventional high-explosive missiles.
****

Admiral Bill Robinson had taken over command of NORAD roughly seven months ago, shortly after the new president had been sworn in. He was ecstatic about getting this command; it was going to be his final command before he retired from the military after 34 years of service.

He had risen through the ranks of the Navy largely by pioneering the advancements in ballistic missile defense systems. Once he'd realized the value of a defense system that could be repositioned anywhere in the world, he had gone to bat for it, vigorously advocating for the Navy to get those resources to the point that he drowned out the other branches. It was only because of him that they had the *Arleigh Burke* guided-missile destroyers and the *Ticonderoga* guided-missile cruisers as the lead defensive platforms. These guided missile ships could be positioned anywhere in the world where there was a ballistic missile threat, giving the US and the Navy the ability to interdict them.

When the time came for a new commander to take over NORAD, he had worked every favor and pulled every string he had to try and get this final posting—the last hurrah of his career. He wanted to make one final mark and ensure the country had a well-established, multitiered missile defense system fully operational by the time he retired.

Despite obtaining this critical post, he knew he was also in the twilight years of his career. Privately, he would admit he was looking forward to the retired life and fly-fishing. He and his wife had bought a couple of acres near the Perry Park area, north of Colorado Springs. They planned on starting construction of their dream home this coming spring.

Since the start of the war with Russia, he had been baffled by trying to figure out how the situation had escalated into a full-scale war.

His mission at NORAD had suddenly become a lot more serious. Not since the days of the Cold War had the US seriously faced a nuclear threat, but now it was at war with a nuclear power that was capable of pulverizing it if it chose to use those weapons, and it had just gone to war with a second country that had spent the better part of a decade saying it would obliterate the US with nuclear fire. He found himself wishing his organization had a lot more fighter aircraft and a much more robust missile defense system than it currently did.

The opening salvo of the war with Russia had not only caught NORAD and the US by surprise, it had temporarily disabled most of the US's surveillance and communication satellites, along with the majority of the world's GPS satellites. Between the distributed denial of service or DDoS attacks on the satellite links and the malware attack against many network-connected devices, the creativeness of the cyber-attacks had caught them off guard. It had taken nearly two weeks to regain control of the satellites and get new ones launched to replace the ones destroyed by the IoT attack.

As the war with Russia continued, it looked more likely that at least that particular conflict would stay conventional, which was good for all involved. As the war with Russia progressed and China annexed much of Southeast Asia, military activity began to pick up heavily inside North Korea. Admiral Robinson watched in horror as the unavoidable conflict with North Korea unfolded. He began to lose sleep at night, trying to prepare for a war that would almost certainly turn nuclear.
****

It was midafternoon, and Admiral Robinson was on a secured video teleconference call with the Pentagon operations center, getting an update on the progress of the war in Korea. As they were going over the progress of the strategic air strikes, the klaxons began to blare, alerting them to a potential ballistic missile launch.

Between the obnoxious noises, the admiral managed to say, "I need to see what's going on. I'll get back to you shortly."

While one of his staff officers was disconnecting the call, an officer from the ops center burst into the room. "Admiral! We have confirmation of ballistic missile launches from North Korea!" he shouted, to the shock and horror of those in the room. The admiral quickly got up and began to race back to the ops center.

He rushed down the hall with several of the other officers and senior NCOs hot on his heels. "Make a hole!" he yelled as he nearly ran several people over trying to get to the command center.

As soon as he ran into the room, he saw the tracks of twenty-three ballistic missiles as they headed towards their intended targets.

"Move us from DEFCON 3 to DEFCON 2 immediately," Robinson said to the nearest officer. "Alert our missile interceptor bases that we have confirmation of ballistic missile launches."

Turning to another officer, he ordered, "Send a FLASH message to all US and Allied forces in Asia and let them know about the ballistic missile launches."

While the messages were being sent, the THAAD missile defense system near Seoul engaged the enemy missiles. The four *Ticonderoga*-class guided-missile cruisers and the guided-missile destroyers also joined the fray, engaging the incoming missiles as well. So far, everyone was acting according to the well-choreographed defensive plan they had rehearsed so many times in training.

Admiral Robinson reached down and grabbed the red hotline phone to the White House. It rang twice before the President picked up.

Gates was shocked when he saw the red phone ring. No one had ever called his desk on that phone before. He knew that something terrible had happened, or was in the process of happening, and he wasn't completely sure what to say.

"This is the President," he answered tentatively.

Robinson cleared his throat before proceeding. "Mr. President, this is Admiral Robinson from NORAD. I'm calling to inform you that we have positive confirmation of twenty-three ballistic missile launches from North Korea towards US and South Korean forces. We've activated our missile defense systems and are engaging the missiles as we speak. What are your orders, Mr. President?" he asked.

The President slowly sat back down in his chair as the general relayed the situation. Just then, the Oval Office began to fill with Secret Service agents. "Mr. President, we have to get you out of here *now*!" his head agent said urgently as he approached the president.

Gates held up a hand and pointed at the red phone. They paused for a second, letting him finish talking to NORAD. "Admiral, I'm being told by the Secret Service that we need to evacuate right now. I want you to intercept those missiles. Keep our nuclear capabilities at a high state of readiness, but don't launch a counterstrike yet. We need to see if we're able to neutralize the threat first. I'll call you back once I'm on Air Force One," the President directed, and then he hung up the phone.

The Secret Service agents breathed a sigh of relief. They immediately rushed him towards Marine One, which was just approaching the White House.

****

NORAD
Peterson Air Force Base

Master Sergeant Collins was reading the trajectories of the missiles when she saw that the two US air bases in Korea were being targeted, along with several points along the DMZ. These were positions where the bulk of the ROK and American forces were marshaling prior to advancing across the border.

She watched nervously as the THAAD missiles accelerated to intercept the incoming missiles, followed quickly by SM-6 and SM-3 interceptors from the naval battlegroups.

While everyone was collectively holding their breath, the klaxons sounded again, indicating another missile launch had been detected. Her computer screen zoomed in to a part of Korea they had never looked at before. The small flash occurred near the North Korean-Chinese border. Her computer program identified it as originating from the Paektu mountain range.

She zoomed in further, locating the source of the launch. To her amazement, she realized these were hardened missile silos they had been completely unaware of until that moment.

How could we have missed that? she thought in a panic.

As far as they'd known, the North's ballistic missile program only consisted of mobile missile launchers and several open-air missile platforms. They had only tested the Hwasong-14 missile this past summer, and it wouldn't have been possible for them to ready those missiles for mass production yet or place them in silos.

What in the world is going on?

Within seconds, the Pine Gap tracking facility out of central Australia had identified the missiles as Chinese-made Dongfeng 5 ICBMs. They were able to make that assessment based on the missiles rate of acceleration and subsequent booster phase. As the processor estimated the flight path and probable targets, it quickly became clear that the ten ballistic missiles were on a trajectory that would take them towards the continental United States.

Admiral Robinson walked into the room, and nearly all eyes turned to him. He looked up at the screen and saw the ten new missile tracks, in addition to the twenty-three that were already halfway to their targets.

"Seal the building immediately!" he yelled to the watch officer. "Bring us to DEFCON 1! Scramble our alert bombers, and make sure the Secret Service knows we have incoming ICBMs to the continental United States!"

Everyone went into action, their training taking over as they methodically raised America's defense posture to "nuclear war is imminent." This change in orders would put into motion a series of actions seldom ever drilled or seen.

The Air Force began the process of scrambling all their aircraft and equipment they could disperse to their secondary positions and await further orders. The Army would likewise begin to disperse their vehicles and critical equipment to secondary locations near their bases. If one of those missiles was headed towards their base, then hopefully at least some of their equipment and people might survive.

The Navy was doing the same, rushing to put their ships to sea, even without full crews. As long as they had enough people on board to get the engines running and steer the ships out of the ports, they would move out to a secondary location to wait for further orders and hopefully save those vessels from a tragic fate.

The continuity of government group, which was a small cadre of emergency operations personnel, would initiate the government's COG program. This would begin the evacuation of the Cabinet, the Supreme Court justices, and the Congress to a myriad of hardened nuclear bomb shelters outside of Washington, D.C., and then disperse them further throughout the country if need be. This was critical in keeping the US government alive and functioning should the capital be the target of one of the nuclear missiles.

Helicopters from Joint Base Anacostia-Boiling and Fort Myer took to the air and headed to a series of designated landing zones at the

Capitol and Supreme Court buildings to begin evacuating as much of the government as they could.

In minutes, D.C. and the surrounding area was going to turn into pure chaos as word got out about the incoming nuclear missiles. The military had to act swiftly to get as much of the government to safety before panic set in and the city ground to a halt. A DF-5B would take roughly 34 minutes to hit D.C., so time was short to get key personnel out of the city.

One of the operations officers turned to the admiral. "Sir, the President just boarded Air Force One. They should be airborne shortly. Secret Service also reports they're starting to evacuate the Capitol and moving the cabinet members to a secured bunker."

The admiral just nodded, almost not sure what more to say.

This isn't supposed to be happening, he thought. This was supposed to be an easy final tour, a last command before retirement.

A colonel on the hotline phone connecting him to the Russians called out in an urgent tone. "Sir, we're receiving a FLASH message from the Commander of Russian Strategic Rocket Forces. He's calling to let us know that Russia has no intentions of launching any ballistic missiles at the US or Europe, and he claims that Russia was completely unaware of the North Koreans' intentions. He further reiterated that the Russian Strategic Rocket Forces will not be moving to a higher state of readiness and wants to assure us that they're not launching a coordinated attack with the Koreans."

The ops center had direct hotlines to Russia, China, Israel, Great Britain, and France. These lines were meant to speed communication between each country's nuclear commands, deescalating potential conflicts and hopefully ensuring no miscommunications occurred.

"Call the Chinese and tell them we demand to know if this launch came from them," ordered Admiral Robinson. "The launch of those missiles occurred on the Chinese-Korean border, and we have confirmation that those missiles are DongFeng-5s. Those are PLA missiles, not Korean."

While they were contacting the Chinese, he turned to the group manning the country's missile defense system. "Alert Fort Greely that we have ten inbound ICBMs to the United States. They are to begin intercepting the missiles immediately! Does anyone know if those missiles are MIRV-capable?" he barked at his operations officers.

Master Sergeant Collins had been on the phone with Pine Gap. They had been analyzing the missile as they sought to make that assessment. She spoke up before anyone else could. "Yes, Admiral, the DongFeng-5B version *is* MIRV-capable. It can carry up to six warheads. The team over at Pine Gap have confirmed that some of the missiles are carrying MIRVs while at least three of them are carrying a single warhead. All warheads have been determined to be nuclear of unknown size. Several of the missiles with the MIRVs are also carrying dummies, decoys meant to throw our interceptors off."

The admiral felt sick to his stomach, but this was the kind of data he needed. He gave her a curt nod and turned back to look at the large monitor tracking the incoming missiles. It was now time to see if his decades of work and focus on the ABM strategy was finally going to pay off.

Looking at the large monitor, they could see the THAAD and SM-6 missiles starting to intercept the original twenty-three ballistic missiles. Scores of them were blotted from the sky. The numbers were rapidly thinning as they began their trajectory downwards toward their targets.

The missiles heading towards the US battlegroup had been successfully intercepted. So had the three missiles heading towards Seoul. The two most important assets had survived.

One hundred and fifty miles to the south of Seoul, two of the three missiles headed towards the American Air Force Base Kunsan were struck from the sky by the THAAD and Patriot missile batteries, positioned there for this very purpose.

Then, the screen whited out—the third missile detonated its 30-kiloton warhead over the joint airbase.

In that second, nearly 40,000 US and ROK service members and civilians were killed instantly by the blast. Another 60,000 or so would be injured, possibly dying painfully later from the exposure to radiation. North Korea had just detonated the first nuclear weapon against another nation since World War II, with devastating effect.

Despite the klaxon alarms, the room suddenly seemed silent. But there was no time to mourn the dead, at least not right now. While everyone was digesting the fact that Kunsan Air Base had just been wiped out, another missile detonated over Wonju Air Base, home of the ROK's Northern Combat Command. That missile killed another 52,000 people and injured nearly 100,000 more. It had also effectively wiped out nearly 40% of the entire South Korean Air Force, along with the majority of their leadership. The screen showed that the remaining missiles were successfully intercepted, though that did little to comfort those who had just died or were gravely injured.

Admiral Robinson spoke loudly to the stunned members of the ops center. "Listen up, everyone. We still have incoming missiles heading to the US. Get your heads in the game. We can grieve the losses later. I need everyone to focus on the tasks at hand," he said, breaking them out of their initial shock.

Turning to his targeting officer, he demanded, "What nuclear assets do we have ready to respond with right now?"

One of the targeters responded, "We have an *Ohio*-class submarine in the area. We also have a B-2 armed with nuclear weapons that can respond immediately."

The admiral thought it over for a moment. He was about to call Air Force One and request permission to launch a counterstrike against the North. The incoming missiles still had close to twenty minutes before they would be over the US. They still needed another ten minutes before the interceptors would be in range.

His mind also raced back to China. *Was this a Chinese missile strike?* he wondered. Those *were* Chinese missiles, but they had been fired from inside Korea.

Chapter 40
I Am Death, the Destroyer of Men

Andrews Air Force Base, Maryland
Air Force One

President Gates had just taken his seat and clipped his seat belt on when Marine One began to take off towards Andrews Air Force Base, where Air Force One was located. The chopper was clipping through the air at a faster pace than the President was used to, and he started to feel a bit of motion sickness as they whizzed through the air.

As Marine One settled down onto the tarmac near his presidential aircraft, one of his Secret Service agents received a call. "Sir, one of the ICBMs is heading towards Washington D.C.," the agent informed him.

It was terrifying to think that a nuclear missile was headed towards Washington and there was virtually nothing he could do other than hope the military was able to save the city. *Is this my fault?* Gates wondered. *Did I somehow cause all of this to happen?*

There wasn't any more time to think. The President was rushed from the helicopter by a host of agents, who practically carried him up the stairs to the aircraft. Once Gates was aboard Air Force One, the door immediately closed. The President looked over and saw his wife, Melissa, and his twelve-year old son, Connor, safely strapped into their seats. He sat down next to them.

"Pat, I'm so worried," his wife said nervously. It had been a while since the President had heard anyone address him by his first name, and only his wife used that nickname for Patrick; usually, when she called him Pat, she was on the verge of tears.

Gates grabbed his wife's hand. Unsure what to say, he simply replied, "Me too."

Connor interjected, "Dad, what is going on? Why did the Secret Service come grab me out of my class at school and throw me in a car to rush me here?"

"I can't really tell you all the details right now, son, but it's serious. All we can do right now is pray and trust our soldiers will be able to protect us," the President explained.

A horrible feeling hit him in the pit of his stomach, and it wasn't from his crazy helicopter ride. *Here I am, being evacuated from D.C. with my wife and son while a nuclear missile is heading towards the city,* he lamented. *Lord, I really hope the missile defense system will work.* His senior advisors and generals had all insisted it would, but those were the same people who told him that Russia would never go to war with NATO over Ukraine.

The roar of the engines was louder than usual as the pilots frantically pushed the heavy plane to get airborne and put as much distance between them and the incoming nuclear warheads as humanly possible. Within a couple of minutes, the aircraft leveled out, though it continued a slow climb. The President looked out one of the windows and saw a pair of F-22 Raptors escorting them away from the city.

Has it really come down to this? Nuclear war...the end of civilization, or America? he wondered.

With the plane settling into its flight plan, the President's National Security Advisor, Tom McMillan, walked up to him. "Mr. President, we need you to come to the conference room. We have the Commander of NORAD on the video link, and we need you to issue some orders that require your authorization," he said urgently.

The President was still trying to take in the surreal scene unfolding around them, but he quickly undid his seat belt and followed his NSA to the briefing room. Several generals were already seated at the table. He also saw some new faces. Some of his staff had either not made it aboard the plane or were being taken to a different facility in case Air Force One went down.

The Secretary of Defense was being flown to Site R, at Raven Rock, along with many other defense officials. Members of the Cabinet and Congress were being flown to Mount Weather, per the COG plans. The VP was being sequestered in the PEOC, deep under the White House in what had been deemed a nuclear-proof bunker, barring a direct hit by anything larger than ten megatons.

Seated across from the President was a man who had just joined his staff a few days ago, the new Chief of Staff, retired Army General Liam Greeson; he was still getting up to speed after Gates had replaced his predecessor. Despite being new to the position, he was still a retired four-star and knew how to take charge of a situation when it was needed.

214

The video conference call was already running, and despite traveling through the air, they could clearly see and hear the commander of NORAD.

He looks nervous, thought the President.

General Greeson didn't mince any words. As soon as Gates sat down, he asserted, "We need an update on the missile strikes, Admiral Robinson."

"Mr. President, we have confirmation of two nuclear detonations in South Korea. One hit our air base at Kunsan, the other hit the ROK air base at Wonju. We estimate that close to 100,000 people were killed, and twice that number injured. We're also tracking ten DongFeng-5 ICBMs heading towards the US—"

One of the Air Force generals at the table interrupted, "— Admiral, did you say a DongFeng-5? That's a Chinese ICBM. Did these missiles originate from China?" he asked with obvious concern in his voice.

"Yes and no," replied Admiral Robinson. "We have confirmation that it's a DF-5. What we don't know is if it's a B model or not. We have spoken with the Chinese, and they are insisting that they did *not* launch any missiles at the US, but have not denied giving the DongFeng-5 to the North Koreans," he replied, knowing that he had still not fully answered the question.

The President felt he needed to get a word in. "So, we have ten Chinese-made ICBMs heading towards the US, but the Chinese are telling us they didn't launch the missiles? Am I missing something?" Gates asked.

Liam followed the President's question. "How in the world did the North Koreans obtain ten DongFeng-5 missiles if the Chinese didn't hand them over? Do we have a way of talking with them? We have to make some very important decisions in a few minutes, and we need more information than we presently have."

"We're working to get them on the hotline right now. We have spoken with the Russians, and they said they're not involved in this and are not raising the alert status of their own strategic rocket forces, as a sign of good faith. They're wanting to make sure we know they're not involved," Robinson replied.

The President surveyed the faces around him, then turned to the Commander of NORAD. "What sort of response do you think we should make? And when will our interceptors begin to take those missiles out?"

"Sir, the first missile interceptors have been launched from one of our *Arleigh Burke* destroyers in the Pacific. Vandenburg and Fort Greely have also fired off their missile interceptors as well. They should start to intercept the missiles within the next five minutes," replied Admiral Robinson. "As to a response, I believe we need to send a strong message. We need to retaliate with our own nuclear weapons. We have one B-2 loaded with twenty B61 guided nuclear bombs in the air now. These bombs are equipped with a variable yield dial, meaning they're designed to give us a yield option of 0.3 kilotons to 340 kilotons of explosive power. This allows us to adjust how big of a nuclear response we want to send. There is also an *Ohio*-class ballistic missile submarine operating in the nearby area that can launch one of its Tridents."

"We also have our missile silos, correct?" the President asked, a bit naïve as to how the nuclear triad worked.

"Yes, Mr. President. We still have our silos, but they won't be able to respond nearly as quickly as the assets we have in theater," Robinson replied.

There was a brief pause as the President considered his options.

"Sir, the first set of missile interceptors will be reaching their targets shortly," said the admiral. "We could decide on the retaliatory targets and weapon platform after the immediate threat is neutralized."

Where the President had been unsure of how to respond a moment before, his facial features suddenly changed, and his eyes burned with determination and anger. "Admiral, before the war started, I gave operational authority to General Bennet and the Commander of the Pacific Forces to use nuclear weapons if the North Koreans detonated a nuclear bomb on the Korean Peninsula. Inform the two commanders they are to initiate a retaliatory strike against the North Koreans. I want them to hit the North Koreans with eight nuclear bombs. One is to hit Pyongyang. I'll leave it up to them to determine what other seven targets they want to hit. Make sure they look to hit targets that will help to bring a quick close to the war, but I'll leave it to them to determine what targets will be best."

While the military members were placing numerous calls to get the ball rolling on the President's order, the missile tracks heading towards the US continued to move steadily closer to their targets. As the group collectively watched the enemy missiles arching towards the US, their worst fear was confirmed; these DongFeng-5B missiles were the recently upgraded missiles with a MIRV capability. Seven of the missile warheads split apart, turning into 42 independent warheads.

Admiral Robinson turned around, screaming to the others in the command center, "Launch more interceptors!"

The targeting computer recalculated the new trajectories now that the warheads had split. Within seconds, the graphics on-screen showed the new targets. The admiral read off the names of the cities. "San Diego, Pearl Harbor, Fort Hood, Washington, D.C., Seattle, Chicago, New York, Oakland, El Paso, and Fairbanks, Alaska—all of these appear to have a single warhead directed at them."

The admiral turned back to the group. "Mr. President, it's likely that most of these warheads are decoys. There is no way that the North Koreans had 45 nuclear warheads in their possession in addition to the short-range missiles they just launched at South Korea."

"Then again, the North Koreans weren't supposed to have DongFeng-5B missiles either," Gates said under his breath.
****

The first wave of missile interceptors fired by the Navy began to reach their targets. Of the twenty SM-6 missiles fired by the destroyer USS *Gonzalez*, fifteen of them hit their targets. A few minutes later, the next round of interceptors began to arrive from Fort Greely and Vandenburg. They managed to hit twenty-seven of the remaining thirty missiles.

Of the three warheads left flying towards the States, one warhead was headed for the Port of Oakland, another towards El Paso, and the third towards New York. A last-ditch barrage of missiles was fired from Vandenburg; those last interceptors would be cutting it close since the incoming warheads were now traveling at speeds approaching Mach 25 as they reentered the atmosphere and began their terminal approach. This was like hitting a bullet with a bullet.

One of the interceptors raced towards the warhead that was targeting New York City. Fortune was on the side of the Americans in this case, because that interceptor met its mark and collided in a spectacular display of precision-guided technology. A second interceptor moved quickly to catch the warhead that was careening towards Oakland. However, Lady Luck did not smile twice. Just as the interceptor looked like it was going to impact, it sailed right past the warhead.

Less than a minute later, a miniature sun was born as the one-megaton nuclear warhead detonated at approximately 5,000 feet above the Port of Oakland. In that second, it vaporized everything within the harbor as well as the entire city. The immediate fireball expanded outwards in a half-mile diameter, consuming everything in its path. Buildings, ships, homes, and people just ceased to exist as the temperatures began to exceed 6,000 degrees Fahrenheit.

The thermal radiation radius swelled rapidly to 7.57 miles from the epicenter, further expanding the destruction caused by the blast. Anyone outside during the blast would suffer third-degree burns across any exposed skin. The five-psi overpressure from the air blast was enough to destroy most structures located within 4.37 miles of the epicenter.

As the initial blast wave and flames swelled out from the epicenter, the secondary blast effect of 1.5-psi continued to as far as 10.2 miles. This was still strong enough to blow out the windows of nearly every home, office, and car in the entire city of San Francisco, causing tens of thousands of injuries from flying glass and debris. The tidal wave of water thrown out from the epicenter of the bomb created a nearly 50-foot swell that hit downtown San Francisco and the surrounding coastal areas of the Bay Area.

The force of the water's surge was then quickly followed by an enormous pull as the sea tried to replace the inordinate amount of seawater that had just been vaporized. Despite the recent earthquake retrofitting, the extraordinary rip tide caused by the bomb was enough to damage one of the main piers on the iconic Golden Gate Bridge. The northern side of the bridge leaned over towards the ocean until the force of gravity caused that portion of the structure to collapse into the sea below.

In a swift deadly blow, 225,000 Americans were vaporized, while another 585,000 more-received a near-fatal doses of radiation and severe third-degree burns. Because the nuclear missile had exploded at 1430 hours, many people were at work at the time of the attack, increasing the number of casualties. As the mushroom cloud began to build, the firestorm that would consume the neighboring cities and forest preserves near the edge of the blast zone began to rage out of control. Many thousands more were blinded by witnessing the searing light of the bomb, even from across the Bay.

While this horrific scene was unfolding, another warhead was still streaking through the sky, careening towards the city of El Paso, Texas, the home of the 1st Armored Division at Fort Bliss. A glimmer of hope still existed as two remaining interceptors raced for the incoming missile, which was now traveling at Mach 25. Unfortunately, the first interceptor just missed the warhead, sailing right past it. El Paso's fate now rested in one final chance. In an extraordinary triumph, the second interceptor scored a direct hit, slamming into the warhead and destroying it before a second US city was blotted from existence.
****

The President breathed a huge sigh of relief as the remaining warhead was destroyed. Without allowing himself to spend any time dwelling on the emotions of the human tragedy on the West Coast, he turned to his advisors and started issuing orders. "First, we need to get whatever government aid we can to California. Those people are going to need immediate assistance. I want FEMA to deploy immediately."

He then turned to face the image of his Secretary of Defense, who had just joined the conference call at the secured bunker. "Jim, what are we supposed to do now? Do we strike China for providing the North Koreans with the DongFeng?" the President asked.

Secretary of Defense Jim Castle heard the President's question, but he needed a minute to think through what they should do. His gut told him to nuke the two countries into the abyss, but he knew they had to be cautious right now. They had just expended nearly 80% of their land-based ballistic missile interceptors. They couldn't adequately protect against another strike like this one.

"Mr. President," he began, "the North Koreans just launched twenty-three nuclear tipped missiles at South Korea and our forces there. Two of them got through our defenses and probably killed and injured over 300,000 people. We need to counter that attack with a severe nuclear response of our own. We cannot allow another nation to use nukes against us or our allies; it will not go unpunished."

219

"Furthermore, the B-2 that is currently carrying the B61 guided nuclear bombs should hit the North Koreans with the maximum yield these bombs can inflict. A message needs to be sent. Now, the second strike is a completely different matter. It is now apparent that China provided the North Koreans with ten Chinese-made ICBMs. They may not have launched the missiles, but they're just as complicit in the annihilation of Oakland and the near-destruction of nine other American cities. That cannot go unanswered. The challenge is—how do we respond to that? Do we nuke one of their cities in response? Do we carry out a first strike against them and attempt to wipe out their nuclear missile capability?"

Castle sighed loudly, taking it all in, then continued, "We also have to keep in mind that we just expended a large percentage of our ballistic missile interceptors. If the Chinese respond by launching a counterstrike against us, we're most likely not going to be able to stop it. We could lose dozens of additional cities," he cautioned.

The group discussed what to do, with several factions arguing for a first strike against China. Another faction argued for a limited strike, hitting one of China's cities in exchange for the destruction of Oakland. After taking a few minutes in private to think the scenarios over, the President made his decision.

Chapter 41
Retaliation and Retribution

Misawa Air Base, Japan

Lieutenant Colonel Tyler Scott's aircraft had just returned to Misawa Air Base, Japan after a successful bombing run over North Korea. They had delivered a series of bunker busting bombs against several suspected nuclear missile sites. As he taxied his B-2 to their hardened bunker, a voice came over the radio.

"Don't shut down the engines!" the voice ordered. "You're going to do a hot refuel and rearm for an emergency mission."

Their emergency alert message came alive and spat out their new orders. The two pilots looked at each other; this wasn't something either of them had expected, though they had trained for this very scenario their entire careers. The EAM system was only used in cases of extreme emergency, or to issue the use of nuclear weapons.

Major Bryan Jordan looked at the code and pulled out his code book. He compared the numbers and confirmed it was a valid code. They then looked at the message to see what their new orders were. After they read the message, they both sat back in their seats for a second, digesting what they had just been ordered to do. Meanwhile, the ordnance teams outside the aircraft wheeled out a B-83 nuclear bomb. This was the largest nuclear bomb still in the US arsenal, with a combined yield of 1.2 megatons. They could see their fuel gauge now read half-full; they would be ready to head to their target shortly.

Then, a voice came over the radio. "Ghost Nine, this is Control. Do you copy?" asked their commander.

"This is Ghost Nine, we copy, Control," Lieutenant Colonel Scott responded.

"Ghost Nine, stand by for the SecDef," the voice said. The two pilots looked at each other in surprise. They had never met or spoken with the SecDef. This was extremely unusual for someone this high on the food chain to call them directly.

"Ghost Nine, can you hear me?" asked a gravelly voice they immediately recognized.

"We copy, Sir."

"Listen up, Ghost Nine. Ten Chinese-made ICBMs were launched from North Korea at ten US cities. These were MIRV-capable missiles. We managed to intercept forty-four of the forty-five warheads. However, one detonated over the Port of Oakland. It wiped out the city and caused significant damage to San Francisco. The President has decided to retaliate against the Chinese for providing the North Koreans with these missiles. We lost one city, and we're going to wipe out one Chinese city in retaliation. One of the other B-2s is currently hitting the North Koreans with nukes in retaliation."

The two pilots looked at each other, mouths agape. They could not believe an American city had just been obliterated by a nuclear missile. This was like something out of a fiction novel, not real life. The voice of the SecDef continued, "The President and I want to wish you luck on this mission, and let you know that the entire country is depending on you."

Twenty minutes later, their aircraft was airborne and heading towards China. They took a flight path that would take them over North Korea once again. They had already wiped out the enemy's air defenses; their best chance of penetrating Chinese airspace was going to be across this border.

As they approached North Korean airspace, they received a warning that several nuclear detonations were about to happen. They closed the blinders on their windows and watched their radar scope and instruments. A few minutes later, they saw the screen white out from one, and then multiple nuclear detonations. Once they confirmed that the bombs had detonated and the flash danger was over, they opened their window screens again and saw eight mushroom clouds rising into the air.

The US had hit North Korea with eight 340-kiloton bombs, obliterating the North Korean capital along with three other cities and four military targets. The government of North Korea had been essentially wiped out, and so had the vast majority of their military leadership, command and communication systems. They were a rudderless country and military at this point.

Within seconds of the American nuclear bombs going off, the search radars all across China began to light up. They were watching to see if any US aircraft or cruise missiles were headed towards them. The *Spirit of California* moved towards its target, methodically and deliberately crossing into Chinese airspace undetected. They had already carried out six deep-strike missions in Russia and one in North Korea. Now they were testing the limits of the Chinese air defense.

It took them roughly fifty minutes to reach their target after the nuclear bombs hit Korea. They were trying to time the two strikes to happen relatively close to each other. Approaching the city at what was now 1040 hours, the pilots could see below that the metropolis below was full of life and people were early in the work day. A sinking feeling sat in the pit of their stomachs as the weight of what was about to happen started to sit on them.

When their bomber neared the drop point, they armed their nuclear bomb and prepared to release it. Without allowing themselves too much time to think, they opened their bomb bay doors and released their single bomb. They waited to turn the aircraft until the doors registered as closed, ensuring their stealth capability was still intact. Then they turned and headed back for home, having delivered America's response to the Chinese for providing the North Koreans with MIRV-capable ICBMs.
****

It took the B-83 bomb less than two minutes to fall to 3,000 feet, at which point, the arming mechanism registered that it was at the programmed altitude. It then sent the signal to detonate. The 1.2 megaton warhead exploded over the city center of Shenyang, China, the largest city in northern China with a population of 6.3 million people.

The blast wave from the explosion reached out to 10.8 miles from the epicenter, instantly killing 4.87 million people and leaving millions more terribly injured. The firestorm the explosion created would wreak havoc on the surrounding boroughs and countryside, destroying one of China's most important industrial centers.

Chapter 42
Pure Shock

Beijing, China
Central Military Commission Bunker

The ruling members of China hurried to the command bunker for yet another emergency meeting. They knew the Americans would most likely launch a preemptive attack, but what they could not anticipate was Pak Lee being dumb enough to launch his nuclear missiles at the Americans and South Koreans. They had warned him to keep the war conventional—a conventional war could have ground on for weeks, if not months, and with China and Russia's assistance, it would have led to a satisfactory outcome.

When two nuclear missiles detonated over South Korea, the Chinese knew the Americans would respond with an overwhelming nuclear response. The members of the CMC had just started the discussion of how to handle the situation when a report came in that the DPRK had launched the ten DongFeng missiles they had given them the year before, and the missiles were on trajectories that would take them to the US mainland.

Legitimate panic set in.

President Xi slammed his fist on the table and let out a long stream of obscenities that was so angry and vulgar that several men in the room blushed. "That was a terrible idea to give them those missiles!" he finally yelled when he had calmed down enough to speak in non-curse words.

"The fools have just doomed us all! The Americans will know we gave them advanced missiles, and if one of them destroys an American city, they'll take their retribution on us!" He aimed most of his shouting at the generals who had advocated to give the Koreans the missiles.

General Xu, the commander of the Chinese Air Force, calmly declared, "We have to get our defense ready for an American attack. If one of those missiles does hit an American city, the US will either go after our nuclear missile capability or they will look to hit one of our cities in retaliation. We must alert our nuclear forces immediately."

Everyone in the room looked at the President for direction.

General Kuang, the Defense Minister, spoke up before anyone else could respond. "No," he asserted. "We need to keep our alert level where it is. We need to assure the Americans that China is not a part of the Koreans' attack. That we have not coordinated with them or encouraged them to use these terrible weapons. We need the Americans to understand that we had no part in this, or they'll retaliate against us with even greater furor."

The President sighed loudly and rubbed his temples. *This is not how things were supposed to happen*, he thought. The Koreans were supposed to bog down American, South Korean, and Japanese Forces so they could carry out their annexation of Formosa.

President Xi finally looked up at his military leaders. "Here's what's going to happen. We're going to inform the Americans that we aren't coordinating a nuclear strike with the Koreans. We have no intentions of using nuclear weapons against America or anyone else, just as Russia has insisted with their ongoing war with NATO. Second, if one of those ICBMs does hit the US and an American city is wiped out, we won't respond to an American counterstrike unless it is a disproportionate response. If they lose one city and they choose to hit one of ours, we will let it stand and not retaliate. We can use it as a propaganda tool, but we will not use that as the pretext for a nuclear war, one we would undoubtedly lose."

"The Americans still have ballistic missile submarines and enough nuclear missiles to wipe our country out. We can only win a war against America if we keep it conventional. If it goes nuclear, then no one wins, and all of this will have been for nothing. This drastically hurts us, but it does not derail our current plans. Does everyone understand?" he said, looking at his military leaders with a gaze that seemed to reach through their very souls.

The men in the room just nodded.

Chapter 43
Mourn with Those Who Mourn

33,000 Feet in the Air
Undisclosed Location over the Continental US

The President's Chief of Staff had just finished working on Gate's speech with the Communications Director and Press Secretary as they prepared to present it to the boss. The press was pushing for a comment and wanted to know when and if the President would be making an address to the nation. It had been nearly four hours since the city of Oakland and most of San Francisco had been destroyed. Over a million people had been killed or injured in the blast, and nine other cities had almost been nuked as well. The public was in a panic, and the media wasn't doing anything to help the matter.

The Dow Jones Industrial Average had fallen nearly 10% in the final forty minutes of trading before it was closed to prevent a possible run on the market. When the government began to evacuate Washington, D.C., the news media immediately went to the air, informing the country that a nuclear attack against the capital and potentially other cities was underway.

People began to flee several of the major cities as fast as they could. No one knew for certain which cities had been targeted or when the nuclear missiles might arrive. Then, new reports came of several explosions occurring in the sky. Military advisors spoke out through various news networks, informing everyone that these were most likely the vaunted missile interceptors, destroying the incoming nuclear missiles.

As soon as the nuclear explosion occurred in California, word spread on both local media and social media about the detonation over Oakland. Images showed a growing mushroom cloud where the city and critical port had once been. Beyond the telltale intimidating cloud, fires were visible all throughout San Francisco, along with numerous damaged buildings. The hills surrounding the area were also ablaze, threatening nearby communities as the destruction from the bomb spread well beyond the initial blast area.

Some people posted videos from closer to the blast site on Facebook Live, Snapchat, and Twitter. The images were horrendous.

Torn, twisted, and burnt bodies could be seen everywhere. One student at UC-Berkeley was filming parts of the campus that had been destroyed by the blast. There were bodies everywhere—some alive, in agonizing pain from third-degree burns and pleading for help, some crying out for death to come, just to end their agony.

****

As the President read the draft, he nodded in approval. It was a good message, and something needed to be put out to calm the country and let them know their government was functioning and that FEMA and other emergency response services were on the way to California.

"Liam, when I'm done with this speech, I want to meet with the National Security Council. We need to discuss what to do next about China. So far, they have not responded to our nuking of Shenyang, but this was clearly an act of war committed by them," Gates said.

"All right, people, we go live in two minutes," one of the comms people announced.

Everyone who didn't need to be in the room scurried their way out while the President took several deep breaths to calm his nerves. This was possibly the most important speech of his life, and he wanted to make sure he got it right.

The camera light turned red, indicating he was now live. He looked up at the camera and began to read from the teleprompter.

"My fellow Americans, today is perhaps the saddest day in our history. Approximately four and a half hours ago, the Democratic People's Republic of Korea fired twenty-three short-range ballistic missiles at United States and Republic of Korea Forces on the Korean Peninsula. The THAAD missile defense system and several of our naval ships were able to intercept twenty-one of the missiles, destroying them before they could hit their targets. However, the US Air Force base at Kunsan was hit with a nuclear missile and subsequently destroyed. A second nuclear missile hit the Republic of Korea's Northern Air Command at Wonju, obliterating the base and the surrounding city."

He paused to let that sink in. Gates looked down for a second before continuing, trying to keep his own emotions in check. "Pak Lee then ordered his only ten inter-continental ballistic missiles to be launched at the US homeland. These missiles were highly advanced, multiple independently targetable reentry vehicle or MIRV missiles. Our

227

intelligence agencies were unaware that North Korea had these types of systems. Within minutes of these ICBMs being launched, we were able to determine that these were, in fact, Chinese-made missiles that had been provided to North Korea."

"When the missiles began their downward trajectory towards the US, the MIRVs released a total of forty-five nuclear warheads aimed at American cities. NORAD directed our ship-and-land-based missile interceptors towards the incoming threats, successfully eliminating 44 of the 45 warheads. Unfortunately, one of the warheads detonated a one-megaton nuclear explosion approximately 5,000 feet above the Port of Oakland in California." He paused for a second, genuinely choked up. He wiped a tear from his left eye before continuing.

"Our hearts go out to the families of those who have been injured or killed by this attack. I can report to you that the imminent threat of nuclear attack against our nation is now over."

"The cities that had been targeted were El Paso, New York City, Washington, D.C., Fort Hood, San Diego, Chicago, Seattle, Pearl Harbor, and Fairbanks. As of right now, there are no additional missiles headed towards the United States, and we have made it clear to both Russia and China that if any missile launches are detected from their countries at the US, we will respond with overwhelming force."

"In response to this devastating attack, I have ordered the Air Force to respond with a nuclear attack of our own. Two hours ago, the Air Force dropped eight 340-kiloton nuclear bombs on North Korea's largest four cities and four separate military targets. Because the Chinese provided Pak Lee with the advanced ICBMs that resulted in the destruction of Oakland and San Francisco, I directed the Air Force to bomb one of China's cities in retaliation. The city of Shenyang was destroyed by a 1.2-megaton nuclear bomb, the largest nuclear bomb in our inventory. I have personally informed the Chinese president that any further nuclear launches against the US or our allies would result in a crushing nuclear response from America."

"I want to assure you, the American people, that our great military is doing everything in its power to protect our nation. Our service members have suffered some horrific losses since the start of the war with Russia, and now North Korea. We must continue to support our men and women in uniform and all of those who serve our country to protect us."

"I am asking that we all come together as Americans in this tragedy, working together and supporting one another during these trying times. Please keep the people of California and our armed forces in your thoughts and prayers. For now, I wish you all good night. May God bless the United States," he said, concluding a short, but informative statement.

Now we have to figure out what to do next, he thought.
****

When the President finished his address to the nation, he headed towards the conference room to meet with the National Security Council. As he entered the room, he saw they had several video monitors up and running on the walls.

Good, it looks like everyone is here, he thought.

He took his seat and jumped right into it, asking, "What's the situation in Korea right now, and what's going on with China?"

To say McMillan was stressed was an understatement. A half-eaten bottle of Tums sat in front of him, and he briefly rubbed his chest where the pain of a possible ulcer was forming. "Our forces in the South are ready to move across the DMZ. We're holding off on sending them in while we try to make contact with whoever is still in charge in the North and see if we can convince them to surrender before we start the ground war. If we can force them into conceding, then we can save countless lives."

"The Chinese, for their part, have not moved to engage our naval battlegroup or air assets yet. I think they're trying to figure out internally how to respond to our nuking one of their cities—"

The Chairman of the Joint Chiefs, Admiral Meyers, interjected, "—We have to decide if the Chinese providing the North with MIRV-capable ICBMs constitutes an act of war, which I believe it does. If so, how are we ultimately going to respond to that?" he asked.

Secretary Johnson signaled that he wanted to speak, and the President nodded for him to proceed. "Mr. President, while I share the CJC's anger, I would argue that calmer heads should prevail. Let's see if we can get the North Koreans to surrender first. If that doesn't work, then we move forward with the ground war.... As to the Chinese, let's see what they do next. Maybe the loss of one of their largest cities will caution them against any further aggressions towards our forces or the annexation of any further countries. Keep in mind, we still have an active war going on in Europe, and we cannot afford to attack China right now."

Several of the members at the table nodded in agreement. It was sound advice, even if it was hard to accept with everyone's emotions running so high.

A moment passed as the Secretary of State's words soaked in. Then the President turned to his SecDef and asked, "When do we start to win some battles in Europe?"

All eyes turned to Secretary Castle, who smiled a devilish grin and began to explain the new strategy.

Chapter 44
Surprise Attack

Mons, Belgium
NATO Headquarters

General Cotton was fuming.

What were the Chinese thinking, giving that madman that kind of nuclear weapons' capability? he thought.

When he'd heard the US was going to respond with nuclear weapons, he had been stunned. Then he had seen the images coming from San Francisco, and he'd no longer cared about how many Chinese or North Koreans had just been vaporized by American nukes.

Just after the "incident," as the Russians were calling it, they had assured him that Russia had no intention of turning the war nuclear. They had also insisted that they had no foreknowledge of this event. To him it didn't matter if they knew in advance or not.

As long as they don't use nuclear weapons themselves, we can win this fight in Europe, thought the SACEUR confidently, pumped up with national pride and a desire to put America back on top.

The arrival of Three Corps brought 49,000 fresh soldiers to bolster the NATO army group. The addition of the 1st Infantry Division, 1st Cavalry Division, 1st Armored Division and the 4th Infantry Division brought with them battle-hardened combat veterans from Iraq and Afghanistan, along with a very combat-experienced NCO cadre—something the NATO forces desperately needed. The European units that were making up the bulk of the fighting thus far lacked any serious combat experience, and their training had done little to prepare them for the onslaught they had faced against Russia.

General Cotton looked down at the field report he'd been given several hours earlier and decided they were now ready to start a new offensive. The Navy had rushed nearly 1,600 main battle tanks to Europe, along with 3,500 infantry fighting vehicles. Together with the British, German, French, Dutch, and Polish forces, that brought his tank numbers up to nearly 4,000 main battle tanks and over 20,000 assorted infantry fighting vehicles. His troop numbers had swelled to 180,000, with fresh Reserve and National Guard units being airlifted to Europe daily from the States. He still had another 65,000 soldiers of V Corps that were re-forming in Germany, and they would be ready by the end of November.

In was now mid-October, and the war was nearly seven weeks old. If the Russians thought NATO was going to roll over and play dead, they had another thing coming. Cotton smiled mischievously at the plan he and Secretary Castle had come up with.

We're going to catch the Russians by surprise with this next move, he thought, *but the key to making it work will be getting the politicians to go along.*

The Russians had staged the 6th Tank Army in Belarus, tying down the entire Polish army from being able to commit to NATO in Ukraine. The Russians hadn't invaded the Baltic States, the presence of several Russian divisions forced him to keep the bulk of the 82nd Airborne spread across the three countries to keep the Russians in check.

While Belarus wasn't looking to become further involved in this conflict, the fact that they were allowing the Russian 6th Tank Army to set up camp in their country was keeping 90,000 troops that General Cotton needed in Ukraine tied down to defend Poland and the Baltic States should it be necessary. It was a brilliant move by the Russians, and General Cotton had had enough of it.

Everyone has a plan until they get punched in the face, Cotton thought.

As SACEUR, he brought this problem to the SecDef. He needed to get permission from the President to deal with the threat and try to end the Russian war quickly. His plan called for the Ukrainian forces in the south to hold their positions, with assistance from the Romanians; this would protect his southern flank. The 108,000 NATO soldiers near Rivne, Ukraine would conduct a feint and appear as if they were going to smash directly into the Russian lines. This would force the Russians to move additional divisions forward in order to block the allied forces' advance. Then, the US Three Corps (along with the Polish 11th Armored Cavalry Division and the 12th Mechanized Division) would launch a surprise attack on the Russian Tank Army in Belarus from Białystok, Poland in the north and a southern push from Ratne, Ukraine.

Once they had captured the Russian army group, they would advance on Minsk and then look to threaten Moscow directly. This would force the Russian army group in Ukraine to fall back and defend the capital. Then NATO could liberate Ukraine and bring an end to the war no one thought would happen. It was an audacious plan, and it just might work.

Chapter 45
Punched in the Face

Highway E67
Lithuania

Major General Paul Austin of the 4th Infantry Division was looking out the window at the countryside whipping past his vehicle as his division raced through Lithuania on their way to Vilnius, the capital city. It was still dark, but he could make out some buildings and petrol stations just off the deserted E67 Highway as they drove along.

He had nearly 2,000 vehicles in his column, snaking across twelve miles of the highway. The decision had been made the day before to change the invasion of Belarus slightly and have his division race north into Lithuania so they could make a more direct move on Minsk. His 11,000-man division was going to try and capture Belarus' capital, and then seal off any possible retreat of the Russian 6th Tank Army.

Following General Austin's division into Belarus would be service members from the Lithuanian army. They would be responsible for the occupation and garrison duty once the primary objectives had been achieved. They spoke the language, unlike the Americans, and shared more of a common history and culture since both countries were former Soviet republics.

Austin's division had been on the road now for nearly five hours, but they still had close to 40 kilometers to travel before they reached the outskirts of the city and then made their way to the jump-off point. They were going to cross the border at Medininkai on the E26 Highway, which would lead directly to Minsk, 155 kilometers away. He looked down at his watch.

The rest of Three Corps and the Polish army should be crossing into Belarus right about now, starting the new offensive, he thought.

At 0700 hours, his division began to roll through the tiny border town of Medininkai, with a population of 528, when they spotted the first sign of enemy activity. A small contingent of armored vehicles and soldiers was gathered along the road. They must have been very nervous at the sight of hundreds of American military vehicles amassing not far from their position.

General Austin could see enemy soldiers scrambling to get in their vehicles and race away from the border. They knew they were outmatched—his division had 62 M1A2 Abrams battle tanks, 96 Bradley fighting vehicles, and 126 Stryker vehicles. They also had an artillery brigade for direct fire support. His forces were ready to pounce; now they just had to wait until it was time.

As they approached the border, he deployed his scouts and forward observers to start getting eyes on possible enemy units they may encounter. Soon he had scouts as deep as 40 kilometers inside Belarus. Shortly, the action would pick up and he would lead his division in a mad race to capture the capital city of Minsk.

What an exciting time to be a soldier, he thought.

****

"Viking Five, this is Hammer Three. We have three T-80 tanks and six BTRs at grid Golf Kilo 743 597. Do we have permission to engage? Over," asked Sergeant First Class Tim Hanse.

His forward observer platoon had crossed the Belarus border nearly two hours ago, slowly moving along various dirt roads towards possible enemy positions. They had been shown several potential enemy positions via satellite reconnaissance and were tasked with getting eyes on them. His platoon had split up into squads to cover more ground as they tried to find targets for the guns.

His squad had found about a company-sized element located at Palyany, roughly thirty kilometers from the border, just where the satellite photos had said they would be. Now it was up to the folks at Division to determine if they wanted to blow them up now or let them live a little longer.

The radio chirped briefly. "Hammer Three, this is Viking Five. We copy. Proceed with fire mission, over."

Sergeant First Class Hanse smiled; they had been given permission to engage. He looked at the coordinates one of the soldiers had given him, and briefly nodded. "Viking Five, this is Hammer Three. Requesting three rounds, HE at grid Golf Kilo 743 597. Fire for effect. How copy?"

A second later, they responded and read the fire mission back to him. He acknowledged, and they stood by, waiting for the rounds to impact, ready to adjust fire as needed.

A couple of minutes later, the radio crackled to life again. "Shot out."

After another pause, the radio came to life again. "Splash," said the voice, indicating the rounds were about to impact.

"Copy that," Hanse responded, and they waited for the sound of the incoming rounds.

Suddenly, a sound like a freight train raced over their heads as the artillery rounds began to fly in and saturate the area they had called in. One of the tanks took a direct hit, and so did two of the BTRs. Several others had been damaged. Most of the troops near the tanks dropped to the ground. The survivors of the initial blasts immediately ran to their vehicles, knowing all too well that they needed to move to a new location.

Sergeant First Class Hanse called in a second fire mission—this time destroying nearly all the remaining vehicles and flattening this small village in the process. As the buildings and vehicles lay in ruins, oily black smoke rose into the air. Sergeant Hanse's scout group got in their two Humvees and drove to their next location, continuing to scout for their artillery brigade.

Chapter 46
Reinforcements

Moscow, Russia
National Defense Management Center

General Boris Egorkin was reading through the reports coming in from Ukraine and Belarus. It would appear that NATO was launching an all-out ground offensive against their forces in Ukraine and had now opted to invade the peace-loving people of Belarus.

The 6th Tank Army commander was reporting contact with Polish and American ground forces. As he looked at the map, he could clearly see what SACEUR was trying to do. He was hoping to cut off the 6th Army and capture Minsk. This would force him to withdraw his forces from Ukraine to defend Moscow.

Before President Petrov arrived, he sent a quick message to his commander in Belarus. "Have your forces fall back to the outskirts of Minsk," he directed.

We're not going to allow ourselves to get surrounded and cut off, no matter what, he determined.

While he was mulling over possible military responses, the President walked in and sat at the head of the conference table. "What is going on in Belarus?" he asked. "How does this change our plans?"

General Egorkin responded first. "Mr. President, General Cotton, the SACEUR, has devised a plan to try and force us out of Ukraine by threatening Moscow."

Petrov raised an eyebrow at that response. The Minister of Defense, Alexei Semenov, replied, "I believe Comrade Egorkin is getting a bit ahead of himself with that statement. The Americans have launched a multipronged attack across Ukraine and now into Belarus. The 6th Tank Army had been tying down too many NATO forces while it was deployed to Belarus. They're now moving to encircle the army group and then capture Minsk and remove that threat."

Egorkin was not one to back down when he knew he was right; he jumped right back into the conversation. "Comrades, if NATO secures Minsk, where do you think they will move next? The obvious answer is Moscow. If they look to threaten Moscow, then I'll have to pull most of my forces out of Ukraine to defend the capital. That is what they're going to do. The question is—how do we stop them from doing that?" he asked.

Petrov leaned back in his chair for a second, thinking what to do next. *Since that fool in North Korea used nuclear weapons against US and South Korean forces, using them here in Europe is completely out of the question*, he realized. The American president had proven to everyone that he wasn't afraid to retaliate with them either. *No, we'll have to find another way.*

"What forces can we draw from that we wouldn't take away from General Egorkin's forces?" asked Petrov.

General Alexei Semenov thought for a minute while the others at the table looked at him, waiting for his response. "We have the 16th Spetsnaz brigade, which we have not deployed yet…we can rush them to Belarus. We can also move the 76th Guard's Air Assault Division from Pskov, and the 106th Guard's Airborne Division from Tula. Those two divisions and the brigade would give us an additional 26,000 soldiers that can rapidly deploy to Minsk. We can have them there within 72-hours. Shoot, the Spetsnaz brigade can get in position within twenty-four hours, once we give them the go."

Petrov raised a hand to interject a comment. "That addresses the short-term need of getting forces into Belarus, but how are we going to address the bigger problem of stopping NATO from capturing the country and then threatening Moscow? Unless we heavily reinforce the 6th Tank Army, they're going to be in trouble."

General Semenov responded, "I recommend we move the 90th Guard's Tank Division from Chebarkul in central Russia, along with the reserve forces we've been mobilizing since the start of the war. We should also have the Air Force start to hit NATO ground forces with a lot more cruise missiles. We need to bombard them constantly from the air, so we can keep the pressure on them."

Semenov took a breath and then continued, "The Chinese are going to attack the Americans within the next 24 hours. When that happens, the Americans won't be able to support and sustain NATO *and* their forces deployed on the Korean Peninsula. They just don't have the sealift capability or the personnel."

"That is partially true," Petrov corrected. "The Americans are conscripting a massive army, and they'll be able to deploy hundreds of thousands of soldiers by February 2018. The Chinese have to take the

Americans out of the war quickly, and that is not something I am confident they can do."

Chapter 47
Missile Swarm

20,000 Feet Above Tangshan, China

Major Chen's squadron of H-6 bombers, which were essentially Russian Badger bombers, were now entering their maximum range for their anti-ship cruise missiles as they flew over the city of Tangshan. Off in the distance, the pilots of his squadron could still see the orange glow at the edge of the horizon from the destruction of Shenyang. It boiled his blood to know that such a great and beautiful city had been so violently taken from them. His squadron, along with the rest of the H-6 bomber squadrons, would now exact China's revenge on the Americans who had killed so many of his countrymen.

Their bombers were each carrying two YJ-12 "Eagle Strike 12" anti-ship cruise missiles. The YJ-12 had a maximum range of 400 kilometers and carried a 551-pound high-explosive semi-armor-piercing warhead. The missiles could also travel at speeds of Mach 3.2 if launched from high altitude, making them very hard to hit. The Chinese Air Force had learned from the Russians the swift effectiveness of a missile swarm, and they planned on hitting the Americans with them as often as possible.

Twenty-eight hours had passed since the Americans had destroyed the city of Shenyang, and they were still determining how many people had been killed there. Initial estimates had placed the casualties somewhere between four and five million. The people of China had been shocked and then terrified when news had broken of the city being bombed by a nuclear weapon. Then, as the images of the devastation—the dead bodies littered everywhere, and others with horrific wounds—began to circulate on social media, anger began to boil over. People took to the streets, demanding the government retaliate.

As Major Chen's bomber droned on, they moved ever closer to the American battlegroup, which was in the process of steaming away from the Yellow Sea back towards Japan. When they had moved to within 300 kilometers of them, they started to detect the powerful American search radars. Several of the advanced reconnaissance aircraft turned on their own potent search radars and began to feed the targeting data back to their squadron. Chen's weapons officer programed the missiles and let him know they were ready for launch.

A voice came over the radio to the squadron. "Everyone, prepare to fire your missiles."

It was a very tense 60 seconds until the voice from the radio commanded them, "Fire all missiles and return to base!"

Chen's weapons officer followed the order, letting loose the cruise missiles on board. Seconds later, Chen felt the aircraft lift slightly as the weight of those missiles was suddenly released from his wings. He saw the flashes as the rocket motors started and the YJ-12s approached their cruising speed.

He nodded in satisfaction; all his missiles had been successfully launched without incident or failure. Then Chen turned the aircraft and headed back to their base, presumably to rearm for another mission.

Chapter 48
Ambushed

Yellow Sea

Commander Paul Jensen was on his last deployment with the Navy before he planned on retiring. This was his third deployment as the Captain of the USS *Howard*, and while he loved the Navy and would probably be selected for captain O-6, his wife and family were done with the long deployments and moving every three or four years. His kids were going to start high school soon, and his wife had told him in no uncertain terms that it was important for them to be able to settle down and stay in one place for a while. He knew she was right, and it would be best for the kids if he retired, but he loved the Navy. To be in command of a warship on the high seas was the most rewarding professional experience of his life. Still, he loved his family, so Jensen had determined that when he returned from this deployment, he was going to see if he could perhaps find a desk job that would allow him to spend four or more years on shore duty, at least until his kids could finish high school.

When the war in Europe had broken out, Commander Jensen had seen it as an opportunity to serve his country one more time before retirement. When the 6th Fleet had been sunk by the Russians during the opening hours of the war, he'd felt simultaneously glad that he hadn't been assigned to the Atlantic fleet and angry that so many of his colleagues had been killed and he wouldn't get a chance to avenge their deaths. However, just as he'd thought his ship might end up sitting out the war, tensions had rapidly escalated on the Korean Peninsula. It looked like Jensen and his ship, the USS *Howard*, would get their chance to fight after all.

Just as Commander Jensen was gearing up for battle, orders came down from General Bennet and the 7th Fleet Commander to change course. He received a FLASH message, which read, "All ships withdraw from the Yellow Sea immediately and proceed to the Sea of Japan. Abort amphibious assault missions and move forward with alternate battle plan B-11. Possible retaliation by the Chinese forces for attack at Shenyang imminent. Move at the maximum speed that can be maintained while continuing to sail in formation."

Jensen had felt a huge letdown after receiving this message, but he had changed course as ordered. It was still early in the morning, and Commander Jensen poured himself another cup of coffee from the hot plate in the combat information center. As Commander Jensen lifted the hot liquid to his lips, he thought, *God, I just hope we live through the next week.*

The USS *Howard* had continued to screen the right rear flank of the 7th Fleet as they moved out of the Yellow Sea. Any action could not be ignored at this point. All the radar operators were extremely tired after pulling extra shifts.

Petty Officer Maria Ramirez rubbed her eyes briefly and then looked back at the computer display she had been monitoring as if trying to make sure her eyes weren't playing tricks on her.

At first, her screen just showed one large Chinese aircraft. Her systems identified it as an H-6, which meant it was a bomber, but it was alone. That would mean that it was most likely a reconnaissance aircraft monitoring their fleet. Then, as the aircraft moved closer to them, a new group of contacts appeared. Her eyes grew wide as saucers as she counted them. She immediately raised her hand to get the attention of the watch officer.

"What have you got for us, Ramirez?" the watch officer asked as he approached her console.

"Sir, a mass of aircraft just came into our radar range," she responded, showing him her screen.

The watch officer's eyes got a little wider, and he became nervous at what this might be. He immediately told Ramirez, "Move your screen to the big board in the CIC so everyone can see what we're seeing."

As the display screen changed, Commander Jensen put his coffee down and examined the big board. He counted more than 60 Xian H-6 bombers, along with several reconnaissance aircraft in the lead.

This is not a drill, he realized. *The Chinese are launching a raid against the battlegroup.*

He turned to his communications officer. "I'm sure the rest of the fleet is seeing this," he said, "but send a FLASH message, alerting them of a possible raid."

Commander Jensen got the attention of his XO. "Bring the ship to Condition One. Sound battle stations for probable air attack," he ordered.

Nearly five minutes went by as the Chinese aircraft continued to move closer to the fleet. They were still outside of their engagement envelope, so they needed to wait for them to get a little nearer before they could attack them with their missiles.

While the Chinese bombers continued to move closer to the fleet, the carriers' combat air patrol was being vectored towards the bombers, and additional aircraft were being scrambled. It looked like Admiral Kinkaid wasn't waiting for the Chinese to fire a missile before he scrambled both carriers' air wings.

Suddenly, the USS *Howard* detected that the lead reconnaissance aircraft had turned on its powerful search radars.

One of the electronic warfare officers yelled, "They're going to start targeting us and every other ship in the fleet! Start jamming the enemy signals and prepare the ship's defensive systems!"

Less than a minute after they were targeted, the first cruise missiles began to appear. At first it was just a handful, then the numbers steadily rose, until there were 120 anti-ship missiles headed towards the battlegroup. As if things couldn't get worse, they received a FLASH message from NORAD letting them know they detected the launch of eighteen ballistic missiles. These were most likely the famed "carrier killer missiles," judging by where they were launched from.

Captain Jensen jumped out of his seat and began issuing orders. "Engage the incoming missiles with our SM-2s once they get in range. Start having our SM-6s engage their carrier killer missiles. We need to try and take them out while they're still in their first phase of launch," he directed, hoping they might be able to get lucky and take a couple of them out.

Jensen grabbed the mic as he addressed his bridge crew. "Bridge, CIC. Move the ship to flank speed and have us tighten up our position with the rest of the fleet for defense."

He could feel the power from the ship surge as the engines approached their peak capability, driving them closer to the rest of the fleet and what he hoped was mutual protection. Thirty seconds later, the first of a series of SM-6 missile interceptors fired from their magazine towards the carrier killer missiles.

Please, Lord, let this work, he prayed. *We can't lose another carrier after the* Bush.

Minutes seemed to tick by as they stared at the big board, watching the cruise missiles bear down on the battlegroup. They were just about to enter their SM-2 engagement range. At that point, they would most likely empty their entire magazine as they attempted to swat the missiles from the sky.

While Commander Jensen knew it was coming, the sudden firing of their entire battery of missiles, one every second until all 67 missiles in the battery were exhausted, still startled him.

The sky above and around the battlegroup was filling with missile interceptors as the other destroyers and cruisers added their own ordnance to the conflagration. The carriers' air wings would soon be going after the cruise missiles as well. It was now a race to see how many missiles they could take out before the enemy scored some hits.

****

The sea was a bit choppy as the USS *Carl Vinson* moved with the waves, causing Captain Michael Richards to work a little harder to balance his coffee a bit more than normal. He had just finished a cold cut sandwich the galley had brought up to the bridge crew when they received a FLASH message from one of the destroyers. He took the paper from the petty officer and quickly read it.

So, they're finally coming for us, eh? thought Richards. *Well, we'll make them pay for it.*

He immediately turned to his executive officer and said, "Sound general quarters for a probable air attack. Order the CAG to get his aircraft airborne and intercept those bombers. If the Chinese bombers fire off their cruise missiles before our fighters can intercept them, then have our fighters attempt to engage the missiles before they hit our air-defense screen," he ordered.

Following the destruction of the *George H.W. Bush* strike group in the Black Sea, the Navy had implemented an immediate change in strategy to combat future potential missile swarm attacks. They had removed nearly all the Tomahawk cruise missiles from the carriers' destroyer escorts and replaced them with additional SM-2 missile interceptors.

245

For the Pacific fleets, they'd also added SM-3 and SM-6 missiles to the destroyers. This would help them counter the possibility of the Chinese or North Koreans using ballistic missiles. It looked like those decisions might just save the fleet.

"XO, you have the bridge. I'm heading down to CIC with the admiral," Captain Richards said.

The XO nodded and responded, "XO has the bridge, sir."

While the captain was walking out, he saw a flurry of activity as everyone on the bridge put on their helmets and flak vests.

Even after Richards had left the room, the crew on the bridge continued their preparations. The armored blinders soon covered the bridge windows--they didn't need to see to steer the ship, and this move would help ensure flying shrapnel didn't explode into the bridge, damaging equipment or injuring sailors. The carrier then turned slightly to angle itself into the wind, providing the alert fighters more lift during their takeoffs.

The roar of jet engines increased steadily until the air sounded like it was filled with a very loud rushing wind. Multiple alert fighters went to afterburners, getting themselves airborne.

Dozens of crew members moved the next set of fighters to the catapults, while others worked to bring additional aircraft to the flight deck from the hangars below. It was a mad flurry of activity on the flight deck as the crews worked to get the carrier's air wing into the air to intercept the enemy bombers, or at least the cruise missiles that they would certainly launch.

As Captain Richards moved from the bridge down into the gangway that would lead him to the CIC, he could see dozens of sailors running to and fro, heading to their various battle stations. Several of the sailors yelled, "Make a hole!" as he continued to walk past them on his way to the CIC.

When he walked into the CIC, he saw it was abuzz with activity. Admiral Lomas was on the radio, presumably talking with Vice Admiral Dan Kinkaid, the 7th Fleet Commander, who was aboard the USS *Blueridge*, the command and control ship that was sailing at the center of the battlegroup, flanked by the *Carl Vinson* and the *Reagan* carriers.

"Captain! The Hawkeyes are reporting the Chinese recon birds have activated their targeting search radars. We're being painted by them!" yelled one of the chief petty officers who had been manning one

246

of the countless radar screens. A second later, the same petty officer announced to the group, "Vampires, Vampires, Vampires! We have missile launches from the bombers."

Everyone in the CIC tensed up at the announcement, even though they had all expected it when they saw the formation of bombers.

"What type of missiles are they shooting at us?" demanded Admiral Lomas, who had concluded his call with the 7th Fleet Commander.

"Sir, they appear to be YJ-12 'Eagle Strikes,'" responded the chief petty officer.

Those are going to be incredibly hard to shoot down, he thought, remembering that those missiles could reach speeds in excess of Mach 3.

Another radar operator, who had been monitoring the Chinese shoreline, yelled out, "Vampires, Vampires, Vampires! We have coastal missiles inbound from Yancheng and Qingdao!"

One of the battle managers quickly moved to the petty officer calling out the new threats. "How many missiles are we looking at?" he asked.

Many of the officers turned to hear what the petty officer would say in response. "The computer is still tallying…" he began. "There are 350 missiles coming in from the coastal area."

At first, no one said anything, almost ignoring the fact that 350 additional missiles had been fired at the fleet. Then they quickly went back to their collective tasks of vectoring missile interceptors, aircraft and other defensive systems towards the incoming threats.

Every few minutes, the men and women in the CIC could hear the roar of aircraft taking off from the flight deck above them. The CAG was working hard to get his aircraft airborne as quickly as possible.

In addition to the fighters, they were scrambling several of the EA-18G Growlers. These were the Navy's electronic warfare aircraft and would be pivotal in defeating the incoming missiles. The fighters below-decks were being equipped with additional AIM-9X Block II Sidewinder missiles to assist in going after the incoming cruise missiles. It was a race against time to get enough missile interceptors and aircraft in the air to take those threats out before they started to hit the fleet.

Another petty officer manning one of communications terminals added to the growing noise level, shouting above everyone else, "Captain! We just received a FLASH message from NORAD. They've detected multiple ballistic missile launches originating from China."

The admiral turned his head towards the petty officer, and before the captain had a chance, he asked, "Do we know what type of missiles those are?"

The room suddenly grew a little quieter as everyone waited for the petty officer to respond. "Yes, Sir. NORAD says they appear to be the Dong-Feng anti-ship ballistic missile."

Everyone sat there stunned for a second, trying to figure out what to do next. These missiles were practically impossible to hit once they began their terminal attack. They could reach speeds of Mach 25 and dive straight down on their target, as opposed to flying in an arching trajectory.

They'll have to be intercepted by a missile, since the CIWS can't turn vertical, Captain Richards realized.

One of the targeting officers picked up the phone receiver next to his terminal. He listened to the information being relayed to him and then hung up. He turned to face the admiral and captain, explaining, "Captain, I just received a message from the missile defense group in South Korea. The THAADs are starting to engage the ballistic missiles now."

Thank God we have the THAADs. I hope they can take them out before they hit any of our carriers, thought Admiral Lomas.

"Have the ships in the fleet start to take evasive maneuvers once those ballistic missiles are less than five minutes away from impact. We need to make it as hard as possible for them to zero in on us," the admiral told one of the action officers, who rushed off to send the message out to the ship commanders.

The next ten minutes went by agonizingly slow as they watched the fleet's SM-2s begin to intercept the incoming missiles. The number of threats was thinning out; only 197 of the original 470 missiles remained. Now it was time for the carriers' air wings to start their attacks.

The Hornets swooped in and began to fire off their barrage of AIM-9X Sidewinders. The heat-seeker missiles immediately went after the Chinese missiles, which were now maneuvering themselves to evade the new threat. The challenge was that these new YJ-12 were incredibly fast, reaching speeds of more than Mach 3. The Sidewinders essentially had one chance to hit an enemy missile before they ran out of speed.

As the enemy missiles closed to within fifteen miles of the battlegroup, it was now time for the five-inch guns and other close-in support systems like the Mk 57 Sea Sparrow and the RIM-116 to take over. By this time, the missiles had been thinned down again from 197 to 63, which was unfortunately far too many for the CIWS to destroy. The fleet was going to take some hits.

In seconds, the fleet's CIWS began to spit out thousands of rounds, creating a wall of lead as the missiles zeroed in on nearly every ship in the fleet, including the *Carl Vinson*. While this was taking place, the THAADs had successfully intercepted twelve of the eighteen anti-ship ballistic missiles; the SM-3s took out two more. That left four of them still heading towards the fleet, most likely towards the *Carl Vinson* and the *Ronald Reagan*.

The crew manning the CIC heard the familiar yet terrifying sound of fabric being torn. The carrier's CIWS came to life as it spat out thousands of rounds to destroy the incoming missiles.

Suddenly, four nearly simultaneous explosions shook the ship violently. Alarm bells went off in the CIC, indicating the ship had taken damage in a number of areas. Then, two more blasts could be heard and felt. They had been hit again.

"Damage report, now!" yelled the captain to one of his officers manning the engineering monitors.

"Sir, it looks like we took one hit at the waterline on the port side. Crews are working to seal off the damaged corridors and decks. We took two more hits in the hangar deck, and one hit near the rear elevator. One of those last two impacts nailed the superstructure and the front elevator...it looks like the bridge is a total loss," the damage control officer said in a shaky voice. The reality set in that many of their friends and colleagues who had been working on the bridge several floors above them had just been killed.

"What's the status of those incoming ballistic missiles?" the captain asked next.

"They're almost to us. Not sure if they're targeting us or not," responded one of the radar operators. The crew nearby was nervous as they waited to see if the next missiles would hit them or not.

Admiral Lomas called out to one of the radar operators who was monitoring the incoming missiles, "How many missiles hit the battlegroup, and did we lose anyone?"

"Sir, it appears the battlegroup took around 63 missile hits. The fleet tracking system shows every ship in the fleet has been hit by at least one missile. It looks like three of the destroyers have been sunk, along with one of the *Ticonderoga* cruisers. The *Reagan* took six hits, but still appears to be functioning, and the *Blueridge* took four hits. She's on fire, but they believe they can bring it under control."

Everything was happening so fast, yet it felt like they were seeing everything in slow motion. Hundreds of sailors had just been killed or injured and there was little the admiral could do to stop it. It saddened and angered him all at the same time.

"*This must have been what Admiral Munch felt like when his carrier was sinking*," he thought.

As the crew of the *Carl Vinson* worked feverishly to get the damage and fires under control, they heard a thunderous boom. One of the ballistic missiles had plowed into the center of the USS *Blueridge*, the 7th Fleet command and control ship. Crew members on the upper decks saw a massive fireball expand upwards and outwards from the explosion. Then the ship started to split in half as the hull broke apart from the numerous hits it had sustained. Within minutes, the vessel would slip beneath the waves with hundreds of crew members still aboard.

While the men and women were observing the destruction of the *Blueridge*, a roar came in from above. All of a sudden, the *Carl Vinson* shook violently, throwing most of the crew to the floor.

One of the ballistic missiles had just landed near the front part of the carrier deck, just behind the catapults. It threw shrapnel across the deck, killing or seriously injuring the deck crew with the flying shards of metal. The missile's semi-armor-piercing warhead, coupled with the kinetic energy of traveling at Mach 25, drove the missile through eight decks of the ship before it finally exploded its 1,100-pound warhead. Less than a second after the first ballistic missile hit the ship, a second one plowed into the *Carl Vinson*, hitting the rear half of the flight deck further back.

Captain Richards was thrown to the floor along with nearly every sailor who wasn't seated in the CIC when the ballistic missiles hit.

The lights in the CIC briefly flickered out as sparks shot out from several cable sections that had split open. A couple of large TV monitors crashed to the floor from the sudden jolt, adding their own crashing sound and additional sparks. A small fire started as some of the papers near one of the exposed wires lit up like kindling. The CIC filled with smoke as the fires spread.

As the emergency lights flickered on, Captain Richards placed his hands in front of his body and began to lift himself off the floor. He looked over and saw Admiral Lomas sitting in his chair, a dark red blotch growing across the front of his uniform. He staggered over to the admiral and saw a small piece of metal had pierced his stomach, and blood was oozing around the wound.

At least he's unconscious, thought Captain Richards. *He would be in a world of pain if he were awake.*

"Corpsman! I need a corpsman!" the captain yelled to anyone in the room. A couple of sailors came over to him and saw the condition the admiral was in. He needed medical attention quickly.

"Sir, please step aside," said a corpsman as he began to examine the admiral. After just a moment, he looked up at the captain. "We need to get him down to medical. I need some people to help me carry him down." He pointed to a couple of sailors and then directed them to get one of the medical stretchers.

The sailors carefully moved the admiral from his chair and placed him on the stretcher while the corpsman set up an IV. A young ensign led the way, yelling for people to make a hole for the admiral. Crew members who had been running throughout the corridor paused to let the stretcher with the admiral through.

Once the admiral was carried out of the CIC, Captain Richards immediately turned his focus back to the emergency at hand. "Damage report! How badly have we been hit?" he demanded.

Before he got an answer, one of the chief petty officers grabbed the fire extinguisher from the wall mount and quickly put out a small fire that had started in the CIC. Then he opened a doorway leading to a hallway, to let the smoke escape the confines of the CIC.

The engineering officer was on the phone receiving an update when she covered the mouthpiece and turned towards the captain. "Sir, it's not good. It looks like the missiles punched through roughly eight decks before they exploded. We have fires spreading throughout the

251

ship, and one of the fires is headed directly for the magazine room," she responded with a grim face.

Another phone rang, this one at Richard's station. He quickly picked it up. "This is the captain. Go ahead."

"Sir, this is the lower deck damage control room. I've been trying to get through to CIC to give my report. I need to let you know that we're taking on a lot of water. We had several of the lower decks sealed that had been hit from the cruise missiles, but that last missile that hit us busted open several new areas. We're trying to control the flooding right now, but I need your permission to seal off the lower two decks of the ship if we're going to save her," the officer said, almost pleading for someone to give him orders on what to do.

"How many men are still down in the lower decks, Lieutenant?" demanded the captain. He wasn't about to seal them off until he knew all his people were out of there.

"I don't know, Captain. A lot of those decks are flooded. It could be a handful, it could be a couple dozen. If we don't seal them off now though, the water is going to make its way to the decks above them, and if the flooding makes it to deck three, we're toast. That would expose half the ship to flooding, with no way to seal it off," he replied.

Richards stood there for a second, trying to think. This was a nightmare scenario.

What if I still have sailors down there, desperately trying to get out? he worried.

He knew he had to save the ship though. "Seal the lower decks, Lieutenant," he ordered. "Do what you need to do to save the ship. Keep us apprised of what you're doing." Then he hung up the phone.

He waved his senior engineering officer over and explained what had just transpired. Seeing that there was nothing left he could do in CIC, Captain Richards left and headed to the flight deck to survey the damage and see how he could help. He wanted to see the damage to his carrier and the rest of the battlegroup for himself, and he couldn't do that while bottled up in the CIC.

As he was on his way out, he saw several stretchers coming in from the flight deck. He ran over and helped hold the door open so another sailor could assist in carrying the wounded sailors to medical. Then he proceeded out onto the flight deck.

What he saw was sickening. There was a huge hole in the center of the flight deck, just behind the catapults, and several demolished aircraft nearby. Turning, he looked aft and saw a second gaping hole with flames and thick black smoke rising from the cauldron of death that had been created by the enemy missile. As the captain surveyed the damage, he saw dozens upon dozens of brave sailors manning fire hoses, trying to put the massive flames out.

There were also bodies everywhere. Some sailors were missing legs or arms. People all over the place were crying out for help, begging for their loved ones as they wailed in agonizing pain. Some of them obviously knew they were in the process of dying.

Richards walked over to a young sailor, who was trying to apply pressure on the chest of a fellow seaman who had a terrible gash. He saw the young woman crying as she desperately tried to stop the blood soaking through the bandage she had applied. Then he saw that she had been injured as well. She had a small gash on her forehead that was bleeding badly, and was cradling one of her arms like she had broken it.

He knelt next to her, pulled out a bandage from a first aid bag she had sitting next to her, and applied additional pressure to the wound of the man on the ground.

Captain Richards told her, "I'll take over with him until a corpsman can help. Go ahead and get a bandage on your forehead."

He yelled out to a couple of corpsmen who had just run out to the flight deck, getting their attention. When they saw it was the captain hailing them, they quickly ran to him. He directed them to take care of the sailor with the chest wound and told the young woman to follow them down to medical and get her arm taken care of.

Then Captain Richards got up and made his way to the edge of the flight deck so he could survey the rest of the fleet around them. He looked off to the right and saw that the USS *Reagan* must have been hit by multiple ballistic missiles; nearly the entire flight deck appeared to be in flames and the ship looked to be dead in the water. Everywhere he looked, ships were on fire, billowing thick black smoke into the air. Many of the ships were dead in the water, while others still managed somehow to keep themselves moving.

Captain Richards turned around to examine his own ship. The superstructure where the bridge had once been was now a twisted metal hulk with flames licking around the few undamaged parts.

We've lost the 7th Fleet, Richards realized. *We've lost the* Reagan, *and I may still end up losing the* Vinson...
****

Following the Chinese attack, the carrier *Carl Vinson*, along with four destroyers and one cruiser, were able to limp away to the protection of the Japanese Navy. While the *Carl Vinson* had survived, the damage to the flight deck, hangars and superstructure would require months, if not years to repair. The *Reagan* and the *Blueridge* were sunk, along with three *Ticonderoga* cruisers and fourteen *Arleigh Burke* destroyers. The 7th Fleet Commander and 13,200 other sailors had lost their lives, and another 7,000 were injured. This was a crippling blow to the US and would leave Japan vulnerable to the Chinese Navy until additional naval assets reached them.

Chapter 49
Air Force One Has Landed

Killeen, Texas
Fort Hood

After 32 hours in the air and four midair refuelings, the President directed the Secret Service to find a safe place to land the aircraft so they could resupply it and begin to get things back to normal with his regular briefings and staff.

When the ICBMs had been launched at Washington, the President had suddenly found himself separated from nearly his entire staff. While Air Force One had an exceptional communications array and the ability to hold any level of classified briefings, it could not replace the sidebar or one-on-one meetings and discussions he needed to have with his staff.

The military, along with the Secret Service, had determined that it was probably safe to land, since the Chinese hadn't launched any ICBMs at the US following the nuking of Shenyang. It was determined that Air Force One would set down at Fort Hood, Texas, for the time being, until it was safe to return to Washington.

The sprawling base could be easily defended and still had a contingent of nearly 12,000 soldiers. Once the aircraft had been refueled and resupplied, it would be moved to the runway and made ready to take off again, should the need to get the President airborne quickly again arise.

The civilian side of the airport had been shut down, and a plethora of additional security had been added to the surrounding area. The Air Force was also flying combat aircraft near the base for added protection. As Air Force One pulled to a halt on the military side of the airfield, a chair truck moved up to the aircraft so the President could walk down and get back to the business of running the country on the ground.

When the outer door opened, several Secret Service members emerged and surveyed the area around the aircraft. They descended the stairway, and the President emerged and followed suit. The Army had sent over several Stryker vehicles to take Gates to the command building, along with a contingent of Special Forces. The armored convoy was also being escorted by several attack helicopters and additional Blackhawk helicopters. No one was going to attack the President on this installation if the base commander had any say in the matter.

"Mr. President, it's a pleasure to meet you, sir," said Lieutenant General John Abrams as he extended a hand in greeting. "If you will please come with me, we can ride together in the Stryker," he directed. Abrams was the commander of US 1st Army, the Army command responsible for mobilization, readiness, and training, which had now become a critical command as the Army was in the process of increasing in size substantially.

The President reached out and shook the general's hand, smiling warmly at him. "Thank you, General, for meeting me here and for allowing us to land at your base. I don't think I could have taken any more hours cooped up in that plane." Both men smiled and briefly laughed, breaking some of the tension they were both feeling.

The President ducked his head slightly as he climbed inside the back of the Stryker vehicle.

So, this is what our men and women ride into battle, he thought.

As he got himself situated in the vehicle, a couple of his Secret Service agents also hopped in and kept their weapons at the ready. Despite being surrounded by armed soldiers, they trusted no one around the President.

"Before we get to the base and I become inundated with briefings and decisions, how are things going on the mobilization front?" the President asked General Abrams. "Are we drafting enough soldiers? Are they going to be ready for what they're going to face?"

General Abrams answered, "It's going to take some time, Mr. President, to get the soldiers trained. Depending on the number of casualties we take in Asia and Europe, these numbers should be sufficient. However, we need to be ready to double the size of the draft should the situation warrant it. My biggest concern is whether or not our forces will be able to hold the line long enough for the recruits to be trained and for our manufacturers to produce the vehicles and munitions needed to win. We are stretched incredibly thin everywhere right now."

Gates had been pondering that same conundrum while on the plane. Things were moving so rapidly. "Thank you, General, for the insight. Those are big concerns of mine as well. Just do your best to get our men and women ready to fight."

After his brief conversation with the general, the President made some small talk with several of the soldiers in the vehicle. He wanted to know what they were thinking and let them know he was just as concerned about them as they were about their families. The soldiers also offered up words of encouragement to the President, and urged him not to forget about the people of Oakland and San Francisco with all that was going on with the war. As it turned out, two of the soldiers in the vehicle were from the Oakland area and had lost their families during the bombing.

The President really did like to spend time with the enlisted soldiers and junior officers. They tended to be the ones implementing the President's orders and often provided invaluable feedback on their effectiveness that senior leaders might not fully understand or appreciate.

As Gates arrived at the command building, he was greeted by the base commander and several other senior military leaders and members of his staff that had flown to the base to be with him. He extended his hand and thanked them for accommodating him. Then the base commander led the President and his small entourage to a secured conference room, which had been outfitted with several trays of sandwiches and plenty of drinks for anyone who wanted to grab a bite to eat.

While several additional members of his staff had flown out to Fort Hood, the Secretaries of Defense and State remained at the Raven Rock facility for the time being, while most of the congressional leaders were at Mount Weather. The Pentagon would make an assessment in another twenty-four hours as to whether or not they felt it was safe for everyone to return to the capital.

A lot of congressional and senate leaders weren't happy about being sequestered at Mount Weather. They desperately wanted to get back to Washington or to their constituents. They also hated the fact that none of them could communicate with the press, who had been explicitly excluded from accompanying them to Mount Weather. The only press that was with any members of the government right now was the White House press pool, who had just arrived at Fort Hood. The media was going crazy with conspiracy theories about what was happening or not happening while they had no one from the government to interview.

The sinking of the 7th Fleet and the war in Korea were keeping the pundits and talking heads speculating on what the President might do next, and how the US would respond to the loss of so many naval ships and sailors. The sooner Gates could get back in front of the cameras to calm the public, the better.

Back in the conference room at Fort Hood, the President walked past the sandwiches and grabbed a water bottle before making his way to a seat that had a "POTUS" placard in front of it. Seated next to him were his National Security Advisor and the Chairman of the Joint Chiefs, who had been traveling with him on Air Force One.

"It's good to see everyone again," Gates said warmly. After a marathon flight, the President was glad to be back on the ground.

"Before we get going, I want to personally thank Admiral Robinson and his team for the outstanding performance of NORAD and our ballistic missile defense program. I know everyone feels terrible about the missile that got through in Oakland, but please remember gentlemen, you also saved the lives of countless millions of Americans when you shot down the other 44 warheads. Given what has happened, I would like to petition Congress for an emergency funding bill to triple the size of our ballistic missile defense interceptors. Without such an important system in place, millions more Americans would have perished," he said, nodding towards the congressional leaders who were participating via secured video teleconference.

He was pleased to see them smile and nod in agreement. No one was going to stand in the way of providing additional money to the one weapons platform that had saved tens of millions of Americans, regardless of party affiliation. Especially because they could see that if the US had had more missile interceptors, the cities of Oakland and San Francisco might have been saved.

"Getting back to business—how in the world did we lose the 7th Fleet? And what is going on with the ground war in Korea?" he probed, bringing everyone's focus back to why he had called this meeting in the first place.

A naval captain walked up to the front of the briefing room. He opened with a monologue of what had transpired, almost like a news anchor would recap clips of a breaking story.

"Sir, in response to the nuclear attack on Shenyang, the People's Republic of China officially declared war on the United States, Japan, and South Korea." The briefer paused for a second to let that part sink in.

He saw the President nod in acknowledgement and continued, "Within an hour of declaring war, the Chinese launched an all-out attack against the US, ROK, and Japanese naval forces in the Yellow Sea. The supercarrier *Carl Vinson* was nearly sunk by a Chinese anti-ship ballistic missile. As it was, the carrier will have to undergo extensive repairs once it arrives in port. The supercarrier *Ronald Reagan* did sink, along with the USS *Blueridge*, which was the 7th Fleet command and control ship. Sadly, only the *Carl Vinson* and five other surface warships survived the missile swarm attack."

Audible groans and gasps were heard from those in the room as the reality of the loss of so many sailors and ships hit them. In this single naval battle, the Navy had sustained over 20,000 casualties and lost nearly 20% of its surface ships.

"Despite the loss in surface ships, we had maneuvered a few dozen attack submarines into the area in case Chinese warships did decide to enter the area. Our subs, along with several Japanese submarines, managed to sink twelve Chinese Navy submarines, at a loss of only two Japanese subs and one American sub."

"One of the *Ohio*-class submarines, which we had converted to become a cruise missile platform, fired off its complement of 154 Tomahawk cruise missiles at many of the Chinese navy surface fleet vessels within a 1,300-mile radius of the battlegroup. They successfully sank 43 patrol boats, corvettes, and destroyers, along with three cruisers. They also hit five Chinese naval facilities, causing significant damage. A second *Ohio*-class submarine fired off their complement of 154 Tomahawk cruise missiles, disabling eight different Chinese air force airfields, ground radar stations and command-and-control nodes across the Shandong Province, directly opposite South Korea."

Most of the military members in the room nodded and smiled, satisfied with the results of the Navy's silent service. The submarine force was really coming through for the US in its desperate time of need.

As the naval captain finished briefing the naval situation, he signaled for the Air Force briefer to make his way to the front. A lieutenant colonel changed the briefing slides to show the Air Force activity. Like the briefer before her, she also stuck to the facts.

"Following the massive cruise missile attack by the Navy, the Air Force sent in two squadrons of B-1 Lancers, which hit a series of additional air-defense systems, critical railways, roads, bridges and tunnels throughout the Shandong Province. Our goal is to degrade the Chinese military's ability to carry out any additional strikes against our naval forces, South Korea, or the Japanese home islands." Her brief continued for another ten minutes before the President asked a question.

"Colonel, my understanding is that the B-2s are still in Japan for another week. Are there specific targets they're going to go after before we have to split the bomber wing up and send half of them back to Europe?" asked Gates.

The colonel clicked through a couple of slides to the one highlighting the B-2s. "The Pacific Commander wants to use the bombers to go after the Chinese transportation and logistics capability. The bombers themselves can carry six 5,000-pound joint direct attack munitions or JDAMs, and fifteen of the 2,000-pound versions, so each bomber can hit a lot of different targets on a single mission. The admiral wants to focus on going after their rail networks, hitting critical bridges, tunnels, and major switchyards. Targets that will hinder their military's ability to move troops, equipment, fuel and munitions across the country," she concluded.

She gave the President a moment in case he had any additional questions. When he didn't have anything further, she passed the briefing on to the Secretary of Defense.

The SecDef eagerly jumped into his part of the brief. "While you were in the process of landing, Mr. President, the South Korean and US ground forces officially crossed the DMZ and are now engaging the remaining North Korean forces. They initially met stiff resistance at the DMZ. However, once they started to break through the frontline soldiers, they started to encounter massive numbers of enemy soldiers surrendering. In many cases, they had dozens of North Korean units approaching our forces with white flags, pleading to surrender."

"The ground war is roughly four hours old, and so far, we have collected over 39,000 prisoners. This could be a fluke, and perhaps we'll start to hit more die-hard units, but this is promising, Mr. President," Secretary Castle said with a look of optimism.

"*Finally, some good news*," thought Gates with a smile.

Castle continued, his expression more serious now. "Sir, we have two other major problems that have developed over the last hour. The first being the Chinese ground forces near the North Korean border. Prior to hostilities, the Chinese had deployed roughly 80,000 troops near the border, and those troops have now crossed over and are moving down the peninsula towards our forces. Right now, we aren't 100% sure who is technically in control of the North Koreans' military or government, and the Chinese may be moving their forces into the country to assume control of what remains of their army and country."

"The second problem we have is that the Chinese just launched a massive missile and artillery attack against Taiwan."

Cursing could be heard from those who hadn't been brought up to speed on this latest development just yet. Everyone's worst fears were starting to play out; despite pleas for calm and peace, the war continued to widen.

Secretary of State Johnson jumped into the conversation to add, "Sir, the Taiwanese president has asked us for military assistance, if we're able to provide it."

Gates couldn't help but snort before responding. "Does the president of Taiwan understand that China has also declared war on the US, Japan, and South Korea, not to mention that NATO is currently at war with Russia? I'm not sure there is any real military support we can give them right now."

The President was numb as the reality of war with four countries at one time began to settle in. *What in the hell are we supposed to do now?* he thought.

Gates sighed audibly, then took a drink from his bottle of water. "Jim—what is our next move here?" he asked, almost pleading for his Secretary of Defense to give him an answer.

SecDef Castle had known the President would most likely ask him this question. That was one of the traits he admired about Gates; he wasn't afraid to admit he didn't know something and ask for advice from those who did.

"Mr. President, the Chinese attack on the 7th Fleet hurt us, but it was expected and anticipated," Castle began. "We survived the initial shock and awe they tried to lay on our fleet, and now we're hitting them back hard. Per our previous discussions, when the Chinese declared war and attacked our battlegroups, I ordered the new commander at PACOM to initiate Operation Trident. As our briefers began to describe, our Navy has hammered the Chinese navy and air force facilities that posed the greatest immediate threat to our forces. This was quickly followed by action from our Air Force."

261

He paused only long enough to take a breath before continuing, "Our B-2s are just now taking off from Japan and will begin to carry out a series of deep strikes within China, going after their critical rail, bridge, and tunnel networks. We're going to make the logistical challenge of moving men and material around their expansive country a bit more difficult for them. The carriers *Nimitz*, *Theodore Roosevelt*, and *John C. Stennis* will arrive in the Sea of Japan tomorrow. We've also relocated the cruise missile SSGNs *Florida* and *Georgia* from the Atlantic to the Pacific. Those additional cruise missile submarines will arrive at Yokosuka Naval Base around the same time the *Ohio* and *Michigan* return to rearm. While the loss of the *Reagan* and the crippling damage to the *Vinson* hurt us, it could have been worse.

"In my opinion, the Chinese wasted the element of surprise when they attacked the 7th Fleet. Had they waited until the entire Pacific Fleet had sailed into the Yellow Sea or near the Straits of Taiwan, they could have sunk all our carriers. As it is, they revealed to us the capabilities of their anti-ship weapons. Now that we know what they can do, we are developing strategies and plans to deal with this threat."

Jim paused for a second as he turned to look at someone off-camera, then returned his gaze to the camera and leaned in closer. "I have ordered our cyber-warfare groups to go after the Chinese logistics capability. We're scrambling their barcode and computer systems. It doesn't sound like much, but when a unit sends a message requesting more ammunition, they will instead receive toilet paper or some other useless supply that won't help them. These may sound like little nuisances, but I assure you, as our cyber guys infiltrate their electronic logistics system, it's going to wreak havoc on their ability to keep their army groups running at full speed. We're also going after their satellites, just as the Russians went after ours. In addition to that, as we identify where their cyber groups are operating out of, we're having the Navy and Air Force launch cruise missiles at those facilities. This is going to have a huge impact on their cyber groups if they know we're actively targeting each site individually," Castle said with a devilish grin.

"As to the ground war, we had to withdraw the US and ROK Marines from landing near Pyongyang once it appeared that war was inevitable with China. We needed to protect the amphibious assault ships and the support ships needed to sustain a ground invasion. Now that China is moving ground forces into the DPRK, I recommend that we have the Marines redeploy along this area here," he said, pointing on the map to the city of Hamhung on the Sea of Japan. "This was the second-largest city in the country, and the only top-four city in the DPRK that we didn't nuke. It is, in all likelihood, the alternative headquarters for the government, if anyone survived the first day of the war."

"This will give us a beachhead from which to land additional forces behind the North Korean frontlines, and hopefully allow us to cut them off. It'll also give us exceptional defensive positions along these ridges here, when the Chinese forces do eventually reach ours."

The President thought over what his SecDef had explained, feeling a bit more hopeful. "OK, Jim, you've convinced me of the merits of the landing. Do it," he responded. "Let's also make sure the Air Force hammers the living daylights out of the Chinese forces entering Korea. Hopefully we can butter them up really well before they even reach our soldiers."

The Secretary of State broke into the conversation again. "Mr. President, while I understand we don't have conventional forces we can deploy to Taiwan to help them, perhaps we can send them some Special Forces, or maybe one of our *Ohio*-class submarines can deliver a barrage of cruise missiles at the Chinese ports near Taiwan, like they just did in the Yellow Sea."

Gates sat back in his chair for a second, thinking about that, when Admiral Meyers interjected, "Mr. President, while I would like to send Special Forces to Taiwan, the limited number of units we have in the Pacific need to stay focused on Korea and any potential incursions we may make into China directly. Once our two cruise missile SSGNs have rearmed in Japan, we could redirect them to head down to Taiwan and hit the Chinese navy. But we also have to remember, the Chinese have their three carriers down there as well. There will also be an increased presence of enemy submarines in the area. I don't want to risk losing any of the cruise missile submarines. We're going to be relying on them a lot more going forward with the loss of two of our carriers." The Chairman of the Joint Chiefs hoped to kill the idea before it could take root.

"Perhaps we can have the B-2s try and provide some sort of direct support?" the President inquired. "Maybe they can hit a troop transport or part of the rail or port facilities in the area," he offered.

263

Castle jumped back in, "That we can do. I'll place a call to PACOM and have him send a B-2 strike that way. It's about as much support as we can offer Taiwan for the moment, until we have additional soldiers and ships."

"How are we doing in that department, Jim?" asked the President, hoping the rebuilding of the army was at least moving along.

"The first batch of 150,000 recruits has just arrived in training. We have a new batch of 150,000 trainees starting each week. Roughly three quarters of these recruits are going directly into the infantry, so their training is roughly three months. Normally, the training would have taken four months, but we need those replacement soldiers at the various frontlines ASAP. The remaining 37,500 trainees from each cycle will be receiving a variety of additional training in communications, medical, aviation and other critical jobs, so their training time is going to be closer to four to six additional months. We're working with the technical training schools to shorten it down as much as possible while not diminishing the required training."

Castle sighed. "It's going to take some time, Mr. President, but the first batch of 112,000 infantry soldiers will start to arrive at the frontlines in December. Approximately 112,000 additional soldiers will continue to arrive each subsequent week, until all five million draftees have been trained," he concluded.

The President's senior advisor, who had just flown in to Fort Hood that morning, asked, "How long is each draftee's service agreement again?" This was a detail that hadn't been finalized, despite previous debate.

Castle bristled a bit at the question, but answered it anyways. "The term of the draft is for the duration of the war. We'll look to do a large-scale demobilization once the war has concluded, just as the US did following the end of World War II. We learned a lot from the Vietnam draft, and the Pentagon has determined that giving a set date to the draftees is not an effective way of building the sustained army needed to win this war. Plus, we would have to continually draft people each week to replace the ones that finished their term."

"This also allows us to keep unit cohesion throughout the war. We won't have units constantly losing good, experienced soldiers just when they're needed most. The Pentagon and I are in agreement that this will greatly cut down on the number of casualties as well," Castle concluded.

The President nodded in approval, as did his NSA and the CJC. The rest of the Joint Chiefs also seemed reasonably pleased with the decision. That had been a major disadvantage during the Vietnam War. Nearly all the experienced soldiers would rotate home and get out of the military, leaving just inexperienced junior soldiers who suffered a very high casualty rate to take their place.

Chapter 50
Cyber-Warfare

Shanghai Shi, China
Agricultural Bank of China

Colonel Xian sipped on his tea as he observed his small cadre of hackers from his office, hard at work. The group, which mostly consisted of young men and women, sat there glued to their oversized computer screens with headphones on and energy drinks strewn about their work stations.

Kids these days…sloppy and messy, he thought as he looked at them. *If they weren't such exceptional hackers, I would never tolerate such filth.*

Now that war had been declared against the Americans, his unit was free to carry out unlimited and direct cyber-attacks against a plethora of US targets. His specific unit had been tasked with going after the civilian sector of the US economy and making the daily life of Americans difficult. He had 36 highly skilled hackers in his unit to accomplish this task, which he thought was more than enough. His first order of business was to break his team down into smaller groups and assign them specific regions in America to target. Their main targets were the American entertainment sector and the transportation industry, areas that continually lagged in cyber defense.

One group of hackers was specifically causing problems for Amazon, Hulu, Netflix, and YouTube streaming services, hitting them continually with distributed denial of service attacks and other malicious activity. A different group was hacking into various small towns across the US, shutting down traffic cameras or changing commuter rail times so that people would show up after the trains had already left. Their mission was to cause general chaos and anxiety for the American civilian population and let the people of the United States know that China, though many thousands of miles away, could reach out and touch them wherever they lived. Judging by the comments they were seeing on Facebook, Twitter, and the other social media platforms they monitored, their attacks were having the desired effect. People were becoming increasingly angry about their mundane, boring online lives being interrupted.

As satisfying as it was to know his team was impacting the daily lives of the enemy, he wished they were able to carry out more malevolent types of attacks, like shutting down the US electrical grid. But he had been warned not to try that. His leadership feared that if they succeeded in taking the country's grid down, the Americans would retaliate and do the same to China. As much as he hated to admit it, China had grown just as dependent on electronics and the power grid as the US had. It was almost as if an unspoken mutually-assured destruction doctrine had been implemented between the warring factions. There were still areas that were off-limits, even during a time of war. Since President Gates had nuked Shenyang, the Chinese leadership had been hesitant to test him further by straying from the unofficial electronic détente.

Just as he was about to walk out of his office to check on one of his hacker teams, the building shook violently, throwing him to the floor. In a fraction of a second, he saw the ceiling above him collapse on top of him and his fiefdom, just as a large fireball consumed them all. Unbeknownst to Colonel Xian and his hacker group, the National Security Agency had acquired their physical location and sent that data over to the Air Force and Navy. A B-2 bomber that had been carrying out a strike against a rail bridge nearby had been redirected to drop a JDAM on the Agricultural Bank of China. Within seconds of the blast, the myriad of persistent cyber-attacks taking place across the US suddenly ceased.

Chapter 51
A Desperate Fight

Smalyavichy, Belarus

The sounds of heavy machine gun fire and various explosions beat out a deadly rhythm in the distance as US and Russian forces continued to clash near the outskirts of the capital. As Major General Austin walked up the steps to the city hall building, he could see the exterior of the building had been scarred by a few nearby explosions and riddled with bullets. Most of the windows had also been blown out. When his forces had entered the city, a small contingent of Belarusian soldiers had tried to prevent the Americans from capturing it, but that fight had ended quickly, with deadly results for the soldiers who had thought they could prevent the 4th Infantry Division from securing the city.

As the broken glass crunched against the boots of General Austin, he saw his staff hard at work, getting the new headquarters building set up. The last two days had been a mad dash to capture the city and cut off the Russian supply lines. The United States' surprise attack in Belarus had caught the Russians off guard, and they were playing defense now. The rest of Three Corps and the Polish divisions had the Russian 6th Tank Army fully engaged further south, and now it was time to force them to surrender or slaughter them on the battlefield.

"What's the status of that Russian airborne division at the edge of the city?" General Austin asked his G3.

"Colonel Pippen's brigade is engaging them now," the operations officer began. "They have that Spetsnaz brigade pinned down near Minsk International Airport. There's a lot of heavy fighting in that area. Colonel Pippen wants to know if we can give him more artillery support while his brigade continues to box them in."

General Austin just nodded. They needed to keep those Spetsnaz guys cornered in the airport region. If they broke out into his rear area, they could cause him a lot of problems. It had been foolish of the Russian commander to drop nearly his entire brigade on the airport without also trying to secure the nearby villages. They were paying for that miscalculation now.

"Where is the 3rd Armor Brigade now?" asked Austin, hoping they had finally made contact with the Russian paratroopers. They had been dropped behind his forces near Maryina Horka. If they were able to get themselves organized, they could pose a serious problem to his grip on Minsk.

"Colonel Eddy says they should be engaging the paratroopers within the next thirty minutes. His lead elements have already started to call in a series of artillery strikes. He did ask if there would be any air support available. What should I tell him?" asked the same operations officer.

Austin turned to his Air Force liaison officer or LNO for an answer on the air situation. "We should have six F-16s on standby for air support operations within an hour. They'll be in orbit over our current position for roughly thirty-five minutes before they need to return home for fuel. We also have six F-15s, which will stay in continuous orbit to provide fighter cover."

"I thought we would have more aircraft than that for close air support," one of the other operations officers responded. They had been promised a lot more air support than what was apparently being provided.

"We have more aircraft in the area, but they're performing Wild Weasel missions, going after the SA-10s and SA-21s. We have to keep the Russian air-defense suppressed or we won't have *any* air support," retorted the air LNO.

Holding up a hand to stop the back and forth, General Austin replied, "Send the F-16s to support Colonel Eddy's brigade. We'll use our aviation brigade to support Colonel Pippen's unit at the airport. Tell 1st Stryker brigade to be ready to roll to either position if additional troops are needed."

General Austin's division was expected to hold his ground for the next 96 hours. By then, a Danish infantry brigade, along with an Italian mechanized brigade, should arrive to support them. This would bolster his forces by another 7,000 soldiers. It was hoped that by the time they arrived, the Russian 6th Tank Army would have either surrendered or been destroyed.

Chapter 52
I Just Wanted the GI Bill

Camp Casey, South Korea

Sergeant Ian Slater had just made sergeant when the war in Russia had started. He was thankful he was stationed in Korea, away from the fighting. All he wanted from the Army was the GI Bill to pay for college. He wanted to get his degree in automotive mechanical engineering like his brother Marcus had and get a decent paying job.

Marcus had started working for Tesla two years ago. All he talked about was how cool it was to be part of a design team that was helping to change the future of the automotive industry. Ian wanted to be like his brother, but he didn't have the same stellar grades Marcus had in high school, so he was unable to get a full-ride scholarship to any of the colleges that specialized in his major.

His dad wanted to help pay for college. He was just financially unable to do so, so he had suggested that Ian look at the Army for help with paying for tuition. Their grandma had dementia and needed constant care, and that was costly. Since his dad was an only child, all the financial responsibility fell on him. Ian knew that his father was making the right decision, but it didn't make his own path any easier. Ian hated violence, and the last thing he wanted to do was be placed in a situation where he might have to kill someone.

When he'd spoken with the Army recruiter, they'd told him that if he joined for four years, with two of them being in Korea. They could not only get him the GI Bill, they could also get him a $25,000 signing bonus. He didn't like the idea of joining the military, but the immediate money meant he'd be able to pursue his passion when he got out.

Two and a half years later, he was sitting in a Bradley fighting vehicle, slowly moving across the DMZ in the Second Korean War.

The first day of the ground war had been horrific. The fighting was brutal, often devolving into hand-to-hand combat as they fought alongside their South Korean counterparts to penetrate the North's defenses. The Air Force and their own artillery had hit the North's positions hard. There was hardly a part of the North's positions that wasn't bombed out or cratered. Even still, the soldiers they encountered fought on like men possessed.

As Sergeant Slater sat in the vehicle, reloading an empty magazine for his M4, he saw one of the privates across from him drawing yet another dark line in his journal, denoting a kill. Slater told the private, "It's a bit morbid to keep track of death like that."

The 19-year-old shrugged; he didn't seem to care.

I hope this guy doesn't turn out to become some kind of serial killer when he leaves the Army, Slater reflected as he placed the newly loaded magazine back in his front ammo pouch.

While their Bradley continued to move forward, an explosion rocked their vehicle slightly. It was probably a near-miss from an artillery round. They heard pieces of shrapnel slap against the armored walls.

Dear God, I hate that sound, thought Slater.

The Bradley's gunner fired off a short burst from the turret's 25mm chain gun, aimed at some unseen target. The vehicle commander then called out to the soldiers in the back, "Another enemy troop position has been identified—we're going to rush the position."

The Bradley lurched forward as the tracks began to pick up speed. The gunner fired the chain gun a few more times as they got closer to the enemy positions. A series of bullets bounced loudly off their armored walls before the gunner managed to silence the attack.

"RPG!" screamed the gunner.

A second later, their vehicle was jolted by a forceful thud as the RPG slammed into their front right track, bringing the Bradley to an abrupt halt. Everyone inside grabbed onto something to steady themselves and keep from being thrown around like ragdolls.

"Gunner, give us some covering fire! Everyone else, dismount!" yelled the vehicle commander.

The vehicle commander and his driver also got out of the Bradley. He wanted to examine where they had been hit and see if they could repair it themselves, or if they would have to call for a wrecker vehicle to tow them back to the rear for maintenance.

"Fan out on the left side," the vehicle commander directed. This would give him the space he needed to go and assess the full extent of the damage.

As soon as they exited the vehicle, they came under instant ground fire from several enemy positions. Bullets whipped through the air, kicking up dirt and rocks near his soldiers and ricocheting off the armored body of their Bradley. His men scattered, looking for cover and praying they wouldn't get hit by one of the hot pieces of lead flying through the air.

As Sergeant Slater ran to a bomb crater for cover, the smell of smoke and death hung in the air all around them. As he looked down below his feet, he saw several dead and rotting enemy soldiers. It startled him just a little bit. Many of the deceased remains were missing limbs.

He pushed the horrific sight out of his mind and looked up over the edge of the crater. Ian spotted several enemy soldiers popping up and down from two foxholes, firing at his squad. They were probably no more than 100 yards from his position. He squinted and rubbed his eyes...

Just as he was trying to figure out how they were going to deal with the gun bunker he'd spotted, the 25mm gun from the Bradley fired a string of rounds into it, silencing it. Then the Bradley's gunner fired two rounds at the enemy soldiers in the foxholes before Slater heard the gun jam.

"Alpha team, lay down covering fire! Bravo team, advance!" he yelled as he jumped up from the edge of the bomb crater he was leaning against. He raised his M4 to his shoulder and fired single-round shots at the group of enemy soldiers who were firing at his team, attempting to shoot at his soldiers. As he and the rest of Bravo team made it to their next set of covering positions, Alpha team bounded beyond their position while it was Bravo team's turn to lay down covering fire.

As they got closer to the enemy positions, several of the soldiers in his squad began to throw some hand grenades at the enemy soldiers. A couple of booms shook the earth in the distance, and then there was silence. His two fire teams advanced cautiously towards the enemy positions, making sure they had their weapons trained where the North Korean soldiers had been.

When they approached the foxholes, they found six dead enemy soldiers. One of his men poked at each of the bodies with the barrel of his rifle, just to make sure they were dead. Then they moved on towards the enemy machine gun bunker, which had remained silent since the Bradley had lit it up.

As they made it over the lip of the bunker, they encountered the remains of five dead soldiers. Before moving on, they made sure to spike the barrel of the gun in the bunker so it couldn't be used again.

Slater turned to look back at the Bradley. There was a wrecker vehicle, maybe a mile back, very slowly making its way towards their disabled vehicle. It looked like his squad would be moving forward on foot for a while.

Now that they had disabled the machine gun bunker and neutralized the threats, several columns of light infantry soldiers steadily moved towards them. Sergeant Slater reached for his radio and let his platoon sergeant know about their situation and told him that they would link up with the rest of the platoon when they could. For the time being, his eleven-man squad would continue forward on foot to the company's main objective and hope to meet up with the rest of their comrades there.

Chapter 53
A Marine War

Seoul, South Korea
Yongsan Garrison

The Second Korean War was now four days old, and just as bloody as everyone had imagined it would be. The casualties continued to pour in by the hour, but progress was being made as US and ROK forces continued to press the Korean People's Army into retreat.

The Allies were at the outskirts of what had once been Pyongyang when all of a sudden, large swaths of the KPA simply began to surrender. With no political or military leader in charge, the local commanders began to take matters into their own hands and started to capitulate in mass. Most of these units were running low on ammunition, water, food, and other essential supplies. They had also been mercilessly bombed by aircraft and artillery for four days straight. For them to fight on at this point meant certain death, and they knew it.

The Allies were offering them hot food, water, and medical support if they surrendered. For the starving army, that was all the motivation they needed to throw in the towel.
****

General Bennet walked over to the digital map displayed on the wall of a 72-inch LED touchscreen, and looked at the overview of the entire war. There was an interactive high-resolution image of the Korean Peninsula on-screen. His operations staff members kept it updated with various Allied unit positions, Special Forces team whereabouts, and known enemy troop locations. If he wanted greater detail or information on a specific area, he just needed to touch that location and it zoomed in, providing an additional layer of information. He could see all the way down to the battalion level if he chose to look that deeply.

As he studied the map, the area that concerned him the most was the northern part of the country that butted up to China. The Chinese had moved tens of thousands of soldiers across the northern border on the second day of the war, and now they were moving those forces down the peninsula towards his troops.

The frontlines were continuing to move forward at a decent clip now that the US and ROK forces had pushed through the first ten kilometers of the KPA's defensive line. It certainly helped that the further they moved into enemy territory, the more enemy soldiers were surrendering—especially once they learned that Pyongyang had been destroyed.

The landing force of 65,000 US and ROK Marines that had been scheduled to invade near Pyongyang was being moved around the Korean peninsula and would conduct an amphibious assault at Hamhung, on the Sea of Japan. It was hoped these forces would catch the remnants of the KPA off guard and potentially force the remainder of the Korean soldiers there to surrender.

It would also provide the Allies with a strategic strongpoint as the main Chinese force continued to advance down the peninsula. The US Air Force had been pounding the living daylights out of the Chinese ground forces as they made their way down the Peninsula, destroying vast numbers of tanks and other armored vehicles. By the time they would reach the Allied forces, they were going to be thoroughly demoralized, or so it was hoped.

General Bennet was done surveying the map. There was no substitute in his mind for one-on-one human interaction. He eyed the group around him and walked over towards his Special Forces LNO to see if he had spoken with any of the units directly about their progress on reaching the DPRK capital.

"How close are our forces to the outskirts of what's left of Pyongyang?" he asked.

Colonel Franklin, who had taken over as General Bennet's operations officer, replied, "A brigade from the 2nd Infantry Division is starting to approach the outskirts now. They've been told not to get too close to the epicenter of the blast until the chemical warfare guys have said it's OK to approach. That should happen before the end of the day."

The general and others in the room nodded.

Very little of the city was left standing after the US dropped a 340-kiloton nuclear warhead on it. What was left were burnt out hulks of buildings. Until they could confirm the level of radiation still left in the blast area, they weren't going to have any US or ROK units operate near or in it. Since this was an airburst at five thousand feet, there shouldn't be a lot of residual fallout after the first couple of days—

especially since a storm came through the area the day before. The rain had finally put out most of the remaining embers still burning in the city.

"How close are the Chinese?" Bennet asked his Special Forces LNO. 1st Special Forces Group had inserted several SF teams near the Chinese border to observe troop movements and to call in air and cruise missile attacks as targets presented themselves.

"The last team reported in a couple of hours ago. They spotted several enemy formations approaching our lines. They are roughly sixty miles from our most forward units. As you know, I've moved ODA teams to a number of locations along the most likely routes they'll use to engage our troops. When an aircraft comes available for an air strike, they hit them hard. I reckon we've probably cost the PLA close to 5% to 10% casualties since they crossed the border," the SF colonel said with a satisfied grin on his face.

Bennet smiled at that knowledge. He only wished they had more aircraft. With the war still raging in Europe, the amount of aircraft the US could send to Korea was extremely limited. Turning to Colonel Sutherbee, his Air Force LNO, Bennet asked, "How are we doing suppressing the enemy's air-defense units?"

Colonel Sutherbee had been a fighter pilot in charge of his own fighter wing in Germany when he had been injured during the surprise cruise missile attack. He had unfortunately caught a piece of flying shrapnel in his left eye during the attack. He was lucky that he hadn't lost his eye or his sight. They had had to fly back to Bethesda Hospital to have the shrapnel removed. After a couple of weeks of recovery, he was sent to Korea to become General Bennet's Air Force LNO when another person had taken over his old command. Sadly, his flying days were over because of the damage to his eye. However, with the war raging now in the Pacific, the Air Force had deemed him more than qualified to be the senior Air Force LNO to Allied Forces-Korea.

"Better than we were yesterday," Sutherbee answered. "We flew 67 Weasel missions yesterday and lost nine aircraft. We thinned out the enemy air defense in this sector here," he said, pointing to an area on the map near what was left of Pyongyang. "Right now, we're focusing our efforts on these two sectors, where the Marines are getting ready to land their forces. It's also the last place where intelligence showed a sizable North Korean military element remaining."

Sutherbee pointed at several places inside China next. "The issue we're running into now is along these areas in China. The PLA Air Force is starting to make a concerted effort there to intercept our aircraft over the Yellow Sea and in Northern parts of Korea. Our F-15s and F-22s are starting to tangle it up more and more over this section of the DPRK," he explained.

"Are you going to be able to contain and defeat the Chinese Air Force going forward? I have a feeling the Chinese are only just getting started here in Korea," said General Bennet.

Colonel Sutherbee sighed before answering, "It's going to be tough, General. It looks like the brunt of the Chinese air force is down south, beating the tar out of Taiwan. The Taiwanese are faring better than I thought they would, but that'll only last for so long. Once they've secured Taiwan, those aircraft are going to shift North. When that happens, we're going to be heavily outnumbered."

So much for ending this war swiftly. This is going to drag on for a long time..., Bennet thought.

"What additional aircraft do we have coming from the States?" he asked.

"We have one squadron of F-22s and two additional squadrons of F-16s due to arrive within the next week. Those are unfortunately only going to replace our losses, not increase our actual force. We lost a lot of good people and aircraft when Kunson was nuked. The additional aircraft we were hoping to get from Australia are having to beef up our defenses in Guam, so we can't rely on any additional help from the Aussies on this one," the colonel said glumly.

Another captain walked up to the general. "Sir, the SecDef is on the video conference for you," he said, pointing to a computer monitor.

Bennet walked over to the desk and sat down in front of it. "It's good to see you, Sir. What can I do for you?"

Jim Castle leaned in, which made his face appear larger on the computer screen. "I'll get right down to it John. How soon can you mop up operations in Korea?"

General Bennet sat there, not sure what to say for just a moment—that question had kind of caught him off guard. "That's hard to say right now. I have over 80,000 Chinese soldiers moving down the Peninsula, and we still haven't finished off the North Koreans yet," he replied, knowing that wasn't exactly the answer the SecDef was looking for.

"How many prisoners have you taken in the last five days?" Jim asked.

"Last count was somewhere around 162,000. I can't tell you for certain how many of them are left. We wiped a lot of them out during the 'Shock and Awe' campaign, and then a lot more when we nuked them. The Japanese are moving 65,000 ground forces to our new beachhead at Hamhung once it's established. That will strengthen our position there as we move to sever the country in half."

Bennet took a quick swig of water and then continued. "The ROK is moving the majority of their forces to meet the Chinese head-on. My plan is for US forces to support the ROK while they lead the way in battling the Chinese. How many reinforcements are coming my way, and when will they arrive?"

Jim Castle leaned back in his chair. "John, I don't have any reinforcements I can send you right now. Nearly everything we have is heading to Europe. The Russians are throwing everything they have at NATO right now. We are so close to turning the tide of that war. The President wants me to focus all our efforts on finishing off Russia. Then we can pivot everything to the Pacific."

"The President said the Pacific was going to be a Marine war. When will additional Marines start to arrive? Will I stay in command of ground forces in the PACOM area?" asked General Bennet, hoping to get some good news this time.

Smiling for a second, Jim replied, "In January, the first batch of 20,000 Marines will start to arrive. Once they do, 20,000 more will arrive each week from then on. You're going to remain the overall commander for Allied forces in Korea. We'll be appointing a new Marine Commander to take over as the PACOM Commander. As the President said, the Pacific is going to be a Marine war, at least until the war in Europe is finished," he said with a smile on his face.

The Marines are coming, thought Bennet with a smirk. *God help the Chinese once the new Pacific army is fully formed up.*

Chapter 54
Beyond the Beachhead

Hamhung, North Korea
Chakto-dong Beach Area

The USS *Bataan, Iwo Jima* and *Makin Island* amphibious assault ships had finally moved to within a couple of miles from the shoreline of Hamhung as the Navy and Marine air wings continued to pound the beach areas and any visible troop concentrations they spotted. The North Koreans knew the Americans might attempt a landing in this area and had gone to great lengths to ensure the beach had been heavily laced with concertina wire and landmines. The KPA's objective was to bleed the Americans dry on the beach and then contest every inch of ground they tried to secure.

As the amphibious assault ship slowly rocked with the waves of the ocean, Sergeant Tim Long placed his final thirty-round magazine in his front ammo pouch on his body armor. He then grabbed a bandolier that held another eight thirty-round magazines and slung it over his shoulder.

I think we're going to need all the ammo we can carry, he thought.

Tim grabbed four hand grenades from the crate nearby, placing two of them on each side of his ammunition pouches on his body armor. As he finished getting his own personal gear and weapons ready, he turned to make sure the rest of his squad members were ready as well. He especially wanted to make sure the two machine gun teams had their extra barrels and gloves with them in addition to extra ammunition.

As he walked down the line, each machine gun crew was carrying four 100-round belts, just like he had planned. Six other members of the squad carried an additional 100-round belt to help supply them. In addition to the extra ammo, four of his squad members were bringing four antitank rockets in case they encountered a fixed machine gun bunker that needed blowing up.

After nearly an hour of getting themselves ready, their lieutenant walked by and said, "It's time to start loading up in the vehicles, Marines. This is happening, so get psyched up! This is what we live for! NCOs, move your squads to the vehicles, and let's get rolling!"

he shouted, adrenaline clearly pumping through his veins as he tried to whip up his platoon into a fury.

Sergeant Long echoed that sentiment. "Grab your gear and let's go, Marines! It's time to earn our keep and go kick those communists where it hurts."

The Marines from his squad put on their individual body armor and grabbed their patrol packs. They had loaded them down with ammunition and two days' worth of food and water. In a somewhat orderly process, they headed down to the lower well deck, where they would load up into the amphibious assault vehicle or AAV that would carry them to the beach.

The AAV had a crew of three Marines to drive it and man its various weapon systems. In the rear, twenty-one Marines were crammed into quarters so tight it would make a person with claustrophobia hyperventilate. As they sat in anticipation, they could smell diesel fumes wafting into their compartment, along with the overwhelming scent of sweat.

Seawater seeped in through the seals. This uncomfortable journey somehow filled the men with adrenaline. When they arrived, they would be ready to hit the beach and advance to contact as soon as the rear ramp had been dropped.

Because of the number of Marines involved in the landing operation, and the fact that this would be an opposed landing, the AAVs would be needed to transport more than a few waves of Marines to the shore. Once the first load exited, the vehicles would return to the ships to bring in the next load of Marines.

Fortunately, some of the LCACs—essentially large hovercrafts—would be accompanying them. They would hold off on hitting the beach for thirty minutes to give the initial batch of Marines some time to get things cleared. When they landed, the LCACs would bring ashore a handful of Abrams main battle tanks and their light-armored tactical vehicles for armored support.

As everyone settled into the vehicle they had been assigned too, they began to do a final once-over on the weapons and equipment. While this was being done, the loading deck began to move slowly, and the conveyor belt moved the vehicles to the back of the deck to be dropped into the water. Once in the water, they would begin their watery drive to the beach.

Sergeant Long's driver slowly revved the engine, making sure they were ready as their vehicle got closer to the water's edge. A minute or so later, the vehicle slipped off the loading deck, and for a brief moment went beneath the waves until the buoyancy of the vehicle forced them to pop up to the surface like a buoy.

As their vehicle broke the surface of the water, the driver revved the engine and built up speed, joining the formation of other AAVs now heading towards the beach. As the first wave of AAVs approached the coast, enemy artillery rounds landed in the water around them, throwing up geysers of water intermixed with shrapnel. From time to time, the scraps of metal would ping or clang off their armored shell, reminding them that this was no training exercise.

Several missiles streaked out from various positions on shore towards some of the AAVs. One missile smashed into the front of a vehicle as it was cresting a wave, exploding in spectacular fashion, killing everyone on board. They were now less than 50 yards from the shore. Bullets bounced harmlessly off their armor as the turret gunner fired back.

Sergeant Long felt the treads of the vehicle catch on the gravel floor of the beach and move quickly up the sandy coast. Prior to leaving the troop ships, the AAV commander had determined that the vehicles would drive just far enough up the shore to create a hole through the concertina wire before backing out to head back for their next load. This would save the Marines on the beach a lot of time in trying to breach the wire while potentially being under a lot of heavy fire.

"We're coming up on the wire now!" yelled the vehicle commander to Long's team. "Get ready to disembark and then get away from the vehicle. We're going to start backing up once you guys are all out!"

"You heard the man!" shouted Sergeant Long. "I want Alpha team to break right and advance to cover. Bravo Team, you break left and advance to cover. Once we're on the beach, look for targets and engage them. Remember, controlled shots—do *not* blow through all your ammo! Fire team leaders, remember fire discipline!"

Seconds later, they could hear the vehicle grind through a bunch of barbed wire. A landmine went off, but their vehicle shrugged it right off. Then, the back hatch opened, and they disembarked rapidly under a hail of gunfire.

Once they were out of the vehicle, the deafening roar of war was almost overwhelming to their senses. There were thunderous explosions from artillery and mortar rounds going off all around them, blistering hot shrapnel flying everywhere. Then there was the constant chattering of machine guns from all directions. Screams of agony rose up from the wounded as the shrapnel and bullets slapped against the soft human flesh of the Marines assaulting the beach.

Within seconds of exiting the vehicle and getting away from behind it, Sergeant Long saw the vehicle lurch backwards as it tried to get back into the water to go pick up the next set of Marines. He then turned his attention to his squad; most of them had found shelter against a small sea wall at the edge of the beach, where the grass and sand met.

One of his soldiers was lying on his back, dead after taking several bullets to the neck and face. Sergeant Long couldn't even recognize his fellow Marine without seeing his name tape. He was reduced to a torn and bloody mess of bone and muscle chunks.

A second Marine lay on the ground a dozen feet away from him, screaming in pain as he reached down to the ragged remnants of his left leg, blood squirting with each pulse. Sergeant Long didn't waste a moment and quickly ran to the man, dropping down next to him. Bullets whipped past his head, kicking up dirt, rocks, and sand all around him and his wounded comrade.

He grabbed the man's belt buckle, undoing it and pulling it out from his trousers. He then wrapped it just above the wound and tightened it as hard as he could to stop his friend from bleeding out. Then, he reached under the wounded Marine's left armpit, and in one strong *oomph*, he threw him over his shoulder and began to run towards the break wall. Shots were whizzing past him like crazy. All he knew in that moment was he needed to get his friend to safety so a corpsman could start working on trying to patch him up.

When he made it to the break wall, he placed the Marine up against it just as a corpsman ran up to them and applied a proper tourniquet just above the wound to try and stem the bleeding.

Tim just lay there for a minute, trying to catch his breath and collect his thoughts. He grabbed at his CamelBak hose and took a couple of long drinks of water from it as his heart raced out of control.

"Sergeant Long, there's a machine gun position in that house, near those resort buildings," one of his Marines said, pointing in the direction where the enemy fire was coming from.

Tim inched his head slightly above the wall they were hiding behind and saw the house with the machine gun. Green tracers flew towards their position, raking the beach behind them. The building itself was a single-story house with a front door and three forward-facing windows. The windows had sandbags built up around them, and several heavy machine guns could be seen with their barrels sticking out, shooting flame and death at his fellow Marines.

Turning back to face his friend, he yelled to be heard above the sounds of war. "Get one of the guys with an antitank rocket to put a round in there and see if that solves the problem."

Then he turned to look at the corpsman working on the wounded lance corporal he had carried to the seawall. "How's he doing?"

The corpsman had tied off the leg a couple of inches above the wound and applied a pressure bandage. Then he pulled a small bag of plasma out of his aid bag and started an IV. "It's a pretty bad wound," the corpsman explained. "If we could get him back to the ship, he might still keep his leg. He needs a medevac. What are the chances of that happening?"

Tim looked back towards the beach. In the distance, he saw another wave of AAVs heading towards them. Then he had an idea. "See if you can get some volunteers to help you with the wounded. I'll try to have the squad give you as much covering fire as possible."

The corpsman nodded. "I'll do my best to get as many of the wounded Marines loaded into the vehicles as possible."

One of Long's heavy machine gunners let loose a long burst of automatic fire at the house that had been converted into an enemy bunker, while another Marine rose above the seawall slightly. He aimed the antitank rocket and fired it off at the house.

Long heard the loud popping noise and then the sudden *SWOOSH* as the rocket headed right for the building. From their spot behind the seawall, they still heard the loud explosion and a splattering of sparks. Then they waited...silence.

With the machine gun neutralized, Sergeant Long yelled at the top of his lungs, "Alpha team, assault forward and secure that building!"

Then he turned to his left and looked in the direction of his other fire team. "Bravo Team, lay down covering fire now!"

Both teams reacted to his orders and began to assault the building.

Sergeant Long stood up and climbed over the seawall, advancing towards the cluster of buildings where the enemy was held up. As he ran forward, he raised his M4 to his shoulder and fired off a series of controlled shots into the enemy positions in hopes of keeping their heads down, or maybe getting a lucky shot and killing one them.

The rest of Alpha team followed him forward. It was a mad dash to the buildings being used by the enemy. Alpha and Bravo teams unleashed a hail of bullets as they sprinted toward the enemy. In this situation, speed was life. It was several hundred yards from the seawall to the enemy positions, with little in the way of cover in between them.

His fire team moved methodically, delivering accurate fire at the enemy while they charged. Hundreds of other Marines saw their charge and joined in, adding their own firepower to the mix.

As the Marines advanced, a pair of AH-1W Super Cobra attack helicopters banked in towards the shoreline and raked several of the buildings with 70mm antipersonnel rockets. They blew apart several vehicles Sergeant Long's men hadn't spotted. They had been lying in wait behind the buildings, waiting for the Marines to expose their positions.

As the helicopters flew low over the enemy, the Koreans launched several MANPADs or shoulder-launched surface-to-air-missiles at them. A slew of anti-aircraft guns also joined the fray.

The choppers swerved from one side to the other in an effort to duck and dodge the enemy missiles and gunfire. One of the helicopters took multiple hits from one of the anti-aircraft guns. It started spewing heavy black smoke from its main engine. The pilot was doing his best to try and maintain control of his chopper, but it was clear he was going down. The helicopter thudded into the ground near the sandy beach where the Marines were landing.

Another pair of Cobras flew in and unloaded their rockets on the enemy lines, and then they fired their own heavy machine guns on the anti-aircraft gun positions. The assistance was unfortunately short-lived. Within only a few minutes, both of the new helicopters exploded when multiple surface-to-air missiles were fired at them from farther behind the enemy lines.

It took nearly five minutes and several short starts and stops before Sergeant Long's squad made it to the first series of buildings overlooking the beach. They threw a handful of grenades into the buildings facing the beach, making sure everyone was dead before they began the process of securing them.

While this was happening, the rest of their platoon double-timed it to his position and set up a new perimeter. Other platoons arriving on the beach moved forward as they now focused their efforts on securing more and more of the city, expanding the beachhead so additional Marines and heavy equipment could be offloaded.

Tim paused for a moment to catch his breath and looked back at the beach. He saw several of the LCACs make their way up the shore, dropping their front gates. Now that some of the beach had been secured, Sergeant Long could see the occasional Abrams battle tank or light-armored vehicle roll off onto the sand.

Finally, he thought. *Those vehicles are exactly what we need to expand the beachhead.*

Within the first hour of the invasion, the Marines had moved off the beach and secured nearly a quarter mile inland, along with most of the coastal villages nearby. Dozens of tanks and other armored vehicles were now being brought ashore as additional waves of Marines continued to join them. It wouldn't be long until they were able to secure the entire surrounding valley and other key objectives.
****

Fourteen hours later, as the Marines tightened their grip on the city of Hamhung, several North Korean soldiers waved a white flag out of one of the government buildings they had been trying to assault for hours.

Sergeant Long yelled at his men. "Hold your fire!"

As the other platoons also stopped shooting, a slight sense of calm enveloped the area. Gun battles raged on in other parts of the city, but in the bubble around Sergeant Long's position, the cacophony of war and death had been paused.

Three enemy soldiers emerged from the building, holding a white flag. They walked towards the American positions, shouting

285

something in Korean that none of them could understand. As they approached Sergeant Long's position, he and a couple of his Marines stood up and motioned for them to stop. Once they had stopped, his Marines moved forward and searched them for weapons or booby traps.

One of the Koreans appeared to be a high-ranking officer. He spoke in barely intelligible English. "I want to speak with the Marine Commander to discuss surrender," he requested.

Their company commander, Captain Dwayne Pepper, came up to them and talked with the Koreans. They repeated their request to speak with the marine commander to discuss terms of surrender. Captain Pepper, along with several additional Marines, escorted the enemy soldiers further back behind the line while they sent a message to battalion HQ.

It took a few minutes, but eventually, they were able to speak with the brigade commander, who arranged for the officers to be brought to the beachhead. Lieutenant General Roy Cutter had just landed and was establishing his new headquarters. They wanted the Korean officer brought over to meet with the general.

****

When Cutter was told a Korean commander wanted to talk surrender, he was caught by surprise. They hadn't been battling them all that long. At the same time, he wasn't about to look a gift horse in the mouth, either. If a local commander wanted to discuss terms of surrender, and he could possibly save the lives of more Marines, then he was more than willing to talk with them. As the enemy soldiers arrived, his executive officer joined him, along with an interpreter.

The senior Korean officer introduced himself. "I am Colonel General Ryu Shin, and I am the senior ranking military member left alive. In the absence of other military commanders from Pyongyang or the other major military headquarters, I have assumed overall command of North Korean forces. I want to discuss terms of surrender with the Marine Commander and find a way to put an end to the killing."

This announcement was music to General Cutter's ears. He hadn't expected to be talking with someone who was now implying that he was the overall commander of North Korea. He invited them to sit down and had some of his aides bring in some hot coffee, tea, and whatever food they could muster. The Korean officers gladly accepted the hot drinks and ate the warm grub like men who hadn't eaten a meal in days.

While the officers were ravenously chowing down, Cutter excused himself to go make contact with General Bennet and the PACOM Commander.

Once General Cutter had explained the situation, Bennet asked, "Can you find out if this man is legit? And can we verify if his claim to be the new overall commander is true? Because if it is, then we might be able to put an end to this conflict sooner rather than later."

Over the next couple of hours, the intelligence community, along with the South Koreans, confirmed they had made a number of signal intercepts that indicated that Colonel General Ryu Shin was, in fact, the new leader of North Korea, or at least he had been asserting himself as such. The South Koreans sent over their terms for what they would accept for surrender, and so did General Bennet and the US PACOM Commander. President Gates and SecDef Castle were also made aware of the development.

It was determined that these gentlemen should be flown out to the *Theodore Roosevelt* supercarrier, where they could meet with senior representatives from the South Korean and the US governments. By the early hours of the following day, a deal had been reached.

The North Koreans were set to announce their unconditional surrender and would make a formal request to the United Nations to have the Chinese withdraw their military forces from North Korea and end the fighting in their country. As hostilities ended between the two Koreas, a transition period would occur, and UN observers would help to disarm the Korean People's Army. After a three-month period and full disarmament, the two Koreas would once again be united.

It was determined that a formal cease-fire and peace agreement would be signed later. It was imperative to get Colonel General Ryu Shin back to his forces, so he could begin to issue the cease-fire orders. While he could not control what the Chinese did, he would do his utmost to have his forces lay down their arms and end the hostilities.

Within an hour of General Ryu returning to his lines, Allied forces intercepted a transmission of him issuing cease-fire and surrender orders to the North Korean People's Army.

"The war is lost," he told his people. "It is now time to start taking care of your families, if they're still alive. The US and South

287

Korean soldiers will bring us food, medicine, and water, but you must lay down your arms. You cannot fire on them. I hereby order you to surrender and return to your homes."

While this order was being carried out, the Chinese government issued a stern warning to the North Korean Army, telling General Ryu that he didn't have the authority to surrender to the Allies. The Chinese said they would shoot any North Korean soldiers who surrendered or abandoned their posts. They also pushed more of their own soldiers across the border in an attempt to hold the country together while they worked on pushing the Americans back across the DMZ.

As the war now dragged on into its 18th day, North Korean military units surrendered in droves, dozens upon dozens of them trying to capitulate before the Chinese army was able to assume control of them. It was a crazy 48 hours as nearly 300,000 Korean soldiers tried to surrender while the Chinese Army raced to get its own military commanders to take charge.

With nearly half of the Korean People's Army killed during the short eighteen days of fighting, close to half of the forces that had survived surrendered before the Chinese assumed control. However, China made it much farther south than the Americans had thought possible.

The rest of the North Korean soldiers ended up being rounded up by the People's Liberation Army. While there were still many thousands of North Korean soldiers in terms of sheer numbers, the vast majority of them were hungry and demoralized. They lacked adequate weapons to be considered combat effective. They were nothing more than a disorganized mob.

As the Chinese moved farther into North Korean territory, these ragged soldiers were marched back towards the Chinese border by their new masters. They were going to be reequipped and reorganized into new units with Chinese officers and NCOs before they would be thrown back into the fighting.

Chapter 55
New Day, New Alliance

Washington, D.C.
White House
Situation Room

President Gates was glad to finally be back in the White House after having to essentially go into hiding. He had only been back in the White House for three days when word came in about the North Koreans seeking terms of surrender. As Gates walked into the Situation Room, everyone rose. He quickly signaled for them to sit back down and took his own seat at the head of the table.

"OK, everyone, bring me up to speed on what's going on in Korea before we transition to anything else. Do we have a cease-fire in place, and what are the Chinese doing in response?" the President asked.

Admiral Peter Meyers, the Chairman of the Joint Chiefs, answered, "Mr. President, we have confirmed that Colonel General Ryu is the highest-ranking military commander left alive in North Korea. He has largely assumed control of the government and military, and they have responded by acknowledging him as their new commander."

"Upon reaching a cease-fire agreement with our forces and the South Koreans, he has agreed to surrender the military and the country. By and large, hundreds of thousands of Korean People's Army units have been surrendering. The units in the far north and units that have linked up with the Chinese Army have been unable to surrender—the Chinese have now assumed control of the remaining KPA forces and have said they'll continue to fight on and unify Korea under their communist rule."

Secretary of Defense Castle piped in at this point, "This was a huge political and strategic victory, Mr. President. While the Chinese plan on continuing the fight in Korea, we have gotten the DPRK to officially surrender within eighteen days of combat. Casualties have been high, but not nearly as high as we had anticipated. As of right now, we have lost 21,248 killed in action, most of those deaths occurred when the Kunson Air Base was nuked. We have also suffered roughly 42,345 wounded, with roughly 60% of them returning to duty within the next couple of weeks."

His demeanor darkened. "Sir, I don't mean to be a pessimist, but the real fighting is still ahead of us as the Chinese continue to move more than 100,000 soldiers across the border. The Air Force is doing their best to bomb and harass them as they make their way down the peninsula, but we're also suffering horrific aircraft losses."

The President's National Security Advisor posed a question to the group. "With the losses we're sustaining in Korea, how is that going to affect our efforts in Europe?"

"That's a good question, Tom," said the President. "We have a major offensive underway in Belarus, Ukraine, *and* the Baltic States. We're starting to sustain some heavy losses there, both in troops and equipment. The last eighteen days of fighting in Korea have also cost us dearly in the way of equipment, aircraft, and soldiers. How are our armed forces faring with all of this? Are we on the verge of utter collapse? Do we need to take a pause in operations to get new trainees deployed and additional equipment built and replaced?"

Several of the military officers sat back in their chairs, looking at Admiral Meyers to see how he would respond. While the military wanted to keep fighting and stay on the offense, they also knew they were running out of soldiers and equipment. They had already signed a series of DoD contracts to plus-up their support operations and private security contractors at their forward deployed bases. The need for support and security personnel was crucial. However, getting everyone a security clearance and getting them deployed to where they were needed was proving to be a logistical challenge they were having a hard time meeting.

Admiral Meyers signaled that he would answer this question, letting the national security advisor off the hook. "We're stretched beyond our breaking point, Mr. President. While we've won a major victory in Korea, the Navy was hit hard. We lost a supercarrier, and the *Carl Vinson* is going to be out of action for several months while it undergoes major repairs at the shipyard. We've hurt the Chinese navy in northern China, but we haven't gone after their blue water navy that is now taking up station around Taiwan. That force has already sunk or heavily damaged much of the Taiwanese navy. The continual air and missile bombardment of the country has also caused significant damage to their air force and their ability to defend the island. It's only a matter of time before they launch their invasion."

290

He plowed on. "In Europe, the 82nd Airborne has neutralized the Russian incursions into the Baltic states. While they've prevented the Russians from capturing them, they're in no position to push across the border into Russia. They are purely trying to hold the line. Our incursion into Belarus by Three Corps has been met by extremely hard resistance. While we maintained control of Minsk for several days, ultimately our forces were pushed back and forced to give up the city. We had thought Three Corps would have been able to capture the Russian 6th Tank Army, but after they rushed in significant reinforcements, including a Russian Spetsnaz brigade and two airborne brigades to Belarus, they have successfully beaten our forces back. In Ukraine, we have bloodied them up but were unable to obtain a breakthrough."

The President sighed heavily, then looked back to his military advisor. "So, what exactly is the problem, then? We had the forces in place after weeks of shuffling units around and moving our forces forward. Why are the NATO member states not contributing more forces to help us defeat the Russians? This war has been going on for nearly eleven weeks. The Russians should have been pushed out of Ukraine already. Why haven't we been able to make that happen?" asked an exasperated Gates.

The Secretary of State spoke up for the first time since the start of the meeting. "Mr. President, NATO is a mess right now. We have some member states contributing as much as possible to the alliance—Canada, Bulgaria, Romania, Albania, Croatia, the Baltic states, and Norway—but these countries' forces are small. Their air forces have been invaluable, but they have also sustained heavy losses, just as our aircraft have. The unfortunate part is that these nations do not have the financial means or the industrial capability to replace the losses they've been sustaining."

"Hmm," said Gates, deep in thought.

Secretary Johnson continued. "Moving to the larger member states—the UK has committed their two most capable brigades. They have been performing exceptionally well and have been a huge help. But even with the activation of their reserves, their forces are just not large enough to be a turning point in the war. The RAF has been a godsend. They are performing better than expected, but again, they're limited in the number of aircraft they can provide. The Royal Navy is in even worse shape. Their aircraft carrier is still not operational yet, they lack the aircraft to support it, and they only have three escort ships available for it. We aren't sure when their navy will be able to get into the war."

"As to Germany, the units they have committed have performed exceptionally well, but they have also sustained heavy casualties. Chancellor Schneider has announced a conscription of two million men and women into their military. They have also started retooling their industry to crank out military equipment. The Germans are no longer sitting on the sidelines militarily. It'll take time, but the German war machine is once again turned on, it will start to make an impact. But it won't be apparent until sometime in the spring. Moving to France—like the Germans, they're doubling down on their military. They've sent their best units forward and are currently conscripting two million additional soldiers."

Johnson then squirmed in his chair for a minute before continuing, "The issue we're having is with Spain, Portugal, Italy, Greece, and Hungary. They're not wanting to release their militaries to NATO, nor are they mobilizing their armies or doing anything to increase their military capability or defense readiness. I believe that we need to follow the example of what happened to Turkey and remove any noncontributing nations from the alliance."

Gates looked like he wanted to hit something. Fire was burning in his eyes as he sat there and listened to the failings of NATO. "Look, it's become pretty clear that NATO is just a boys' club, not a serious military organization. I propose that we end NATO as an organization and look to create a new global military alliance force that includes countries like Australia, Japan, and South Korea, along with those European countries that are willing to be a part of the new alliance."

The President paused for a minute, thinking about what he wanted to say next. "I believe we should form a new global alliance—one that can address the threats of the 21st century and will work together for the common good. As to its name, let's call it the Global Defense Force, or GDF. It will function like NATO. An attack on one member would be considered an attack on all, but unlike NATO, it would be US-led. Participating nations would have to commit 3% of GDP to military spending and a minimum troop count level. The members would be required to maintain a certain force composition and structure, so they could effectively contribute to the alliance. Thoughts on this?" asked the President.

Admiral Meyers was the first to speak. "I believe this could be great. We could integrate new members that aren't geographically dependent but are willing to be a part of an alliance of mutual defense."

Secretary Castle was next to speak up. "I have to agree with Admiral Meyers. I say we move forward with this. This conflict has shown us how ineffective NATO has become, and we're going to need to think globally and look to integrate new allies that share our same global interests and goals."

For the next thirty minutes, everyone discussed this new proposition and came to the conclusion that it should be formally developed and created. The President signaled for them to get to work on creating this alliance while he directed the rest of his military leaders to continue to execute the war.

The plan in Europe was to slow things down while they waited for the new troops to finish their training and for additional equipment to be produced. It was already mid-November, and winter was starting to set in. It was a good natural time to pause the conflict and consolidate their positions while they rebuilt the military. Meanwhile, the war in Korea would progress as the Chinese tried to secure as much of the country as possible.

Chapter 56
Battle of Hwangsuwon Air Base

Hilltop 079

After ODA 1110's initial strike against the KPA's mobile ballistic missile launchers a couple of days earlier, CW4 Charles "Chucky" Lee moved his team to Hilltop 079, overlooking the Hwangsuwon Air Base. Their new overwatch position sat above a small reservoir and dam that also gave them a view of not just the base below, which had already been bombed multiple times, but also provided them with an overwatch position of the main highway that ran from north to south across the country.

The Chinese army would have to move along this path if they were going to secure the lower half of the Korean peninsula and prevent the Marines from establishing a solid foothold behind the KPA frontlines. ODA 1110's new mission was to continually monitor the traffic on the road and call in air strikes as often as possible.

Sergeant First Class Mark "Maverick" Wilson placed his small utility shovel down on the small dirt mound in front of him and took a long drink of water. Since arriving at their hilltop observation point a day ago, they had been hastily digging in and creating a defensive perimeter. While they had no plans to stand and fight against a larger force should they be discovered, it would have been foolish to not prepare some fighting positions in case it became necessary.

Technical Sergeant Jordan "Jordy" Mitchel moved over to Chucky and announced, "I just received a situation report from Henhouse. They said we have a large formation of Chinese soldiers heading towards the air base. They want to know if we can be ready to call in a series of air strikes as they start to arrive."

Chucky nodded. "Tell them we'll be ready. Make sure you get a good idea on what strike packages we have on hand. Also, find out from Henhouse—if we need extraction, what's the plan? I don't like not having an exit strategy this deep behind enemy lines," he said, speaking in a low enough voice that only he and Jordy could hear.

A couple of hours went by before they spotted the first columns of Chinese soldiers. It looked to be a mechanized unit of some sort. They had armored personnel carriers and a slew of air-defense vehicles, tanks, and other troop transport vehicles. It looked to be at least a battalion's worth, maybe more of vehicles.

Chucky turned to Jordy, signaling him silently with his hands and asking if he had a good grid on the targets for an air strike. Jordy smiled and nodded in reply. Chucky indicated he should go ahead and call in the strike. The entire ODA team had gone silent at this point. They were only communicating with hand signals, and if necessary, very quietly through their throat mics.

"Henhouse, Watchman Five. We have positive ID on a Chinese armored column at grid November Kilo 764 576, break. They are on main road heading towards destroyed DPRK air base, Break...we observe multiple IFVs, MBTs, anti-aircraft artillery vehicles. How copy, over?" Jordy said over his mic.

Roughly ten agonizing seconds later, Henhouse responded, "Watchman Five, that is a good copy. Can you give us a better description on the air-defense vehicles? Over."

Chucky crawled closer to Jordy at this point and pulled out his binoculars. He scanned the enemy vehicles, attempting to identify the specific air-defense vehicles traveling with the column. Speaking softly into the mic, he said, "They look like SA-22s and SA-19s, so be advised they have air-defense support with the column." It was only fair to pass along as much of information as possible to the pilots who would have to fly in for this mission.

Their command acknowledged and told them to stand by while a strike package was put together.

Three minutes later, Henhouse came back over the radio, informing them that a pair of Vipers would fly in to suppress the enemy air defense while a couple of pairs of Marine F/A-18 Hornets brought the pain. Jordy and Chucky exchanged smiles, knowing what was heading towards that Chinese column. They passed the word down to the others to be ready. So far, they hadn't spotted any enemy soldiers near them or looking for them, but that might change if the Chinese believed their positions were being monitored from the hills above.

Fifteen minutes later, as they continued to observe the vehicles arriving at the destroyed DPRK air base, a flurry of activity began. The men manning the air-defense vehicles began to get them ready to engage an unseen enemy. The other armored vehicles and tanks in the group scattered to different portions of the air base while the infantry soldiers ran to various dugout shelters.

The few remaining North Korean forces at the base waved in the direction the air attack would most likely come from. The SA-22, which had both missiles and twin 30mm cannons, turned and swung its weapons in that direction.

In seconds, the two cannons opened fire, throwing hundreds of projectiles in the direction of the American aircraft. These were quickly followed by several SAMs being launched at the incoming threats. A few seconds later, an American missile streaked across the sky and plowed into the vehicle, exploding it into a million little pieces.

The second SA-22 and the SA-19 Grison both opened up with their 30mm autocannons and their own anti-air missiles. A second American missile plowed into the Grison, shattering it in spectacular fashion. At this point, the remaining SA-22 had turned off his radar and moved his vehicle back several hundred feet at high speed. Another American missile plowed into the dirt where it had just been. The SA-22 turned its search radar back on and fired off four anti-air missiles at the incoming F/A-18s and the Vipers still trying to kill them.

As Chucky and Jordy observed the fighting going on below them, they couldn't help but marvel at the skill of the men on both sides trying to leverage their technology and weapon systems in an effort to defeat each other. When the SA-22 fired off four anti-air missiles, they watched as one of them zeroed in on an F-16. The missile exploded below and just behind the aircraft. It was clear the fighter had sustained heavy damage. The F-16 began trailing smoke and tried to maneuver back towards friendly lines.

One of the F/A-18s that had dove in on the airfield to attack the armored column flew in fast, releasing a series of 500-pound bombs, ripping multiple vehicles apart in their destructive wake. As the Hornet angled skyward to gain altitude, the lone remaining SA-22 was tracking it and fired a string of 30mm cannon fire in its direction. The American aircraft jinked hard from one side to another in an attempt to dodge the incoming enemy rounds.

The first F/A-18 was lucky and gained enough altitude to escape the enemy fire. However, his partner flew right into it. The second F/A-18 was blown into a million little pieces before it was able to release its ordnance. The pilot was able to eject, and as luck would have it, the aircraft came apart as it flew over ODA 1110's observation point. When the pilot ejected, he was nearly on top of them. As his chute opened and descended, several members from Chucky's team were there to greet him and keep him silent. They brought him into their lines, along with the other pilot they had rescued earlier.

Chucky walked up to the Marine aviator and held his hand out. "I'm Chief Warrant Officer 4 Charles Lee. I'm in charge of this Special Forces A-Team you dropped into. Until we're relieved or extracted, you are now going to operate under my control. Is that understood Major…Woods?"

Major Woods wasn't sure what to make of the men in green faces who had just rescued him. He had practically been on top of them when he'd ejected from his aircraft. Ultimately, he was just glad *they* had found him and not the Chinese or the North Koreans.

Woods chuckled quietly and then smiled. "It sounds like you have a deal, Chief. I can't thank you guys enough for recovering me. I thought for certain I'd be captured," he said as he shook Chucky's hand. Chucky led him to the center of their perimeter so they could talk a little more freely for a few minutes.

Turning to look at the Marine aviator, Chucky explained, "Listen, we've been deep behind enemy lines since before the start of the war. So far, we haven't been spotted, but it's only a matter of time. If the Marines establish a beachhead, do you think you could speak to them and have them bail us out?" he asked.

They hadn't gotten any sort of confirmation from Henhouse on their extraction, but with them recovering this second downed pilot, the likelihood of them needing an extraction was increasing by the hour. It wouldn't take the Chinese or KPA long before they sent a search party in this direction.

Woods thought about this question for a minute, not sure how much information he should disclose. Seeing that his own life might depend on the answer, he decided to be direct and give them the truth. "The Marines have already secured a beachhead. They've pushed about ten miles inland, so believe it or not, they're only around ninety miles from this position. The fact that the PLA is moving a lot of units here is not good. It means they're going to try and push our Marines back into the ocean. As for an extraction, I'm not sure. As you just saw, the enemy air-defense capability around here is pretty strong. I'm not sure our helicopters would survive. If the Air Force can get a few more Viper missions to suppress them, then yeah, I think it's possible."

The two of them talked for a few minutes longer before they gave the major a commandeered AK-47 and about a dozen magazines. They placed him in a fighter hole near one of the other SF soldiers on the perimeter and told him to stay silent and watch while they reported their position to higher headquarters and asked for an extraction.

For the next ten minutes, they went back and forth with Henhouse on the details. It was determined that the Air Force would have to conduct additional Wild Weasel missions in the area. Once the enemy had been thinned out, then they could try for an extraction.
****

DPRK Hwangsuwon Air Base

Brigadier General Cho wasn't happy. His division had been getting harassed from the air for the past several days by the Americans and Japanese, greatly slowing down his progress. He should have arrived at this DPRK air base two days ago. His orders were to get it operational for the People's Liberation Army Air Force. However, just as his lead battalion arrived at the base, they came under additional air attacks by American F-16s and F/A-18s.

"Colonel Fang, I need you to keep these Yankee aircraft off our backs! How soon until the rest of your air-defense brigade is able to set up a perimeter at the DPRK air base and stop these attacks?!" Cho demanded angrily.

Colonel Fang had been doing his best to provide air defense for the 39th Army, but it had been nearly impossible to keep the Americans from getting through. Between their stealth aircraft and electronic jamming, his air-defense systems were having a hard time suppressing the American air superiority.

"I understand the problem, General Cho. We are working on solving it. I just lost two of the three SAM systems I sent to the air base earlier today. The air force is supposed to start providing us with more fighter support. That should help the situation until I can get additional SA-21 systems set up," he responded.

The accusation that his brigade wasn't doing the best they could made him hot under the collar. He had been getting yelled at by nearly every division and brigade commander since their army group had crossed into North Korea at the start of the war.

Walking over to Colonel Fang, General Cho leaned in and said in a low voice, "Look, the American Marines are less than ninety miles from the Hwangsuwon Air Base. Once they land enough forces, they're going to make a concerted push in this direction. With the North Koreans having surrendered to the Allies, we have to secure as much of the country as possible. What can you do to establish some sort of air-defense corridor to allow us to marshal enough forces to push them back into the sea?" he asked in a much calmer tone.

"Sometimes the best way to get what you want is to apply honey when the vinegar has clearly not worked," Cho remembered.

The sudden surrender of the North Koreans had caught the Chinese army off guard and certainly made things a bit more complicated. The PLA now had to secure as much of the country as possible.

Pausing for a minute before responding, Colonel Fang replied, "I need you to secure the surrounding hills and ridges around the air base. We need to make sure there are no enemy soldiers nearby calling in air strikes on us. From the reports I read from one of my units at the base, they came under air attack almost as soon as they arrived at the base. Clearly an enemy force is operating in the area. Find and destroy them, and I'll get you an air-defense corridor."

General Cho nodded. "I'll have my division start to clear the surrounding hills and ensure there are no Americans observing the base. In the meantime, please move additional air-defense vehicles to the base. My infantry forces will work with your men to identify new positions to locate the SAMs and anti-aircraft guns to best protect the base."

The two men talked for a few more minutes and then went their separate ways to get things moving.

General Cho waved to his executive officer for him to come over to him. Cho unfolded his map on the side of his command ZBD-04A infantry fighting vehicle and spat the piece of gum he had been chewing into his hand. Then he applied it to both corners of the map and pressed them against the side armor of the vehicle.

"You didn't want to use one of the tables?" his XO said with a slight chuckle as he approached his commander.

Smiling and then laughing at what he had just done, he responded, "Sometimes when you have an idea, you just have to run with it before it fades away. Come here and look at the map of the DPRK air base. I just got done talking with Colonel Fang from our air-defense brigade. He insisted that there must be an American, ROK, or Japanese unit operating on one of these ridges or hilltops near the air base, calling in air strikes. He has asked if we could help clear these areas, so he can bring in additional air-defense systems. Then the engineers can work on getting the airfield operational again for the air force."

General Cho showed his XO multiple hilltops and ridgelines in the vicinity of the air base. "Colonel Fang also said they had shot down two aircraft. One of the pilots was able to eject in the vicinity of this hilltop, roughly a mile and a half from the air base, but no one has gone looking for the pilot yet."

The XO gave a puzzled look. *Why didn't anyone send a search party?* he wondered. *Seems like someone isn't doing their job...*

"I'm going to call Fifth Brigade and find out why they haven't secured that downed pilot yet. They should have," he replied. "We have a Special Forces battalion we can call and see if they'll support us in trying to ferret out this enemy force in the area. Would you like me to give them a call and see if they can spare any units?" his XO offered. He knew his commander was under a lot of pressure to secure the air base and then move to the coast to make contact with the American Marines.

General Cho nodded and signaled that it was time for them to get back on the road. "Have the rest of the division continue to move towards the air base. We need to get it secured and operational within the next 24 hours, if possible."
****

Hilltop 079

Maverick signaled Chunk, their demolition expert, to crawl over to his position. Sighing, Chunk slowly crawled out of his fighting position and made his way over to Maverick's little foxhole, which was fifteen yards away from his own. "This had better be good—I just opened my tortellini and cheese. It's now getting cold," he said in reference to his MRE, snickering at his desire to eat such a meal.

Maverick ignored the joke and handed him his spotting lens. "What do you see down there at the base of the hill?"

Chunk grudgingly took the glasses from Maverick and began to scan down below. The bottom of the hill was roughly 4,000 yards below them and had a fairly steep elevation. A soldier on foot could easily scale it, but not a tracked vehicle. As he peered through the trees towards the clearing at the bottom of the hill, his eyes spotted something. At first, it was just a couple of what appeared to be Chinese soldiers. But as he scanned the area, he spotted dozens of infantrymen, all heading up the hill towards their position.

"I see we have company joining us for lunch," he replied as he handed the binoculars back. "You better tell Chucky."

Keying his mic, Maverick said, "Chucky, we have company heading our direction from the base of the hill. Chunk and I spotted at least a couple dozen infantrymen. How do you want us to proceed?"

Chucky had been hoping they could stay undetected for a little while longer, but with the downing of the Hornet pilot, he had known that was becoming less and less likely.

This is going to get ugly fast, he thought.

Keying his own mic, Chucky responded, "Stand by and monitor them. I'm going to raise Henhouse and advise them of our situation."

"Henhouse, this is Watchman Five. We have enemy soldiers heading towards our position. What is the likelihood of us being able to get an extraction?" he asked for probably the tenth time in the last three hours.

A couple of minutes went by before they heard the familiar voice of Henhouse. "The Air Force is going to vector in two pairs of Wild Weasels to your position. Depending on their success, we may be able to arrange for an extraction on the back side of Hill 079, roughly 2,000 yards from your current position. How copy?"

Chucky smiled at that news. They had been going around and around, trying to get an extraction. "That's a good copy, Henhouse. How soon until the Vipers show up?"

The radio came back to life quickly in response. "They should be inbound in less than five mikes. Stand by, and report back on any battle damage assessments."

As the enemy soldiers slowly climbed up the hill they were dug in on, additional armored troop carriers and tanks fanned out around the air base. Several pieces of construction equipment showed up as well; two bulldozers and a couple of graders had begun the process of filling in the craters on the runways and taxiways. Two more SA-22s had also shown up, and it looked like an SA-10 was being set up not far from the dam and the edge of the reservoir. Then, they heard the unmistakable sound of jet engines.

Once the jets could be heard, the SA-22s and SA-20s began to fill the sky with surface-to-air missiles, intermixed with their 30mm anti-aircraft guns. Several PGZ95 Chinese self-propelled anti-aircraft vehicles also opened up with their quad 25mm autocannons, filling the sky with green tracers and SAMs.

The overwhelming rumble of war was incredible; the thunderous booms of hundreds of 30mm and 25mm autocannon rounds echoed throughout the valley and filled the sky. Then Chucky and the rest of his team saw several missiles impact against the body of two PGZ95s, which blew up violently, throwing flames and shrapnel in all directions.

Then, one of the SA-20s exploded in spectacular fashion, just as the others had earlier in the day. Only this time, they saw one of the F-16s explode in midair as one of the SAMs collided with it. As more SAMs flew after the F-16s and additional anti-aircraft fire continued to light up the sky, another Viper pilot was hit, though he managed to limp his aircraft away. Fortunately, before he had to leave the battle, he managed to shoot down two more of the anti-aircraft vehicles.

There was just one more SA-22 left in the vicinity of the air base as the last two Viper pilots zoomed in to go after it. They both released a series of snake eye 500-pound bombs as they banked hard to the north. The two aircraft lit up their afterburners, putting as much space as possible between themselves and the bombs they had just released.

The four bombs landed near the SA-22 and several other ZBD infantry fighting vehicles, tearing them apart and killing the crews and the nearby soldiers instantly. As the remaining American aircraft headed out to sea and the relative safety it provided, the carnage they left below was impressive.

While they had lost one F-16 in the short engagement, they had also eliminated the remaining SAM and anti-aircraft vehicles near the DPRK air base. Meanwhile, additional tanks, infantry fighting vehicles and other self-propelled artillery guns continued to arrive with little to no air-defense systems left to protect them. It wouldn't be long until additional SAMs were brought in. However, until that happened, Chucky signaled for Jordy to try and call in as much air support as possible on the enemy vehicles marshaling at the base below.

As Jordy was on the radio setting up the air strikes, a company-sized element of Chinese infantry moved steadily up the ridge, towards the spot where their team had dug in. Chucky was left with two hard decisions: they could maintain the tactical advantage they held right now of controlling the top of the hill and being entrenched, or they could leave the safety of the high ground and try to evade down the backside of the slope. If they chose the second option, they would have to try to set up a new landing zone and hope for the best.

Chucky realized that the problem with escaping was the two downed pilots with them. Neither of them had the equipment or training in how to evade to the level that his team did. It would slow his team down, and in all likelihood, they'd end up giving their position away.

In that moment, he made his decision. They would stand and fight while they waited for their extraction to get close enough for them to bug out.

"Henhouse, this is Watchman Five. We have good battle damage assessment from the Vipers. There's only one SA-22 left at the air base. However, we're also seeing additional armor, self-propelled artillery, and infantry fighting vehicles arriving at the base—looks to be about a battalion in size, though that number continues to increase each hour. Requesting immediate extraction at landing zone Papa. How copy? Over." Lee spoke into the mic softly but succinctly.

It took a few minutes before they heard a response, "Watchman Five, this is Henhouse. That's a good copy. We're dispatching the extraction now. Expect two CH-53K Sea Stallions and four Cobra gunships, courtesy of the Marines. ETA ninety minutes."

"Good copy, we'll stand by. Out," Lee replied. He turned to his team's private net. "Heads up, guys. We have an extraction inbound, ETA 90 minutes, at LZ Papa."

Maverick looked down at the enemy troops moving towards them and made the quick calculation in his head that they would arrive before their extraction. Keying his mic, he said, "Chief, those PLA soldiers below us are probably less than fifteen mikes away from making contact. What's the plan?" he asked

Lee sat there next to the log he was using for cover. He craned his neck and looked around the hilltop. About one hundred yards further down the hill, on the opposite side of the Chinese soldiers, the ground leveled out and there were only a few small trees.

What if we cut those smaller trees down and move the LZ closer to us? he wondered. That way, they wouldn't give the enemy a chance to take the hilltop just as their rescue helicopters started to arrive.

Keying his mic, he said, "Chunk, I want you to take your explosives and head down the slope behind us. Roughly a hundred yards away is a plateau with a few smaller trees on it. I want you to rig those trees to be blown down with some det cord. We need to create a new LZ closer to us, so we can defend the hilltop for the extraction. How copy?"

Chunk turned to look back to the area Chucky had just mentioned, and sure enough there was a small plateau just large enough for a CH-53K helicopter, assuming they removed a few of those trifling trees.

Yeah, that can work, he thought as he smiled.

"No problem, Chief, I'm on it," Chunk replied, and then he scurried away to get their new LZ ready.

"Henhouse, this is Watchman Five. We have enemy troops converging on our position. Estimate contact within ten minutes. We're changing the landing zone to grid November Kilo 7657 8684. It's a small plateau near our existing position. Please be advised that this will be a hot extraction. How copy?" he asked.

They acknowledged the change in plans and informed him that the gunships would lead the way into the area to pick them up.

Lee then turned to Jordy, his Air Force tactical air combat controller, and said, "See what kind of air support you can raise to hit the base below and provide us with some air support, OK?"

Jordy had a grim look on his face as he nodded. He had already been working the air support angle before Chucky had even asked.

The enemy soldiers had now advanced to within 300 yards of their current position. When they had set up their position a couple of days ago, they had placed a series of roughly twelve Claymore mines in front of them. Eight of them were roughly 50 yards away, while the remaining four were less than twenty meters away. Lee, however, didn't want to let the enemy get that close to them. He hoped to save the Claymores for when the helicopters arrived and they needed to bugout.

304

When the soldiers got within 250 yards, Chucky keyed his throat mic. "Everyone, mark your targets and be ready. When you hear me fire the first shot, open up and let's cut these guys down. Our choppers are now 45 minutes away. We need to make sure these guys aren't able to interfere with our extraction."

Everyone was tense. Up to that point, they hadn't engaged any enemy soldiers since their infiltration. They had managed to stay below the radar, hidden, while they called in relentless air strikes. But in a few seconds, everyone in the valley below and at the enemy air base was about to know they were there.

Lee looked down his rifle sights and spotted who he believed to be the Chinese officer in charge of the group. He was holding a pistol and yelling, pointing in the different directions where he wanted groups of soldiers to move to.

Knowing this was likely the officer in charge, Lee moved his right thumb ever so slightly to the selector switch and turned it from safe to single-shot. He slowly applied pressure to the trigger with his right index finger until he felt the firing pin slam against the primer. This ignited the cartridge, sending the 5.56mm projectile 2,841 feet per second down the length of the barrel to impact in the center mass of the Chinese officer he had been aiming at. The officer clutched at his chest and then collapsed to the ground.

This all happened in less than a second, and it took a moment for the sound of the round being fired to reach the rest of the Chinese soldiers before they reacted. Within that fraction of a second, the eleven other members of ODA 1110 opened fire with their own weapons. The downed pilots also joined in the chorus with the additional rifles the Special Forces had given them. As the fourteen Americans began to pour accurate and heavy fire down on the Chinese soldiers, nearly forty of them were killed outright before they even knew what was happening.

The remaining enemy soldiers dropped to the ground and scrambled for cover as they slowly returned fire at the Americans. The Chinese soldiers were now desperate to escape the ambush they had walked into. As an officer or sergeant was identified by the Americans, they were killed off, leaving the remaining enemy soldiers leaderless at a critical moment. In less than two minutes, the enemy soldiers who were still left alive tried to break contact and began to fall back further down the hill, trying to escape the killing field

Five minutes after they had opened fire on the Chinese soldiers, the short engagement had ended. Now, all they could hear was the cries of agony from the wounded and the dying that had been left behind by their comrades. They could still hear some of the enemy soldiers further down the hill shouting something in Chinese, but they were unable to make it out.

"Is anyone hurt?" Lee said over the team net, trying to do a quick assessment. Everyone reported back that they were fine, and they had only burned through a couple of magazines of ammunition. The machine gunners reported they had each burned through two 100-round belts but were otherwise good to go on ammo.

While the team continued to assess their situation, they spotted dozens of vehicles now heading towards the base of the hill they were on. These vehicles were undoubtedly bringing additional reinforcements.

Chucky tried to get in touch with Sergeant First Class Obed "Eagle Eye" Perez, the ODA's resident sniper. "Eagle Eye, set up that M82 and see if you can slow down some of those vehicles," Lee ordered.

"Copy that, Chucky. Give me a minute, and I'll start hitting them," Perez replied.

He placed his M4 on the ground to the right of his position and unpacked and assembled his M82 Barrett .50 sniper rifle. As he snapped the optics on, he placed his first 10-round box magazine in the rifle. He pulled the bolt back and chambered the first round, sighting in on the lead truck, which was carrying close to twenty enemy soldiers.

Eagle Eye placed the red dot of his sight on the engine and pulled the trigger. The rifle recoiled hard into his shoulder, but no more than what he had expected. The half-inch round reached out nearly a mile and slammed into the engine block of the truck. A trail of smoke emanated from the hood as the truck rolled to a stop. The soldiers in it immediately jumped out of the vehicle and took cover, not sure if another bullet might be aimed at them next.

A second truck, an infantry fighting vehicle, moved around the now disabled truck and began to head towards Hill 079. The turret gunner turned his 30mm autocannon in their direction and began to fire. Everyone dropped down behind their cover as the 30mm rounds tore through the trees and vegetation around them.

As branches and leaves fell on Eagle Eye, he aimed at the turret, hoping he might kill the gunner or vehicle commander with his next shot. He squeezed the trigger and felt the weapon kick as his next round hit the turret, punching a small hole into it. Then he aimed just slightly to the right of his first round and fired again. He put two more quick shots in the turret, and it stopped firing at them. He wasn't sure if he had killed them, but he had stopped them from shooting at his comrades, and that was all that mattered.

While he had been focused on that ZBD-04, two more had opened fire with their own turrets. One was equipped with a 30mm autocannon like the first one that had fired at them, and the second was equipped with a 100mm cannon. As the Chinese began to fire, a tree not more than twenty yards below them exploded. Additional 30mm rounds raked their position as well.

While the 30mm gun was causing them problems, the 100mm cannon needed to be taken out first. Eagle Eye aimed at the turret of this ZBD just like he had the first one and fired several quick rounds. He dropped the box magazine and replaced it with a fresh one.

Just as he took aim at the third infantry fighting vehicle, a Type 99A main battle tank fired its 125mm cannon in his direction. The tank's high-explosive round hit not more than fifteen feet away from his position. Eagle Eye felt like multiple sledgehammers were hitting his back, legs and right arm. He momentarily blacked out.

When he opened his eyes, he hurt everywhere. He tried to move his right arm, only it didn't respond. He turned to look at his right arm and saw that it was barely being held together by some muscles and tendons. With each pulse, he saw more blood squirt out, pooling on the ground around him. "This is Eagle Eye. I'm hit bad. I need help," he managed to say in a weak voice that was barely audible over the sound of battle.

The team's medic, Sergeant First Class Rich "Doc" Tory came out of nowhere and landed right next to Eagle Eye.

"Let me look you over, buddy," he said, assessing his friend's wounds. He cursed under his breath.

Eagle Eye's limb was nearly ripped off, and he had several deep gashes in his back. Doc pulled a tourniquet out of his bag and tied it off an inch or so above the wound. He applied pressure on it until he saw the wound had finally stopped squirting blood. Then he applied several

307

bandages on Eagle Eye's back, pouring some quick-clotting powder in an attempt to stop the bleeding. Then he pulled out a bag of plasma and started an IV.

While Doc was working on stabilizing Eagle Eye, the rest of the team were doing their best to keep their heads down as the Chinese moved hundreds of soldiers to the base of the hill. The PLA started storming up toward them, firing at the team as they went. Just as the enemy fire peaked, with the armored vehicles and tanks below adding their own fire to the battle, Jordy signaled to Lee that he had a pair of Marine F/A-18s inbound to provide support.

The valley below and the area around the enemy airfield lit up with anti-aircraft fire, throwing hundreds of 25mm and 30mm rounds into the air. Then they heard the unmistakable sound of jet aircraft flying through the valley at high speed.

Multiple 500-pound bombs landed among the armored vehicles below, scoring direct hits against the tanks and other armored vehicles. Hundreds of enemy soldiers who hadn't yet started up the hill were also caught in the bomb's blast, which killed or maimed many of them.

The remaining enemy soldiers continued to advance toward the Americans, who were not in a position to escape. Occasionally, several of the Chinese would pause to launch an RPG at them. One of the downed pilots screamed out in pain after an RPG hit near him. He yelled for a medic at the top of his lungs, clearly in agony. Doc left Eagle Eye bandaged up with the IV bag of plasma and ran over to Major Wood's position.

The Marine aviator had a horrible gash in his abdomen. His intestines were partly visible, poking through the wound. He was trying to use his hand to push them back inside his own stomach.

Doc immediately grabbed a pressure dressing from his bag. "Woods, I need you to lay down. I know this hurts. I'm going to give you a quick shot of morphine, but I need you to lay back so I can wrap up your wound, OK?"

Major Woods nodded through gritted teeth. As he lay flat on his back, Doc could better see the wound. He grabbed the intestines and pushed them back into the wound, pouring some water over the wound and then applying the pressure dressing to hold everything in place. Then Doc grabbed the syringe of morphine, biting the cover off with his teeth to expose the needle. He immediately stuck it in Major Woods' right thigh and let it work its magic.

He spat out the cap. "Hang in there," he told his patient. "Our extraction chopper isn't that far away."

Meanwhile, 30mm rounds, RPGs, and high-explosive rounds from the various cannons, not to mention bullets from the hundreds of infantrymen coming their way, filling the air with hot lead and shrapnel.

Doc heard the other members of his team viciously returning fire. They were throwing hundreds of 5.56mm and 7.62mm rounds down the hill at the enemy, in a volume of fire that far exceeded the team's limited number of personnel. Like most ODA teams, they were punching way above their weight class and making the enemy pay for each foot of distance they traveled up the hill.

Lee looked over at Jordy. "Can you get us any more air support? We need them to place some bombs danger close, several hundred meters below us!" Chucky yelled to his tactical air combat controller.

Jordy was already on the radio to a flight of Marine F/A-18s, begging for air support. "We have troops in contact—multiple US forces casualties and in danger of being overrun. Requesting all available air support," he said frantically over the radio net to any fighter aircraft monitoring this frequency.

A new pair of F/A-18s heard the cries of distress. "We still have two 500-pound bombs each. We will come in hot and heavy on the coordinates you provided."

Then a pair of A-10 Warthogs came over the net, saying, "We have a full load of bombs. We can assist." Jordy vectored them in towards their position and warned them of the enemy anti-aircraft guns near the enemy air base.

The F/A-18s came in first, hitting several of the armored vehicles and anti-aircraft vehicles and guns near the enemy airfield. When the A-10s arrived, they dropped a series of cluster bombs across the base of the hill and near their positions, obliterating the enemy soldiers advancing up the hill towards them.

While the A-10s tore into the enemy, one of the 25mm anti-aircraft guns stopped firing at the F/A-18s and took aim at the Warthogs. Within seconds, one of the A-10s' engines was riddled with 25mm rounds, causing the engine to explode.

Black smoke billowed out of the aircraft as it banked hard to the left, trying to gain altitude and move away from the anti-aircraft gun. The Warthog continued to take hits, until the pilot realized that he wouldn't make it if he stuck around. He opted to limp back toward home. The other A-10 did his best to rake the enemy positions with his 30mm gun and his remaining bombs before turning to home to escort his wounded comrade back to base.

While these attacks were taking place, they began to hear the familiar sound of helicopter blades beating against the air in their rhythmic thumping.

Jordy heard a call over the radio from the Cobra gunship pilots. "We're going to make a few quick passes to hit the enemy positions. We need you to move while we cover you. Fall back to the LZ now," they told him.

Chucky spoke into his mic. "Chunk—it's time to blow those charges on the trees in our makeshift LZ."

Seconds later, he heard a series of smaller explosions. Chunk came over the radio, shouting, "The alternate landing zone is ready."

Then the pilot in the lead CH-53 came over the net. "We're on our final approach to the LZ."

"Maverick, I need you to buy us some time to get the pilots on board the helicopters before you join us at the LZ. I want to blow the Claymores if the enemy gets close enough. When I give you the signal to head to the helicopters, blow the Claymores whether there's enemy nearby or not. Got it!?" Chucky yelled before he got up to look for the pilots.

He ran over to Major Woods. Noticing his stomach injury, he pulled him off the ground. Doc was helping Eagle Eye move to the LZ, and a couple more of the wounded were also making their way to the CH-53K, which had settled down on the plateau they had just cleared.

As the wind from the rotor wash hit Chucky's face, he felt a sudden relief as he approached the back ramp with Major Woods on his shoulder. A Navy corpsman ran forward and assisted in taking the wounded pilot from him before assessing his injuries in the helicopter.

Chucky sent the final message to Maverick. "It's time. Blow the charges and beat feet back to the LZ!"

Chucky couldn't hear the Claymores going off, but he saw a small cloud of smoke rise from their old positions. He knew they must have gone off. Then he saw Maverick come running over the hilltop towards them. The second CH-53K was still in a low hover a couple of hundred meters behind them; the door gunner opened fire on something he saw.

One of the Super Cobras flew in low and fast, firing off several 70mm antipersonnel rockets and using his chin gun on something. As Maverick made his way into the helicopter, the tail gunner let the pilots know they had everyone on board. The chopper lifted off and turned away from the Chinese positions and down the opposite valley.

The Cobras stayed behind for a few minutes longer, tearing into the enemy vehicles and positions below. Out of nowhere, a pair of Chengdu J-10s flew in and blew three of the four Cobras out of the sky. Before the J-10s could go hunting for the two CH-53Ks and the remaining Cobra, a pair of F/A-18s joined the fray. The fighters took their fight high in the sky, allowing the rescue helicopters to escape.

Chief Lee took his helmet off and rubbed his hand through his sweaty, greasy hair with his right hand, still in a bit of disbelief that they had made it out. He was completely unaware of the enemy fighters in the area, or the fact that three of the four Cobras had just been shot down.

All he knew was that everyone in his team and the two downed pilots appeared like they were going to make it. They had been hidden behind enemy lines now for twenty days and accomplished multiple missions given to them. Now it was time to recover, rearm, and get ready for the next mission.

An hour later, their helicopter flew over the beachhead and they got a good glimpse of what was going on down on the ground. They could see the city had been hit hard during the fighting. It looked like the military officially had the logistics "gravy train" fully up and running. Ships were now docked and offloading heavy armor and other equipment, along with thousands of additional Marines.

Their helicopter continued out to sea, until they arrived at the USS *Iwo Jima*. The chopper hovered and then slowly settled down on the deck. Several Navy members ran up to the ramp of the helicopter, along with several corpsmen and stretchers for the wounded.

A Marine officer approached Chucky. "I'm Major George," he said, extending his hand. "Are you Chief Warrant Officer Lee?"

311

He nodded. The major guided him away from the helicopter to the tower and opened a hatch. Once they were inside, he turned and said, "Chief, Colonel Bigsby wants to speak with you in the operations room." "What about the rest of my team?" Lee asked.

"They're being escorted below to one of the SEAL team rooms. They can rest up in there for the time being," Major George replied as he continued to lead Lee through the winding corridors of the ship.

When they entered the operations room, Lee could see they had a lot of maps up on the walls, marked with the positions of various enemy and friendly troops. Lee was still wearing his body armor and weapons when he walked in, so he looked a bit intimidating. He also had a three-week beard going and hadn't showered in that time either, so he was sure he stank to high heaven.

Colonel Bigsby walked towards Lee and extended his hand. "Well done out there, Chief. Your team did a bang-up job. I've been reading over your contact reports. Impressive. The Air Force was able to destroy a number of those mobile ballistic missile launchers before they could fire their missiles. Then you guys directed a number of air strikes that prevented the KPA, and later the Chinese, from pushing my Marines off the beach into the sea. You guys saved a lot of lives," he said with genuine conviction and gratitude.

Lee wasn't sure what to say. He just nodded in acknowledgment.

"Here, let's walk over to the map board," Bigsby directed. He pointed at Hill 079, where they had just come from. "Our latest signal intercepts place an entire Chinese division moving down this road, heading towards the air base you were over-watching and our beachhead. The Air Force is going to order in an arc light mission to carpet-bomb the entire valley, stretching from the air base to this point here," he explained, pointing to a spot on the map several miles further north. "If we're lucky, we're going to obliterate a lot of that division tonight when the strike happens," he concluded with a smile.

"Sir, I appreciate the congratulations and giving me the big picture of what's going on and what we accomplished. I'll pass it on to the rest of my team...but once we've had the chance to clean up, sleep, and rearm, where are we needed?" Chucky asked.

The colonel just smiled. "I like you snake eaters, all business. You just want to get right back to the business of killing the enemy—

just like Marines," he said jokingly. "Now that you've made it to the ship safely, I've got to let your command know and find out where they want me to send you guys. You may head back to Korea or maybe Japan. I'm not sure if you guys had heard, but the Chinese just invaded Taiwan. I'm not aware of us sending any forces down to support Taiwan, but I suspect if they did, it would be snake eaters like yourselves, and some of our SEAL teams."

This certainly was news to him. He had known the Chinese had joined the war once they'd started to see PLA soldiers, but he had been completely unaware Taiwan had been invaded.

This war really was starting to spill over into a lot of countries. *If this isn't the start of World War III, then I don't know what is,*" Chucky thought.

Looking back to the colonel, he replied, "Thank you again, sir, for pulling our butts out of the fire on this one. We owe you guys big-time. If it's all right with you, I'm going to go get a hot shower and try and get some sleep for the next few days before they throw us back into the meat grinder." He spoke with a devilish grin on his face. Lee was tired, sore, and hungry, but he was ready to go another round with the enemy if needed.

Later that evening, an hour or so after evening chow, Bigsby passed him a note. "You're going to be flown to Seoul for further orders from First Group."

The following morning, ODA 1110 boarded a V-22 Osprey, along with a handful of sailors and Marines as they began the trek to Seoul and an uncertain future.
****

Camp Kim
Seoul, South Korea

Four hours later, after two pitstops for fuel, ODA 1110 arrived at Camp Kim, located adjacent to Yongsan Garrison in Seoul, South Korea. Camp Kim was the new home to the Combined Joint Special Operations Task Force-Korea. Once the Osprey landed and the back ramp was lowered, Chucky's team grabbed their gear and headed out the ramp. Lieutenant Colonel Hank Mitchel, their battalion commander, was there to greet them with a warm smile.

"Welcome back to the world, gentlemen! Come this way. We have a van ready to take you guys back to the team room. We have a lot to brief you guys on, but before we do that, I want to congratulate you all on a really successful mission. You guys rescued two downed pilots, and your intelligence nearly destroyed an entire PLA division after that arc light mission last night," the colonel said, beaming with pride.

The team members threw their gear into the back of one van and got in another that would take them to their unit's team room. Their battalion sergeant major was also there with Lieutenant Colonel Mitchel, and like their commander, he was heaping praise on them for a job well done.

While none of their comrades had been killed, three of them were gravely injured, and the likelihood of them returning to the team was slim. Chief Lee climbed into the passenger seat while Colonel Mitchel drove the van the short distance to their building so he could find out how his men were. "How are Eagle Eye, Chunk, and Tig doing?" Lee asked.

Lieutenant Colonel Mitchel didn't say anything for a second, "Tig will be fine. He may even be able to come back to the unit in a few months, once he's recovered. Chunk's done with the military, and so is Eagle Eye. Chunk's back got messed up from some of the shrapnel. I talked with someone at the hospital this morning. He has partial feeling in his legs. They're confident it'll return, but it'll take some time. Eagle Eye unfortunately lost his right arm. The damage was too extensive, and they couldn't save it. The shrapnel in his back and legs didn't cause any lasting damage, but they'll medical him out of the Army...I wish I had better news for you, Chuck, but that's what I've got," Mitchel said.

Chuck nodded. "They're alive. That's all that matters." The two rode in silence for the last mile of their trip.

An hour after they arrived back at the unit building, Chucky walked down the hall to the operations center to see what all was going on and when his team might be needed again so he could dismiss his guys to get some proper rest and downtime.

"Ah, there you are, Chief," Major Witten said as he motioned for him to come over to his desk. Lee walked over and plopped himself in the chair next to the major.

"Whatcha got for us, Major?" asked Lee with a smile that hid his tiredness.

"We have a possible mission for you guys. We're still getting all the details, but you guys are going to be on deck for it. You want to know about it?" he asked with a wry grin on his face.

Lee smiled; it must be a good mission for Major Witten to smirk like that.

"Sure, why not?" Chucky replied.

Witten brought up a picture on his screen and turned it towards Lee. "You see this guy? His name is Liang Zhang Wei. He's a Deputy Minister in State Security and is the right-hand man to Chairman Zhang Dejiang. Chairman Zhang is the third-ranking member in China and believed to be the second-most powerful man in China next to President Xi. If the mission gets approved, it's going to be a snatch and grab."

Lee studied the picture of Liang and then asked, "Why is this guy so important that they want to capture him?"

That was a good question, and honestly something Major Witten was still working on getting the answer to. "I'm not sure why he is so important. I only know that one of those guys with no names, from an agency that doesn't exist, came in and handed us his information. He said they're still working out the details on where and when, but when they get that locked down, they want a team ready to snatch him immediately. Since you guys just got back from a long mission, they selected you guys for it. Until we get more information, your team should probably rest up and stand by."

Just then Lieutenant Colonel Mitchel walked over. "Take the next 24 hours and get some rest. Tell your team to be back here at 1300 hours tomorrow, and we'll have more information for you guys then."

As Lee left the operations center, a man in khaki pants and a 5.11-button-down shirt walked over to Mitchel and Witten. "You sure you want to handle this mission? I can see if the SEALs have a snatch team that can do this, if you think your guys need more time to rest and recover," he offered.

Both Witten and Mitchel looked at each other and then back to the man, who was most likely CIA. "We'll be fine," Mitchel replied. "But since you're here—why is this guy so important?"

The CIA man eyed the two of them suspiciously for a minute before responding, "We have a source within the Chinese government that says Chairman Zhang Dejiang is the mastermind behind the recent attacks by the Chinese. He also says China and Russia planned this entire war out years ago. Chairman Zhang is too heavily guarded, and our source says he spends most of his time in various command bunkers with the President. Liang Zhang Wei, on the other hand, handles a lot of the meetings Zhang can't make or is too busy to attend. Our plan is to snatch Liang and then interrogate him and find out what he knows."

He leaned forward, speaking more quietly. "This whole war seems to have come out of nowhere, but what if it was engineered and planned years in advance? That's what we want to find out. That's why Liang is important enough to risk one of your teams to capture him," the man explained.

"Our guys will be ready. Just make sure this isn't some sort of suicide mission," Lieutenant Colonel Mitchel said.

This is a tough one, he realized. He hated the idea of passing on a mission, but maybe this would be a better mission for the SEALs or Delta. They specialized in snatch-and-grab missions, far more than his conventional Special Operations Forces did. His teams were usually busy conducting deep penetration and reconnaissance raids behind enemy lines, not grabbing political prisoners.

The CIA man turned and left them wondering how much this Liang truly knew and if what he said was true. This whole thing had been planned out for years.

I guess they'll find out soon enough...

From the Authors

Miranda and I hope you've enjoyed this book. To continue the action and read the next book in the series, *Battlefield Taiwan*, please order your copy on Amazon.

If you would like to stay up to date on new releases and receive emails about any special pricing deals we may make available, please sign up for our email distribution list. Simply go to https://www.frontlinepublishinginc.com/ and sign up.

If you enjoy audiobooks, we have a great selection that has been created for your listening pleasure. Our entire Red Storm series and our Falling Empire series have been recorded, and several books in our Rise of the Republic series and our Monroe Doctrine series are now available. Please see below for a complete listing.

As independent authors, reviews are very important to us and make a huge difference to other prospective readers. If you enjoyed this book, we humbly ask you to write up a positive review on Amazon and Goodreads. We sincerely appreciate each person that takes the time to write one.

We have really valued connecting with our readers via social media, especially on our Facebook page https://www.facebook.com/RosoneandWatson/. Sometimes we ask for help from our readers as we write future books—we love to draw upon all your different areas of expertise. We also have a group of beta readers who get to look at the books before they are officially published and help us fine-tune last-minute adjustments. If you would like to be a part of this team, please go to our author website, and send us a message through the "Contact" tab.

You may also enjoy some of our other works. A full list can be found below:

Nonfiction:
Iraq Memoir 2006–2007 Troop Surge
Interview with a Terrorist (audiobook available)

Fiction:
The Monroe Doctrine Series

Volume One (audiobook available)
Volume Two (audiobook available)
Volume Three (audiobook available)
Volume Four (audiobook still in production)
Volume Five (available for preorder)

Rise of the Republic Series
Into the Stars (audiobook available)
Into the Battle (audiobook available)
Into the War (audiobook available)
Into the Chaos (audiobook available)
Into the Fire (audiobook still in production)
Into the Calm (available for preorder)

Apollo's Arrows Series (co-authored with T.C. Manning)
Cherubim's Call (available for preorder)

Crisis in the Desert Series (co-authored with Matt Jackson)
Project 19 (audiobook available)
Desert Shield
Desert Storm

Falling Empires Series
Rigged (audiobook available)
Peacekeepers (audiobook available)
Invasion (audiobook available)
Vengeance (audiobook available)
Retribution (audiobook available)

Red Storm Series
Battlefield Ukraine (audiobook available)
Battlefield Korea (audiobook available)
Battlefield Taiwan (audiobook available)
Battlefield Pacific (audiobook available)
Battlefield Russia (audiobook available)
Battlefield China (audiobook available)

Michael Stone Series

Traitors Within (audiobook available)

World War III Series
Prelude to World War III: The Rise of the Islamic Republic and the Rebirth of America (audiobook available)
Operation Red Dragon and the Unthinkable (audiobook available)
Operation Red Dawn and the Siege of Europe (audiobook available)
Cyber Warfare and the New World Order (audiobook available)

Children's Books:
My Daddy has PTSD
My Mommy has PTSD

Acronym Key

AAV	Amphibious Assault Vehicle
AG	Attorney General
ASAP	As Soon As Possible
ASROC	Anti-Submarine Rocket
ASW	Anti-Submarine Warfare
AWACs	Airborne Warning and Control System
BMP	Boycvaya Mashina Pekhoty (Russian infantry fighting vehicle)
BTR	Bronetransportyor (Russian armored personnel carrier)
CAG	Commander Air Group
CIA	Central Intelligence Agency
CIC	Combat Information Center
CIWS	Close-in Weapons System
CJC	Chairman of the Joint Chiefs
CMC	Central Military Commission
COG	Continuity of Government
C-RAM	Counter Rocket, Artillery, and Mortar systems
CSM	Command Sergeant Major
CW4	Chief Warrant Officer Four
DCM	Deputy Chief of Mission
DDoS	Distributed Denial of Service
DEFCON	Defense Readiness Condition
DF-5B	Dongfeng-5B
DIA	Defense Intelligence Agency
DoD	Department of Defense
DMZ	Demilitarized Zone
DPRK	Democratic People's Republic of Korea (North Korea)
EAM	Emergency Alert Message
FSB	Federalnaya Sluzhba Bezopasnosti (Russian intelligence agency that came after the KGB)
GDF	Global Defense Force
GDP	Gross Domestic Product
GM	General Major
G3	Head of Operations Staff
HALO	High Altitude-Low Opening (military free fall)

HEAT	High-explosive Antitank
IBA	Individual Body Armor
ICBM	Intercontinental Ballistic Missiles
IoT	Internet of Things (all network-enabled devices)
JCET	Joint Combined Exchange Training
JDAM	Joint Direct Attack Munition
KPA	Korean People's Army (North Korea's Army)
LCAC	Landing Craft Air Cushion (hovercraft)
LCDR	Lieutenant Commander
LNO	Liaison Officer
LT	Lieutenant
LZ	Landing Zone
MAD	Mutually Assured Destruction
MANPAD	Man Portable Air Defense System (shoulder-launched surface-to-air-missiles)
MIRV	Multiple Independently Targetable Reentry Vehicle
NATO	North Atlantic Treaty Organization
NORAD	North American Aerospace Defense Command
NSA	National Security Advisor OR National Security Agency
ODA	Operational Detachment Alpha
ODC	Office of Defense Cooperation
OP	Observation Post
PACOM	Pacific Command
PLA	People's Liberation Army
PLAAF	People's Liberation Army Air Force
PLAN	People's Liberation Army Navy
POTUS	President of the United States
PSI	Pounds Per Square Inch
QRF	Quick Reaction Force
ROK	Republic of Korea (South Korea)
RORSAT	Radar Ocean Reconnaissance Satellite
RSO	Regional Security Officer
SAM	Surface-to-Air Missile
SCIF	Sensitive Compartmented Information Facility
SDO	Senior Defense Official
SecDef	Secretary of Defense
SF	Special Forces

SSGN	Ship, Submersible, Guided Missile, Nuclear
S2	Intelligence Officer
TACP	Tactical Air Control Party
THAAD	Thermal High-Altitude Area Defense
XO	Executive Officer

Printed in Great Britain
by Amazon